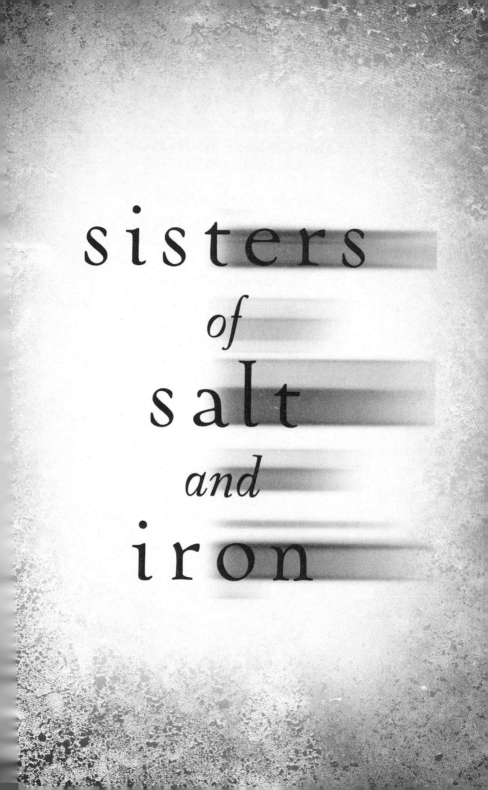

sisters of salt and iron

**Also available from Kady Cross
and Harlequin TEEN**

Sisters of Blood and Spirit

SISTERS OF BLOOD AND SPIRIT
SISTERS OF SALT AND IRON

The Steampunk Chronicles

THE STRANGE CASE OF FINLEY JAYNE (ebook prequel)
THE GIRL IN THE STEEL CORSET
THE GIRL IN THE CLOCKWORK COLLAR
THE DARK DISCOVERY OF JACK DANDY (ebook novella)
THE GIRL WITH THE IRON TOUCH
THE WILD ADVENTURE OF JASPER RENN (ebook novella)
THE GIRL WITH THE WINDUP HEART (coming August 2016)

KADY CROSS

sisters
of
salt
and
iron

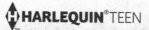

HARLEQUIN®TEEN

ISBN-13: 978-0-373-21176-0

Sisters of Salt and Iron

This book is for Kenzie and Zoe.
I hope you grow up to be best friends as well as sisters.
And for Steve, because I couldn't do this without you.

chapter one

LARK

Ghosts are *such* douche bags.

My sister, Wren, was the exception to this rule, but other than her I'd *never* met a ghost that wasn't a colossal pain in the ass. And this one was starting to *seriously* piss me off.

I hit the wall of the girls' locker room hard, my head cracking the plaster. Fortunately, I had a hard head, and a high tolerance for wraith-inflicted pain. I dropped to the floor on my feet, and came at her swinging as the DJ in the gym played a bass-thumping dance song that shook my joints. My fist connected with her face hard enough to knock her off her feet—which was funny, because it wasn't as though her boots actually touched the floor.

Truth be told, I wasn't much for school dances, and I wasn't a huge fan of Halloween, given that it was the one time of the year that the worlds of the dead and living merged. The veil weakened in the spring as well, but human celebrations and lore had given All Hallows' Eve even more strength. Still, I would rather be dancing with my friends than getting the snot beat out of me by an angry grunge girl who had been dead longer than I'd been alive.

I was covered in salt dust, ghost-juice and plaster, and bleeding from a cut above my eye where she'd rammed me headfirst into a locker. I was dressed like Harley Quinn from Batman, so it only added to the costume.

"Listen, Courtney Love, you can't be here. Why don't you just move on? Whatever's waiting for you has to be better than this."

Really, who haunted a high school Halloween dance? No, wait—who haunted a high school at all? Seriously, you had to have lived a pretty lame life if the place that held the most pull for your spirit was Samuel Clemens High.

The ghost—her name was Daria Wilson, and she'd died when she crashed her car into a tree after the Halloween dance in '91—rose up. "Says who?" she demanded. "You?"

I smiled, trying to ignore that I could see her brain glistening through the crater in her skull. Her hair was almost as white as mine beneath the blood and gore, but mine was natural. "That's right."

She glared at me, her eyes nothing but bottomless black pits. She opened her mouth, unhinging her jaw a good twelve inches. In the dank, yawning cavern of her mouth, her teeth were jagged razors, and her tongue rippled and writhed like a worm. She roared.

The scream of a vengeful spirit was like having your eardrums punctured while being tossed around in a tornado of rot. Her rancid breath burned my skin, and I could feel something warm and wet trickle from my left ear. My nose, too. I staggered forward as my left knee began to buckle.

She was *not* going to take me down.

The scream stopped abruptly. I almost fell down anyway from the release of it. I grabbed at the wall to steady myself.

"You can't make me go, bitch," she snarled, moving toward me. "If you could, you would have already."

I lifted my gaze, swiping my hand under my nose to wipe the blood away. "I'm working on it, skank."

Where the hell was my sister? Wren and our friends had gone off in search of the item that was so important it kept Daria here rather than where she was supposed to be.

Don't ask me where we go when we're dead. I'd only died once, and I didn't get any farther than the halfway mark between this world and the next before getting pulled back. But I knew how to banish ghosts from this plane, and that was good enough for me.

Daria grabbed me by the throat, her fingers like steel clamps. I wheezed for air as my toes left the chipped tile floor. She lifted me like she wanted to hold me up to the light and get a better look.

I seized her wrist with my left hand, holding myself up to ease the strain on my neck. Then, I shoved my right hand into the hole in her head. Wet tissue and sharp bone filled my palm as I closed my fingers into a fist.

Daria cried out.

I fell to the floor, this time landing on my knees. Hard. I was too busy sucking in air to cry or even swear.

My hand burned, ectoplasm sizzling as it met the salt residue on my skin. Ghosts didn't like salt.

My phone made a noise—like a groan. I took it out of my boot and risked taking a look while Daria was keening in the corner. The text screen came up. It was from Wren—we'd been working on her communicating through electronics since we couldn't actually project words at each other.

On my weight. I hoped that was a typo. I shoved the phone back into my boot.

If my knees had been capable of sound, they would have sobbed as I pushed myself to my feet. I limped to the sink and turned on the faucet, shoving my hand into the cold water. The pain rinsed away with the salt—thank God.

Something grabbed at the back of my neck. I looked up into the mirror and saw Daria behind me. I twisted, just in time to avoid having my head smashed into the glass, and threw a wide punch into the side of her head—the gooey side again.

She stumbled back, giving me room to come at her again. This time, I hit her as hard and fast as I could before drawing back and landing a solid kick to her chest that sent her crashing into the same wall she'd knocked me into just minutes before.

She recovered quickly, shaking it off. When she stared at me, her blacked-out eyes sparked with rage. She looked murderous.

And scared. I got that a lot from ghosts. Ones that had been around for a while usually figured out how to mess with humans in one way or another, but they were *always* surprised to meet one who could mess back. I didn't know why I could do these things, no more than I understood why I could interact with my dead twin. It didn't matter—I *could*.

The parts of Daria's bleached hair that weren't matted with blood started to lift off her shoulders—like the static electricity experiment I'd done as a kid by rubbing a balloon against my head. I'd been lucky up until now—she was just having fun. If she manifested, I was going to be in trouble.

Ghosts in their natural form were one thing—I could interact with them, and we were on fairly even footing, but when they gathered enough power to take form in the real world—to gather mass—that's when things got serious. I would still be able to fight her, but I was going to get hurt, and the locker room was going to take some damage—not to mention what might happen to all the people out in the gym if Daria decided to get her party on.

The hair on my arms lifted. The back of my neck tingled. *Oh, hell.* This wasn't good.

I punched her in the face. A little reminder—to both of us—that I was the one in charge. Unfortunately, my heart didn't get the message. Damn thing hammered against my ribs like it was trying to get out.

Daria lifted her hand to her nose. I'd drawn blood, a little payback for the coppery taste in the back of my throat.

"*What* are you?" she demanded. Surprise laced her raspy voice. She probably hadn't felt pain since the night she died.

"I'm Lark Noble," I informed her as I hit her again. It was the best explanation I had.

I'd knocked her jaw off center. She pushed it back into place as her eyes—still filled with wisps of black—widened. "Sister of the Dead Born?"

Okay, so I hadn't been expecting that. "I think of her as *my* sister—I came out first."

She stared at me. "The Living-dead."

"Uh, no. Just living, thanks."

She drifted closer. The smell of her filled my nose and throat, coating them like oil. "You shared a womb with death. You died, but you live."

I wasn't comfortable discussing my suicide attempt with a stranger. "I shared a womb with my sister, not death."

She smiled. I'd seen a similar expression on Wren's face before. It usually meant something really, really bad was about to happen. "I wonder what would happen if I ripped your throat out?"

"You want to kill me?" I challenged. I was afraid, but not like I should have been. Death wasn't scary. The act of dying was, but if you were lucky, that didn't take too long. "Go for it. I could hang out here for eternity. With you."

Obviously she didn't like the idea of a roommate, judging from the way she screwed up her face. Her hair fanned out from her face as she drew back. I could see the spot where the vertebrae in her neck had splintered and shattered. One of her shoulders hung lower than the other, limp and disjointed.

"There won't be enough of you left to haunt anything." Her voice had deepened, the words coming to me on air that had dropped several degrees. My nose was cold, and my fingertips tingled. Out of the corner of my eye I saw the mirror on the wall frost over.

I stepped to the right, keeping my eye on Daria as she grew as dark and ominous as a thunder cloud. That gaping crater in her head glistened with black ooze—the same black that filled her eyes. I reached into the shower stall nearest me and felt along the wall until I found what I wanted.

It was a wrought-iron rod. Nothing too fancy, though it had a bit of a twisting pattern along its length. My boyfriend Ben had given it to me a while ago, and it was still my favorite ghost-beatin' stick.

Normally I avoided salt and iron because of Wren—all ghosts have a sort of allergic reaction to both. Maybe because they were of the earth, where the dead were generally buried? I didn't know. Didn't care.

I stood facing the ghost, the iron rod in my hand. This was normally the time I'd make some kind of snarky or smart-ass remark. To be honest, I was biting my tongue. I wasn't supposed to bait her—just keep her busy and distracted.

She was going to pop any second. Then I was going to have

to fight her and hope that everyone at the dance continued on in blissful ignorance. I'd been warned when I came back to school after my time in Bell Hill Psychiatric Hospital that I was only there because of my grandmother, and that I'd better not make trouble.

Wrecking the girls' locker room counted as "trouble." The ghost didn't matter. It never did. People always found a way to explain the supernatural, and in my experience the favorite explanation was that I was a troublemaking, attention-starved emotionally unstable delinquent.

Which, actually, wasn't too far from the truth.

I glanced in the direction of the door. The line of salt I'd poured a few feet away from it was still whole, as were the lines in front of the opaque windows. They weren't infalli-ble—Daria could possibly create enough energy to break the lines, and then she could get out—but for now it was just me and a drunk ghost.

C'mon, Wren.

Then I sensed it—the subtle shift that might have been just in my head but felt like it was outside of me. My sister was there, and everything clicked into its rightful place.

"About freaking time," I told her.

"The others are coming," she replied, coming to stand be-side me. Wren and I were identical except for two things—my superior fashion sense, and the fact that my hair was almost snow-white while hers was a comic-book shade of red.

She had her hair in pigtails and was wearing a blood-soaked pinafore and blouse, tights and Mary Janes. She looked like a demented rag doll.

Daria looked impressed—or as impressed as someone with only part of a head and drunk out of her mind could look. "Dead Born."

My sister frowned at her. "I don't like that name."

The two of them watched each other with the same amount of hostile wariness. Wren's anger wavered around her like heat off pavement. She wasn't immune to the approach of Halloween either, and that made me wonder, just what the hell did I intend to do if *both* of them manifested?

"Did you find what's keeping her here?" I asked.

Wren glanced at me. "Yes, but it's not what I expected."

Daria chose that moment—when Wren's attention was distracted—to attack. She hit my sister square in the chest. Wren barely moved. Daria's surprise would have been funny in any other situation.

"You are so stupid," I said. Now she'd gone and pissed off Wren. If I made it out of the locker room unsuspended and alive, it was going to be a miracle.

My sister is usually a gentle soul, but she's a ghost and ghosts have notoriously short fuses. Wren's eyes had already gone black, and I could feel her spectral energy reverberating in my bones along with the new song playing in the gym.

I put my hand on her arm. "Don't."

Her head whipped around. My heart jumped into my throat. There was nothing so terrifying as Death wearing your face. I held her gaze and her arm, watching as the darkness slowly left her eyes.

The door to the locker room opened—the music from the dance increased in volume for a few seconds, then faded back to its muted thumping.

Three familiar faces came into view—my friends, Roxi and Sarah. Well, I wasn't completely sure if Sarah was a friend or not, but whatever. They had the history teacher, Mr. Fisher, with them.

Fan-freaking-tastic. Busted.

"That's why she's still here," Wren whispered.

"Him?" I looked at Mr. Fisher. He wasn't a bad-looking guy. Fairly young.

She nodded.

Mr. Fisher turned to me. "Who are you talking to?"

"Her." I pointed at Roxi. "Did you tell him?"

Roxi's big brown eyes widened. "That he was needed in the girls' locker room."

"That's it?" I demanded. She nodded. Great.

"What's going on here?" Mr. Fisher demanded.

Daria stood up and walked toward him with a stupefied look on her face. "Danny?"

"Your name's Daniel, right?" I asked.

He nodded. "One of you girls had better tell me what's going on. Why did you bring me here?"

"You wouldn't happen to know a girl named Daria, would you? Smashed into a tree a few years back on the night of the Halloween dance?"

He went white. "What do you know about Daria?"

I could try to lie—make it sound less crazy than what it was—but I was pissed off at having to be doing this instead of having fun with my friends. "You believe in ghosts, Mr. F.?"

He looked at me—saw the salt dust on my clothes—and the lines of salt on the floor. He looked at Roxi and Sarah, both of whom shrugged. A lot of help they were.

"He's gotten so *old*," Daria remarked, walking around him.

Mr. Fisher shuddered. "It's cold in here," he said. "You girls are in a lot of trouble."

I glanced at the ghost. The way she looked at him froze my blood. She reached out and tapped him on the shoulder. Frowning, he turned around.

Daria shoved her hand into his chest.

He looked so surprised. He looked down at his chest, then up again. "Dee?" His voice was little more than a gasp.

"You're the reason I'm dead," she snarled. "It's all your fault."

She was so close to taking form I was terrified I was going to end up with a dead teacher to explain. Never mind suspension; they'd lock me up and throw away the key.

There was no doubt that Mr. Fisher could hear her. "I tried to stop you," he protested, as his dead girlfriend held his heart in her icy fingers. "You ran away."

Daria actually growled. "Because I found you screwing my best friend!"

"Wren?" I glanced at my sister. "Little help?" This was going to hell fast.

Daria turned her attention to me. "This is between me and him. One step and I'll crush his heart."

"Isn't that what you plan to do regardless?" I asked.

She smiled. "Yeah, but if you make me do it quickly I won't enjoy it as much." The smile faded, morphing into something that was going to wake me up at night for weeks to come. "Now, back off, bitch."

Everything happened in a blink. One moment my sister was beside me, and the next she was on Daria, shoving the teacher aside as she threw herself onto the other ghost.

Sarah gasped. Roxi stared. Mr. Fisher made a small mewling sound in the back of his throat as he sank to the floor, clutching his chest. I ran to him.

"What do you have of hers?" I demanded. When he gave me a blank look, I added, "Of Daria's!" Who else could I possibly mean?

He reached into his pocket and pulled out a key ring. There was an aged brass *D* hanging from it. *D* for *Daria*, not *Daniel*.

I fumbled with the keys, trying to pull the large letter off the ring. Freaking hell! Who invented key rings, anyway? Couldn't they have thought of a more user-friendly setup?

Wren and Daria smashed into the row of shower stalls, buckling the metal frames.

Finally, the letter came free. I pulled a plastic baggy partially filled with salt from my pocket and opened the seal, dropping the letter charm inside.

A few sparks, but other than that, nothing. *Shit.* If it wasn't the letter anchoring Daria to the world of the living, then what was it?

Anger. Vengeance. I didn't know how to break that, and Mr. Fisher wasn't going to fit into a sandwich bag of salt. If I didn't do something fast, Daria and my sister were going to wreck the locker room.

Mr. Fisher, Roxi and Sarah were on the floor near the wall of lockers, huddled together. They looked terrified, and I didn't blame them. I dropped to my knees in front of them as Daria flew toward me, crashing into the lockers above my head.

"Get out," I ordered. "Get out now!"

I didn't have to tell them twice. They scrabbled across the floor, keeping low until it was safe to stagger to their feet and run for the door. Mr. Fisher paused and looked back at me.

"Dee, no!" he shouted.

My brain froze, but my body didn't. I dropped to the floor, twisting so that I landed on my back. Daria leaped onto me like a cat on a mouse, all darkness and stink and sharp teeth.

"Hold her!" I cried.

Wren seized her, fingers like talons as they restrained Daria's arms. I tried not to look at her. I didn't want to see my sister looking like something out of a horror movie. I ripped open the bag of salt and shoved my hand inside, scooping up the sharp grains and the charm. I looked up into the ghost's fathomless eyes; there was no shred of humanity left.

"Do it," my sister growled. Her voice was like the drag of a shovel across a gravestone, and it was all the encouragement I needed to end this shit storm fast.

I bolted upright, slamming my fist into the gaping side of Daria's skull, burrowing my hand deep into the ectoplasm of her brain. I gagged.

It's not really her brain. She's dead. A ghost—she has no brain, not physically. Telling myself that was the only thing that got me to open my fingers and release the salt and charm inside her. She reared up, screaming.

I fell back on the floor, hands over my ears. It felt like my head was going to explode. I gasped for breath as tears streamed down my cheeks.

And then, it was quiet. No other sound but the muffled music from the dance, reverberating through the floor.

Daria was gone, and my sister sat beside me, her back to me, legs splayed and shoulders slumped.

"Wren?" My voice sounded small.

She held up her hand—it still looked like claws. I knew not to say another word. Instead, I sat up and took that hand in my own. Once we made contact it didn't take long for it to morph back into its usual state. I didn't understand my effect on my sister any more than I understood any part of our existence, but it didn't matter. I was the one thing that could bring her back from a manifestation.

"You okay?" I asked.

She nodded. "Yes. You?"

"I'm covered in salt and ghost-goo, but, yeah, I'm okay." I

was sore, but that would be gone by morning—another side effect of this whacked-out life.

"This room's a mess."

I glanced around at the damage. It was too much for me to undo. "We need to get out of here. Is she gone?"

Wren nodded. "She's gone. How did that even work?"

I shrugged. "Don't know. Don't care."

"We need to start figuring these things out."

"Yeah, but not tonight." I pushed myself to my feet. She followed—much more gracefully, of course. "There's one thing we need to do before we go home."

"What's that?"

I grabbed her hand and pulled her toward the door. "Let's dance."

chapter two

WREN

There really wasn't any reason for me to stay at the dance once Daria moved on, but I knew it bothered Lark sometimes when I manifested, and that had been happening a fair bit lately. I couldn't help it—Halloween was coming, and my ties to the world of the living were already abnormally strong. I knew Lark was having a difficult time with the number of ghosts she had to deal with, but I don't think she realized how hard it was for me to try to remain hidden when All Hallows' Eve demanded I come out and show myself.

Anyway, I stayed at the dance so that Lark and I could have a little fun together—not that she paid that much attention to me. She had her boyfriend, Ben. And now that she had real, loyal friends, she didn't need me so much. I was happy for her, and I knew I could hang out with her group anytime I wanted. But being in a room with people who couldn't see or hear you seemed more like punishment than fun.

I danced a little with Lark and *our* friends—she insisted they were mine, too—to a few faster songs. Even though Lark and Kevin—who I was trying to avoid—were the only ones who could actually see me, I still enjoyed myself—laughing as they took silly selfies and made what Sarah called "duck lips."

"Oh, my God," Roxi said, as she looked at the screen of her phone. "There's Wren!"

Everyone crowded around to look. I drifted between Sarah and Kevin, knowing they'd feel the chill of my presence. Kevin looked right at me. I ignored him. He'd hurt my feelings and proven that he wasn't the person I thought he was. I was having a hard time forgiving him for it.

"That's so weird," Gage, Roxi's boyfriend, remarked. "She looks so real."

I glanced at him at the same time Lark said, "She *is* real."

He rolled his dark eyes. "Realer, then."

Roxi kissed his cheek. "I think you mean *tangible*."

Gage shrugged. "Whatever. It's just cool to see her, that's all."

Everyone else agreed, and I smiled. Lark smiled, too.

But then everyone broke into couples for the slow dance, and Kevin looked at me. "It is good to see you," he said. No one else would ever hear him above the music, his voice was so low, but I could hear it, and he knew it. It took all my strength not to stick my tongue out at him—or rip his eyes out.

I left instead. I couldn't trust myself to be around him, not when that dark and angry part of myself was so close to the surface. I might hurt him, and I didn't want to do that, no matter how much he'd hurt me.

I let myself drift through town, wandering aimlessly along the dark streets. My kind were everywhere—strolling along the sidewalks, peeking in windows, sitting on benches. To-morrow there would be even more of them as even the weaker ones gathered strength.

Halloween was still days away, but that time of year has

always been hard for me. This year it seemed even rougher. The veil between the world of the living and the world of the dead grows thinner as the calendar counts down to the end of October. It's our holiday—when we can cross between dimensions and interact with the living if we wish. We can be our true selves. Those who have become violent or despondent remember who they were, and decide if they want to try moving on, or give themselves over to the darkness.

A lot give up, but there are an equal number who move on.

But not me. I stayed exactly where I was. I don't think I had a choice.

Halloween's approach had to be hard on Kevin, as well. He was a medium, and his abilities had only gotten stronger since our encounter with the ghost of madman Josiah Bent at Haven Crest Hospital.

I liked Kevin, and I thought he liked me, but then he told me we shouldn't spend so much time together since we could never really have a relationship. Then I caught him kissing Sarah—Mace's girlfriend. Mace, his best friend. That had stung, but the disappointment I'd felt was worse.

I kept drifting. The town of New Devon wasn't very big, and there wasn't much more for a ghost to do there than there was for a living sixteen-year-old. I didn't feel like going home, but I wasn't going back to that dance.

I suppose I shouldn't have been surprised to find myself at Haven Crest. The abandoned asylum was incredibly haunted from years of treating those who were considered insane or were locked up by their families. The graveyard on the property contained hundreds of cremated remains—and those were just the ones the families hadn't claimed.

Haven Crest was full of, as Lark would put it, her people. Though, unlike Lark, most of the residents really were insane. If they hadn't been when they went in, they had been by the time they died. It made for a lot of spectral energy in one spot, and like any ghost, I was drawn to it, because no one lived at Haven Crest anymore—they were all ghosts, and that made them *my* people.

I stood on the lawn facing the main building—a large, red-brick building with a wing on either side of the central block and a large white domed-roof tower. It had staging and construction materials piled up in front of it. The town was in the process of reclaiming as much land and buildings as they could, turning them into offices and public spaces.

Because what could possibly go wrong when disturbing the ghosts of more than a century's worth of mental patients?

On the light post near my head someone had recently stapled a poster: One Night Only—Dead Babies!

I frowned. Why would anyone in their right minds want to see deceased infants? In my experience that kind of thing was very disturbing to the living. As a ghost, a baby was just another ghost. I hadn't seen one myself—they tended to move on quickly.

Oh. Wait. Dead Babies. Yes, this was a musical band that Lark enjoyed listening to. I remembered dancing around our bedroom one night pretending to play a guitar while she sang into a hairbrush. I smiled at the memory. We didn't do things like that anymore. Lark was always with Ben, or there were other people around. The times we were alone were rare and usually when she had homework to do, or needed to sleep. I would never actually say it to Lark, but sometimes I wished we could go back to a time when she didn't have friends, and people stayed away because they thought she was crazy.

Dead Babies was going to be holding a concert here at Haven Crest on Halloween night. I'd heard Lark and Ben talk about a concert that Lark proclaimed was "a farking bad idea." This had to be it. All that music and energy at a place like Haven Crest? The dead wouldn't be able to resist, and there would be so many living to interact with—who wouldn't think anything of a peculiarly dressed stranger dancing next to them. It would be Halloween, after all.

I would have to attend this concert. It might be fun. Or dangerous. If I was lucky, maybe both. All those warm, breathing bodies, ripe with fear, practically begging to be terrified. *Delicious.*

"Hello."

I didn't jump. It's a well-known fact that ghosts don't scare easily. I turned my head. Standing there beneath the lamp across the drive from me was a boy who looked to be a little older than I was. From the way he was dressed, I'd say he was actually a century older than I was. Young men didn't wear suits much anymore, especially not jackets with tails.

"Hi," I said.

Hands in his pockets, he crossed the pavement toward me. He was tall and pale with thick black hair and bright blue eyes. He had a nice smile—the sort that made my heart flutter. I might not actually be alive in this dimension, but I was fully intact in my own. Even if my heart didn't actually beat, I was still capable of the sensation of physical response.

"I haven't seen you around here before," he remarked.

I folded my arms over my chest like my sister did whenever she felt defensive. "I haven't seen you, either."

He stopped right in front of me, still smiling. "I'm Noah."

"Wren."

His left eyebrow lifted. "An unusual name. One I've heard before. You wouldn't be the ghost who helped destroy Josiah Bent?"

I stiffened. Bent had been a terrible creature, and he'd hurt Lark's—our—friends. Because of that, and because I believed he needed to be destroyed, it hadn't occurred to me that anyone at Haven Crest might harbor resentment for us getting rid of him.

But I wasn't afraid, and I wasn't going to lie. "Yes."

His grin widened—he had nice teeth. "I have to thank you for that. Bent was a first-class bas—uh, scoundrel."

"You can say *bastard* in front of me. Women aren't considered delicate creatures anymore."

His smile turned rueful. "That is a pity. Still, I'm happy to see that the loss doesn't extend to beauty nor grace."

Was that a compliment? "Are you flirting with me?"

Noah leaned a little closer. "Perhaps. Is it working?"

"I think so." I smiled at him. I liked this game. It was fun, and it made me feel silly and light. "Maybe you could do it some more just to be certain."

His dark eyes brightened. They were like a night sky—I could see stars reflected in them. "I've met many girls on these grounds, and you're the first with whom I wanted to flirt."

I laughed. "I don't believe that."

Noah's head tilted as he shot me a bashful look. "Fair enough, but you're the first one I hoped would flirt back."

Oh, he was good. Lark wouldn't trust him. In fact, I could hear her making retching noises in my head. But my sister wasn't there. I was alone with a cute boy who wanted to spend some time with me, and there wasn't any drama around it. We were both dead, so what was the worst thing that could happen?

I smiled. "I don't really know how to flirt."

He made a clucking sound with his tongue. "For shame. I would be happy to instruct if you are in want of a teacher."

We were so close I could feel his spectral energy mingling with mine. It was like a warm breath on bare skin. We weren't tangible to the living, or in their world—unless we manifested—but to each other we were solid. Real.

My gaze drifted to his mouth—he had perfect lips—before rising to meet his. God, those eyes! "Do you really think you could teach me?" I asked with a smile.

He arched a brow. "I think you have a natural talent for it."

I laughed. "Maybe you're just so good that I'm learning already."

A bright smile parted his lips. "That may be true." He offered his hand. "Would you care to dance with me?"

I said the words that I'd heard said countless times in romantic movies—"There isn't any music."

As though on cue, the sound of a cello and violin playing together in perfect harmony drifted around us, soft as a breeze.

"How did you do that?" I asked, looking about. I actually expected to see a couple of ghosts nearby, playing for us.

"When you've been around as long as I have been, you learn how to tap into lingering spectral energy."

I nodded. "You found a looper."

A looper was a common kind of ghost—the kind that are stuck, either knowingly or unaware, in a particular moment or action. Some are doomed to jump off that bridge night after night, or walk the same stretch of road, scream the same blood-chilling scream. They're like ghost-zombies, mindless and driven only by compulsion. Sad, really.

"There are quite a few of them here," he said. "I've just brought them a little closer. I'm not hurting them."

The concern in his tone made me like him more. "I hadn't thought you were."

Noah looked relieved. "You'll dance with me, then?"

I nodded. "I'm not very good. I've never really learned."

"Ah." He grinned. "Something else for me to teach you." He held out his hand. I took it and put my other hand on his shoulder as his arm went around my waist.

"Just look into my eyes and follow me," he instructed.

I did. The next thing I knew we were whirling and twirling around—easier to do when your feet didn't have to touch the ground. Following really wasn't all that difficult once I realized there was a pattern to the steps. It was fun.

There were ghosts in the windows of nearby buildings watching us. Some even came outside, but they didn't approach us. A few found partners or danced by themselves, but they didn't try to interrupt. Noah spun me over the top of the security patrol car as it drove by, and I laughed as we flew up into the air.

Lark reached out to me an hour or so later. It wasn't a summons, just a gentle prod to make sure I was all right. We really did have the whole twin-ESP thing going on, but I didn't know if it was because we were twins or because I was dead. The why wasn't really important, it was convenient to be able to feel one another when we weren't together. My sister had a habit of getting into trouble—though she'd probably say the same about me.

I let her know I was fine, and she seemed to respect that because she didn't summon me—a command that I didn't seem to be able to ignore, and Lark only used it when it was urgent. She was probably with Ben anyway.

"What's it like to have lived?" I asked as we danced.

His smile seemed almost sad as he whirled me around the chimneys of one of the older buildings. "Terrible and wonderful. Anxious and joyous. Things hurt and stink and rot.

And then, you'll find the most perfect flower, or watch the sunrise, and every pain will have been worth it."

I felt hollow inside. "I wish I could experience it."

He looked me in the eye. "My dear girl, you don't have to be alive to *live*. There are plenty of living people in this world who sleepwalk through it and never hate or love any part of it. You are more alive than almost anyone I've ever known."

Noah and I danced and talked some more. We flirted and we laughed. And then, the sun peeked its head up over the horizon.

We were sitting beneath an old tree that still had most of its leaves—which were almost as dark a red as my hair. Noah lifted his head.

"You should go," he said. "Your sister will wonder where you've been." Of course he knew about Lark if he knew who I was.

He was right. She'd worry if I wasn't there when she woke up, even though she wouldn't be up for a while yet. It was Saturday, after all.

"Is the daylight difficult for you?" I asked. It was a known fact that most ghosts were weakened by the sun. I wasn't one of them, though I did feel more "alive" at night.

He glanced away—as though it was something to be ashamed of. "Yes. I'm sorry."

I placed my hand over the one resting on his thigh and gently squeezed. "Don't be."

Suddenly, his face was right there in front of mine, and his fingers touched my cheek as though I was made of the most delicate glass. "If I could I would spend all the hours of this day and the next, and all the others that follow, in your company."

My throat tightened. Lark would have thought of something witty to say at such a time. Me? Not so much. "Me, too."

His face brightened. He rose to his feet, helping me stand at the same time. He held both my hands in his. "Will I see you again tonight?"

I nodded. "Yes. If you want."

"I can think of nothing that would give me more pleasure."

He talked like something out of a romance novel—like Mr. Darcy. I loved it. I grinned. "Well, I would hate to deny you."

A slow smile curved his perfect lips. "I was right—you do have a natural talent for flirting." His smile faded. "I must go. Until tonight."

I started to say something, but he cut me off by pressing his mouth to mine in a quick, firm kiss. Then, he was gone, leaving me standing there, stunned.

I pressed my fingers to my mouth and smiled. I felt light— ridiculously happy. Who knew that boys held such power in their lips?

I spun around, laughing out loud as I whisked myself away from Haven Crest. As I drifted away I saw two leaves fall from the tree. They drifted down to the ground where Noah and I had sat. They each fell alone but ended up together on the grass, stems entwined. Somehow, they'd found each other.

I danced all the way home.

LARK

I woke up late, a little sore from the fight with Daria, but otherwise fine. I would have been up earlier, but I'd stayed out late with Ben. Memories of how we'd passed the time made me warm all over. God, that boy knew how to kiss. Where to touch...

What the hell was that sound?

Slowly, I pushed myself up onto my elbows and looked out into the dimness of my room. There was Wren dancing and singing under her breath in front of my mirror. She kept changing her outfits and hairstyles like a movie montage. All she had to do was think it, and she could look it. I hated that about her. It took me forty minutes to get ready. It took her four seconds.

I'd never seen her like this. She was grinning like an idiot, and I'm pretty sure she was singing a Taylor Swift song. She was also wearing a dress exactly like the one Belle wore to dance with Beast in the Disney movie.

"That yellow clashes with your hair," I grumbled, beating down the blankets.

She yelped, and so did I. What the hell? I'd never startled her before.

"Are you okay?" I asked, frowning at her. She looked… sheepish. I guess I would be, too, if I'd been caught in that dress.

"I'm fine," she chirped. "Just bored waiting for you to wake up. It's about time."

My gaze narrowed. There was definitely something up with her. "Where did you end up last night? I was surprised you weren't here when I got home."

She shrugged and looked away. "I went to the Shadow Lands for a while. Nothing exciting."

My ass. But, hey, if she didn't want to talk about it, she didn't want to talk about it. I didn't like it when she nagged me, so I wasn't going to nag her.

Except… "You'd tell me if you were in trouble, right? Like if something awful happened?"

She frowned, dark red brows lowering over eyes that were

exactly like mine. "Of course. Just because I wasn't with you doesn't mean something terrible happened."

But *something* had. I was willing to bet it was Kevin. He'd left the dance early, too. At the time I'd assumed a high school dance wasn't all that interesting for a guy in college, but now I suspected he'd run off to hang out with my sister. If he broke her heart, I was going to break his head.

"Why are you looking at me like that?" Wren demanded, the ball gown melting away into leggings and a long, slouchy sweater.

"Like what?"

"Like you want to punch me in the face."

"Sorry. It's not you I'd like to punch." I threw back the covers. "Gotta pee."

She came into the bathroom with me, phasing through the wall. Ghosts didn't have the same personal boundaries as the living. Wren never had a full bladder, the cow, so she didn't get that emptying it was often a private thing.

"Did you have a good time last night?" she asked, sticking her fingers through the shower curtain as she turned her back to me. At least she gave me a little privacy.

"I did—obviously after we got rid of Daria."

Wren frowned. She looked disappointed. "I was so sure that it was her love for Mr. Fisher that kept her here, not revenge."

"When love goes bad, it goes bad. Happens all the time." I flushed and washed my hands. "Not like they had a chance at happiness with her being a ghost."

"You know, for a girl with a boyfriend, you're terribly cynical about love."

"No, I'm not." I pulled on my pink fuzzy robe. "I just be-lieve it works better if both people are on the same side of the veil." I gave her a pointed look, hoping my meaning hit home.

She thought about it. "Well, that certainly makes intercourse easier."

I stared at her. Gaped, actually. "What?"

Wren looked at me like I was slow. "Intercourse. You know, interaction between two people."

"I think you mean *discourse*. *Intercourse* means sex."

"Oh." A look of understanding took over her face. "It really would make that easier, then, wouldn't it?" Then, she burst out laughing and so did I.

Our grandmother wasn't home when we went downstairs. Sometimes Nan and a couple of her girlfriends went shopping on Saturday mornings and then went for tea afterward. I didn't expect to see her anytime soon.

The coffee was still hot. I filled the biggest mug I could find and dumped in some flavored sweetener until it was the perfect color. I drank it while waiting for my bagel to pop.

"That's a lot of cream cheese," Wren remarked when I sat down at the table, breakfast in hand.

I picked up half the bagel and took a big bite. I could feel cream cheese smear against the outside edges of my mouth. I had been a little heavy-handed. "It's the best part."

She shrugged. "If you say so." Wren had experienced food before. Sometimes I'd let her possess me so she could experience things, but while she enjoyed the taste of cookies or chocolate, or even hot wings, she didn't understand eating for pleasure. To her a little cream cheese was the same as a lot.

I actually felt sorry for her when it came to that.

"Hey, can ghosts have intercourse?" I asked as the coffee kicked in. "The sex kind, not the conversational type."

She stuck her tongue out at me. "We have all the same parts the living have, so I have to say yes."

But she didn't know for certain. My sister was still a virgin.

The idea that she might remain that way forever was a little…
depressing. It wasn't any of my business, but sometimes…
Sometimes it was upsetting thinking of all the things I could
experience that she never would.

Then again, I'd never know the sublime pleasure of being
able to scare someone so effectively their bladder never worked
properly again.

"Mostly ghosts merge their energy," she continued. "It's
more of a literal 'becoming one' with one another."

"What if everything gets all mixed and you, like, leave part
of yourself in the other ghost?"

She frowned. "I don't know."

Yup, virgin. I finished the first half of my bagel. "Hey, I
want you to practice with my phone a bit."

Wren rolled her eyes. "Do we have to?"

"Yes. If Kevin hadn't been at the dance last night you
wouldn't have been able to lead them to Mr. Fisher." I didn't
add that the less time she had to spend around Kevin, the better. "The message you sent me was wrong. You need to be
able to communicate with people, and electronics have always
been a popular medium of supernatural communication."

Red brows shot up. "You've been watching those ghost
hunting shows again."

"Yes," I admitted. "They're ninety percent crap, but they
get the electronic stuff right. Most of the time. Look, I'm not
expecting you to download any apps. I just need to know that
if something took me out, that you could talk to someone." I
held her gaze, even though it was uncomfortable.

When I'd cut my wrists in a much-regretted suicide attempt, Wren had had to find a medium in order to get help.
That medium had been Kevin. If she hadn't found him—and

if he hadn't called my neighbor, Mace—I would have died for sure. As it was I had been technically dead for a few seconds.

It had felt much, much longer.

I wasn't in any hurry to die now, and I needed to make sure she could get help if it was needed.

I set my phone on the table. "Okay, go."

Wren sighed, but she didn't put up a fight. She closed her eyes and tilted her head back. A few seconds later my phone vibrated, and the text notification came up. I swiped my finger over the screen and brought up my new messages. One was from Ben, but the other had no name attached. Even though I was pretty confident it had worked, I held my breath as I opened the text.

BOO!

I looked up. My sister sat there grinning like a freaking idiot. "Really?" I said. "That's the best you can do?"

She shrugged. "You're sitting right next to me. What was I supposed to say?"

"I don't know. Something a little less stereotypical?"

My phone vibrated again. I looked down. A new message.

BOOBOOBOOBOOBOOBOOBOOBOOBOO.

"Ass," I said. Wren laughed. "Fine, you can use a phone right in front of you. Now I want you to send a message to Ben—and try to put a little more thought into it, please."

"Fine." She closed her eyes again, and I started in on the second half of my cream-cheese-laden bagel. I checked my email as I chewed.

I was scoping out the latest designs on the Fluevog website—I loved me some shoes—when my phone buzzed yet again.

It was Ben. His first text said that he'd dreamed about me last night, followed by a bunch of winky faces. The second read, How is Wren able to text me? And why did she ask me if you and I have ever had intercourt?

Intercourt? I started laughing. Auto-correct spared no one, not even the dead.

Wren smiled. "Is that from Ben?"

I set my phone aside. "He said to tell you that he's saving himself for marriage."

"Saving himself from what?" she asked. I didn't know if she was serious or not.

"Forget it." I took another bite of bagel. "You're good with text. Next we work on actually making a phone call."

My phone rang almost immediately. I glanced down at the display and sighed. Wren started laughing.

"Cow," I muttered.

On the screen, underneath Calling, it simply said: BOO.

My twin was still chuckling to herself when my phone buzzed again. I looked down expecting to see another message from Wren the comedian, but the name that came up was Emily, and the message read: Darkness is coming. You must save her.

My heart skipped a beat. I only knew one Emily—we were related, and she'd been a twin, as well. She was also dead.

Save who? I typed, then hit Send.

No reply. Awesome. Who the hell was this mysterious "her"? But more importantly, what did she mean by "darkness is coming"? That wasn't cryptic or anything.

God. Ghosts were *such* douche bags.

chapter three

LARK

We met at the local Goodwill later that day to shop for Halloween stuff. The dance the night before had just been the beginning of what Roxi was calling "The Halloween Season." There was a party tonight at Kevin's because his parents were on a cruise—his parents were away a lot—and then there were a couple of ghost walks through the week that I'd probably bow out of, leading up to the Dead Babies concert at Haven Crest on Halloween.

I'd already let everyone know what a bad idea attending the concert was, and we had all agreed to go anyway, despite the fact that ghosts from the hospital had tried to kill us. Were we mentally deranged? Probably, but Dead Babies were *awesome*. One of my favorite bands. Yes, enough that I'd risk going to see them at the most haunted place I'd ever visited, on the night the barrier between the realms of the living and dead was at its thinnest.

I justified it like so: I had to be there in case anything happened. It was my duty as someone who could combat ghosts to protect the concertgoers—and the band—from spectral harm. I had told my friends—and myself—so many times I almost believed it.

Bottom line—I wanted to go more than I was afraid of the ghosts. And that was stupid. No getting around it. I was the chick who went into the dark basement to find out what had made that scraping sound, armed with nothing but a pair of nail scissors. The idiot who decided to help the creepy little bare-footed, black-eyed kid who wore a tattered nightgown and stank of stale well water.

Hey, at least I owned it.

So, we were at Goodwill getting last-minute items for tonight, and also for Halloween night.

"I think you should go as Daenerys Targaryen," Roxi remarked, holding up a pink stuffed dragon.

"Ugh," I said, digging through a rack of dresses. "Do you know how many times I've been called 'Khaleesi' since that show started? Too many."

"But your hair is perfect for it." She looked genuinely upset that I didn't jump on the idea. "And I found a dragon."

I sighed as she wagged the toy. "Throw it over."

She grinned and tossed it over the racks. I caught it with one hand. "It smells like puke."

"It will wash," she chirped.

Roxi was one of those people who were almost always happy. I could hate her for it, but I think she kept me from being too emo. She was a little shorter than me, with long dark hair, a tan complexion and big brown eyes. She said her mother was Romanian and her dad was half-black. It didn't matter much to me, but she was gorgeous all the same. My mother was a bitch, and my father was a half-ball-less wonder. I was jealous that her parents even liked her, let alone loved her.

"I think I'm going to go as Cleopatra on actual Halloween night," she announced, holding up a long white dress that might have been fashionable in the late '70s. It was hideous by way of fabulous.

Her boyfriend, Gage—cute, dark-eyed, needed a haircut—bounded up beside her. "Does that mean I can be a gladiator?"

The way they smiled at each other made me turn away. PDAs were not a spectator sport as far as I was concerned.

Ben walked over. We'd been dating for almost two months, and I saw him almost every day, but I still smiled whenever I saw his face. Call me biased, but he's one of the hottest guys in school. Funny, smart—and he knows how to kick ghost-butt. His grandmother was Korean, and she'd taught me how to make *pujok*—basically a protection sigil against ghosts and evil spirits. I thought she liked me, but sometimes she looked at me like she wasn't quite sure what I was.

I got that a lot. I'm a teenage girl with stark-white hair whose mental state had been seriously questioned, and who could interact with ghosts the same as the living. I probably wouldn't like Ben's granny nearly as much if she just welcomed me with open arms.

"What are you wearing?" I asked, trying not to laugh.

Ben grinned and did a little twirl in front of me. "Do you like it? I might get it."

"It" was a full-length silver fur coat that was too big for him and too short in the arms. My guy was tall and lanky, and for a former chubby kid, he seemed to have no issues with self-confidence. One of the things I liked about him was that he was comfortable in his own skin and rarely worried about what other people thought of him.

"It's a little big," I said. "But it's a good look."

"I feel sexy."

"You smell like mothballs."

He sniffed his shoulder and made a face. "Yeah. Who even uses those things anymore?"

I shrugged. "People against moths, I guess. I have no idea what to wear to the party."

"You could go as Elsa," he suggested, slipping the coat off his shoulders. "You've got the hair for it."

I rolled my eyes. "Me and my damn hair."

He hung the fur up and stepped closer. He took a piece of my hair and wrapped it around his finger. "I like your damn hair."

Oh. When he lowered his voice like that and smiled that little smile…

"Get a room," Mace growled.

I turned around and shot him a grin. Mace was tall with light brown hair and hazel eyes. He was gorgeous, and someone I never thought I'd be friends with, especially after he found me bleeding to death and called 911. But we were friends. In fact, he was one of my best friends, though I doubted he knew it.

He had a fedora on his head. It actually didn't look too bad. "Who are you supposed to be?" I asked.

He made a face—like he'd bit into something sour. "Sarah wants us to be Bonnie and Clyde."

"We'll look fabulicious," his girlfriend called from four aisles away. "Stop making that face."

Mace made the face again and went back to pawing through the racks.

Suddenly, Wren popped out from between two dresses in front of me. It was so weird seeing her do that and the clothing not move. She was so real to me that it was easy to forget she was no more substantial than breath in this world.

"Haven't you figured out what you're going to be yet?" she demanded. "I've had my costume sorted out for weeks."

I wasn't feeling quite snarky enough to inform her that no one but me—and possibly Kevin—would be able to see it. "Yay, you."

Ben glanced at me. "You talking to me?"

I shook my head, glancing around to make sure no one else was paying attention.

He smiled. "Hey, Wren."

She waved, even though he couldn't see her. "Hi!"

"You could help me look for a costume," I told her.

Her eyes lit up. If she clapped her hands I was going to slap her. Instead, she turned around and whipped down the aisle toward evening wear. Mace shivered as she flew by. He turned to me. "Was that...?"

I nodded. "Yup."

He grinned. "I knew it."

My chest tightened. I looked from Mace to Ben, to Roxi and Gage, and even to Sarah. Kevin hadn't come because he was prepping for the party, which was just as well. Each of these living, breathing people made an effort to acknowledge or be kind to Wren. They were thoughtful of her, and that meant more to me than any of them could ever know. After years of being told my sister wasn't real, that she was only in my mind, it was so *freaking* good to know that not only were they wrong, but that Wren had become real—in her own way—to others.

I blinked back tears.

"Lark!" Wren cried a few seconds later. "I found it!"

Had she ever. It was a vintage pink slip-dress from the '70s. Normally such a piece would be fairly expensive, but this one had slight stains on the front and was only five bucks.

I knew exactly what to do with it.

Half an hour later we left the store. Everyone but Ben had a plastic bag full of items. He'd bought a pair of sunglasses and that was it. He still hadn't told me what he was going as that night, so I decided to keep my costume secret, as well.

I crossed the parking lot, swinging my plastic bag, as I laughed at a joke Gage had made. I turned to say something to him, but he was gone. They were all gone. The cars and the parking lot—the box stores that made up the rest of the plaza—everything was gone, and I was standing on cobblestones in a world where everything was muted and soft. The street I stood on seemed taken right from the pages of a BBC historical production, with gas lamps and horse-drawn carriages rattling along.

A woman in Edwardian clothing stopped on the opposite side of the street and stared at me. She looked scared. I glanced up and saw another woman peeking out a window from behind a curtain. Her mouth was open.

"Lark?"

I turned toward the familiar voice. It was Wren. She stood right beside me. "You're not supposed to be here," she said, taking my hand. "Come with me. Now."

I entwined my fingers with hers and stepped toward her. My ears popped, and suddenly the other world was gone, and I was back in the Goodwill parking lot, with my sister and all of my friends staring at me in concern.

"What happened?" Ben asked, pulling me in for a hug.

"I don't know," I replied. I was shaking, and there was no hiding it. "It felt like I stepped into another world."

"You did," Wren informed me. She had a strange expression on her face. My sister wasn't easily frightened, but she looked worried. Not just that, but she was looking at me like she didn't quite know me. "Lark, you were in the Shadow Lands."

I frowned at her. "I couldn't have been."

"Couldn't have been what?" Roxi asked, looking from me to the empty space occupied by my sister.

"In the Shadow Lands," I replied. "It's impossible. Only the dead can go there."

"You were dead," Mace reminded me softly. "Once."

I shook my head. "It had to have been my imagination."

My sister stomped up to me, so close our noses were almost touching. Of course, no one else could see it. "It was real. You were between both worlds."

Like her. Our gazes locked. I didn't have to say it for her to understand. This was weird. And it was big.

"Are you okay?" Ben asked, giving me a squeeze.

I nodded, looking away from my sister. "It's probably because Halloween's so close."

"Maybe," Wren allowed. "Or it might be something else."

I ignored her. "We'd better get going."

In my pocket my cell buzzed. I had a text. I pulled the phone out of my pocket and glanced at the message.

We're going to talk about this whether you like it or not.

I shot Wren a snotty look. She didn't look impressed, but I didn't care. I'd been to the Shadow Lands when I died for, like, two seconds. It felt like a lot more time there. And with the veil thinning it made sense that I'd be sensitive. Last year I was still in Bell Hill, so the meds might have kept me from experiencing the same thing then.

"Want to grab some lunch?" Mace asked us. "Mexican?"

A big plate of cheesy nachos was exactly what I needed.

"Sure," I said. And then to Ben, "Unless you need to go home."

"No. Lunch sounds good."

Everyone else left ahead of us. Wren said she'd meet us there. I didn't know where she was off to, but I suspected it was the Shadow Lands. I got into the car.

Ben opened the driver-side door and slid in. He put the key into the ignition, but instead of turning it, he turned to me. "Be honest. Are you okay?"

I leaned my head back against the seat and smiled. "Yeah, I'm good." It was mostly true. I mean, yeah, it was weird, but my whole life was weird. If I freaked out every time something strange happened, I'd spend 99 percent of my time a basket case.

He leaned over and kissed me. For those few seconds I didn't think. I didn't worry about anything.

Like what those two women in the Shadow Lands saw when they looked at me. Or why my sister had been afraid.

WREN

"She just didn't look *right*," the woman with the cockney accent explained. "There were something dreadful odd about her, for such a pretty girl."

She looked odd because she was alive, but I didn't say that. I only asked this woman—and the one who had been on the street when Lark had popped into the Shadow Lands—about what she'd seen because I didn't want it getting around that my sister had slipped past the barrier.

It made sense that if the dead could easily cross at this time of year, then the living could, as well. It felt strange, though. I'd never heard of it happening before, but that didn't mean it hadn't. I wished our ancestor Emily—who had reached out to both Lark and me before—would decide to show up and give us some advice on how this living/dead twin thing worked, but we hadn't seen her since the night she helped Lark tap into her ghost-fighting abilities.

I hadn't had any glimpses of her sister, Alys, either—who had occasionally shown herself to me at my grandmother's house. It was frustrating, because I felt like their appearances *meant* something. Shouldn't they have moved on?

I wanted to find Emily and Alys. I wanted them to tell Lark and me why we existed. What was the reason? What was our destiny? I wanted *answers*. But it seemed that Lark and I were destined to wind up with nothing but an endless list of questions.

The one thing that struck me as I left the woman to wander the streets of shadow-Edwardian London, was that neither of Lark's witnesses had remarked that she looked like me. That meant that she looked different here—maybe like how I looked when I manifested in the living world? No wonder the women had been afraid of her.

What would happen if Lark manifested here for any length of time? We spent so much time trying to make sure I didn't cause harm in the living world with my abilities, but we'd never considered whether she could be a danger to the dead.

And why hadn't we discussed it? I'd seen her punch a ghost. Seen her hurt a spirit. Those ones had deserved it, but what if she went after someone who didn't? She might hurt someone, just like there was the danger of me doing harm when I manifested among the living.

I was getting ahead of myself. There was no need to get anxious. This might have been an All Hallows' Eve aberration. Yes, that was the best way to think of it for now. If it happened again, I'd consult the Shadow Lands library.

I drifted back into the earthly realm. I spent more time among the living than I did the dead. It wasn't completely because of Lark and our friends, but because I found the living more interesting.

The Shadow Lands was made up of bits and pieces the dead had assembled—not quite Heaven, but a more idyllic version of what their lives had been. There wasn't the amount of emotion and drama going on that there was in the living world. Lark turned her nose up at many of the reality shows on the television, but she didn't seem to realize that, to me, *her* life was a reality show! Even the simple act of shopping was interesting to someone who only had to "think" her appearance and make it so.

I ended up at Haven Crest. I didn't wonder why—I wasn't totally vacuous. It was obvious that some part of my mind had been thinking about Noah. Other than Lark's realm-jumping, I hadn't thought about much other than him all day.

It was late afternoon, and while the daylight hours had shortened considerably in New England, there was still an hour or more of daylight left. Noah wasn't a young ghost, so there was a chance he might be about, especially if I could find the spot he haunted.

Finding another ghost wasn't easy in a place like this. The dead recognized each other's energy, so if I was in a house with one or two ghosts I could probably seek them out without much trouble. A place like Haven Crest, though… Well, there were so many ghosts that trying to find just one was like that old saying about needles and haystacks.

Maybe not quite that hard. I had interacted with Noah. Our spirits had brushed together. That would make it a little easier to find him once I found the right spot—just like Lark knew the scent of Ben's soap, I would recognize Noah's energy.

Based on the way he'd been dressed I knew he had to have died in the late nineteenth/early twentieth century. There had been fewer buildings back then, and of those only the main residence and one other had been used to house patients. I knew this because, after Josiah Bent, Lark and I both wanted to make sure we knew as much about this place as we could. Haven Crest was so haunted it was practically a spiritual entity itself. That was something that needed to be watched.

I moved toward the main building, where there had been a wing for male patients and another for female. A building to the left of that, some distance away—closer to the forest and former garden—had been segregated in a similar manner, but with one difference. It had been for the wealthy patients. The wealthy white patients. I'd learned that the "colored" inmates had been divided by gender and affluence and were housed in a separate building.

Lark had tried explaining racism to me in the past, and while I understood the concept, I couldn't wrap my mind around the sentiment behind it. People ought to be judged by their character, not their color.

Based on the fact that Noah had fair skin and had been well dressed, it was probably a valid assumption that he haunted the upper-class residence, so that's where I went. Thankfully, this was not where Josiah Bent and his followers had haunted, because I probably wouldn't be welcomed there by many of them. As an outsider, Dead Born and free to go wherever I wanted, I was going to be resented, regardless.

That knowledge didn't keep me from entering the old building. Its once beautiful windows were mostly broken and boarded up. The large, double doors were locked but hung loose on rusted hinges, dirty white paint peeling. It reminded me of photos I'd seen one time Lark was browsing some internet site—photos of celebrities who had ruined their looks with drugs and alcohol. This building had been beautiful once, but it had been abandoned to the ravages of time and neglect.

I walked through those sad doors and stood in the middle of a reception area with a high, vaulted ceiling. It looked as though there had been some plasterwork on the walls at one time, but it had been pried off. Broken pieces lay scattered on the dirty hardwood floor. Not just neglected, this building had been pillaged, as well.

Vandals. Their kind had no respect for anything. How terrible it must be for those who haunted this place to see it slowly stolen away. It hurt me—offended the deepest part of me.

In response to my anger, the building cried out. To living ears it would have sounded like a low groan—creaking floors or old pipes. To me, it was an anguished wail.

Yes, Haven Crest was more than just a collection of old wood and stone.

"Wren?"

I turned my head. Standing on the stairs to my left was Noah. He looked concerned. "Is something wrong? I felt… a disturbance."

I shook my head, but my heart was full of sorrow. "This place must have been beautiful once."

"It was." He continued down the stairs. He was wearing different clothes today—a white shirt and gray vest with black trousers and boots. His thick hair was tousled as though he'd been running his hands through it. He was beautiful. I just stood there and watched as he approached me.

"Would you like to see it as it once was?" he asked.

I didn't know if seeing its former glory would make what I felt better or worse, but I knew that I *wanted* to see it. "Yes."

"Take my hand."

I slipped my hand in his, feeling the warmth of his fingers around mine. Slowly, the faded wallpaper gave way to a beautiful pale blue damask. The plasterwork reappeared as frames on the walls and bouquets of flowers in the corners of the ceiling. The wood floor gleamed, the stairs, as well, and they were covered by a strip of cream carpet with roses printed on it. Above our heads a sparkling chandelier hung, its brass chain shining. Even the reception desk was a thing of beauty. And the windows! They were flanked by pale gold velvet curtains, pulled back to let in the sunlight.

"It's prettier than I thought," I said, my voice a little hoarse.

"This is how I choose to see it," Noah told me. "Rationally, I know that it's a ruin now, and that soon it will either collapse or they'll tear it down, but in my heart, it will always be a grand old girl to me."

"What will you do if they tear it down?" I asked.

"I suppose I'll have to learn to like whatever they build in its spot, or find someplace new." He smiled, but I could tell it was forced. "Perhaps I'll move on. Whatever happens, I suppose it shall be an adventure."

I think I fell in love with him at that moment, watching him trying to be brave when faced with losing everything he had left in the world. Someday, everything I held dear would be in ruins, as well.

I squeezed his hand in mine, and in that moment I made a decision. I looked him in the eye and smiled. "Would you like to go to a party with me tonight?"

chapter four

LARK

"Oh, my gawwwwd!" Roxi squealed. She was dressed in a Day of the Dead costume complete with elaborate face makeup and roses in her hair. "Your costume is amazeballs!"

I did a little twirl on the back step of my grandmother's house. I was wearing the long pink slip dress I'd bought earlier that day. It was covered in fake blood—fabric paint, so I didn't have to worry about getting red on everything. I was also wearing a "blood"-splattered long strawberry-blond wig, a tiara and a sash that said Prom Queen.

"Did you do the makeup yourself?" I asked as we climbed into Nan's car—a purple Volkswagen Beetle with flower-shaped brake lights.

The wreath in her hair brushed the ceiling of the car. "Yeah. I watched a couple videos online first."

I fastened my seat belt and started the engine. "What's Gage going as?"

"Baron Samedi," she replied. "I know it's hokey to do the matching thing, but it was his idea."

"I think it's cute." And it was, which suited the two of them.

"What's Wren's costume?" she asked as we pulled out onto the street.

"I'm not sure," I replied. "She said she'd meet us there." To be honest I thought it was really weird that she wasn't with me now. She'd been acting a little off lately.

"Oh, hey. I meant to tell you that she showed up in a few more photos from the dance. Like, fully visible."

"Really?" My mother used to accuse me of doing "something" to make it look like there was someone beside me in photos when we were kids. She never believed me about Wren. She thought I talked about my sister to upset her.

"Yeah, she totally photo-bombed a couple of shots. Want to see?" She started digging through her purse for her phone. The purse wasn't much bigger than a tablet—how hard could it be to find a phone in it?

I pulled into the local middle-school parking lot. I wanted to study what Roxi had to show me, and I couldn't do that and make sure I didn't drive into a tree.

I turned on the dome light just as Roxi found her phone. It took her a few seconds to get into the photo album and find what she was looking for, but finally she handed me the phone.

The image on the screen was of me, Sarah, Gage and Ben dancing. Mace was out of frame. And there, just behind me, was Wren dancing with wild abandon.

My throat tightened. I don't know why it choked me up to see her, but it did.

"Scroll to the next one," Roxi instructed. I did.

And burst out laughing.

It was the whole group of us, clustered in for a dance-floor selfie. There, sticking her head in by mine—while standing practically *in* Roxi—was Wren, making duck lips.

How the hell did she know about duck lips?

Roxi grinned as I handed the phone back to her. "Awesome, huh?"

I nodded. "Can you text that to me?"

"Already on it."

I was still smiling as I steered the Beetle out of the lot and back onto the road.

New Devon wasn't a big town—like most places in Connecticut it just sort of melded with the other small towns around it. Kevin lived not far from Haven Crest and the town cemetery, where he used to take care of Wren's grave. He didn't do that anymore—I did. I never asked Wren why he stopped, and she never offered to tell me. Kevin's house was in a neighborhood that had a lot of space between homes, which was great for a party. The brick house with its white trim was supposed to look warm and homey, but it still screamed *money!* which I found a little intimidating. Not that I'd ever let Kevin know that.

There were already several cars parked in the drive and on the street when we arrived. I pulled in behind Mace's car.

Kevin answered the door a few seconds after Roxi rang the bell. He was dressed as the main character from *Kick-Ass*. It suited him. He grinned when he saw us, but he didn't hold my gaze. "You guys look awesome," he said, stepping back so we could enter.

A Taylor Swift song was playing when we walked in. I arched a brow. I hadn't taken Kevin as a fan, but when we walked into the living room and I saw Sarah by the stereo system, shaking her head and butt to the beat, I understood who was in charge of the music. Sarah was dressed like an old-time female gangster. Not far away was Mace, looking very gangster-ish. Bonnie and Clyde had won out after all.

I looked around the room. There were easily twenty or so people there already—an assortment of "sexy" cops, Disney characters, superheroes and guys dressed as horror-movie villains. What—or rather who—was Ben? I didn't see him. I had offered to pick him up in case he planned to drink, but he'd turned me down.

It made me anxious. Was he tired of me already? My heart told me that was stupid, but my head couldn't help it. I didn't trust in good things. And I didn't trust myself to be able to keep a guy like Ben around. He was good and nice, while I thought of myself as something of a hot mess—emphasis on *mess*.

Gage—or rather, Baron Samedi—showed up and claimed Roxi, leaving me standing alone by the snack table. The huge bowl of chips looked so tempting now that I was all anxious. I grabbed a can of soda from the cooler instead and made myself walk away rather than dive headfirst into salty, greasy temptation.

"Nice costume," came a familiar voice as I leaned against the wall—far away from food.

I turned to smiled at Mace. "Thanks," I said. "You, too."

He made a face. "When Sarah gets her heart set on something, it's easier sometimes just to go with it." He gestured at my head with his own soda. "Weird to see you with different hair."

Self-consciously, I touched the "blood"-soaked wig. "Weird-bad, or weird-good?"

Mace shrugged. "Weird-different. You always look good."

I blinked. The compliment was so unexpected I wasn't sure how to take it. "Oh. Thanks."

He looked away. I followed his gaze and saw that Sarah and Kevin were standing together by the stereo, and she was laughing at something Kevin had said. Mace didn't look too happy about it.

"I hate Taylor Swift," he said, turning his gaze back to mine. I could tell he suspected there was something between his best friend and his girlfriend, but I wasn't going to ask. Not here.

I watched as his expression brightened. He was looking at a point over my shoulder, a grin spreading across his face. "That's too cool."

I turned. Practically everyone had stopped to watch the guy who had just entered the room. He was tall and dressed entirely in black as Neo from *The Matrix*. The costume was perfect—long black coat, boots with silver buckles, cargo pants with weapons strapped on. His black shirt was snug enough to cling to his defined chest and abs. Even the hair and sunglasses were perfect.

A "sexy witch" and a "sexy Freddy Krueger" straightened up as he walked by, eyeing him with obvious interest. But "Neo" didn't even give them a glance. In fact his attention was focused on just one person.

Me.

If it had been anyone else, I would probably say something sarcastic about the amount of detail in the costume, but this was Ben. *My* Ben. And he looked freaking incredible.

"He wore that to New York Comic Con last year," I heard Mace say. "He's got new sunglasses, though. Killer costume."

That was one way to describe it. I would also describe it as "hot" if I were capable of speech.

"Hey," Ben said when he reached me. "You look amazing."

"So do you," I replied.

As if to prove my point, Gage walked by and slapped him on the back, saying, "Awesome costume, man."

Ben smiled. "I kinda feel like I should give you my coat. There's not much to that dress."

It was a thin material, but it wasn't like I was naked underneath. It was October in New England, after all. That said, spaghetti straps don't provide that much warmth.

"Keep it," I said. "Enough girls are staring at you already."

His grin grew. "Jealous?"

I rolled my eyes. "No." And then, with a smile, "Maybe." It was true. I liked knowing other girls thought he was gorgeous, but I didn't like feeling that someday he might find someone he liked better than me. Certainly there were girls out there who were less work and weren't always getting into fights with dead people.

He laughed and put his arm around my shoulders—he was so warm!—pulling me in for a kiss.

"Get a room," Mace drawled—as he always did—before walking away. I flipped him off, but he didn't see the gesture. Ben gave me a hug before letting me go, but he took my hand in his.

"So, *Carrie*, huh?" he asked, giving me the once-over again. "Points for going with the original."

"Thanks. It was an easy costume—Wren found the dress."

"Is she here?"

"Not yet. I'm not sure she's going to show. It's getting harder for her to keep herself hidden. She showed up in a lot of Roxi's photos from the dance. She might not want to risk other people seeing her." It was weird, but after years of wishing people would believe my sister was real, I was suddenly very worried about what might happen if they did.

More people began to arrive, and we gravitated toward what I considered my main group of friends. I was eating chips—my willpower having evaporated—when Wren arrived. Chewing was the only thing that kept my mouth from falling open at the sight of her.

She looked amazing. She was dressed in a gorgeous gold ball gown—the kind they wore in the Victorian era—and her hair was all piled up on top of her head with pins that glittered in the light. She looked like a princess.

She turned her head and said something. That's when I realized that the guy standing next to her, dressed in a tux with tails, was also a ghost.

And they were holding hands.

My breath caught. How had she managed to bring him with her? I didn't even know she could do that. Ghosts could travel, but it required some sort of connection with a person or object. Josiah Bent had been able to follow us to the hospital after hurting Gage because he'd gotten a "taste" of us. Normally the dead were bound to the place they haunted. Wren didn't have a haunt and wandered about as she pleased at times. She wasn't a normal ghost, and this only made that all the more clear to me.

But I had more important questions than how she'd managed to bring another ghost with her, such as who the hell was he, and why didn't I know anything about him?

And why did that hurt so much?

WREN

My sister was *not* happy to see me. I suppose I ought to have told her that I was bringing a date, but asking Noah to come with me had been an impulsive thing, and I hadn't really given Lark much thought while I was with him. It wasn't as though she told me everything she did.

Lark didn't like surprises, and Noah was the second of two

I'd just sprung on her. The first being that I could tether to another ghost. It wasn't a big deal. Not like Noah could come here without me afterward. It wasn't that easy either, though the fact that it was almost Halloween helped. It also helped that I was me. I could do things that other ghosts couldn't, and what was the point of it if I didn't take advantage on occasion? All I had to do was share a little of my energy with the other spirit.

I knew from the look on Lark's face that she was going to have a lot to say to me later, and I admit that I felt a little guilty, but I was allowed to have my own life, wasn't I? Maybe *life* wasn't the best word. I was allowed to have *something* of my own. Did she think being invisible and mute to the people she called "our" friends was fun for me?

Lark jerked her head—which was covered by a reddish-blond wig that looked like she'd sustained a major head wound—toward a doorway that led to a quiet corridor. If she intended to give me a hard time, she was in for a surprise. I was ready to fight it out with her, and I couldn't blame the sudden aggression entirely on Halloween. I rarely told Lark how to behave, but she was always ordering me about like a dog.

"Come meet my sister," I said to Noah, tugging on his hand. He was the most handsome of any of the boys there, I thought a little smugly. It was just too bad that I couldn't show him off to anyone but Lark.

"This is extraordinary," Noah remarked, his head slowly turning from side to side as he took everything in. "There aren't any chaperones. In my day this amount of young men would never be allowed to socialize with these young ladies without supervision. It would be ruinous for the females, their very virtue called into question."

I loved the way he spoke, the words he used and how they rolled off his tongue. I held his arm as we followed after my sister. "Are you telling me that you never managed to sneak off with a girl at a party?" I teased. "Never stole a secret kiss?"

He smiled coyly. "Maybe once. Or twice." The smile faded. "But still, had we been caught, there would have been serious consequences."

"Would you be grounded?" Our parents had subjected Lark to such a punishment once for insisting I was real despite all their attempts to make her say otherwise. We were ten at the time.

"Grounded?" he repeated. "I'm not familiar with the term. No, we would have been forced to marry. I would have been duty-bound as a gentleman to save her reputation."

Married! I tried to think of Lark having to marry Ben because they'd been caught making out in his car. My sister would probably rather have her reputation ruined than be forced to do anything—even if it was something she might enjoy.

"Did that happen a lot?" I asked, swerving to avoid walking through a girl wearing a ridiculously skimpy costume. She shivered as I passed. I resisted the urge to run a finger down her spine just to watch her do it again.

"Occasionally." He nodded at the girl. "I remember when women wore more clothing than that to go swimming. The world has changed so much since my death."

There was a sadness to his voice that made me want to hug him. I squeezed his arm instead, drawing another one of his smiles. "Do not worry yourself about me, Miss Wren. It happens to all of us eventually—whether we be living or spirit."

We crossed the threshold into the corridor where my sister paced. She was halfway down the length of the hall when she stopped, back stiffening. I didn't know how she sensed us, but she did. She always did. She pivoted sharply on her high heels and stomped toward me.

"She looks ill-tempered," Noah remarked.

Lark shot him a glare. "And you look like a butler."

I don't know which surprised him more—the insult or the fact that she had heard what he'd said. Noah had said he'd heard of me before, so I assumed he knew about Lark as well, but he obviously didn't know as much as I'd thought.

"She can see me?" he asked, incredulous.

"Even when it's not Halloween, Mr. Darcy," Lark retorted.

I frowned at her. "Don't be rude."

She looked as though she could cheerfully punch me. What was wrong with her? She needed to get over it, and quickly.

"Noah's my friend," I informed my sister. "I asked him at the last moment to come with me so I can talk and dance with someone who isn't you. Someone who can see me. Someone I can touch."

Lark's expression could only be described as annoyed contrition. She wasn't happy about the situation, and I knew part of that was because she distrusted any ghost that wasn't me. I couldn't blame her—she had an awfully violent history with many of my kind—but Noah wasn't like that.

"You should have told me," she said. "What if someone sees the two of you? It's too close to Halloween for surprises."

"What if someone *does* see us?" I asked. "You've spent most of your life trying to prove that I'm real."

She looked surprised at the question. "Because I don't know what people would do to us if they figured it out."

People could be such...*douche bags.* "They can't do anything. Not to me." The words felt hard in my mouth, but they slid out anyway. "And I don't care if someone sees me. I'm not afraid of a bunch of teenagers."

My sister stared at me. I didn't like the suspicion in her gaze. I hadn't meant to upset her, but I was through behaving as though I was something to be ashamed of. Tugging Noah with me, I turned around. "Let's go dance."

"Hey, Lark," Roxi cried from further up the corridor. "Smile!"

A flash went off, and for a second all the world was sharp and bright. The eyes of the dead don't need to physically respond to light or dark, so the light didn't blind Noah or myself like it had Lark.

Roxi stared in my direction, her eyes wide.

"Something wrong, Rox?" Lark asked.

The dark-haired girl shook her head. "No. I thought I saw something, that's all." She shook her head, and her normally cheerful expression returned.

In the next room the music for "Thriller" began to play. I pulled Noah out into the small group dancing in the middle of the living room, leaving Lark behind. She could be as upset as she wanted. I was going to have fun, and if my sister didn't like it she could…well, she could just not like it all she wanted.

I spotted Kevin talking to Ben and Gage. Was it wrong of me to wish he could see me with Noah? I wanted him to know I wasn't crying over him. That I didn't miss him, because I didn't.

"This music is strange," Noah remarked. He gestured to the small group around us. "Is this what qualifies as dancing these days?"

I laughed. He looked horrified. "Just move to the music,"

I instructed, raising my arms over my head and moving the rest of me to the beat. "Do what feels right."

He was awkward, and a little stiff, but the best part of being a ghost meant that very few people could see you make a fool of yourself.

But this was Halloween week, and I'd forgotten what that meant. I bumped into a girl—and felt it. She didn't go through me. And when she turned around, she looked surprised not to see someone there. I moved away. Maybe dancing wasn't such a good idea after all.

"I'm sorry about my sister," I said to Noah as we drifted away from the dancing.

He shrugged. "She's very protective of you. I cannot fault her for that."

I rolled my eyes. "I don't need protection. I'm supposed to be the scary one."

"Scary?" He frowned. "Is that what she thinks of you?" The look he shot my sister was one of indignation. Thankfully, Lark was paying attention to something Ben was saying and not my date.

My date. I never thought I'd call someone my date. Never thought I'd ever meet a boy who was a ghost like me.

"No," I said, putting my hand on his arm. "Lark doesn't think I'm scary at all." That was a lie. There were times when I knew my sister found me terrifying, but she loved me anyway. I never understood why I was so frightening until I saw Lark in my world. Sometimes people didn't have to be hideous or monstrous to be frightening. In fact, simply looking "not right" could be disturbing enough.

Noah relaxed. "Good." He turned to me with a soft smile. "I cannot imagine anyone thinking you anything but perfect."

"Oh." That was the only word I could remember at that

moment. He was so handsome, and so tall, and so saying everything I wanted to hear. Lark would tell me he was too good to be true. That I shouldn't trust him.

Sometimes, my sister didn't know what she was talking about.

"Are you having fun?" Noah asked. "Do you want to stay? Or can I steal you away?"

I glanced around the room. I was having fun—sort of. As much fun as a dead girl could have in a room full of people who couldn't see her. But then my gaze fell on Kevin.

He was staring straight at me. Or rather, he was staring at Noah. With the veil between worlds thinning, his abilities as a medium were magnified. My wish that he could see me there with another boy had just come true.

He looked like someone had punched him in the throat. I had hoped for regret, not pain. The satisfaction I had thought I'd feel wilted under an emotion I couldn't quite identify.

I turned away, facing Noah, who thankfully hadn't realized we had an audience. It wasn't too difficult to smile at him. "Let's go," I said. "This isn't as fun as I thought it would be."

Noah took my hand, and then we were gone, back to the grounds of Haven Crest where we talked and danced to our own music for hours. And I concentrated all of my attention on the boy I could have, rather than the one who could never be mine.

chapter five

LARK

Wren had taken off with Casper the Friendly Douche a few hours earlier, and I hadn't seen her since. It wasn't like her to just disappear on me, which meant she was all twitterpated over Mr. Darcy. Noah. Whatever.

I was *not* jealous. I was, however, worried. What if this guy was a jerk? Wren didn't know anything about relationships outside of TV and movies, and Noah had spent at least part of his existence among the living. Any guy that polished and pretty had to be a player as far as I was concerned.

I really wanted to be wrong, but something about him bothered me.

I was *not*—repeat—*not* jealous.

A few of us stuck around after the party to help clean up. It wasn't a terribly late night. Mace and Ben volunteered to drive those who'd had too much Halloween "spirits" home.

Carrying a recyclable bag full of soda cans, I walked into the kitchen. Sarah and Kevin stood in front of the sink. He leaned back, slightly, as though trying to put as much distance between them as he could when she had him practically pinned between herself and the counter.

"He's my *friend*," Kevin said, his voice low, his hands gripping the edge of the sink behind him.

"What am I?" Sarah demanded.

Okay, I didn't have to be a genius to figure out what was going on. "The friend's girlfriend?" I volunteered. Was this any of my business? Nope. But Mace had saved my life, and had become a good friend. I felt strangely protective of him, and in the hierarchy of friends, both Kevin and Sarah were near the bottom of my list.

Sarah jumped back, putting several feet of distance between them. She looked pissed. Kevin looked guilty—and maybe a little relieved? Sarah must have seen that relief as well, because she made a noise of disgust and pivoted dramatically on her heel. She shot me a glare as she stomped past me and out of the kitchen. I raised a brow and said nothing.

I took the bag of cans over to the blue bin and set it inside before turning to look at Kevin. He was flushed. "Thanks."

I tilted my head. "For what? Keeping you from becoming even more of a jerk?"

He laughed. I hadn't expected that. He laughed so hard, his eyes watered. Or maybe those were tears. I couldn't tell. He was a hot mess.

"Yeah," he said with a nod as he wiped at his eyes. "For that."

I never understood what Wren saw in him, but at that moment I felt bad for the guy. He looked really effed up.

"Do you really like her?" I asked, moving closer to him.

Kevin shrugged. "Not enough to lose Mace over her. He's been my best friend since elementary school." He swiped at his eyes with the back of his hand. "Did Wren tell you about us?"

Both my brows shot up. "Wren knows?"

"Shit." He closed his eyes and shook his head. "She didn't tell you that she saw us kissing?"

"Uh, no. Otherwise I would have taken you aside and kicked your ass long before this." Wren was keeping all kinds of secrets, it seemed. Didn't she trust me? Or did she just not want to hear what I might say? If she'd told me about Kevin and Sarah I would have shot my mouth off, and I would be the first to admit just how much of a bitch I could be.

Or worse, my sister had felt too awful to even talk about it—which really made me want to take a swing at him. No wonder she'd grabbed onto Mr. Darcy.

Folding his arms over his chest, Kevin looked me in the eye. "I didn't mean for it to happen. I just wanted to connect with someone." He laughed again. "God, I sound so pathetic, don't I?"

I frowned. "No, not really." And then, as the thought occurred to me, "You love my sister, don't you?"

A look of horror washed over his face. "Is she still here?" He even glanced over his shoulder as though he expected to find her standing there.

"No, she's gone."

His shoulders slumped. "Good. Stupid, right? Not like we can ever be together."

I shrugged. "Not until you're dead."

This time when he laughed, it seemed more out of a sense of amusement. "Something to look forward to."

I smiled. "Sure."

Kevin's brows drew together. "Who was that guy she had with her? Do you know him?"

"You saw him?" It had taken Kevin a long time to be able to see Wren, and even then it had taken a lot of focus for both of them. It made sense, I guess, that with Halloween's approach his abilities would sharpen.

"Yeah. He looked familiar. Who is he?"

"Noah," I replied. "That's all I know. I called him Mr. Darcy."

He grinned. "You would. His clothes were more Victorian, though."

"You're splitting hairs, Sixth Sense." He hated when I called him that. And when had he become a historical fashion expert? "If you don't want to discuss your feelings for Wren with me, that's cool."

"It's not that I don't want to, I don't see the point. You've figured me out, and talking about it just hurts. She hasn't told you about this new guy?"

"No. I just met him tonight. I don't think she's known him long. She's just thrilled to find a cute dead guy, I think."

"I know him from somewhere, though." His frown deepened. "You think he's cute?"

Somehow, I managed not to laugh. I smiled, though. "I think she does, though my sister seems to have a thing for dark hair and blue eyes." I didn't mention that I actually thought Noah and Kevin looked a bit alike, because pining over a dead girl was no way to spend your life.

Kevin nodded. "Yeah. Anyway, thanks."

"If you remember where you know Noah from, let me know, okay? Wren hasn't been exactly chatty about him."

"Sure."

"Hey—" I felt the sudden need to change the subject "—you want some help taking this garbage out?" I knew from previous visits to the house that his parents put the recyclables and garbage in bins in a little shed out back to wait for pickup.

"Yeah, thanks."

We each had two bags as we walked outside. Everything at

the party had been disposable to cut down on dishes to wash—and to narrow the margin on dishes that idiots could break.

It was dark out and chilly. It had been a warm fall, but October nights in Connecticut were going to be cold, no matter how warm the day had been. I had my arms wrapped around myself as we hurried back to the house.

There was a guy standing right in front of the door, blocking our path. It took me a moment to realize he was a ghost—they looked as solid as real people to me for the most part, but there was a weird "feel" to them that I couldn't quite explain.

This guy had been in his late twenties when he died. He had long shaggy hair and was wearing bell-bottoms. I was going to guess he died in the '70s, and from the smell of patchouli, sweat and vomit that seemed to cling to him, I figured it had been an overdose that did him in. Although, he looked pretty clear-headed now. And angry. And all of that anger was staring at Kevin.

"Hey, Woodstock. What's up?" I chirped, trying to draw his attention.

His dead gaze flickered to me and then dismissed me, as though I were nothing more threatening than a mote of dust.

"Kevin McCrae?" he asked.

Kevin was still, tense, but his expression was blank. "Yes. Who are you?"

Woodstock grinned, revealing teeth that had seen better days. "Death," he replied.

And then he lunged.

WREN

"Who was that boy?"

I glanced up at Noah. We were back at his building at

Haven Crest, dancing to the music that lingered from many, many years earlier. Spectral energy was like that—it hung around long after it was created, waiting to be discovered. It was like tuning a radio station to the right frequency.

"What boy?" There had been so many at the party.

"The one in the strange green long johns. I swore he looked right at me."

Oh. *Him*. "That was Kevin. He's a medium."

"Ah. That explains it. This time of year must be difficult for his kind. What is this Kevin's last name?"

I didn't want to tell him. I don't know why, but talking about Kevin with him felt wrong. "McCrae."

"Irish."

"American." Kevin's family had come over from Ireland so long ago it hardly mattered anymore.

Noah gave me a little smile. "Still Irish, dear girl."

I arched a brow. *Dear girl*? "Are you still English?"

"Of course," he replied. "A man's country is all he has. It's what defines him as a man."

"I thought it was character that defined a man."

He laughed. "Cheeky girl. You have me there." He glanced over my shoulder at something I couldn't see, his gaze narrowing. He nodded once. When I was able to glance in that direction, there was nothing there.

"Beg your pardon," Noah said. "I was just shooing away another resident who thought they might join us."

I smiled. I liked that he wanted me all to himself. "I'm sorry that the party wasn't more fun for you."

He whirled me around. "I don't understand most modern social behaviors, but it was pleasurable to me to simply spend the evening in your presence."

"I could listen to you talk all night," I told him with a sigh. "Hurray for English boys."

"Hurrah for the Melinoe."

"What's that?"

He smiled, and tucked my hair behind my ear. "Just an old Greek term for beautiful girls. For you."

I couldn't hide how that made me feel, so I glanced away. I didn't know much about boys and dating, and flirting. I couldn't even tell if he was being sincere.

I *wanted* him to be sincere.

The tall grandfather clock against the far wall chimed the hour. It was midnight. I felt a frisson of energy race up my legs to swirl in my stomach. In my arms, Noah seemed to glow a little brighter.

"Did you feel that?" he asked. "One day closer to All Hallows' Eve."

"I've never felt a jolt like that before." My fingers tingled.

Noah grinned. "It's because you're here. You don't spend much time with the dead, do you?"

I shook my head. "Not really, no. And if I do, it's in the Shadow Lands."

His handsome face darkened. "That *place*. They expect us to skulk about there, while we've as much right to this world as the living. Did we ask to perish before our time? To be made monsters in our own home? How is it we 'haunt' a place while the living reside there? Or worse, cast it aside like trash to wither and decay?"

He was so angry. "I'm sorry. I didn't mean to upset you."

Suddenly, the tension drained from his face, and the Noah I'd come to know was there again. "Forgive me. Sometimes I give into the unjustness of my plight rather than appreciate what I have." He smiled flirtatiously. "Such as the company of a beautiful young lady."

I preened under the compliment, lowering my eyes to hide the joy his words inspired. Only Kevin had ever called me beautiful before.

"Let's go for a walk," Noah suggested. "I want you to see how the grounds once looked."

He held my hand as we drifted through the peeling wooden door, out into the night. Outside, the exterior of the Haven Crest campus looked as it always had to me—old and run-down. Its beautiful architecture abandoned and left to rot, feeding the malevolence and despair of all the souls bound to it.

"It doesn't look any different," I said, unable to hide my disappointment.

Noah squeezed my hand. "Close your eyes."

I did as he said.

He kissed me—his lips soft and warm against mine. My soul fluttered. When he pulled away, my first response was to pull him back, but he didn't go far.

"Open your eyes," he whispered.

I did, choking back a gasp at the sight that met my eyes. The electric lamps that had flooded the grounds with light had been replaced by flickering lanterns in glass cases on high black poles. The grass was thick and rich green. The trees were shorter, and gravel paths replaced cracked asphalt. But it was the buildings that were truly spectacular. Redbrick with gleaming white trim. Windows lit from within with golden light. Steps unbroken and straight, some with columns that stood straight and smooth rather than pitted and peeling.

"It's beautiful," I whispered.

"Horrible things have happened here," Noah said softly.

"But there were good things as well, things that unfortunately have been forgotten by many."

Other spirits had joined us—ghosts from across the ages. Some were male, some were female. Some were young, some old. There were people of different ethnicities and backgrounds standing together—class didn't matter to the dead. We were all transfixed by the sight of Haven Crest in its prime.

"You did this?" I asked, turning to Noah.

He shrugged. "I merely made it possible for you to see it in another dimension. The Haven Crest you know still exists, but this is how it sees itself. I think this version is much prettier, don't you?"

I nodded. The jolt I'd felt and all this beauty only made me more certain that Haven Crest was its own entity. "It's like something on *Masterpiece Theatre*."

"*Masterpiece Theatre*? Never heard of it."

I laughed. "No. It's a little after your time." I gripped his hand tighter. "Noah, thank you for showing me this."

He smiled. "It's important to me that you see this place as I do, that you understand why those of us who choose to be here are reluctant to go."

My gaze was still busy taking it all in. How different it looked! "I wish Lark could see this."

"The living are incapable of it. They see only death and decay." He said it with a sneer.

"Lark isn't like most of the living," I informed him—maybe a bit defensively. "She would be able to see this, if it was shown to her."

"Well, then, maybe we'll find a way to make her see."

The thought of the look on my sister's face when she saw this beautiful place made me grin. "I'd like that."

"I would do anything to make you smile exactly as you are right now. I've never seen anything as lovely in all my days—alive or dead."

"You're a flirt," I accused, practically fluttering my eyelashes.

"You inspire it in me," he replied with a wink. "Shall I show you about the grounds?"

I hesitated. The last time I'd been in the main buildings Josiah Bent had tried to bend me to his will and badly injured my friends.

"I assure you no harm will come to you," Noah comforted me. "And the man who once tormented you is gone from this place—forever. Your sister saw to that."

I believed that. When Lark put her mind to banishing a spirit, she did a pretty good job of it. I did, too, come to think of it. The last time being on these very grounds. "Won't some of them hate me for getting rid of Bent?"

"Josiah Bent was a terrible man, and we're glad to be rid of him. He thought of nothing but himself, and had nothing but blatant contempt for this place and those of us who had been here long before he showed up. Come with me, you'll see."

I let him lead me up the gravel path toward the main building. The ghosts around us came closer. Some of them reached out as though they wanted to touch me. Others smiled and shied away. But they all looked happy to see me, as though we were old friends. They would never look at Lark like this, not with her belief that most ghosts were evil.

I smiled back at them, and for the first time in my existence, I was happy that my sister wasn't with me.

chapter six

LARK

I punched Woodstock in the face. The blow knocked him back.

The second ghost I'd hit in twenty-four hours. That had to be a record, even for me.

"I can see him," Kevin said dumbly. "Like, *really* see him."

I kept my gaze on the ghost, fists clenched, ready. "It's almost Halloween. Hasn't this happened to you before?"

"No." Out of the corner of my eye I saw him slip something on his fingers—iron rings. I'd yet to find a better weapon against ghosts. "But since you and Wren came back to town, my sensitivity to the dead has increased."

Made sense. Lately I'd been thinking more and more that if I was around people who were in tune to ghosts, I acted as a kind of magnifier for their abilities.

The ghost had shaken off my punch and came back for more. He hit me in the face so hard my vision blurred. I kicked him between the legs. Dead or not, a guy's still got his junk.

I shook my head and delivered an uppercut to Woodstock's jaw. "Do you know this guy?" I yelled at Kevin.

He landed a punch on the ghost, as well. "Never seen him before in my life."

"Well, he knows you." I managed to get the words out before the hippie slammed his shoulder into my gut. "I thought you guys were peaceful!" I shouted as I hit the ground. My head slammed into the paved drive. Black swarmed my vision, followed by an array of stars that spun so fast I thought I might puke.

"You can't run from me, little man!" the ghost shouted with a cackle. I heard Kevin's footsteps pounding against the ground. Through blurry eyes, I saw Woodstock start to follow after him. I reached out and grabbed him by the ankle, pulling hard.

Off balance, the ghost fell, his other foot slamming into my shoulder. I grunted and tried to roll away, but he grabbed me by the hair and yanked me back. My eyes watered at the pain, but I didn't make a sound.

Woodstock straddled my chest. Swimming in and out of focus, he leered at me. The smell of patchouli and pot filled my nostrils. "You're not as pretty as your sister," he told me. "We can still have a little fun, though."

How did he know Wren? And was that a ghost-boner pressed against my stomach? A little tingle of fear raced down my spine. He could rape me if he overpowered me. I'd heard of people being sexually assaulted by ghosts before. Not something I ever wanted to experience.

"Fuck you," I growled.

His expression turned angry. He shifted his weight to lean closer. God, the smell of him was all over me. His movement let me pull my arm out from beneath his knee. I moved fast, grabbing him by the throat and squeezing with all my strength.

Not to brag, but I'm strong—especially against ghosts. I can't explain it and I don't care. It's enough for me that I can fight the dead. I've been a match for most that I've gone up against, and Woodstock was no different. His fingers curled around my arm and hand, trying to pry my fingers loose.

I kept squeezing. Not like I could kill him, but the iron on my finger would hurt him.

Suddenly, I was pelted by a spray of pebbles. No, not pebbles, I realized as one hit my lip with a hard sting. It was salt. The kind you use in winter to melt snow. It hurt as it rained down on my face.

Woodstock howled and exploded into mist, leaving me holding nothing but air. I pushed myself up onto my arm, coughing out pellets that had gotten in my mouth. When I looked up, Kevin stood above me, holding a large bag that was still half-full of the noxious salt. I felt grimy from it—itchy.

"You couldn't have just thrown handfuls at him?" I asked. "You had to dump the whole damn bag over his head?"

"It wasn't the whole bag," Kevin retorted, scowling. "And you're welcome."

He offered me his hand, and I took it, letting him help me to my feet. I was going to be sore tomorrow. Hell, I was sore *now.* "Hey, it wasn't me he was after." Then, in seriousness, "You're sure you've never seen him before?"

Kevin nodded. "Never."

I frowned as something occurred to me. "He said your name like he was asking for confirmation. He didn't know you, either."

"Lark, what's going on?"

I looked around. The salt had scattered the ghost, and usually that was good for a while, but some strong spirits could get it together pretty quickly, and at this time of year all bets were off. I took him by the arm and pulled him toward the house. "Let's get inside. We need to ghost-proof your house for when he comes back."

"You think he'll come back?" Kevin asked as we stepped inside.

"He was sent here to do a job, and he failed. I'm pretty sure he'll be back, yeah."

Kevin set the bag of salt against the wall. "What job?"

I met his gaze. He already knew the answer—I could see it. But he wanted to be wrong, and he wanted me to back him up. "I think he was sent to kill you."

For someone with a spectral hit out on him, Kevin took the news fairly stoically. Instead of freaking out, he went immediately to work securing his house against ghosts. Roxi, Gage and I helped. Sarah had apparently left immediately after I walked in on her and Kevin in the kitchen, so she didn't know about our surprise visitor.

I called Ben. He'd want to help, and I knew he'd be upset if I waited until morning to tell him what happened. His family was as comfortable with the existence of ghosts as mine was, so he wasn't going to get in trouble by staying out half the night helping to protect a friend from a nasty spirit. I gotta say that made life a lot easier for me.

I reached out for Wren, figuring she would want to join the rest of us in determining why the ghost had come for Kevin and who had sent it, but she didn't answer. That was weird. I waited a few minutes and tried again. This time I opened myself up to her. My connection to my sister has always been more soul than mind. We could pick up on how the other was feeling more than what she was thinking, although there had been times when I could've sworn we were telepathic.

I wish I hadn't opened myself up when I realized what she was feeling. It's a little uncomfortable realizing your twin is having warm *tingly* feelings for someone. Especially some ghost wearing a cravat. I mean, *come on*. A cravat?

Here's what bothered me more, though. Wren chose to stay with her douchey Mr. Darcy instead of answering my call. Being a ghost, it was way easier for her to simply "pop" to wherever I was than for me to get to her. Still, if she called me, I'd go, because I'd know it was important. Maybe if she felt that I was in a state of panic or in pain she'd come. Of course she would. I was a cow to think anything different.

But she didn't come. And I didn't feel her reaching out for me, to gauge my emotional state.

I shook my head. So my sister was being a selfish teenager. *Get over it.*

"Do we think this had anything to do with Bent?" Mace asked, his voice coming from the speaker of Kevin's phone. He couldn't justify going out again to his folks, so he was at home.

"Woodstock didn't mention Bent," I said. Ben shot me an amused glance at my nickname for the ghost. I shrugged. "But that doesn't mean anything."

"How was he able to come here if he didn't know Kevin?" Roxi asked, looking around at those of us gathered around the kitchen table. "Isn't that, like, against the rules or something?"

"Usually," I replied. "But this close to Halloween, I don't know. The dead can travel around All Hallows' Eve. Maybe this ghost came in contact with us at Haven Crest when we took Bent out. Bent was able to follow Gage to the hospital, so maybe this guy could follow Kevin home."

"And he waited a month and a half to do it?" Kevin asked. He was still in his *Kick-Ass* costume. I had to admit he looked halfway cute in it. "Does that make sense?"

"It does if he wasn't strong enough before," I replied. Then, I shook my head. "No. This guy didn't just randomly follow you home. He came here for a purpose. He was sent." I was certain of it. Maybe I was just paranoid, but the explanation felt right.

"Who would do such a thing?" Gage asked, his big brown eyes even wider than normal. He was such a puppy. "And why?"

I glanced at Kevin. "Piss any ghosts off lately?" I asked. Okay, maybe I smirked when I asked.

He met my gaze. "Only your sister."

Snap. "Wren wouldn't send someone after you," I informed him—and the others. "She'd come for you herself." They didn't look comforted. Were they still scared of my sister? "It wasn't her."

"Of course it wasn't," Ben said, holding my hand. But they were all still looking at each other. Suddenly, it all made sense. They didn't blame Wren for this.

They blamed me.

I looked at each of them. The only one who seemed comfortable meeting my gaze was Ben.

"I know what you're thinking," I said. My voice shook a little, and that pissed me off. "You're thinking that if you'd never met me you wouldn't have to worry about some crazy-ass ghost coming after you. But you guys came to me, remember? When you'd already poked around in places you had no business poking." My voice rose. "Bent would have come for each and every one of you if I hadn't been here, and he probably would have gotten every one of you with the exception of Ben, who at least knew something about ghosts. So don't you freaking dare blame me for this. You'd still be wandering around thinking I was crazy if you'd stayed away from Haven Crest. You go looking for ghosts, you're going to find them, and surprise! Now they've found you. So, why don't we shelve the blame and try to figure this out?"

Silence. All of them looking anywhere but at me.

"She's right." The voice that made everyone jump was Mace's, loud and sharp, coming from the phone in Kevin's hand. Out of all of them he probably had the most reason to resent me—after all, he'd found me bleeding to death after slitting my wrists. He'd saved me, and I'd...

Well, I saved him, too, that night at Haven Crest. So we were even.

Roxi nodded. "Yeah. Sorry, Lark. I know this isn't your fault. It's just kind of freaky."

"And Daria wasn't?" I asked.

She smiled. "She was just a tiny girl, and she didn't come looking to kill any of us."

"Yeah, well, you could have fooled me. You weren't there when she tried to off me."

Her eyes widened. "I would have hit her with some salt if I'd been there."

"I know you would, Rox." I turned to Kevin. "Are you sure you haven't made contact with any ghost other than Wren lately?"

He shook his head. "None."

I stared at him. "You're sure?"

He frowned. "No, because I channel in my sleep all the time, just like that chick on *Medium*."

"Dude, I loved that show," Gage piped up.

I stared at him, ready to rip him a new one, but he looked

so goofy and harmless. He genuinely loved the show, I guess. I laughed. And then, everyone else did, too.

And just like that, it felt like we were good again, and I was glad. It had been a long time since I'd had friends I could just be me with, and I wasn't in any hurry to lose them.

"Okay," I began once we'd all stopped chuckling. "So right now, all we have is the Haven Crest connection. Do we know if records from the '60s and '70s are available online?"

"They are," Gage said. "I downloaded all the accessible records after we dealt with Bent." He saw us all staring at him and shrugged sheepishly. "You know, just in case."

"I could kiss you," I said, and I meant it. "Seriously, you're a rock star." And so much smarter than he looked, but I didn't say that.

He blushed as Roxi hugged him. "They're on my computer at home."

"There had to be a lot of guys during that time that looked like our ghost," Kevin said, killing my buzz. "How are we going to narrow it down?"

"Description, photos." I shrugged. "Homicidal tendencies."

Kevin actually smiled at me. "A penchant for patchouli."

I grinned, though how either of us could find the attack funny I had no idea. "The hospital would have started photographing patients by then. There were photos of some of the people we thought the ghost could have been before we discovered it was Bent, right?"

"There are pictures," Gage confirmed. He wrinkled his nose. "Some are kind of sick. Wounds and stuff."

Unfortunately, that sort of thing might give us even more information. "Can you email them to each of us when you get home, or in the morning?" I asked.

"Sure. The sooner we figure this out, the smaller the

chance that Woodstock comes for the rest of us." Gage rose
to his feet. "I'll go do it now if we're done here."

I looked around. No one protested. "Yeah, let's go home,"
I said. "Everyone, salt your windows and doors, and keep
iron nearby." Not that I thought the rest of them were in
danger, unless our hippie ass-hat was going to visit each of
them one by one. My gut told me Kevin had been his one
and only target.

They all agreed that they would take precautions, and our
little group broke up. Mace said goodbye and disconnected,
promising to let Sarah know what was going on. Funny that
no one had thought to call her. But then, Sarah didn't feel
like part of the group. It was pretty obvious to me that if she
wasn't Mace's girlfriend, she wouldn't have anything to do
with any of us. He could do so much better.

I made sure Kevin was okay with being left alone before
Ben and I walked out to our cars.

"Do you blame me for this?" I heard myself ask.

Ben shook his head. "You were right. We went looking
for ghosts, and we found them. Had nothing to do with you.
Now stop talking and kiss me."

I smiled as his lips touched mine. Leaning against Nan's car,
we kissed until my head felt light and the world melted away.
If Wren reached out to me at that moment, I don't know if
I'd answer her either.

"I'll be over at noon," Ben told me, when he finally let me
go. "We'll look through the records together, okay?"

I nodded, still a little dizzy. "Okay. Good night."

He grinned and kissed me again. "'Night. You make sure
you protect yourself, as well. This guy's gotten a taste of you,
too."

I didn't want to think about just how much of a "taste" Woodstock had wanted. "I will."

"I'll ask my grandmother if she has any advice," he added. "An attack by a vengeful spirit is right up her alley."

"She's going to want you to break up with me. No one wants their grandson involved in this kind of crap."

He kissed my forehead. "She'd rather have me knowledgeable than ignorant. Besides, she likes you."

I arched a brow but didn't argue. I would just have to take his word for it.

Gage had taken Roxi home, so I was on my own for the short drive back to my grandmother's, where my mother had dropped me two months earlier. Dropped me and walked away. I tried not to think about it. Being abandoned by your own mother because you "broke her heart" sucked.

Wren didn't pop into the car. She didn't meet me at the door when I walked into the house. And after I tiptoed upstairs, I found my room empty. She was still with Noah, I guessed.

I felt strangely alone. I suppose it would be a normal feeling for most people, but not for me. I had no connection to my sister at all, and I hadn't felt that since all the drugs at Bell Hill when I'd actually believed that I was crazy after all, and that Wren was just a product of my sick mind.

I washed my face, brushed my teeth and changed into a tank top and pajama pants. Then I slipped between the sheets and tried not to think about Woodstock. I was getting better at not letting ghosts get to me. Ghosts, I could handle.

I fell asleep in minutes, replaying Ben's kisses in my head. I dreamed.

There was nothing but darkness, and I was in the center of it. All around me I could hear voices crying out. Something brushed by me, but I couldn't tell what it was. I struggled through the dark until I caught sight of a glimmer of light. I tried to chase it, but it was like swimming through a sea of rubber bands. I had to reach that light. I had to break through to the other side, to the place where it began.

The Ruiner is after you, a voice whispered. *He won't be satisfied until you and your sister are destroyed.*

Who was the Ruiner? I couldn't find my voice to ask.

You'll know what to do. When the time comes you will not fail as we did.

Who the hell was "we"? I fought to ask the question, but nothing came out but panicked silence.

I must have fallen deeper asleep, or it was forced upon me, I didn't know, but when I woke up the next morning, sunshine filled my room.

And my sister was still gone.

WREN

I didn't leave Haven Crest until late morning. I stayed inside with Noah when dawn broke, and met a couple of his friends who drifted about the place. They looked like an odd little group, since each came from a different time period! But they were friendly and had some amazing stories, and I so enjoyed meeting others of my kind that weren't insane. It might sound like a small thing, but it didn't happen very often. Ghosts that had lingered on earth for a long time usually became bitter and twisted whether they wanted to or not.

When I finally left it wasn't because I wanted to, but because I knew Lark would be worried about me by now, and it wasn't as though she could check in on me as easily as I could her.

And maybe I felt a little guilty about not coming when I felt her reach out for me last night, but I did not want to return to that party and watch everyone having fun when I could be having fun of my own.

So, I said goodbye to Noah—we didn't kiss because the others were there, and he was old-fashioned—and drifted home. I took my time. I told myself it was because I wanted to enjoy the morning, skirt around trees and cars, peek in windows and spy on the living, and *not* because I wanted to put off facing my sister. Sunday morning was a lazy time in New Devon. Even the brightly colored leaves took their time falling from branch to ground.

Smiling, I caught hold of the breeze and followed it home, to the big old house my grandmother owned. It had a nice yard where Lark and I had played as children, with trees just begging to be climbed, their bare branches thick and sturdy. I slipped through the front door—no more substantial than air—into the kitchen. I thought Lark might be in the kitchen having breakfast, but she wasn't.

"Wren, honey, is that you?" Nan asked, squinting in my direction as she poured a cup of coffee.

Charlotte Noble was in her sixties, but she didn't look it. Her hair—not quite as red as mine—was graying, but there was hardly a line on her pretty face.

I nodded. Normally, she couldn't see me, but she could feel my presence. Nan was sensitive to ghosts, which made sense, because it was her side of the family where all this kind of stuff happened. It was because of her that Lark and I knew about our great-great-grandmother Emily and her twin, Alys—who was Dead Born like me. I'd caught glimpses of Alys in the house when we first moved here, but I hadn't seen her in

a while, and neither Lark nor I had seen Emily, who had appeared to both of us, in just as long.

Nan smiled. "Thought so. You ought to have let me know
when I saw you earlier."

"But I just got home," I said.

She blinked. "Did you just speak?"

"Yes." I moved closer. "Nan, what did you see earlier?"

She stared at me. I don't know just how solid I appeared
before her, but I imagined that it was like looking at someone through a veil of gauze. "I can hear you. See you. Oh,
my dear girl." Her eyes filled with tears.

If I could cry I would have, but I could only feel that pressure in my chest. When she reached for me, I could feel the
warmth of her hand against my cheek like a kiss from the sun.

"It's almost All Hallows' Eve," I explained. "When the veil
between the living and the dead is at its thinnest."

She continued to stare at me as though she'd never seen
anything like me before. Oh, right. She hadn't. Her brow
puckered. "It wasn't you I saw earlier, was it?"

"No. She looked like me, though?"

Her frown deepened. I didn't like seeing that confusion
on her face. "Yes, but she was dressed differently. More old-
fashioned. I suppose I ought to have known."

"Alys," I said—more to myself than her.

Nan didn't look as surprised as I thought she would. "I
ought to have noticed. I've felt her here, you know. I always
assumed it was you because she felt so familiar, but now I realize your energy is very different."

"Where did you see her?" I asked.

She shook her head. She seemed a little scattered. Was that
because of me, the situation or something else? "Around the
bottom of the stairs. If you can talk to me, why couldn't she?"

That explained her confusion. I didn't want to tell her what Lark and I thought—that there was something wrong with Alys. That she was stuck here when she ought to have moved on. If that was true, there was a chance that Alys could be twisting like other old ghosts. She'd better not be a danger to Nan, because I'd rip her apart, family or not.

"Maybe she's confused," I suggested. "If she's become accustomed to you not noticing her, she might have not even heard you. Sometimes we don't notice the living who notice us." That was sort of true.

Nan nodded, and I relaxed. "Maybe you can talk to her, dear." She looked up at me, her eyes watering again. "It's so good to see you, my pretty, pretty Wren."

I threw myself at her, engulfing her in my energy. She gasped, but I could feel her arms around my waist. I could feel her like Lark would feel her, and it was amazing. So much love and warmth.

The TV on the counter came on, and the timer on the stove dinged. Nan and I jumped apart at the same time, but it wasn't my energy that had caused the surge.

Lark stood in the doorway between the kitchen and dining room, her pale hair wild around her shoulders and her eyes bright as gems. She was the one who had set off the electronics. As the veil between worlds thinned, I became more of a part of this world, and Lark became a part of mine.

I'd never been afraid of my sister, but at that moment I had no idea what she might do.

"Where the hell have you been?" she demanded.

chapter seven

LARK

Wren just stared at me, like she didn't understand why I was so upset.

Okay, *I* didn't understand why I was so upset, either. I just was. Bad. It felt like static electricity snapping beneath my skin.

My sister cocked her head, blood-red hair spilling to the side like a long, dense curtain. "Are you manifesting?" she asked.

I glanced around. Everything looked right—not like it had at Goodwill. "I don't think so."

"You are," she said, coming toward me. I stepped closer.

My feet weren't touching the freaking floor. I yanked my head up, gaze locking with Wren's. "What the hell?"

Nan frowned in disbelief, her gaze pointed at my feet. "Lark, what's going on?"

"I don't know," I said. My voice shook. "It's never happened before."

Wren was the only one of us who didn't look freaked out. In fact, she looked at me like I was some sort of science experiment. "It's All Hallows' Eve," she said. "It has to be. If the thinning of the barrier makes me more substantial in this world, it also increases the parts of you that are like a ghost."

Nan nodded. "You do look somewhat ethereal, dear." White hair will do that to you. "More so than normal, I mean."

I drew a deep breath and pointed my toes. As I exhaled, I slowly lowered until my feet were flat on the floor. That was enough of that foolishness.

"I'm going to have to watch out for that," I said. At least I felt normal again.

Our grandmother shook her head. "You girls certainly make life interesting." And then, more seriously, "Is this something I should be concerned about?"

"I don't think so," I told her. "I'll let you know."

"I need a cup of tea," she said, and walked back into the kitchen, toward the stove.

I glanced at Wren. The annoyance I'd felt toward her was returning. "Have a good night?"

I think she actually blushed. "I did."

"Great." And just because I could be such a bitch—"You missed all the fun. A ghost attacked Kevin and me last night."

"What?"

I'll admit, her reaction wasn't quite what I'd expected. I'd thought she'd be shocked, of course, but I expected more emotion. You'd think I'd told her he bleached his hair.

Was this lack of human caring a Halloween thing, too, or was it because of Noah? I understood that she wouldn't be so worried about me—I could take care of myself, but her lack of concern over Kevin was strange. Now that she had a ghost boyfriend, Kevin was yesterday's garbage? I couldn't believe she could be that indifferent.

"A ghost showed up at the party last night and said it was there to kill Kevin." Maybe that hadn't been its exact words, but I figured when someone introduced themselves as Death, they were there for a fairly specific reason.

"Is he all right?" Now she looked concerned.

"Yeah. We fought it off."

"Male or female?"

"Male."

Her gaze narrowed. "Then he's not an 'it,' is he?"

I stared at her. The air between us practically snapped with tension. I grabbed her arm and pulled her away from the kitchen and out of Nan's earshot. I didn't want our grandmother to hear us argue, and I really didn't want either of us around her if things got weird again.

"Regardless of gender identification, the ghost was still a murderous douche bag sent to kill someone you considered a friend until very recently. And *he* intended to rape me as a bonus. You still insulted on *his* behalf?"

"Rape you? Oh, my God, Lark." She threw her arms around me. "Of course I'm not. I'm so sorry!"

Tears filled my eyes. I hadn't realized just how badly Woodstock had shaken me until then. There had been a male ghost in Bell Hill that liked to "mess" with the female patients, but we'd exorcised him. He hadn't hurt me, but he'd come close, and there were others whom he had.

I resisted hugging Wren back. My feelings were hurt that she'd stayed away, but mostly I was pissed because I'd been scared without her there, even if I hadn't known it at the time. We were a team, and I wasn't so tough without her at my back.

And I was jealous of the dead boy who was so fascinating that she'd leave me hanging for him.

She must have felt how stiff I was, because she melded into me, the cheater. I had no choice but to feel how truly sorry she was, her guilt and anger. And I felt her love for me, which made everything better.

Finally, I put my arms around her. Wren always had substance to me, but at that moment, with her energy melding with mine, it felt like I was hugging myself. Weird. I could feel my own arms wrapped around me like she was me and I was her, but we were both still ourselves.

"Does this feel odd to you?" she asked.

I nodded, tears gone. "Much."

She let me go, and I released her. We both took a step back, eying each other warily.

"What's going on?" I asked.

She shrugged. "All Hallows' Eve?"

"That's becoming too convenient as an explanation. If it's the time of year, why hasn't it ever happened before?"

"I don't know. Maybe because we've been using our abilities more often? They're stronger?"

It was a better explanation than anything else—and less panic-inducing. "I wish we had someone to explain all this."

"Emily wrote about Alys in her journal, but never why they were the way they were."

"Yeah?" I knew this already. "We figured she didn't know why they were like that, either."

"But she talked like she did. And she wasn't trying to explain it to anyone who might find and read the journal."

"The journal was given to you in the Shadow Lands. For all we know, she could have burned the real-life copy. No need to explain what no one else was ever going to see."

"Then why write it down?"

I sighed. This was one of those moments when my sister

just didn't get humanity. "Some people just like to write stuff down. Record their lives."

"Like Twitter? People don't explain what they mean on there, either."

Close enough. "Sure."

Wren grinned. Then her happiness faded. "Earlier, Nan said she saw someone she thought was me. I think it might have been Alys. It would be nice if she or Emily would come to us and explain everything."

Wasn't that the truth? "I'd like a manual, thanks."

"A diagram even."

"I'd settle for a Tweet."

We smiled at each other. Something deep inside my chest gave a little—like easing up on an elastic band stretched too tight.

"I don't like it when you're mad at me," Wren said, smile gone. "And I don't like feeling like I'm letting you down if I try to have friends of my own."

Friends of her own. She should be allowed to have them. I should encourage her to do just that. I wanted her to be happy. So why did I feel like she'd just kicked me? "I don't like it, either. I'm sorry. I shouldn't expect you to drop everything and come running when I call."

"I should know that you wouldn't reach out if it wasn't important. I'm just glad neither of you were hurt." Then, she frowned. "Kevin wasn't hurt, was he?"

"No, but I am totally convinced the ghost was sent for him."

"Who would do something like that?"

I shrugged. "No idea. He says he hasn't been in contact with any spirits other than you, so the only thing we could think of was that maybe it had something to do with Haven Crest and Bent."

"No one I know at Haven Crest would do something like that."

I arched a brow. "Know a lot of Haven Crest ghosts, do you?" No, I didn't sound like a jealous cow *at all*.

"A few." Her expression was defensive. "It's different there, now that Bent is gone. The entire place is much happier."

Happy ghosts. That made no freaking sense to me. Other than Wren, I don't think I'd ever met a ghost with any joy in their un-life. Ghosts were generally ghosts because there was some kind of terrible emotion they clung to in death, keeping them trapped here.

"Well, maybe a few of them that you haven't met are unhappy that Bent got snuffed."

She scowled. "If that were the case, you'd think they'd come after you. You did the most damage, after all."

"I wasn't the one that ended Bent," I reminded her. "And I said they were unhappy, not stupid." I mean, really. If a ghost came after me, there was a really good chance I was going to hurt it, track it down and torch its mortal remains. Kind of like what we planned to do with Woodstock.

Maybe he was stupid after all. Or maybe he figured we'd never find him.

Or, my paranoid brain whispered, *Woodstock's got someone way more powerful watching over him.*

Yeah, didn't want to think about that.

"Anyway, Gage has patient records that Kevin and I are going to look through. Ben's coming over later to help. Hopefully we'll find a photo of the ghost and figure out what he's up to."

"And if you don't?"

I sighed at the edge in her voice. "Look, what's up with you defending Haven Crest all of a sudden?" *Oh, shit.* "Was Noah an inm—a *patient*, or did he work there?"

Wren looked down, pretending to pick lint off her shirt. News flash—ghosts don't pick up lint. "It doesn't matter."

"You don't know, do you?" How the hell could she not know? Yes, girls got involved with psycho guys all the time and didn't know it, but when you met a guy at a freaking lunatic asylum you should at least freaking ask if he listed the place as his home address!

"I knew you'd do this!" she blurted, pointing a finger at me. "I knew you wouldn't even give him a chance. You think all ghosts are monsters!"

I almost shouted that all ghosts were monsters, but I caught myself. "If I'd met Ben at Bell Hill, wouldn't you have wondered whether or not he was nuts?"

Now she was the one crackling with energy, her hair standing out. She was pissed. And for once, my main concern wasn't calming her down.

"If you lose it in our grandmother's house I will kick your ass," I warned her, while at the same time part of me itched for a good fight. "Every time something you don't like happens you almost manifest. Get. It. Together."

And she did. For maybe a split second I thought we were going to go at it—which was just plain weird. Really, if Halloween didn't come and go soon I didn't know what was going to happen. Wren and I were never like this with each other. Sure, we got pissed, but not like this.

"Noah is nice," she informed me, a little petulantly, but her hair and eyes were normal, so I'd take it as a win.

"I'm glad," I replied, swallowing a smart-ass reply. "Do you remember Melanie at Bell Hill?"

She nodded, but from the sour look on her face, I knew she had an idea where this was going.

"Mel was nice, too—until she wasn't. I don't want to see you get hurt. And I bet Noah doesn't want to hurt you either, but he's still here for a reason."

Another stiff nod. She really didn't like me much at the moment, but at least she listened to what I had to say.

And if she didn't act on it, I would. How many teenagers named Noah could have been admitted to Haven Crest in the late nineteenth century?

"You didn't give me much of a chance to meet him," I said, using a different tactic. "You just threw him at me."

"I knew you wouldn't like him."

"Why wouldn't I like him? Because he's a ghost? That's stupid. If you like him and he's good to you, I'll like him, too. I'd like the chance to actually talk to him." And maybe ask a few questions of my own.

Wren met my gaze, a hopeful expression on her face that made me instantly guilty. "Really?"

I nodded. "Really." I did not push my luck by suggesting a double date. "Is he going to be at the concert?"

She wrinkled her nose. "He said he'd go if I wanted, but it's not exactly his sort of music."

"It might be the only chance anyone gets to meet him." I said this knowing full well "anyone" would translate to "Kevin" in her head, because I'd want the guy who hurt me to see my current hottie. "They might actually see him."

She liked that idea. Did I feel even the least bit guilty for manipulating her? No. She'd spied on Ben shortly after we got together—after we got rid of Bent. For days she'd tell me what he ate for breakfast, or how he talked to his mother— stuff that was none of her business, and it was none of mine, but she wanted to make certain he was "good enough" for me. Well, I was just returning the favor.

Wren was right about me—I distrusted ghosts. I never tried to hide the fact, but if I was wrong about Noah, then I'd apologize. In fact, I hoped I was wrong about him and that he was nice and sincere, and not at all an insane spirit corrupted by the malevolent energy of the place holding him to this world. I would really, really like to be wrong about a ghost just once. And I would especially like to be wrong about the ghost who made my sister look like any other teenage girl who was hopelessly infatuated with a boy.

Because if I was right about Noah, I was probably going to have to destroy him. And my sister might not forgive me for it.

WREN

The ghosts of Haven Crest were quiet and watchful when I returned later that day. I left Lark with Ben to look into the ghost they'd encountered. I probably ought to have stayed and helped—or at least checked to see if I knew the ghost, but I wanted to be with Noah instead, and Lark would show me a photo of "Woodstock" if and when she found one.

I wasn't normally so selfish. At least, I didn't think I was. Sometimes the expectations of human behavior confused me. Ghosts didn't have the same morals or rules. We were pretty much creatures of instinct, and my instincts wanted to see Noah, even though it had been only a couple of hours since I left him.

I had enjoyed spending time with Kevin, but not like this. True, Kevin and I hadn't been able to interact the same way as I could with Noah, but being with Noah felt so much more electric. When I was with him I felt…alive. At least what I imagined alive would feel like.

The town had started reclaiming two of the old buildings on the property, fixing them up to turn them into offices. Renovation work ran from Monday to Friday, and Noah had told me that so far the ghosts in those buildings were all right with the changes as the buildings were being restored to much of their original appearance. It would be the former living areas—and those who haunted them—that suffered the most. Some of those buildings might even be completely destroyed. None of them knew for certain what was going to happen to their homes.

When Noah told me that, I volunteered to find out. I had meant to ask Lark to see if she could find the town's plans on the internet, but forgot. I made a mental note to make certain I did that later that day.

It was Sunday, and there shouldn't have been any construction on-site, but there were men and women wandering around a section of the property. That's why the ghosts were watchful, most of the residents of Noah's building gathered in front of the windows nearest the lawn where the living stood, talking, gesturing at various areas of the grounds.

"It used to be the sporting area," Noah explained when I asked what the empty space was. "In my day they played croquet. Later they used it for everything from badminton to baseball to picnics."

"They don't seem to be playing any sort of game," remarked Miss April. She was a pretty young girl who looked as though she'd been there longer than even Noah, judging from her long dress, which had a high waist and short sleeves. "If they are, it's most uninteresting."

I smiled. "I don't think they're playing anything. It looks like they're putting up a stage."

A few ghosts murmured in understanding.

Noah nodded, giving me a warm glance for solving the puzzle. "For the impending musical performance."

"It's awfully high," another ghost whose name I didn't know commented as he pushed his head through the broken window for a better look. "A man would break his neck if he fell off that."

"They need to be high," said Robert, a man whose hair was almost as long as mine, "so people can't climb up and attack the band."

"Attack?" Noah asked with a frown. "Is the music so offensive?"

I laughed, and so did Robert. "No, man. People love musicians and get so into the music they just want to get close to the performers. I once climbed a human pyramid to get close to Janis Joplin." He smiled, revealing teeth that had seen better days. "She touched my hand. Best night of my life, man."

"It sounds terribly rude," Miss April commented. "No offense, Robert, but in my day one sat quietly during a recital."

"If an audience doesn't go nuts for you, you're doing something wrong," came a new—and oddly familiar—voice.

I whipped around. Standing there, in the middle of the upstairs gallery, was a tall, thin young man with long dark hair and a lopsided grin. His eyes were outlined in black, and his leather pants were so tight I could see the outline of his kneecaps—and more of him than I wanted—above his boots.

"Joe?" I couldn't help the surprise that filled my voice. "What are you doing here?"

Joe Hard had been dead since before Lark and I entered our worlds. He'd been in some sort of rock band when he died. From what I'd heard he'd been slightly famous. He was a flirt, but he seemed fairly harmless.

He grinned at me—the sort of smile I'm sure he'd used to charm girls when he'd been alive. "Hey, Red. How's kicks?"

I had no idea what that meant. "Uh, good."

Noah stepped up to stand beside me. "Wren, would you mind giving me an introduction?"

"Oh, yes. Of course. This is Joe. Joe, this is Noah."

They nodded, eyeing each other in that way that only men seemed to do.

"So, why are you here?" I asked again. I suppose I should have asked how as well, but it was almost Halloween, and I didn't know Joe's history. The last time I'd seen him was in the police station the night Mace and Lark had been arrested for trespassing on Haven Crest property.

Joe raised a skinny arm and pointed at the window. "That stage they're building? It's for a concert that Dead Babies is performing in my honor. Olgilvie came down to check out construction. You know I couldn't resist coming with him."

Just like some ghosts haunted places, others were attached to people or objects. Joe had attached himself to Officer Olgilvie, a cop against whom he had some sort of grudge. It had to be bad, because when Joe looked at Olgilvie he looked like he wanted to rip him apart, but he hated him enough that he wouldn't do it. He wanted to torture him instead. I couldn't blame him. Olgilvie had it in for Lark, which made him a jerk in my book. I hadn't been around that long, but Joe was the first spirit I'd ever met who tethered himself to a person. Daria had been the second.

"Where's that sweet sister of yours?" he asked.

"Home," I replied.

"She coming to the concert?"

"Yes."

"Are you?"

I frowned. "Yes. Why?"

He shrugged his leather-clad shoulders. "Just wondering. Do you suppose you could tell J.B. that I'd like to talk to her?"

J.B. stood for Jail Bait, and it was a term Joe applied to young women. Apparently he meant it as a compliment, even though it sounded vaguely criminal to me. "I'll tell her."

He smiled again. There was a sadness in Joe's eyes that hurt to look at. It was like all of his pain was in his gaze, and every time he looked at me, an invisible iron blade cut me to thinly sliced ribbons.

"Thanks, sweetheart. Sorry to interrupt your party." And just like he'd appeared in the room, he was gone in a blink.

"Who was that?" Noah demanded.

I stepped back from the anger in his voice. "I told you. His name is Joe."

Noah's eyes burned with blue flame, and his lips were tight. "What is he to you?"

I stared at him. Out of the corners of my eyes I saw the ghosts flicker out of the room, leaving us alone.

"Are you jealous?" I asked.

He stiffened. "Perhaps. Ought I be?"

If I hadn't thought he'd be offended, I would have laughed. "No! Joe is... Well, I'm not sure. I don't know him well enough to call him a friend. But calling him an acquaintance doesn't seem right, either. He's certainly nothing more."

"Ah." Noah's posture relaxed a little. He looked sheepish. "I see. Forgive me for my loutish behavior. I thought he was someone you were once close to. He spoke to you in a very familiar manner."

"I think that's just Joe."

"He must have been someone of great importance if this concert is to be held in his honor."

"I think he was very popular, yes. I don't know his music, though."

"Who is this Olgilvie he spoke of?"

He was asking an awful lot of questions, and I would rather talk about him, or even myself, than all these other people and things. "A police officer. He doesn't like my sister and our friends very much. I don't think he's a nice man."

Noah took my hand in his, our auras blending together. "I don't know how anyone could be anything but charmed by you."

"You're making up for being jealous very nicely," I teased with a smile.

He smiled back. He was so very, very handsome. "I am glad to hear it. Now why don't you tell me what brought you back here so soon. As much as I'd like to think you returned for me alone, I do not think that's it."

My smile faded. "I wanted to ask for your help."

His expression sobered. "Of course." He began moving, and I followed, drifting throughout the building with him. "Anything."

"Last night after we left the party, a ghost attacked my sister and a friend."

"Is your sister all right?"

I loved him for asking about Lark first. "Yes, but the ghost claimed that he was there to kill our friend, who had no idea who the ghost was. It was Kevin, the one I told you is a medium."

Noah's brow creased. "That's odd. Most spirits respect mediums, or want to use them as conduits. I've never heard of a ghost trying to harm one. The ghost had no attachment to the place or your friend?"

"None. Lark thinks that maybe it was retaliation for what we did to Josiah Bent."

"And you want to know if I've heard anything?"

I twisted my hands together. "Yes. I don't want to ask you to break any code of loyalty between the ghosts of Haven Crest, but my sister could have been hurt. Our friend could have been killed."

"I haven't heard of anything. Nobody's even muttered Bent's name since you sent him packing. I think most were happy to be out from under his thumb. But I don't know everything that goes on here. Did your sister happen to mention what the ghost looked like?"

"She said he looked like he was from the 1960s or '70s. And that he smelled of patchouli." I wasn't terribly certain just what that smelled like, but maybe he would. Being dead since I was born meant that I didn't have much of an olfactory sense.

He shook his head. "Would you like me to ask around? I don't know if anyone will confide in me, but I can try."

Oh, what a relief! "That would be so wonderful of you. Thank you."

His expression turned flirtatious. "You can thank me with a kiss." He took my hand and pulled me closer.

I smiled, a sense of intense giddiness washing over me. "Just one?"

Noah's arms wrapped around me. "We can start with one. It may take more for you to fully express your gratitude."

I laughed, and then his lips touched mine, and I stopped laughing. I stopped thinking. In fact, I think the entire world just stopped. At least, that's how it felt.

If Noah found out who the vengeful ghost was, then Lark would have to like him. Kevin, too.

They'd have no choice.

chapter eight

LARK

"Found him!" The words rushed out of me like I'd just won a million dollars.

Ben set his laptop aside and got off my bed to walk over to the desk where I sat. I didn't always use my desk, but I knew that if I sat on the bed with him while searching the files Gage sent, I wouldn't get any work done. Ben was just too tempting.

As it was, it had taken me almost two hours of poring over patient intake records to find him. Ten years equaled a lot of new faces at Haven Crest. People were hospitalized for all kinds of reason back then—even people who were mentally challenged were locked up in asylums. I mean, it was a little disturbing just what could get people committed back then. Don't even get me started on the nineteenth century. It was only for the fact that believing in evolution had been grounds to call someone mad that I hadn't totally violated my sister's privacy and tried to find Noah. For all I knew he could have gotten locked up for using the wrong fork at a dinner party.

I had every intention of checking into Noah, it was just

that Woodstock—aka Robert Alan Thurbridge, Jr.—was more important at the moment.

Ben leaned over my shoulder. He smelled like cinnamon. "*That's* the guy that attacked you and Kevin?"

"Don't sound so impressed," I drawled. "He was a lot scarier in Kevin's driveway, trust me."

In his admittance photo, Robert Alan Thurbridge, Jr. was obviously stoned out of his ever-loving mind. I wasn't all that educated in drugs that weren't prescribed antipsychotics, but I knew what someone looked like when they'd been given some pretty serious shit. Thurbridge looked as though he'd been taking elephant tranquilizers with a side of Xanax.

His long hair was stringy in the photo—not as full and wild as it was as a ghost. His eyes were heavy-lidded and dull, and his face puffy from too many drugs. He was scruffy and looked as though he hadn't showered in days, which he probably hadn't.

"Death was an improvement," I remarked. "He must have gotten at least a little bit healthier at Haven Crest. Physically, anyway."

Ben kissed my temple before looking back at the screen. "It says he was admitted because of bouts of paranoid schizophrenia."

I snorted. "Bet the drugs didn't help."

"He was probably self-medicating. Wow. He tried to kill his own father because he thought he was covering up evidence of alien abductions. And that wasn't the first time he'd been arrested for something violent. Looks like each time it was because of a delusion. He died there in 1973. Hanged himself."

"Poor bastard," I muttered. I knew what it was like to not know if you were crazy or not. For the longest time people told me Wren wasn't real, and for a little while I let myself believe them. Bell Hill Psychiatric Hospital cured me of that. If it hadn't been for Wren, I probably wouldn't have survived.

Then again, if it hadn't been for my sister, I wouldn't have been admitted. But I didn't blame Wren. She couldn't control what we were any more than I could.

"Okay," Ben began. "We know he's part of the Haven Crest haunt. Now what? It doesn't say where he's buried."

"They had a special plot for suicides," I said. "Or, his family sounds like they might have been well-off—maybe he's buried in a family plot somewhere." That was going to be really inconvenient, if it was the case. "It might not even be his bones anchoring him here if he died after the hospital started cremating patients to conserve plot space. Do we know when they started doing that?" I was scrolling through the file to see if it said anything. Ben went back to the bed and sat down with his laptop, clacking away at the keys.

"Google says Haven Crest started cremating their dead in 1980. Our guy's gotta be in the ground, then."

"I'll check that cemetery layout we found when we went after Bent." I paused, my hands dead over the keyboard. "I'm sorry," I said, glancing over my shoulder.

Ben frowned. "For what?"

"That Bent wasn't the end of it. That there's a new ghost and a new danger for me to put you guys in."

He stared at me, his eyebrows coming together in a frown. "None of this is your fault."

He was sweet to say that. "Maybe not, but I feel like I attract trouble, and my friends just get swept up in it."

"That ghost—Woodstock, Thurbridge, whatever his name is—came looking specifically for Kevin. That's not on you."

"But why Kevin?" I asked. "Why didn't he come for me?"

My boyfriend shrugged. "Maybe he thought Kevin would be an easier target."

"Maybe." It was as good an explanation as anything I could come up with, but it still didn't sit well with me. Maybe I just made things more complicated than they needed to be.

But I had a very uncomplicated solution brewing inside the thick walls of my skull. And it was one I wasn't going to share with Ben. I wasn't going to share it with anyone until I had proof, because at that moment, it was driven by nothing more than paranoid suspicion.

"Wren's been spending a lot of time at Haven Crest lately. I'll show her Thurbridge's photo and see if she recognizes him."

Ben closed his laptop. "Does that bother you? Her spending time there?"

It was serious conversation time—not like killer ghosts weren't serious. I closed my computer as well and got up from the desk to join him on my bed. He took my hand in his. He was warm and strong. All he had to do was hold my hand, and I felt like I could take on the world. Or at least the ghosts in it. I wasn't sure I liked that he had that much power where I was concerned, or that it felt so good.

"Yes," I admitted. "It bothers me a lot."

"Because of Bent? Or because of something else?"

We both knew what "something else" was. "My prejudice against mental hospitals? Yeah, that's some of it. A lot of it, actually. Mostly I worry that being around that many ghosts will make her want to be one of them."

He looked at me like I was speaking backward. "She is one of them."

"No. She's not." I tried to pull my hand away, but he held tight. It wasn't enough to hurt me, just to keep me from withdrawing like I wanted. "She's not like them. I don't *want* her to be like them."

"Like them how?"

"Crazy. Mean. Dangerous." My gaze locked with his, and I hoped he could see me pleading for him to understand. "She's never been alive, Ben. She doesn't even have that to keep her from becoming something dark. The longer ghosts hang around, bitter and lost, the more they become monsters."

A little smile curved his mouth. "She's got you."

I snorted. "If Wren goes bad, I don't know if I'll be able to stop it. But I can't ask her not to spend time with other ghosts. Noah seems to really like her, and she really likes him. She wouldn't ask me to leave you. I can't ask her not to see him." But I wanted to. I really, really wanted to.

Ben's expression softened. "You're afraid you're going to lose her."

"Well, yeah." Hadn't I just said that?

"No, I mean you're afraid she'll pick Noah over you. That he'll be more important than you are."

I shifted a little on the bed. I wasn't all that skilled at serious talks. "Okay, so I'm jealous. Big deal. She's never had a boyfriend before."

"That's not what I meant." He let go of my hand and put his arm around me instead, pulling me against his chest. "You're afraid she'll love him more than she loves you, and that's not going to happen."

"You don't know that," I said, listening to the beat of his heart.

"Yeah, I do. Can you imagine ever choosing me over her? Choosing anyone over her?"

Was this a trick question? I wasn't sure, but I think it depended on me answering honestly. "No. I'm sorry, but, no."

"Don't apologize. I'd never put you in that position, and you would never do it to her. You don't have to worry, because there's no contest. Wren would choose you every time, just like you'd choose her. You two are like...like halves of the same whole."

That wasn't the first time someone had referred to us as such. I thought it a lot myself. Sometimes I used to wonder if we were supposed to be one person, but that somehow we split into two in the womb. It wasn't until we found out about Emily and Alys that I'd begun to think otherwise.

I lifted my head and kissed his cheek. "Thanks."

He turned his head, his lips brushing mine. Next thing I knew we were stretched out together on the top of the quilt, kissing each other like we had nothing else to do for the next one hundred years.

I liked Ben *so* much. Like, *a lot.* And I knew all that stuff school and books and TV threw at teenagers about sex. It was a responsibility, and not something to be taken lightly. I also knew it was something awesome if you did it right, and I wanted to do it with Ben.

I was pretty sure he wanted to do it with me, too.

But he never pushed it. We'd kissed and touched and did a lot of things that felt really good, but he never got upset if I wanted to stop. If I was honest I'd have to admit that there had been a couple of times that I was upset that *he* stopped. I guess we'd get there whenever we got there. Right now I was just going to *really* enjoy the trip.

I had my hands under his shirt and he had his under mine when I heard a strange sound from my bathroom.

Ben's head jerked up, his mouth leaving my neck. "Did you hear that?"

I nodded, slipping my hands out from underneath his Henley. He removed his hands as well, and we both sat up.

"Wren?" he asked.

I shrugged. Normally I felt when Wren was nearby—a subtle shift in the air or some extra sense that made her presence known to me. She had the same sense of me. I didn't feel anything like that, but I did feel something wasn't quite right, which was reason enough to worry.

Slowly, I eased off the bed and to my feet. Quietly, I walked toward the bathroom door and pulled it open.

There, standing in front of the tub, her back to me, was a girl with long, blood-red hair wearing an old-fashioned dress.

"Wren?" I asked. But it didn't feel right.

The girl turned around, and I understood why it hadn't felt right. This wasn't my sister. My sister didn't have eye sockets that were completely filled-in black, and she didn't have a long gash in her face that dripped blood onto her gown. Blood covered the fingers of her right hand, and in her left, she held a bloody straight razor.

Her mouth opened, and I braced myself for whatever hellish sound might come out of it, but nothing did. She vanished before she could make a sound, swallowed up in what looked like a cyclone of shadow.

Dumbfounded, I stared at the words dripping down the white tile.

HELP ME.

My heart jammed itself into my throat.

"What the hell is that?" Ben asked, coming to stand beside me. "Is that blood?"

"Yeah," I rasped. If he could see it, too, then it wasn't just a message for me. It was a message for anyone who could see it—and that made it a haunting, which was never good.

"Who was that?" he asked. "She looked a little like you."

"Alys," I replied. My pulse was still hammering way too fast. "I think she's in trouble."

Ben hung around for another couple of hours until he had to go home for dinner. His parents weren't terribly strict, but they liked having a big family meal on Sunday nights. I'd been invited to join a few times since we'd started dating, and I went each time, but tonight I had other plans.

I walked him to the door. "I'll see you tomorrow," I said—hoping that it wasn't a lie.

He gave me a hug. "Are you sure you're okay? I can stay if you want."

I shook my head. I'd accept his help researching things and even fighting ghosts, but when it came to situations that involved Emily or Alys—or anything family—I wanted to handle them on my own, or with Wren.

"You're awesome," I told him, pulling free of his arms. "I don't tell you that enough."

Ben smiled. "Feel free to say it whenever the urge hits."

We kissed and then he left. Nan appeared at almost the exact moment I closed the door behind him. It was like she had some sort of silent alarm set up to alert her when it was just me and her—and usually Wren—again.

"I like that boy," she said as she opened the fridge and starting taking things out to cook.

I smiled. "I like him, too."

"He's very respectful." She glanced over her shoulder. "How does pad thai sound for dinner?"

"Sounds awesome," I replied. "Can I help?"

She gestured to a paper-towel-wrapped block on the counter. "You can cut up the tofu and start cooking it."

We worked together, side by side, for the next half hour, putting all the ingredients together—crushing peanuts for garnish—and then I set the table.

"Where's Wren?" Nan asked as she drained the noodles. "She hasn't been around much the past couple of days."

With Nan honesty was always the best route—mostly because she seemed to know I was lying before I did. "She met a boy."

Nan's head came up. She seemed momentarily transfixed by something she saw through the window above the sink. Then she turned toward me. "A ghost boy?"

I nodded.

"Huh." She turned on the tap and stuck the colander beneath the flow of water. "How does that work, I wonder?"

"I don't know and don't want to," I announced.

"Probably a wise decision. Get us some drinks, will you, dear? Is he a nice ghost boy?"

This was such a weird conversation. I opened the fridge and grabbed a bottle of the fruit-flavored seltzer she liked, and a diet soda for myself. "I've only met him once. He seemed okay—if you like the pompous British lord type who looks like he ought to be on the cover of a Brontë novel."

"Which one?"

I shook my head. "One what?"

"Which Brontë sister? They had fairly different styles, you know."

What the hell? I didn't know which of them wrote what. I didn't even know how many Brontës there were. "Whichever one wrote *Jane Eyre*."

My grandmother smiled dreamily as she plopped noodles onto each of two plates. "I'm a Rochester girl myself." She shook her head as she set the colander in the sink. "Everyone always goes on about Heathcliff, but he was something of a psycho in my opinion."

I'd read *Wuthering Heights* in English and wasn't really a fan—for the very same reason my grandmother just mentioned.

"Well, as long as this boy makes Wren happy, I suppose it doesn't matter what either of us think."

That was the problem. I couldn't remember there ever being a time when my opinion hadn't mattered to my sister. The only time we'd come close was when I'd tried to kill myself and she found help rather than letting me join her in the Shadow Lands.

After dinner, I helped clean up, did what little homework I had and then asked Nan if I could borrow the car.

She took one look at me dressed all in black and shook her head. She knew I was up to something. "You'll be careful, won't you?"

I nodded. "I promise."

She didn't look 100 percent committed. "Will you be taking your sister with you?"

"She's meeting me there." It wasn't really a lie, so I didn't feel guilty and Nan didn't notice. Wren would be meeting me at Haven Crest, she just didn't know it yet.

"Drive safely. Don't get arrested, and be home by midnight. I don't care how tired you are in the morning, you're not missing school tomorrow."

"Yes, yes, yes and nope." I grabbed the keys from the counter, slipped my arms through the straps of a small backpack and gave her a kiss before I left.

I drove the "grape" to the town cemetery that bordered Haven Crest property. The parking area was empty except for me. It was a prime make-out spot for local teenagers, but with school in session it was really only busy on Friday and Saturday nights, which meant I had my pick of a prime parking spot.

I chose to leave the Beetle beside an old giant of a tree that had spots where its bark had been slowly stripped away by the toes of sneakers as kids climbed it to sneak over the fence. This was the best way onto Haven Crest property if you didn't want to get caught. Security guards patrolled the grounds, so any strange cars would get attention, as would a girl with white hair simply strolling up the driveway.

I'd worn a pair of thick-soled boots for the night's adventure and easily climbed up to the heavy branch that stretched over onto Haven Crest property.

I hesitated before jumping to the ground on the other side of the stone wall that divided the properties. Once my feet touched that unconsecrated soil, the ghosts of Haven Crest would know someone was there. They might not care that they had a guest at first, but once I got a little closer, the stronger ones would "taste" me and probably form a not-so-welcoming party. Bent had come to check me out almost immediately when I'd come here with Mace—he'd felt his victim's return.

Not everyone at Haven Crest had been one of Bent's followers, but there had to be a few spirits there who wouldn't be happy to see me.

Who was I kidding? No one there was going to be *happy* to see me. Not even Wren.

I took several iron rings from my pocket and slipped them on my fingers. They'd been made from old nails. They weren't all that pretty, but they were effective when punching a ghost in the face. I didn't usually wear them since they could hurt

Wren, but to not have protection here would be incredibly stupid. Way more stupid than I already was.

I could have brought my iron rod. I probably should have, but I figured that would be like walking into a gang clubhouse with a pistol in my hand. Besides, I wanted to make nice with the ghosts if I could. And I didn't want to cause trouble for Wren, whom I was also counting on to help protect my ass.

She was nearby, my sister. Hopefully she felt me, too.

Taking a deep breath, I climbed down to the ground. The moment my boots hit the grass I felt a tingle run up my legs. Halloween, you had to love it. Even the property of Haven Crest was charged with spectral energy. The night of the Dead Babies concert I was going to be jittery as hell if this was any indication.

Luckily, the tremors in my legs stopped after I took a few steps. It was dark and quiet. Too quiet. I didn't use a flashlight because security would spot it. I'd covered my white hair with a black hat and kept to the shadows as best I could. I had no desire to be caught trespassing here again. No desire to meet up with Officer Olgilvie again, the dick.

I kept low as I ran toward the main cluster of buildings. As used to ghosts as I was, this place was still creepy. The old brick buildings had rotting wood trim and busted windows, but you could tell it had been pretty at one time. That wasn't the creepy part. The creepy bit was all the faces in those broken windows, watching me as I scurried past. That was not something you ever got used to.

I had a fairly decent sense of direction and an idea of where Woodstock's haunt was located, but that wasn't necessarily where I was headed.

I hid behind a tree when I saw a police car slowly move along the paved road that ran throughout the compound. The site had a security guard, but the cops patrolled, as well. From what I'd heard, Haven Crest used to be a lot more popular with the teen population of New Devon and surrounding towns. It used to be a haven for the homeless and runaways until the town reclaimed the property and started renovations. That's when the police added it to their nightly patrol, keeping an eye out for trespassers.

I bet the ghosts hated the police for the extra attention. Suddenly their all-you-can-haunt buffet dried up, and they had to make do with the odd ghost hunter, cop or teenager daring enough to risk getting caught.

Luckily for them, there would always be people who thought looking for a ghost in an abandoned mental hospital was a fun idea. People like me, who were at least looking for a particular ghost.

Once I was sure I was safe from security, I ran across the cracked pavement to the other side of the roadway. From there, I sprinted across the lawn, past the building where we'd hunted Josiah Bent and outside of which Mace and I had been picked up by the cops. On the other side, I slipped into the shadow of the building and waited for my breathing to calm down—I really needed to do more cardio.

"You shouldn't be here," came a voice from my right.

Shit. Slowly, I turned my head toward the darker side of the building. Standing there, dirty arms folded over her narrow chest, was a girl about the same age as me. She was dressed in a plain cotton tie-dyed sundress, and her feet were bare. Long blond hair hung down her back.

Wait. That wasn't dirt on her arms, and her dress wasn't tie-dyed. It was blood. Her forearms were sliced from wrist almost to elbow.

I swallowed. Looking at those wounds made my own scars itch. "I know, but I'm looking for somebody."

Her thin face was void of sympathy. "Last time you came here looking for somebody you upset a lot of us."

"Yeah, sorry about that, but no way was I going to let Bent take my sister."

Her pointy chin lifted. "There aren't too many of us who miss Josiah. Even fewer who would thank you for it. You put a hurt into a lot of us that night."

"They tried to stop me from burning his bones," I reminded her. "And *I'm* not going to apologize for that."

She moved closer—little lurches like when the cable TV feed sometimes got garbled. Japanese horror movies did it all the time. It was scarier in person. I closed my fingers into a fist, just in case she got too close.

"Why are you here now?" she asked. This close I could see that her eyes were bigger than they ought to be—too big for her tiny face. And her eyelashes were thick and kinked like spider legs.

"What do you care?"

She jerked her head back. "We want to know if there's going to be trouble."

I glanced up. There, in every damn window on this side of the building, were ghosts. Men, women, children. All of them peering down on me like a tree full of silent crows, waiting to peck out my eyes.

"I didn't come to cause trouble," I told them. "I just need to talk to somebody, and then I'll leave. I promise." I couldn't, however, promise that I *wouldn't* cause trouble, or that it wouldn't find me.

The ghosts exchanged glances. I turned my attention back to the dead girl beside me. She looked at me for a moment, then nodded her head. "Fine. Do what you have to do, and then leave, please."

"Hanging around is not something I want to do, trust me."

"Trust you?" she echoed, with a laugh that sounded like nails on a chalkboard. "You're living. Why would we ever trust *you*?"

I shrugged. "I got rid of Bent, didn't I?"

She tilted her head to one side. "You're going to have to do better than that, but go. Do what you have to do and then leave us in peace."

"Look, Girl Interrupted, I could be doing that right now if you hadn't snuck up on me. So, why don't you just float back to your bathtub and let me go on my way?"

For a second I thought she might go full-on *Beetlejuice* on me, but she didn't. She simply sneered at me, her lips as red as her blood against her pale face, and then she faded away.

Did she give me the finger? I laughed and shook my head. Then, I took a second to look around and let that part of me that was connected to Wren reach out for her.

There she was.

I jogged toward the building that stood out like a beacon to me—the place that pulsed with unseen energy that I felt deep inside my soul. If there was an upside to Halloween, other than Ben in a tight black shirt, it was being able to find my sister in a sea of teeming spiritual energy. Even on a bad day I'd be able to find her, but not quite like this. Every step felt like I was moving closer to a part of myself. A nail drawn toward a magnet.

If my memory was correct, this building used to be one of the old housing units. I didn't know which one, but it looked like it had been really nice once, so I figured it had been home to the patients with money, or from families with money. And they had probably been white, which increased the probability of this having once been home to Robert Alan Thurbridge, Jr.

The door swung open just as I reached for the knob. I knew who stood on the opposite side of the threshold before I even looked up. I knew the moment I saw her bare feet, the toes painted bright blue.

"Hey, sis," I said, trying to sound casual. "Can I come in?"

She looked worried, nervous and a little angry. "Are you crazy? What are you doing here?" She stuck her head out through the wall beside me and looked around. "Did you come here alone?"

"Yeah. Stick your head back inside. It's freaking me out." Seriously, seeing your sister sticking out of a building while her butt was still in it was really, really weird.

She pulled back in. This time when she looked at me, there was no question as to her emotion. "You are crazy."

I shrugged. "You come here alone."

"That's different."

I arched a brow. "Really? Because last time I checked, we both played a huge part in ridding this place of Josiah Bent. Are you telling me the ghosts of Haven Crest are playing favorites?"

Wren reached out her hand and flicked me in the forehead. "Ow." It stung.

"They're not exactly fans of the living here," she reminded me.

"Yeah, I met up with one of them already." I rubbed my forehead. "She's still in one piece and so am I. I think it's you who really doesn't want me here. Don't worry, I don't plan to stay long, I just need to talk to Noah."

Her mouth dropped open. "Noah?"

I forced a smile. "Yeah. I need some help with something, and I'm hoping he's the ghost for the job. Is he around?" Since she wasn't going to step aside, I crossed the threshold and brushed past her. When the door clicked shut, I pivoted on my heel.

Holy crap.

The outside of this building might look as run-down and decayed as the rest of the campus, but inside was another story. It was gorgeous—the floor polished and windows clean. There was nice furniture and drapes, plasterwork and fresh paint on the walls and ceiling. This must be what it used to look like once upon a time.

"Nice digs," I commented, trying to sound calm. I'd seen places and people through Wren's eyes before, but normally only when we made contact. I didn't think this was all to blame on Halloween, either. This was…magic? No. This… this was *power*. I swallowed.

"You can see it, can't you?" My sister was right in front of me; only inches separated us. The dead had little concept of personal space. "You see this place like I do."

I nodded. "I wonder why that is?"

She shrugged. "The approach of All Hallows' Eve would magnify your sensitivity to spectral energy, but probably because this is how every ghost in this building sees it."

I glanced around again. "Like an altered reality?" I wasn't completely sold. Halloween was becoming an all-too-convenient excuse for anything strange, and this didn't feel natural to me like other All Hallows' Eve weirdness had. It felt contrived. Like someone had cast a spell over the entire building. Or maybe, the building itself was responsible. It was so old and full of so many ghosts, it had become something of a wraith itself, able to revert its appearance to a more beautiful age.

Regardless, it was both weird and awesome to witness.

"Why do you need Noah's help?" Wren asked.

"Oh, we found out the name of the ghost that attacked me and Kevin. I wanted to ask Noah if maybe he knew of him."

Wren's hands went to her hips, elbows out like she was about to do the chicken dance—which would be freaking hilarious. "Because all ghosts automatically know each other?"

"No." I scowled at her. "Because the guy was a patient here, and Noah's been around so long I thought he might know the guy. God! I'm not that much of a bigot against ghosts, Wren, no matter how much you think I hate them. Thanks for that, by the way, because the most important person in my life just happens to be a ghost, so, you know, it's great to know she thinks I'm a total douche."

She made a face. "I hate that word."

I threw my hands in the air. "Then you shouldn't have looked it up!" It was not my fault that she knew nothing about outdated feminine hygiene products. I'd had to look it up myself, and I personally thought it was a fantastic word that rolled easily off the tongue and included a large sampling of the human race.

I wasn't going to think about the fact that she hadn't said she *didn't* think I was a douche.

"Suggesting your sister be less inquisitive is akin to telling the sun not to shine, Miss Noble, but then I'm certain you're already well aware of that fact."

I turned. Standing on the staircase that curved down from the second floor was Noah. He looked like something right out of the pages of Victorian GQ magazine. Any moment I thought someone might come along and challenge him to a duel, or that he might yell for his horse.

Of course he disappointed me by doing neither of those things. He simply walked down the remaining stairs, then toward Wren and me. I could see more ghosts gathered at the top of the stairs, peering down at us like kids spying on a party during which their parents had made them go to bed. I waved.

Someone waved back, which made me smile.

When he stood in front of me—beside Wren—Noah bowed. "It's a pleasure to see you again, Miss Noble." He straightened. "Have you come to collect your sister, or is this more of a social call?"

Okay, so maybe I wasn't completely sold on the guy, but he had an accent that almost made me not care. Seriously. I'd listen to him read the phone book.

I pulled the page I'd printed off at home out of my pocket and offered it to him. "I was hoping you might know this guy."

Long, manicured hands took the paper from me. "Is this the fellow who attacked you and your friend? Because I can assure you, Miss Noble, that none of the spirits in this house are given to violence. Nor are many strong enough to travel to places beyond their own experience."

He didn't really think I'd believe that, did he? The violence part? Most humans were capable of great violence, and ghosts were even more inclined. I wasn't being racist, that was just a documented fact.

"I'm sure that's true," I lied. "But would you mind looking? Maybe you've seen him around." The moment the words left my mouth, a movement on the stairs caught my eye. I turned my head and smiled at the man standing on the landing, staring at me like he'd just seen…well, a ghost.

I smiled at him, not the least bit amused. "Hey, Woodstock. Got a minute?"

Robert Alan Thurbridge, Jr. stared at me. I braced myself for his attack, but then he did the one thing I hadn't anticipated.

He ran.

chapter nine

WREN

Lark ran after Robert, her boots striking the steps hard. I turned to Noah, who stood beside me holding a piece of paper with a grainy black-and-white photograph of Robert on it. It was part of his patient file.

He was the one who'd attacked Lark and Kevin. A tendril of anger snaked up my midsection, obliterating the confusion that had been there just seconds before. Running was the act of someone guilty.

He'd tried to hurt my sister but played friend to me.

I started after them. Noah grabbed my arm. His eyes were bright. Such pretty eyes.

"Where are you going?" he asked, frowning. "Surely you don't believe these accusations?"

"My sister doesn't lie." Lark was a lot of things, and sometimes she made me angry, but she wouldn't have come here if she weren't certain.

"Of course not." He glanced at the paper in his hand. "But she must be mistaken."

I appreciated his loyalty to his friend. Hopefully, he would appreciate mine to Lark. "Robert threatened to rape my sister and kill my friend. The only one who is mistaken is him." I yanked my arm free and ran after Lark. Noah was right behind me.

The ghosts gathered at the top of the stairs had parted into two groups, leaving me an open path. I didn't need to ask where Lark had gone, I simply followed her energy trail like a hound after blood.

I found them in the third room on the right, which had probably been Robert's in life, if he'd chosen it as his refuge. I swept into the room at just the right moment to see Lark kick him hard in the stomach, knocking him against the wall. My sister was bleeding from a cut to her lip.

He'd hurt her. The realization filled me with rage, and the heightened energy of all the ghosts around me—of the building itself—only made it worse.

I lunged at Robert, my hand closing around his throat. I lifted him up until my arm was straight, and he dangled above the floor like a fish on a hook.

"Wren!" Noah cried. He moved toward me, but I held up my hand.

A hand touched my shoulder. Instantly, I felt a little calmer, not quite so cold. It was Lark. She was the only person— dead or alive—to have such an effect on me when I felt myself starting to lose what little humanity I'd worked so hard to cultivate.

I'd never known what it was like to be a living person, with a sense of morality or compassion. What I knew of any human emotion had come from my sister, and the spirits of Haven Crest had no idea how dark and cold I could be.

"Why did you attack Kevin McCrae?" Lark asked Robert.

The man I had thought to be so peaceful and joyful and kind sneered at my sister. "To kill him, you stupid bitch."

I gave him a shake. "Watch how you speak to my sister, worm. Kevin McCrae is my friend." Maybe he'd hurt me deeper than I'd ever been hurt before, but I didn't wish Kevin any harm. I never would.

That sneer transferred to me. He must have felt really brave with his brethren behind me. He had no idea what I could do to him before any of them even thought to stop me.

"We're not *friends* with the living, Dead Born. We're either predator or prey. Which one are you?"

"She's the one with her hand around your throat, dickless," Lark retorted. "And she's not the one you need to be worried about. I am, because I have no illusions about our relationship status. Who sent you after Kevin McCrae?"

Robert smiled, and I saw him as Lark must see him—as tainted and stained. Venomous and twisted. "Fuck you."

I squeezed harder. I couldn't kill him this way—he was already dead. But I could hurt him. He struggled against my hold. He might be older than me, but he wasn't stronger. I tightened my fingers a bit more so he'd learn that lesson quickly. If he wanted to spend the rest of eternity walking about with a crushed throat, that was his prerogative.

"You tried that once," Lark said. "Didn't work out so well for you, did it?"

The ghost winked. "Tell your sister to let me go, and we can try again."

Lark reached out, her hand grabbing Robert between his dangling legs. He cried out, smoke rising from his crotch. Iron. Lark was wearing iron rings.

I smiled. "That has to smart." Even a dead girl like me

knew how attached men were to their reproductive organs—even after death.

"Who sent you?" she asked again.

Robert only whimpered.

Lark released him, pulled back her hand and wiped it on her jeans like she was trying to scrub the skin right off. If she'd hit him, the iron might have dispersed his energy or marked him. She had an iron rod that would have surely knocked him into the Shadow Lands, but the rings were less potent, and she hadn't been trying to get rid of him. She was a natural interrogator, my Lark.

Of the two of us, I was the predator. I was the loose cannon. For all my chastising of Lark for her prejudice against ghosts, I was almost as bad. At least she showed consideration. Mercy. I usually had those things as well, but it was all too easy for me to lose them. At that moment I teetered on the precipice of rational morality and the desire to rip Robert to shreds.

I could do it. They didn't know what I'd done to Josiah Bent. Neither did Lark. They hadn't been there, and I'd had Bent all to myself.

Robert's gaze strayed from mine for a moment. Was he looking to Noah to save him?

"Tell her, Robert," Noah said. Knowing that he was on my side—on Lark's side—wrapped me in a rush of joy.

The ghost in my grip slumped a little as he glared down at me and my sister. "No one sent me. I sought to avenge the spirit of Josiah Bent!"

There was a chorus of gasps behind me. I knew for a fact that most of the inhabitants of this building hadn't agreed with Bent or his violence. Bent had been a monster, and Robert... Robert was no better. Yes, he was one of my kind, but

I couldn't let what he'd tried to do to Kevin slide by. And what he'd tried to do to my sister decided his fate.

"Noah, where are Robert's bones located?" I knew he'd know. They all knew. A coven of ghosts like this always knew where bones and anchors were. It was part of the hive mentality. The property of Haven Crest knew every inch of itself, and therefore, so did the ghosts that haunted its buildings.

Silence answered me. I waited, my gaze never leaving Robert's. It was Lark who turned to address our witnesses. "Noah, I have no problem digging holes above every grave, dousing the entire graveyard in lighter fluid and throwing a match. I'll light up this building, too, if I have to."

"You're a very cruel young woman," he replied.

I glanced over my shoulder at him, my eyes locking with his. "She's my sister, and he threatened her. Robert is the one in the wrong."

"She's right," came a small voice from the back of the crowd. It was a young woman whose name I couldn't remember right at that moment. She looked as though she might be from the same time period as Noah. "Robert's behavior is abhorrent. It's clear that he's become a monster. I know I would no longer feel safe if he is left among us."

Noah crumpled the paper Lark had given him in his fist and hung his head. I knew this had to be hard for him as Robert had been his friend for many years, but surely he could see what a danger he'd become?

He looked up—right at Lark. "I'll take you."

Robert jerked in my grip. "Noah, you can't!"

Noah glared at him. "You brought this on yourself. You know what you must do. What must be done."

Something flickered in Robert's wild gaze. I didn't understand it, but something passed between him and Noah. "As you wish."

Lark leaned close to me. "Will you be okay when I go?"

I nodded. "I'm not in any danger from these people. Or him." Robert wouldn't hurt anyone ever again.

"That's not what I meant."

I turned my head and looked into eyes identical to my own. "I know. I'll be fine. Go. This has to be done, but I don't want to drag it out any longer than necessary."

She patted my shoulder before walking away. I knew she'd finish this as quickly as she could, and I trusted Noah. His honor was important to him.

I heard them leave the room. A look over my shoulder, and I realized we were alone. I lowered Robert to the floor, but I didn't let go. He was still taller than I was, but not by much.

We stood there for a long time, just he and I. Waiting.

Finally, he smirked at me. "This won't change anything. Someone else will take my place. Send me on to the Shadow Lands or the Beyond, it doesn't matter. Someday I'm going to cross paths with that breather sister of yours, and she and I are going to play."

I leaned forward, pushing my hand deeper into his throat. A tenuous thread inside me snapped. I was not prepared for the rush of hunger that followed. It was a wild feeling—like how I imagined birds felt when they realized they could fly.

I smiled—all teeth. "You know, Robert, you have lovely eyes."

He scowled. "What?"

I lifted my free hand to his face, tracing the outline of his right orbital bone. Of course, it was all just energy, not bone at all, but why split hairs? It wasn't the bone that interested me.

"Wren?" he whispered. "What are you doing?"

My finger dipped around the edge of his eye. He had really long eyelashes. They weren't terribly thick, but they were soft, and they tickled my skin like fairy wings.

"You're not going to miss it," I whispered back. "Not where you're going."

His eyes widened—which made my quest all the easier. "Wren..."

I let go of his neck and slammed my hand over his mouth. Then, I shoved my fingers into his eye socket, where it was wet and warm. Robert jerked, crying out against my palm.

"Stop struggling," I commanded. "You'll only make it worse—and you don't want it to get any worse, do you?"

He went still.

"Good boy." I curled my fingers and yanked hard. Robert screamed against my palm. I let him go when he stopped making so much noise and stepped back to admire my prize. I turned away, holding it up so I could see it glisten in the light.

"Beautiful," I whispered. There was something so incredibly perfect about the human eye. The window to the soul, indeed.

Behind me there was a flash. I turned just in time to see the flames vanish, leaving nothing but a small, sooty smudge on the wall where Robert had slumped just seconds before.

It was done. He was gone. For good. Noah had kept his word.

"Miss Wren?" came a voice from behind me.

I turned around, hiding my sticky fingers and bloody prize behind my back. It was the girl who had spoken up before. She was a tiny little blonde in a blue Victorian gown. Her hair was piled up on her head in an elaborate hairstyle that I guessed was from her days before Haven Crest. She was pretty and delicate. She looked sweet and gentle. I bet she'd never ripped someone's eye from their skull.

"Yes?"

She looked about, as though worried that she might have been followed, then rushed toward me like a hawk on a mouse. I held my ground. She was the one who ought to be frightened, not me.

She stopped directly in front of me, eyes darting about in a nervous flutter. Whom was she so afraid of overhearing us?

"I need to talk to you," she whispered. "I have a message."

"A message?" I asked, rolling my prize between my fingers behind my back. "From who?"

"Emily," she replied. It took me a moment to realize who she meant.

"Emily Murray?" I asked. My ancestor?

The girl nodded. "I knew her once. A long time ago. We were friends. She would often come to visit me after I was committed. Even after I died she came a few times to say hello, but the others didn't like her coming by so much. She made them nervous. Your sister makes them nervous, as well."

If they knew I was holding Robert's eyeball in my palm, they'd be nervous around me, too.

"What's the message?" I asked. I didn't mean to be rude or to rush her, but I needed to get the blood off me before Lark returned.

Her wide blue gaze locked with mine. In it, I saw fear, but not of me. "She says you and your sister are in danger. She said that he's coming for you."

"'He'?" I made a face. "He who?"

The girl shook her head. "I don't know. That's all she told me before saying that she didn't want to put me in danger. She disappeared, and I haven't seen her since."

"When was this?"

"Two days ago."

When I'd first met Noah. Emily must have seen me here that night. Maybe she kept tabs on Lark and me all the time. I was really starting to feel conspicuous with this eye in my clutch. "Why are you just telling me this now?"

She drew back. What a little mouse. "This was the first moment I had alone with you. She told me not to trust anyone except you and your sister." Her gaze darted to the smudge on the wall. "Is he really gone?"

"Yes."

"Good." She shivered. "He was an awful man."

I didn't ask what he'd done to her. It wasn't like I could hurt him for it again. "He can't hurt you anymore. Did Emily say anything else?"

"No. She only begged me to tell you and your sister to be careful." Her face lit up. "Wait, she also said that you needed to look for Alys. Does that make sense to you?"

I nodded. I'd seen Alys in Nan's house before, but she hadn't been around lately. Had something happened to her? "Thank you for giving me the message. I have to find my sister."

The girl smiled and then flitted away in a rustle of skirts. I left as well, but I didn't immediately go to Lark. I went to my private little place in the Shadow Lands, where I retreated when I wanted time alone, or felt the need to simply be dead. There, I opened the small box I kept my treasures in and deposited Robert's eye with my other keepsakes. I paused just a moment to admire my collection before putting the box away. Then I cleaned myself up—easy to do in the Shadow Lands, when all you had to do was wish it—and phased back into the realm of the living.

I met Lark and Noah in front of the building. My sister was dirty and smelled of smoke, but she was otherwise fine.

"Are you all right?" Noah asked.

I nodded. "I am. I'm sorry you had to be a part of this."

"Don't be. Anyone who would threaten a woman is no friend of mine. Are you leaving?"

"Yes."

"Will I see you tomorrow?" he asked. I couldn't judge his emotions from his voice. His tone was polite, as it always was around others.

"Would you like to see me tomorrow?"

He smiled, and Lark rolled her eyes. "Get a room," she said. And then, "Security's coming. I've got to run. Thanks for your help, Noah."

I watched as she slipped into the darkness. I'd catch up with her in a moment.

Noah held out his arms, and I walked into his embrace, wrapping my own arms around him. "I don't want you to leave," he whispered.

"I don't want to, either, but I need to talk to Lark. Do you really want me to come back later?"

He nodded. And then he kissed me, and I knew then that everything was good between us. He wasn't angry at me for Robert's destruction. And he didn't know about my trophy.

After I left him, I caught up with Lark just as she climbed into Nan's car in the graveyard.

"You okay?" she asked. "Truthfully?"

I nodded. "I'm good. We need to talk. Emily's in trouble."

She swore as she stuck the keys in the ignition. Her expression was grim when she looked at me.

"Great." But she didn't sound the least bit happy. "I think Alys is, too."

LARK

The moment we arrived home we went straight up to our bedroom. On the drive, Wren had told me about what the ghost at Haven Crest had told her, and I filled her in on seeing Alys in the bathroom.

"There's something going on," I muttered as I yanked open the top drawer of the desk. "Anytime we've seen Emily she's seemed on edge—like she's doing something wrong. And Alys has popped in and out like a newbie ghost. She should be stronger than that."

"They shouldn't even be here. Should they?" Wren paced the length of the room—or rather, she floated along the top of the carpet. "They were different, like us, but they ought to have moved on. The girl said that Emily had a warning for us."

"Yeah, that 'he' was coming for us." I dug through the papers in the drawer. "Whoever 'he' is."

"How did you know?"

I barely glanced at her. "I've been having dreams. I think they're of Alys. Everything's black, and there's danger all around me."

"If Emily wants us to find her, Alys must be in some sort of danger."

"Of course she is." I dug deeper in the drawer. God, I was such a slob! "Would you expect anything less from our ancestors?"

"What are you looking for?"

I pulled the spirit board that had belonged to Emily and Alys out of the drawer and held it up like it was a prize. "This."

Wren made a scoffing noise. "A spirit board? What can that do that I can't?"

I shot her a narrow glance. "Ego much?" I wanted to chalk it up to Halloween, but she was different—I could feel it. Was it Noah? Or was the bigotry Wren claimed I had toward ghosts clouding my judgment? Regardless of the fact that he'd taken me to Woodstock's grave, I had the feeling that he would have been just as happy to turn his back on the whole thing.

"You know what I mean." She drifted toward me. "It doesn't even have a planchette."

I looked at the board, my fingers tracing the image on the wood. It was old, but heavily lacquered, preserving the image on it. Twins—one with white hair, the other with red, standing so that they faced each other from opposite sides of the wood. Their clasped hands were in the center of the board. The way they were linked made me think of a planchette. Maybe that was because of what Wren had just said, or maybe it was a message from Emily and Alys for those of us who came after them.

And maybe it was time for me to do some more digging into the family history.

"I don't think we need a planchette," I told Wren. "I think *we* are the planchette."

She looked at the board where my hand rested in the center. A moment later, her fingers settled on—in—mine.

Bam! It was like a punch to the face that left me seeing stars. I blinked, and then realized we were someplace else. Someplace...dark.

Not just dark. This place was black.

I clung to Wren's hand. Where the hell were we? A light wind ruffled my hair, bringing the smell of dirt and wood.

Was that scratching I heard? And crying? The back of my neck tingled, as though invisible fingers had brushed against my skin.

"Where are we?" I whispered.

"I think it's the void," Wren replied, her voice shaking. "Lark, we're in the damn void!"

Wren rarely swore, and it was even more rare for her to show fear. It was important that I calm her down, even though I was freaking out myself. "We don't know that's what this is." But it fit the description.

The void was a place we'd first heard about as kids. A ghost we'd encountered at a bed-and-breakfast in Maine while on vacation with our parents had explained that it was a dark, endless kind of place, where souls could be trapped or imprisoned. Solitary confinement for ghosts. It was said that ghosts that lingered too long, who became so corrupt they couldn't move on, were sent to the void for eternal torment. I didn't believe that any more than I believed in hell, but this place was scary—like the dark cellar of a house that hadn't been lived in for a hundred years.

Like a grave.

"Why would the board bring us here?" I wondered.

"Who cares? Let's just get out of here. Now!"

It wasn't very often that I was the calm one and Wren was the one hanging on by a thread. "It brought us here for a reason."

"I don't care!"

"Just listen for a minute!"

We fell silent. I listened—hard. Past the crying and the scratching and the wind, I heard a voice.

And it was calling our names.

"Do you hear that?" I asked.

Wren tugged on my hand. "We have to get out of here."

I held tight to her fingers. "Do you hear it? There—it's coming closer."

"Lark, we have to go. How do we get out?"

It was coming closer. I could feel it. It wasn't a constant cry. In fact, I wasn't even sure it was actually a sound. Whatever it was, I understood it, and it was coming to meet me.

"Oh, my God," Wren whispered. She had to feel it, too. But unlike me, she was afraid of it. And I wasn't.

I saw it—a flicker of something in the dark. Just a flash. A face? I tried to take a step toward it, but Wren pulled me back. I whipped my head around to glare at her. Why could I see her so clearly in the dark? It was like the two of us were white shirts under a black light.

Suddenly, Wren's fear was understandable. We were lit up like a lighthouse. Beacons. All around us I saw other flickers, heard their voices.

They were all coming.

My heart seized. *Oh, shit.*

A hand reached for me, disembodied as though the darkness was a lake, and I was the only thing between her and drowning.

More flickers. Closer now.

"Lark," Wren whimpered.

How did I know it was a she? Not just a she.

Alys.

Wren's panic washed over me.

I reached back. It was Alys, I knew it. My fingers brushed hers at the same time Wren let go of my other hand.

It was like being tossed out of a speeding car. One second I was surrounded by blackness, reaching out to Alys, and the next I was on my back on my bedroom floor. Wren sat beside me, arms wrapped around her knees.

"What the hell?" I demanded, pushing myself upright. My head spun. "It was Alys, Wren! I almost had her."

Wild eyes turned to me. She looked terrified. "They almost had us, Lark! Once they get you, there's no getting away from them. And you almost let one take you!"

"It was Alys! Don't you understand? She's trapped there!"

Wren's expression hardened. "If she's there, then she did something to deserve it."

I watched her for a moment, taking in the slight tremor in her shoulders and how her hands were clenched into tight fists. "How do you know that?"

She swiped at her eye with the back of her hand. Was she crying? "I've heard things in the Shadow Lands. The void is ghost hell. It's torment and pain. And there are things there… things that like hurting ghosts. There were so many ghosts in the dark. I could feel their suffering, their pain. Couldn't you?"

"No," I replied honestly. "I couldn't. And just because Alys is there doesn't mean she deserves to be. Didn't you say the girl at Haven Crest told you to find Alys?"

She held up her hand, palm out. "I'm not going back to that place."

Wow, she was really messed up. I didn't argue with her, and I didn't push it, but we weren't done. If Alys was trapped, it was our job—our responsibility—to find and help her. And if I could walk into Haven Crest after all that had happened to me there and at Bell Hill, Wren could suck it up and brave the void.

I watched as she stood up. I wasn't going to be half so graceful, but I struggled to my feet regardless. I didn't like it when we weren't on equal footing.

"I can't believe Robert tried to kill Kevin," she said.

I shrugged. Fine, she didn't want to talk about Alys. I wasn't going to let her avoid it forever. "I can't believe he was a follower of Bent's."

My sister shot me a narrow glance. "What do you mean by that?"

What did *she* mean by that? "Just what I said."

"If he wasn't a follower of Bent, what reason would he have for coming after Kevin or threatening you?"

"Well, he could be just a nut job, but he wouldn't have a reason. Look, what the hell are you so twisted up about?" Then it dawned on me.

Wren's fists went to her hips. "You don't trust the friends I've made at Haven Crest."

I blinked at her. It sounded to me like maybe *she* didn't completely trust her new friends. I could understand that. "I don't really trust anybody—except for you." And sometimes... Well, I wasn't going to go there. "And since Noah took me to Woodstock's grave, I've got no reason to distrust him."

Not to mention that on our way to the grave the one thing he said to me—honestly, we hardly talked—was that he had "the highest regard" for Wren. I figured that meant that he liked her better than any other dead girl he'd ever met. That was a good thing. Anyone who saw Wren's worth was all right by me.

She was still silent. I sighed in frustration. "I don't know what you want from me, and I'm too tired to figure it out. But the way I see it is that at this very moment everything is good. Okay? Now, I'm going to bed." Tomorrow was a school day and after a weekend of parties, Halloween madness and ghosts a-go-go, I was exhausted. All I wanted was to go to bed, but I needed to shower off the grave dirt and soot first.

"Are you sticking around?" I asked as I started for the bathroom. "Or going back to Haven Crest?"

Wren shrugged a shoulder. She didn't look at me. WTF? "No. They need some time to recover from losing Robert. I'd feel like an outsider, and after what he did to you, it's not like I would mourn him."

I wanted to remind her that he'd wanted to hurt Kevin, too, but I didn't. She was so weird lately I didn't know what to say or do. Was Halloween the ghost equivalent of a period? Was my sister caught up in a tide of raging, spectral PMS?

Whatever. I really didn't have the energy to worry about it. I didn't respond or ask any more questions. I walked into the bathroom, shut the door and turned the faucets in the tub. I undressed as the water heated up, so when I stepped into the tub I was hit by a pelting blast of hot water.

My *gawd*, it felt *good*.

I scrubbed myself pink, washed and conditioned my hair. I'd put it in a couple of braids before I went to bed and then finish drying it in the morning. The braids would give me some nice waves, and I wouldn't need to do much in the way of styling, which meant I could sleep a little later. Yay.

After I rinsed the last of the conditioner out, I turned off the water and wrung my hair. I yanked the shower curtain to the side and reached for my towels. The bathroom was full of steam.

I wrapped a towel around my head and dried off with the other. It wasn't until I pulled on my robe and turned toward the mirror that I saw *it*. My stomach dropped.

There, on the fogged glass, was a note. It was written backward—as though from the other side of the mirror.

ƎM Ԁ⅃ƎH

chapter ten

WREN

"Who wrote it?" I asked, when I saw the words fading on the mirror.

"Who do you think? Alys, obviously."

Beside me, Lark scowled in her bathrobe. But when did Lark not scowl? It seemed to me that she spent most of her time with that expression on her face. Sometimes I wanted to hit her. Other times I hoped her face froze like that.

Once in a while—like now, since I'd been the one to make us leave the void, where my sister was certain Alys was trapped—I felt like it was my fault that Lark always seemed to be upset. I mean, if it wasn't for me she'd probably have a normal life, right? Then again, if it hadn't been for her being born alive, I could be the one with that normal life.

What if I grabbed her by the back of the head and slammed her face into that mirror? She'd stop frowning then, wouldn't she? I took a step toward her.

Clarity knocked me back a step. What was I doing? Had I really been about to physically attack my sister? What was wrong with me?

This wasn't me. This wasn't right. It had to be the approaching All Hallows' Eve. I was too young for the madness that came from "lingering" too long in the world of the living. Wasn't I?

I had to do something—something right. I was not going back to the void—I didn't even know if I could do that by myself—and I didn't feel right going to Haven Crest and spending time with Noah when he'd had to destroy a friend. But there was something going on, and Lark had faced too much of it on her own already.

Maybe I would be alive if not for her, but I don't know if I'd want to live if she wasn't with me. That was what was important. As much as I liked Noah and sometimes Lark upset me, she was my anchor. She and I were what mattered.

All that mattered.

"I'll go to the Shadow Lands," I announced. "I'll see if I can find Emily, and if I can't find her, I'll see what I can find out about the void." Iloana—an old woman I liked—might have some answers. There was also this library in my world that held the most wonderful books—some that had never even been written but only dreamed. If I couldn't find something to help us there, then it didn't exist.

The lines in Lark's forehead smoothed. I knew she'd sleep better knowing that one of us was able to do something. In the past twenty-four hours she'd been attacked by a ghost, destroyed him, gone into the void and had two spectral messages. She was due for a rest.

"Thanks, Wrennie."

The weariness in her voice weighed on my shoulders. This was her life, and my death. Our burden. We didn't know how or why, it just was. And there was no running away from it.

Lark had tried that once, and it hadn't been pretty for either of us.

When she turned to me, her arms open, I stepped in and wrapped mine around her. It would probably seem weird to most people, but whenever Lark and I connected in some manner, it felt like I was whole. We hadn't connected as much lately as we used to. She had Ben and school, and I had…well, I had my collection, my own interests and now I had Noah. Still, I needed the other half of my soul, and that's what I honestly believed my sister to be.

I tucked her into bed, stayed beside her, telling her stories like I'd done when we were younger, until she fell asleep. Then, I slipped between worlds, into the soothing, muted atmosphere of the Shadow Lands.

I sighed, just like Lark sometimes did when she got all wrapped up in that fleece blanket she had. I felt centered and strong.

Home.

I really should spend more time there. But there was so much in the world of the living that I liked. My sister—when I wasn't fantasizing about killing her. Noah. Reality TV shows that I couldn't watch in front of Lark because she made fun of me and swore at the people on the show, despite my insistence that they couldn't hear her.

Iloana didn't seem to be around—which wasn't all that odd. If I didn't find any information at the library I'd go looking for her.

The first time I visited the library—and I'd only found out about it recently—I encountered Emily, our ancestor. She had white hair like Lark, but was a little older. She'd given me a book that allowed us to find out information about Josiah Bent. I eventually brought that book back, but Emily hadn't been there. Neither Lark nor I had seen her in weeks, and then she sends me a message via a Haven Crest ghost? Why? Why couldn't she contact me herself?

Was Alys the reason Emily hadn't moved on? It made sense. I wouldn't leave Lark, either. But the void…that was not a place I ever wanted to see again. I'd never been so scared before. Never.

I hated being afraid, and it wasn't something I felt very often.

The library was a large, looming building with columns and a huge front door. Inside, it was all dark wood and rich colors. It felt timeless, and like all things in the Shadow Lands, its outside dimensions were smaller than they ought to have been. The library was infinite. Unmeasurable.

Today there was actually someone at the desk. That was new—not that I was any expert in the workings of this place. I approached the woman. She was tall and thin, with long thick hair that flipped out at the ends. She was wearing a lime-green minidress with white trim. Her tights and shoes were the exact same shade as her dress. Her eyes were heavily rimmed with black eyeliner that flicked up at the outer corners.

Lark would love her look.

"Can I help you?" she asked softly, smiling.

I smiled back. "I need a book on Haven Crest patients between 1879 and 1899. And I would like the book on Emily Murray and her sister, Alys." There was no harm in asking, was there? If there were books on other people in this library, surely there was one about my ancestors. I don't know why I hadn't thought of it earlier.

"I'm sorry," the woman said, handing me a leather-bound

volume, "I can give you the Haven Crest book, but the other is part of Special Collections."

"What does that mean?"

Was that smile stuck on her face? "It means that you can look at it here, but you can't check it out."

This sort of thing happened in the libraries of the living. I knew this because of Lark's various school projects that had required trips to various libraries. But how did those rules apply here? Surely if a book went missing, another would take its place? Or was there actually an author behind these countless tomes? That was too much to contemplate.

"Fine. Where is Special Collections?"

That smile never wavered. "It's by appointment only."

"Then I'll make an appointment."

She consulted a large book in front of her. It had gold-edged pages and had to be at least six inches thick. "The earliest appointment I have available is Wednesday at one."

The day before Halloween.

"Is that Eastern Standard Time?" I asked sweetly, wondering if anyone would notice if I jumped over the counter, wrestled her to the floor and ripped her eyes out of her smiling head.

Some of that must have shown in my face, because her smile wavered. "Yes. Would you like the appointment?"

"I would, yes, thank you." I held the Haven Crest book to my chest and returned her stare. "Don't you need my name?"

"Oh! Sorry, yes."

"Wren Noble," I informed her, but I had a feeling she already knew who I was. It was a feeling I was beginning to grow very, very tired of. It had all started around the time Lark killed herself. She was only dead for a blink, but that's when it seemed that suddenly people—especially dead ones—

knew more about us than we did, and they weren't keen on sharing the information.

It was time for that to stop.

"Wren Noble, one o'clock on Wednesday, October thirtieth for Special Collections," she chirped as she scribbled in the book. Her smile was back in place. "Is there anything else I can help you with?"

"No, thank you," I said. Then, still smiling, I leaned across the counter. "I just wanted to tell you what pretty eyes you have."

She giggled. You'd think we were the very best of friends. "Oh, thank you!"

I flashed a little teeth. She wouldn't be so pleased if she knew what I wanted to do with those chocolate-colored little orbs. But the thought gave me "a happy," as Lark would say, so I took my book and left the library. I could have read it there, but if I had to spend another moment in the same room as that woman—no matter if it was one of infinite space—I was going to make some violence that someone would notice.

When people already knew more about you than they ought, attracting notice wasn't wise.

I went back to the little house that had been mine for as long as I could remember. The thing about being dead—being a ghost—meant that I never really needed care. And what little I did need, Iloana had been kind enough to offer. My link to Lark had enabled me to drift between her world and this one, and I learned everything at the same rate at which she did—how to talk, how to walk. Thankfully I avoided the whole potty-training fiasco. That was just a lesson in humiliation, if you asked me.

We helped each other, taught each other. We took our first steps together, holding each other's hand. My mother used to laugh at how Lark always walked, ran—even danced—with one arm out farther than the other. She never saw me holding on to that hand, no matter how hard I wished she would.

My mother never once realized I was there. My father, on the other hand... There had been a couple of times that I think he felt my presence, and maybe even saw me. Emily was his ancestor, so it made sense that he would have a bit of sensitivity like his mother—my grandmother. Those times that I thought he'd been aware of me, he'd had a little too much to drink, so my mother accused him of being drunk. I don't know if he ever had a sense of me again, because he never mentioned it—at least not to my mother. Not when Lark or I were around.

I called them my mother and my father. Lark at least called him Dad, but neither of us felt much motherly love toward the woman who couldn't see me and then punished Lark because *she* could.

Anyway, I had my little house. It wasn't even that we needed shelter. There wasn't any weather or temperature change in the Shadow Lands. And it was never night or even day—just perpetual twilight. Still, I guess the human mind clung to the idea of shelter, even a human who had never lived.

I had my little box of treasures, but I didn't look at it right now. There was a big, deep armchair in front of a fireplace that I had added after seeing one someplace else. That's where I sat with my library loan, reading by the firelight. Not like I could ever develop eyestrain.

I flipped through the Haven Crest book. I found the girl who had given me Emily's message at Haven Crest. She was admitted in 1901, born in 1885. She would have been the same age as Emily, so her story rang of truth thus far. She had been admitted for hysteria—whatever that was. There was nothing in her record that would lead me to believe that she'd been lying about Emily's message. There was nothing linking her to Emily at all. Didn't they have a visitors log back then? They must have, but it wasn't here.

I kept turning the pages, nervously studying the grainy photos of patient after patient. Then I found it.

Noah Andrew *McCrae*? I stared at the name written in faded cursive. I had to be wrong. It was McCain or something else, and it was just the handwriting that made me imagine Noah's last name was the same as Kevin's. But no, there it was. The penmanship was perfect, as were my eyes.

Maybe they weren't related. They couldn't be, because I'd told Noah what Kevin's name was, and he'd made that remark about being Irish, and that he was English.

But England had controlled part of Ireland for centuries, and a family that started out in England could have moved to Ireland. Maybe it was a huge coincidence, but as I looked at Noah's face, so young and alive, I could see a resemblance to Kevin that went beyond their dark hair and blue eyes.

That would explain why I had been so instantly drawn to Noah. Just when I thought I was over Kevin I went and fell for his ancestor. Not a direct ancestor, of course, because Noah would have been too young to have had children. Wouldn't he?

I was jumping to conclusions. There was no reason for Noah to keep this from me, so either he didn't know they were related, or they weren't. It was that simple. His surname wasn't what I wanted to look at anyway.

Lark had accused me of not knowing anything about him. And she was right. It didn't matter to me what he'd done, but given recent events, it would be wrong of me not to at least be curious.

If Noah and I were alive, wanting to know his last name would not be strange. In fact, it would be strange if I didn't know it. And if he had been mentally ill in life, that sometimes affected how the person was in the afterlife. You didn't die and revert to a perfect version of yourself.

I read through his record. It said that he had been committed to Haven Crest by his father, Patrick McCrae—so Irish!—on the seventh of October 1903 at the age of nineteen. The reason for this was "inconsolable grief."

Oh, no.

Noah's sister Maureen had died earlier that year, and it seemed that Noah had been unable to let her go. He'd told his parents that he could see her and still talk to her. They'd thought their son's mind had broken. They'd thought he was mad, and the more they'd tried to help him, the more intense and violent he'd become that they wouldn't believe him.

My eyes burned with tears. I never had to pee, but I could cry, though I had no idea where the tears came from. They weren't wet, but I could feel them trickle down my cheeks.

Noah had been a medium. He and Kevin had to be related. That talent ran in families. How horrible for him. He could still talk to his dead sister, and no one had believed him.

Just like how no one had believed Lark about me.

LARK

I woke up at five. Not because Wren was there, or because I had some sudden revelation about Alys, but because someone was bouncing on my bed.

Groggily, I lifted my head, opened my sleep-crusted eyes and looked straight into the twinkling gaze of Joe Hard.

"Rise and shine, J.B.," he said.

He was all hair and eyeliner, and it was a good thing ghosts didn't have circulation, because his would have been cut off below the waist, his leather pants were so tight. He'd been a rock star back in the day, and even death couldn't make him give it up.

"What do you want?" I demanded. "And how the hell did you get in here?" I had a few protections up, but couldn't use too many because they'd work against Wren. Still, the house was somewhat fortified against unfamiliar ghosts.

"I knew your grandmother, remember? We have a connection." He grinned. "Olgilvie is at the coffee shop down the street, so I decided to pop over. Your sister tell you I wanted to chat?"

I stared at him. None of what he'd just said explained why he was perched on my duvet at this time of morning, looking as fresh as a dead metalhead could. "No, she didn't. We've been a little preoccupied lately."

He nodded. "All Hallows' Eve, yeah. It's gotta suck for you. Nice to have a little freedom to roam, though."

I sat up. "What do you want to talk about, Joe?"

The smile faded from his face, along with any other trace of pleasantness. "I need your help."

Yeah, so he was a little scary. "With?"

"Making sure the police find a body before Olgilvie gets a chance to move it."

But Olgilvie *was* the police. Oh. *Oh.* "Laura." Back when I'd first returned to New Devon, I'd been unlucky enough to cross paths with the human stain known as Officer Olgilvie, who Joe haunted. I knew it had something to do with a girl named Laura, and I figured that Joe blamed Olgilvie for her death. Now, I realized that Olgilvie had killed her.

"Yeah."

"Where is she?"

"Near the grounds of Haven Crest. It's why the bastard's been supervising construction and why he does security there—so he can keep an eye on her. But with the work the town's been doing, he has to move her or someone will find her."

"And you want to make sure someone finds her."

He nodded. "Her family—this whole fucking town—needs to know what happened to her." I didn't ask, but he told me anyway: "He raped her, and then he killed her when she tried to get away. He says it was an accident, but you don't bury an accident in an unmarked grave and watch over it for more than two decades."

"He's more of a monster than I thought."

"You don't know the half of it. I wouldn't even ask you to tangle with him if it wasn't for Laura."

"Is she anchored to the grave?"

"No. She moved on when he...when she died."

And Joe had made the choice to haunt her killer when his own death came, rather than move on with her. He must have seen my confusion, because he added, "I couldn't be with her, knowing he'd gotten away with it. I loved her, and I should have been with her that night, but we'd had a fight. I thought she'd taken off to LA like she always threatened to do. It took ten years and me dying of an accidental overdose to discover the truth. She came for me, but I couldn't go—not without making him pay."

"Dude, that's messed up, but I get it." I nodded. "What do you need me to do?"

"You're going to the concert?"

"Yeah. Probably one of the worst decisions of my life, but I'm going."

"He's working security, but he's going to move her during the show."

"Isn't that risky?"

"Yeah, but the show will provide some distraction, and give him access to the construction tools that have been stored on-site. The town's going to start excavating the spot where he hid her next week. If he doesn't do it now, they'll find her."

It took me a moment to see what the problem was. "You want them to catch him in the act."

He nodded.

I had no idea how I was going to make that happen, but I'd do it. "I need you to show me where she is."

"I can't take you unless he's there. I'm tethered to him."

I held out my arms and beckoned him to me. "One-time offer, Softie, my friend. Jump on board the Lark train."

A dark eyebrow arched high on his pale forehead. "Possession? How very 1973 of you." He didn't hesitate, though. He jumped into me like a flea onto a cat. It was like being hit by a car and knocked into the air, but without the pain and broken bones.

My head was crammed with a series of images that sped through my brain like a high-speed train. A birthday party for a five-year-old boy, Joe's graduation, cars and guitars and screaming fans. And there were a lot of images of him with the girl I assumed was Laura. They were smiling in every one of them.

And then he showed me her grave, and everything went still—a barren plot of land, overgrown and neglected, covered in tall grass and wildflowers. I wouldn't have thought anything of it had I walked by. The gentle rounding of the ground—the swell of dirt that concealed Laura's body—wouldn't have even registered with me as odd.

I turned my head, and the Haven Crest campus came into view. I knew where I was now—where Laura was.

And I could feel every emotion that Joe attached to her, and to her grave. More importantly, I felt his desire to make Olgilvie pay for what he'd done. That sensation lingered, even after Joe left my body.

"I have to go," he said, rising from my bed. "He's leaving. Can I count on you, J.B.?"

"You can. Now get out so I can go back to sleep."

Joe grinned. "Sorry, sweetheart, but you're about to have more company. Go easy on the poor kid."

And then he was gone—like flipping a switch. When a ghost decided to take off, there was no lingering to say good-bye. What had he meant by more company?

Someone knocked on my window. My bedroom was on the second floor. Who did I know who was crazy enough to climb a tree to visit me this early in the morning?

I crawled out of bed and went to my window. I pulled back the curtains, ready to shoo away a squirrel or scare off a woodpecker.

I was not prepared to see Mace staring back at me, even with Joe's warning.

It was a good thing that I didn't scare easily. I still jumped, and I swore, but at least I didn't scream, because that would have brought Nan running, never mind that she slept like a brick.

I opened the window. Mace sat in the tree outside holding the screen. It was cold and I was only wearing a T-shirt and boxers, but the T-shirt was black and it covered everything, even if some of those bits were stiffly offended by the chill. Besides, he'd seen me in less the night he'd saved my life.

"What the hell are you doing here?" I asked.

"Can I come in?" he asked. Now that I got a good glimpse of him, he looked terrible. He was scruffy, looked like he hadn't slept. And I could smell beer on him, which was really odd, because he wasn't much of a drinker.

That was why I stepped back and let him crawl inside.

It wasn't graceful—he lurched over the sill and pretty much fell into my room, sprawling gracelessly on the carpet while still holding the screen. I took it from him before he could hurt himself with it.

"You're going to be putting that back," I informed him, and shut the window. It was freaking cold out!

He pushed himself into a sitting position. There were a lot of girls who would love to be me right now, and I wasn't one of them.

"Sorry," he said. "I didn't know where else to go."

"Home?" I suggested, wrinkling my nose. "You know, that place where the shower is?"

He lifted his arm, turned his head and took a whiff. "I must smell like ass."

"A little bit, yeah." Since it was obvious he wasn't going to stand up, I sat down. It wasn't even dawn yet, and my room was lit only by the street light outside. Thanks to Joe, however, I was fully awake.

"Is Wren here?" he asked, looking about like my sister might pop out of the closet at any moment and scream "Boo!"

"Nope. Just you and me, stinky." Then, more seriously, because we kinda had a bond and I cared about the guy, "What's up?" I didn't need to ask. I already knew what he was going to tell me.

"Kevin came over last night," he said, his words slurring a little—probably more from lack of sleep than the beer, because I could tell he wasn't really drunk. "He told me he couldn't

lie to me anymore, and that he and Sarah have been screwing around behind my back."

I raised a brow. "Did they actually go that far?"

He looked at me—long enough that I almost squirmed.
"Did you know?"

I shook my head. "I saw them talking at the party, and I
figured it out."

"Huh. Guess I'm the last one to know. I feel like such an
ass."

"For what it's worth, I heard Kevin tell Sarah that you
were his best friend and he didn't want to hurt you." Maybe
that wasn't my story to tell, but I didn't care too much about
Sarah. I cared about Mace, though. And, oddly enough, I
cared about Kevin—and their friendship.

"He should have thought of that before. And, no, he says
he never slept with her."

"You don't sound convinced."

Mace closed his eyes and leaned back against the side of my
bed. "She wanted to. I went to see her after Kevin confessed.
She says he treats her better than I do. She said with me she felt
like she was just a substitute for the person I really wanted."

"What's she talking about? You were totally into her. What
other girl have you even spent time with?"

"You. She was jealous of you."

I swear to God the bottom fell out of my stomach. "Me?
Is she on crack? I'm with Ben." And I totally wasn't Mace's
type. Was I? Never mind, because he wasn't mine. "Why?"

"Because we have history."

"She's jealous because you found me lying on the floor in a
pool of my blood and tears, begging to die? That's fucked up."

He laughed at that—thankfully. "Yeah, I know." His expression sobered. "I can't decide if I'm happy that I know what

she's like and that we're done, or if I'm just really pissed off.
I feel betrayed, y'know?"

I nodded. "Yeah." I didn't really. I hadn't dated much, and
no one had ever cheated on me before because they thought
I was crazy and might go psycho on them if they did.

"Can I crash here for a bit?" he asked. "I don't want to go
home and have to explain it all. Not right now."

Nan probably wouldn't like it, but she'd like me letting him
drive any farther even less. "Sure." I pulled the quilt off my
bed and handed it to him. I gave him the extra pillow, too.
Then I climbed back under the covers. My bed was still warm.

"Hey, Lark?"

I peered over the side of the bed. He was cocooned in the
quilt on the floor so tightly I had no idea how he'd accom-
plished it. "Yeah?"

"Thanks for being my friend."

Aww. I smiled. "You're welcome. And if you're still here
when Ben comes by to pick me up, you get to explain why.
Got it?"

"Got it."

He curled up into a ball and promptly passed out. I watched
over him for a little while just to make sure he was okay. Out
of the small group of people I considered friends, Mace had
been the big surprise. I felt more of a connection with him
than I did even with Roxi. I couldn't explain it, but if I had
to move away tomorrow, Ben and Mace were the people it
would break my heart to leave—and my grandmother, of
course.

The fact that Sarah thought our relationship was romantic
was just one more reason not to like her.

She was obviously nuts.

chapter eleven

WREN

I didn't go to Noah with what I'd learned. I was going to wait on that. There had to be a reason why he didn't tell me Kevin was a relative. Maybe he didn't even know. I wasn't going to jump to conclusions, and I wasn't going to ask about it so soon after him losing a friend. Never mind that the friend was a bastard and a villain. Instead, I stayed in the Shadow Lands a while, letting it balance and recharge my spiritual energy, and then I went home to tell Lark what I'd found out.

And found Mace asleep on the floor of our bedroom while Lark was sprawled across most of the bed.

Was that a window screen leaning against the wall? The strangest things seemed to happen to my sister when I wasn't around.

An advantage to being a ghost is that I was very, very quiet. I sat down on the edge of the bed and waited for the alarm to go off. It did just that a minute later; Lark's cell phone suddenly came to life, blaring a song that always made me want to dance.

Mace bolted upright. "What the hell?"

I laughed. He was a mess. Lark didn't react with the same surprise. "Wren?" she mumbled. "Wren?"

That was my cue. Part of the whole "working on my electronic interaction" agenda apparently included learning how to turn off my sister's alarm, so she could remain wrapped in the warmth of the bed.

I turned off the alarm. Mace fell back to the floor. I heard a thump, and he swore.

"I think he missed the pillow," I said.

Suddenly, a wave of blankets crashed through me. I shuddered. God, I hated the feeling of fabric disrupting my energy. I'd tried to explain it to Lark once, and she said it sounded like trying to floss her teeth with yarn. I had no idea if that was accurate or not, but she understood me better than anyone else.

"Get up!" my sister cried. "Mace, get the hell up!" She almost stepped on him as she jumped out of bed.

He groaned and sat up once again. His thick sandy hair stuck out in all directions, and he looked like he was about five years old, all rumpled and sleepy.

"What?" he demanded groggily. "What time is it?"

"Seven," Lark replied.

He swore again. "Wake me up in half an hour."

Lark grabbed him by the shirt front before he could fall back onto the carpet. She was pretty strong, my sister, though it was more impressive against ghosts than humans. I could see the muscles in her arm straining against the weight of his torso.

"You'll get your ass up *now*," she informed him, holding his upper body a good foot above the floor. "My grandmother will be up soon, and Ben will be coming to get me for school. I am *not* going to be the one who explains why you're here."

Mace glared at her. "Ben won't freak out—he's too zen. And get your morning breath out of my face."

"My morning breath? Dude, you smell like you rolled around in sweaty beer that someone else puked up." But she let go of him and stepped back. "C'mon."

Cursing under his breath, Mace struggled to his feet. Standing, he raised his arms above his head and stretched. This lifted the hems of the two shirts he wore, revealing a thin expanse of flat stomach that was surprisingly tan and surprisingly muscular.

"You're staring," I said to my sister.

Lark rolled her eyes at me. Mace lowered his arms with a frown. "Did you hear something?"

"It was Wren," Lark informed him. "It's the Halloween thing again. Do you want to shower? You can use the one down the hall."

He shook his head. "No. I need to get home. Mom will worry. I'll see you at school."

Lark put on her robe and saw him out. When she came back, it was with a look of relief on her face. "Nan isn't up yet," she said. "God, that was weird. I love the guy, but nothing makes life more awkward than waking up to the friend who drunkenly spilled their heart out to you. Thank God you were here. I didn't know what to say to him."

"What happened?" I asked.

"Kevin told him that he and Sarah had been messing around." Her gaze turned shrewd. "That's why you've been pissy about the two of them lately, isn't it?"

I nodded. The memory of seeing Kevin kiss Sarah after telling me we could never really have any sort of relationship still hurt. "Poor Mace."

"I think Kevin honestly feels bad." Lark removed her robe.

"I respect him for having the nads to confess. It's going to take a while for him and Mace to patch things up."

I could have said at least five things about Kevin at that moment—none of them nice—but Lark was right. He'd done the right thing breaking it off with me, and it probably hadn't been easy. And for every bad thing I could say about Kevin, I could think of ten that were good, so I didn't say anything.

"Mace must think of you as a good friend," I said, following Lark into the bathroom. She turned on the shower.

"I guess he figured since he'd seen me at my most vulnerable, he could let me see him at his." She pulled off her pajamas. "He was pretty messed up."

I didn't ask her if anything had happened between them, because I knew it hadn't. Lark wouldn't do that. And I didn't ask what Mace had said to her because that wasn't any of my business, and she'd tell me if she wanted. Besides, I didn't really care. I had my own things to worry about.

My sister pulled back the shower curtain and stepped inside. "Did you find out anything in the Shadow Lands?"

"To find out about Emily and Alys I had to make an appointment with Special Collections in the library."

"What?" Her voice was slightly muffled by the spray. "That's crazy."

"I know!" I felt better having her agree. "So I can't get to them until Wednesday."

"What about the void? Did you research it?"

"Um, no."

"Wren." My name dripped with disappointment.

"I'm not going back there." And she couldn't make me. Although we both knew she could, really.

"That's why we need to check into it—see if there's another way to help Alys without actually going in there."

"Oh." I was such an idiot. "Okay, I'll look. But there's something else I want to talk to you about. It's about Noah."

"O-kay." The word seemed dragged out of her mouth, as if her teeth were trying to hold it in. "What about him?"

"I think he may be related to Kevin. His last name is Mc-Crae."

The hooks that held the shower curtain to the rod scraped against the metal as Lark yanked the curtain open enough to stick her face out. "Really? Did he tell you this?"

I shook my head. She was going to make a big deal out of this, I just knew it.

Her eyes widened. "Did you go snooping into his Shadow Lands library file?"

When she put it that way it made me feel like a character on one of those TV shows she liked to watch where there was melodrama at every turn. "Sort of."

Lark frowned, obviously unbothered by my snooping. I ought to have known she'd support it. "Do you think he doesn't know?"

"I'm not sure. He asked what Kevin's name was, though. And he didn't say anything when I told him. That's weird, right?"

"Yeah." The curtain slipped closed once more. "It's probably not a big deal, but it is strange. I guess the only way to find out is to ask him. You know, if he did know, that would explain why he gave up Woodstock so easily. The jerk picked on Noah's family."

I hadn't thought of that, but she was right. What surprised me the most was that she actually sounded like she wanted to give Noah the benefit of the doubt. That was weird, too.

Maybe Noah hadn't said anything to me at the time because Robert might have been listening. "I'll go to Haven

Crest later and talk to him." As soon as I said the words, the toothbrush holder on the vanity fell over, and Lark's makeup caddy began to shake, tossing brushes and cosmetics onto the marble counter.

"What the hell...?" Lark muttered. Then she screamed.

I yanked open the curtain without touching it. My sister had her back pressed to the tiles, and held up her hands to deflect the spray from the shower.

It was blood.

Blood poured from the showerhead, ran over her bare feet and down the drain. It covered Lark from head to toe. It was in her hair and eyes, coating her in a clotted glaze.

"Stop it," I said, focusing on that spray as my energy heated. My hair lifted, and I felt that surge of power that came when I got angry. "Stop it. *Now.*"

And just like a flick of a switch, the shaking stopped. Water poured from the showerhead, washing away the blood. Lark jumped under the spray, scrubbing furiously at herself to get clean.

"What the hell was that?" she demanded when she finally stepped out—scrubbed pink and free of blood.

I knew she didn't really expect me to have any answers. "I don't know." Then I felt it—like a shiver down my spine— the presence of something, or *someone*, else. It wasn't close, but it was strong. Powerful. Everything around me blurred for the duration of a blink, and when it cleared I couldn't believe my eyes.

"Lark?"

My sister looked up from tying the belt of her robe. When she saw what I'd already seen, her jaw dropped. "Oh, my God."

Blood ran down the walls of the bathroom, trickling from

the letters that a dead hand had painstakingly printed all around us, some of them several times.

DANGER

HE'S HERE FOR YOU

SALT

IRON

DEATH

AS ONE

BURN

Our gazes followed the words, the letters losing shape as the blood dripped. At the same time we turned toward the mirror. Lark made a small noise. I didn't, but I was just as surprised.

There, on the other side of the glass, was Emily. Her palms pressed against the mirror. Her long white hair hung wildly around her pale face, and her eyes...

Her eyes were hollowed-out black holes. Not gory. Not bloody. Just black. Bottomless.

Lark moved toward the mirror. I reached out for her, but she stepped just out of my reach. She raised her own hands to the mirror, so that they settled over Emily's.

"What do you want?" she asked.

Emily opened her mouth to speak, but then she glanced over her shoulder. I couldn't see what she saw, but whatever it was scared her. For a second, her fingers breached the glass, grasping at this world—at Lark.

I rushed forward as my sister reared back, tugging on Emily's hands. I grabbed her right arm so Lark could switch both hands to her left, and we pulled. First came her forearms, then her head and shoulders, then her torso...

Emily jerked back, taking us with her. "Pull harder!" she cried. "He's got me!"

I glanced at Lark. She turned her head to look at me. I

knew our expressions were the same. Without saying a word, we both dug in our heels—for me that was fairly literal, as I could actually set my heels into the floor—and pulled with all our combined strength.

Whatever—or whoever—had a hold of her on the other side was incredibly strong. Even though we pulled with all our might, my fingers slipped against Emily's energy. She was being pulled back into the mirror, and there was nothing Lark or I could do to stop it—though we tried.

"You need to face It together!" Emily cried as she was ripped from our grasp, the black caverns of her eyes staring sightlessly at both of us. "Together!" Her head phased through the glass so fast it was a blur. Then her arms.

And then she was gone.

Lark took a step toward the mirror. It cracked, spider webbing out from the center with a violent *crack!*

"Duck!" I shouted, flinging myself at her, forcing myself to manifest as I pushed her to the floor. The mirror exploded into tiny daggers that burst from the frame like shrapnel from a bomb. If Lark had still been standing, her face would have been destroyed.

I glanced up and saw mirror fragments embedded in the opposite wall—some were buried all the way into the plaster. Lark wouldn't have just been wounded, she would have been killed.

"What the hell, Wren?" Lark gasped, clutching me as tightly as I clung to her. She had glass dust and shards in her hair and on her shoulders, and a tiny cut on her cheek, but other than that, she looked unharmed. She stared at me for a moment.

"What?" I asked.

"Turn around."

I did as she asked. Lark gasped.

I glanced over my shoulder and saw what made her go so pale.

Shards of glass stuck out of my back like reflective spines.

"Do they hurt?"

"I don't feel them at all." That was interesting. I moved a little closer to the sink so my back was to the vanity, and willed myself to my usual form. The glass fell away as I lost tangibility and clinked against the porcelain. I could actually see myself in them—little fractured pieces of myself.

"What just happened?" Lark asked. "Who grabbed her?"

"I don't know," I replied, my jaw clenched. "But I'm going to find out." Because whoever or whatever it was, it had tried to hurt my sister, and as far as I was concerned, that meant war.

chapter twelve

LARK

I was late to school. There was no way I could leave the bathroom in that state, and it took forever to clean up the glass—it was in my robe, in my hair, in the canister for my makeup brushes, on my towels. It even created a sharp powder that dusted the top of the toilet bowl.

Wren was able to generate enough of a breeze to knock all the fragments and dust—even the ones on me—to the floor so I could vacuum it up.

Nan came up to see what was taking me so long. She took one look at the shattered mirror, and at the little cut on my face, and went pale. "What happened? I heard a noise."

"The mirror broke," I said—as if that weren't obvious. "Sorry, Nan. I'll replace it." And just how the heck I was going to do that was a mystery. I didn't even have a part-time job.

She shook her head. "Don't worry about that, dear. Are you girls okay?" She was looking at Wren.

"We're good," I replied.

She was still looking at Wren. "It's like looking at a reflection in a window. I can see you, Wrenleigh, but not clearly."

Wren waved, smiling happily. We had just been attacked, and she was grinning. Okay, so that was a little annoying, but whatever. If my twin was okay, then I could be okay. What had happened was freaking scary, but we'd survived. Or rather, I had survived. Survival was sort of moot with Wren.

I texted Ben to tell him not to pick me up. So much for being worried about him seeing Mace here. Mace was the least of my worries. Something seriously effed up was going on with Emily and Alys—something I didn't know if Wren and I could handle. I was scared—not that I would admit that to anyone else.

"Nan," I said, "could you call the school and let them know I'm going to miss first period, please?"

"Of course. Come down when you're ready." She cast another worried glance in my direction. "You know, you don't have to go to school at all. Is it safer for you here?"

"I have no idea," I replied, honestly. "Nan, there's something going on with Emily and Alys, and I don't know what it is."

"What can I do to help?"

She was so freaking awesome. I went to the desk and opened the bottom drawer. Emily's journal was there. I'd read through most of it when we'd tangled with Bent, but truth be told, I'd forgotten most of it, too. "Can you look through this and mark any references to Haven Crest? Or people and ghosts who caused trouble? I can't explain it, but this feels personal."

"Of course." She took the book from me.

"Thanks."

"How did the mirror break?" she asked, holding the journal to her chest.

"Emily," I replied. I mean, it wasn't a lie, but it was all the truth she needed to know at that moment.

Her gaze held mine for a long moment. Just long enough for me to start squirming.

"You girls know I'm here for you, don't you? Not just to feed you and put a roof over your head, but to protect and help you, however I can."

She was such an awesome grandmother. My mother would have flipped out over the mirror and not have cared why it happened. And she wouldn't have believed me that it had been broken by a ghost.

"Have you ever seen Emily or Alys here?" I asked.

"My grandmother and her sister? Oh, I don't..." She frowned. "Yes. Actually, I have seen one of them, I think. My grandfather built this house shortly after my mother was born. My grandmother lived here until the day she died."

"How did she die?" I asked. I was half-afraid to ask.

Nan smiled. "She was ninety-six and died in her sleep." Something flickered in her eyes, and her smile faded.

"What?" I asked. Wren moved closer to me and took my hand.

"I remember going to see her in the hospital the day she died." Nan frowned. "Your father wasn't much younger than you are now, and he didn't want to come with me that visit. It was hard on him to see her in the hospital. She told me not to be sad because she was finally going to find Alys. I just thought she meant she'd see her twin in Heaven. That wasn't what she meant, was it?"

"I don't think so," I said. "I think Alys was in trouble. And I think Emily's still trying to save her. That's why she's visit-

ing us." I didn't add that Emily also seemed to be a prisoner
of something powerful.

My grandmother sat down on the bed. "She told me she
was afraid that there wouldn't be any more twins born into
our family because she hadn't produced any, and neither had
my mother, my aunt, my brother or I."

Wren and I shared a glance.

"Was Emily's mother a twin?" I asked.

Nan shrugged. "I don't know. I never asked. I suppose I
ought to have, now, looking back." She sighed. "I suppose if
I'd had a twin we would have been like the two of you, and
she would have explained it all to me, so that I could explain
it to you. I'm so sorry I can't help you girls."

I watched, helpless as Nan swiped at her eye with the back
of her hand. "Please, don't cry. None of this is your fault."

Nan nodded and rose to her feet. "Maybe not, but I could
do more to help you."

"Nan," I said, incredulous. "You took us in. You've given
me more love and understanding than my mother ever did.
I don't know what I—what *we*—would have done without
you." Tears burned my eyes. Damn PMS.

She held out her arms, and I went into them, taking Wren
with me. We hugged, and I pushed the tears away. I wasn't
going to cry, because my mother didn't deserve it, and because
my tears would set Nan off as well, and then Wren wouldn't
know what to do with either of us.

Nan kissed my forehead, and Wren's as well—though I
thought she was just a little off. Not bad for interacting with
someone she couldn't see clearly. "You get ready. I'll make
breakfast."

When she left, Wren and I finished cleaning up, and I
started getting ready. I had a text from Ben:

U OK?

YEAH. I'LL FILL YOU IN LATER. *SO* MUCH DRAMA.

<3

I smiled and sent three hearts back to him. Then I put on my face—doing what I could to minimize the cut from the mirror—dried my hair, got dressed and went downstairs to discover that Nan had made pumpkin-spice waffles.

"Woman, you are a domestic goddess," I told her as I sat down. "Wren, you have to try these."

"Really?" Normally Wren had to ask to inhabit my body. She'd done it without permission in the past, and it usually pissed me off. We'd had to have a discussion about boundaries. She could possess me if I was in danger without asking, but on any other occasion she had to ask, or wait until she was invited.

Having Wren slip into me was a weird feeling that I never quite got used to. It was like walking into one of those big spider webs outside—the invisible kind you didn't know were there until you walked through one and it was all over your face. Anyway, that was what it felt like—soft, gossamer threads settling over me, tickling my skin.

I don't know which of us enjoyed the waffles more, me or Wren, but I ate entirely too much. I was still really full when Nan dropped me off at school.

I gave her a hug before getting out of her ugly little grape of a car, and watched as she drove away.

"I'm going to Haven Crest," Wren informed me. "I want to talk to Noah."

This wasn't something I was thrilled to hear, because I still didn't completely trust the guy, especially now that I knew Wren had some doubts about him. But maybe that ghost who had passed Wren a message from Emily would be there, and maybe she'd be helpful. It was worth a shot.

"Sounds like a plan," I said. "Tell him I said hi."

Her eyes narrowed. "Seriously?"

I shrugged. "Just trying to be nice to your boyfriend."

The suspicion on her face turned to a tiny smile. "Boyfriend. That sounds so strange. Hey, who's that on the roof?"

I turned and looked up. There, on the edge of the school roof, was a boy dressed in relaxed jeans, a white thermal shirt and a plaid shirt over that. Very grunge.

"That's Dan," I said. "He committed suicide in 1998 by jumping off the roof into the path of a van. I met him in the library one day." I waved, but Dan either didn't see me or was caught up in being too tragic and misunderstood for this world to care.

I wasn't mocking him, I just had to make light a little. There were quite a few of them—suicides—loitering around the school. It was sad, really. And if I couldn't treat them like every other ghost, I empathized too much.

It was at that moment, when we were both watching, that Dan jumped. He looked right at us—so *now* he saw me—and stepped into thin air. I cringed when he "hit" the ground— turned my back as a ghostly van plowed into him.

"What's he looking at?" Wren asked.

I turned my attention back to Dan—who had already reset and was back on the roof. He was a rapid cycler. He seemed to be watching something on the far side of the school, which was odd for him. Any other time I'd seen him, he was staring down at the driveway, trying to get his timing right.

I looked in the direction he was staring. I thought I saw

something, but then it was gone. I must have imagined it. The morning's insanity with Emily had freaked me out—more than I would even admit to Wren. Maybe I was having paranoid hallucinations or something.

Walking toward the school entrance, I shook my head. Of course I'd been wrong. I hadn't seen a person standing on the grass staring at me, and the person certainly hadn't been my old pal Woodstock, because he was gone. I'd burned him up myself. It was just my mind—and Dan—playing tricks on me.

Even so, I stopped at the school door and took one last look over my shoulder to make sure I was alone before going inside.

WREN

I arrived at Haven Crest to find Noah with his arms around Miss April, who was very, very upset. So much so that even to me—another ghost—her manifestation had taken on a hideous appearance. Her face was moldy and battered, her lips blue. Her form was skeletal, her hair peeling away from her scalp. Her dress was more moth-chewed rags than expensive silk. She looked nothing like the sweet young woman I knew her to be. If this was how humans sometimes saw her, it was no wonder they ran screaming from this place.

There was a crowd gathered around them. Several of the residents nodded at me when they saw me. They looked somber. And angry.

I obviously wasn't going to get to talk to her in private anytime soon. That was annoying enough that I didn't even feel guilty for it.

"What's wrong?" I asked. I wasn't too crazy about the death grip she had on Noah, either.

Noah looked up at the sound of my voice. There was a

wildness to his expression that spoke to something inside me. A darkness to his eyes that made me think of dangerous things. At that moment, I knew that if I showed Noah my collection of treasures he would appreciate it.

That he would *understand* it.

"Vandals defaced the walls in Miss April's room," he told me.

The young woman pulled from his embrace and whirled around to face me. "They painted the walls and smoked vile, pungent cigarettes. They left refuse on the floor. They...*fornicated* in the corner!"

Had Miss April not looked so completely monstrous I might have laughed, but I couldn't do that to her, not when she was so obviously upset.

"Are they still here?" I asked.

"No." She grinned, revealing brown and chipped teeth. "I finally summoned the strength to manifest and scare them off."

Noah smiled slightly. "*Scared* is far too gentle a term, Miss April. You terrified those children. They will never set foot on these grounds again."

After what Bent and his disciples had done to Lark and our friends, I probably shouldn't have smiled, but I did. The situation was totally different, and people who trespassed on Haven Crest property, knowing all the stories, deserved whatever they got. The spirits of this building kept to themselves and were peaceful—except for Robert, but he was gone now.

Miss April preened under his praise, but her gaze was unsure. "But why can't I stop?"

Noah's smiled faded. "I don't know." He looked to me. "Miss April can't seem to revert to her natural state."

"Oh." I'd never experienced a lingering manifestation my-self, but then I'd always had Lark to calm and ground me.

I reached out and put my hands on either side of Miss April's terrible face and stroked the parchment-dry flesh of her cheeks. She looked surprised, but she didn't pull away as I willed some of my aura—my energy—to mix with hers. I could feel her anger, her distress.

"It's over now," I murmured, pulling some of that negative energy from her and replacing it with my own calm. "They're gone, and they won't ever come back. We'll get rid of the garbage in your room and see if we can remove the graffiti. Would that make you happy, Miss April?"

She nodded. Her hair was thicker now and shinier. Her skin seemed brighter and softer.

"Just let it go," I told her. "Give it all to me and let me put it away for you." I continued the gentle exchange of energy. Too much and I might take her aggression for my own, but if I kept it slow and steady, all would be well.

Finally, after what felt like a long time, Miss April looked as she normally did. She threw her slender arms around me. "Thank you so much!" she cried, and then pulled away from me, whirling and twirling in her gown. "I haven't felt so de-lightful in an age!"

The gathered ghosts were all staring at me. It wasn't a hos-tile situation, but it felt strange all the same. Noah looked es-pecially impressed.

"Well done," he said. "Your talents and abilities continue to amaze me."

I shrugged. I had never done that before, but somehow I knew what to do and how to do it. "I'm nothing if not sur-prising," I said with a slight smile. Miss April's manifestation and the denial of my own agenda had me feeling a little pet-ulant. I hoped it would go away soon.

Noah offered me his arm. I didn't hesitate to take it. We began walking away from the crowd, toward the back of the foyer. "I was worried you might not come back after the un-fortunate events with Robert," he said to me.

"I didn't want to intrude on your grief."

Noah shook his head. "We don't grieve creatures like Rob-ert. He proved himself unworthy with his actions. I hope your sister doesn't hold his behavior against the rest of us."

"No, of course not." I was sure there were plenty of other things Lark would hold against them, given enough time. Why was it that I felt so bitter toward her at times? I'd been so frightened for her at the house, but at that moment, the thought of her annoyed me. That was so very, very wrong.

"That's good to hear." He stopped walking. "You didn't come here to discuss Robert or your sister, did you?"

"Not entirely." I turned toward him. We were standing in front of a window that overlooked the back lawn. "Noah, why didn't you tell me you are related to Kevin McCrae, the boy Robert attacked?"

He glanced away. "I wasn't certain I was when you asked. How did you find out?"

"I saw your photograph and patient information. I didn't read all of it, but I know why you were admitted, and that convinced me you were related to Kevin. You were a me-dium, weren't you?"

He nodded. "I was, yes. And if your friend is as well, then we are most certainly related as I supposed. That particular ability is passed on by blood."

"But why hide the connection?"

His bright gaze locked with mine, and he smiled sheepishly. That expression was all the proof I needed that he and Kevin were related. Of all the ghosts for me to have feelings for, why—*why*—did he have to be related to the living boy I wanted to forget?

"I thought if I told you I was related to your friend that you wouldn't want to see me anymore."

I frowned. "That makes no sense."

"I know, but it's true. And I was afraid that maybe you would think I had something to do with the attack on him."

"Why would I think something like that?"

He shrugged. "I have a connection with the boy, and someone who I considered a good friend tried to kill him. You have to admit it sounds odd."

"I would never, ever believe that you would hurt anyone, let alone have them killed."

"I've hurt plenty of living people, Wren. Those who trespass in my domain are too scared to return, and if they do, they don't do it a third time."

I should have been bothered by his confession, but I wasn't. I understood it as only another ghost could. "Regardless, I would never have thought you capable of hurting Kevin in such an underhanded way."

He lowered his head so that he had to lift his gaze to mine. "But since I didn't tell you then, you're suspicious of me now."

"That's not it." I shook my head. "But I am a little upset that you think I would suspect or turn on you so easily. I thought we were friends."

He took my hand. "Wren, it's because I want to be more than your friend that I behaved so stupidly."

I stared at him. "Oh."

He moved closer, so close that not even a breath could pass between us. "Do you forgive me? Or shall I persuade you?"

I smiled. I knew what sort of persuasion he intended. "I do," I told him, "but I don't mind a little persuasion."

And then he kissed me, and nothing else mattered.

Until the front door burst open and a group of noisy living people walked right into our house of the dead.

chapter thirteen

WREN

They were kids—not much older than Lark and me, but I didn't recognize them from school, which meant they probably went to the local college. There were six of them—four boys and two girls.

"This place is awesome!" One of the boys enthused, stomping around like he owned the place. He took no notice of the spirits staring at him or the ones he ignorantly walked though. There wasn't the barest shred of sensitivity in him, or he'd have felt *something*.

The two girls—one a blonde and the other a brunette—stood close together just inside the door. "We shouldn't be here," the brunette said. "I feel like I'm being watched."

Nice observation, Veronica Mars, I thought.

"Yeah," the blonde joined in. "It feels disrespectful."

Noah and I exchanged glances. I could tell he was surprised to hear that sentiment from someone who was alive, or a "breather," as some of the dead rudely referred to them.

"Why are they here?" demanded Miss April. She'd just

calmed down, and now she looked angry enough to manifest again.

"Did you hear that?" one of the boys asked. He had red
hair and freckles and a friendly face.

"Hear what?" Stompy Boots asked.

His friend looked around. His gaze fell upon the general
area where Miss April stood, but it didn't focus. "I thought
I heard a voice."

"You're trippin'," said yet another boy with dark skin and
a shaved head. "You need to stop watching all those Japanese
horror movies. There's nothing here." But his gaze was nervous as he glanced around.

The ghosts pulled together, forming a horseshoe around the
young people. We watched the living with a shared curiosity
that ranged from benign to openly hostile as they treated the
building as something to which they had a right.

Stompy Boots stood in the middle of the foyer, hands on
his narrow hips. The hoodie he wore looked to be three sizes
too big for him. "This will be great. It's far enough away from
the stage that no one will see us, but close enough that when
they start letting people in we'll be able to get up front."

"What time on Wednesday?" asked the fourth boy, who
looked a bit out of place with his dyed black hair and piercings.

"Just before five," Stompy said. "There'll still be a lot of
people working here, but it will be getting dark, so we should
be able to sneak in here no problem. We'll spend the night
and get so close Eddie's sweat will soak us."

That really didn't sound appealing—I didn't care who this
Eddie was. I assumed he was a member of Dead Babies. Even
with that assumption I failed to see the appeal in getting covered in a waste product from his body.

"They say they're going to spend the night!" Miss April

turned wide, angry eyes toward Noah. "What are we going to do?"

Stompy walked up to what used to be the front desk and hopped up onto it, dangling his legs over the side, kicking his feet against it. "This place definitely has enough room for a dozen people. We can have a party after the concert. Harris says his older sister can score us some Molly. I doubt security can even see this place from the road."

A sound of opposition rose up around me; the ghosts of Acton Hall turned to Noah for a solution. He was their leader, whether he wanted the job or not. The girls in the doorway pressed closer together, their nervous gazes darting about the hall.

"I won't allow humans to take over and further damage our home," he told them. "Wren, you may want to leave."

When I looked at him, my brow raised, he continued, "I intend to rid us of these intruders by whatever means necessary. I know you have living friends, and this might make you uncomfortable."

I did have living friends. And we'd met because they had been foolish like this lot, poking about where they shouldn't and being disrespectful of the spirits there. But they'd also crossed paths with a very, very malicious ghost who'd tried to kill them. Noah wasn't going to hurt anyone; he only meant to scare them away. People who have been scared by ghosts tend not to mess with them again.

I'd be doing these kids a favor, really.

I smiled at him. "I'm with you," I said. Oh! The smile he gave me in return was delicious.

Noah turned to the gathered spirits. "Be gentle, my friends." His voice rang through the hall. I noticed one of the girls looked up, as though she heard it; one of the boys, too.

"Make certain they never come back!" he cried, and then manifested in front of me. *Dear God.*

He was terrifying.

He was monstrous.

He was *gorgeous.*

As the rest of the ghosts manifested, as well—and the screams started—I felt my own humanity slip away like pulling the sheet off a bed. I let my true nature take over for the second time that day, and as I swooped toward the screaming brunette, I smiled.

I was free.

LARK

There was a dead man in my English class.

I watched him as he paced the front of the room reciting Marc Antony's funeral speech from *Julius Caesar.* It was difficult to hear what the living teacher—a substitute named Miss Chaisson—was saying over his booming voice. I was okay with that, as he was much more interesting. Miss Chaisson had to read from the play, and based on her performance, I'd say she hadn't much more experience with the subject matter than her students. As for her enthusiasm, that was about on par.

I'm not a big fan of Shakespeare, but when the lines are read with the right inflection and cadence, it's a *lot* easier to understand. Miss Chaisson had neither.

"Put some life into it, you boorish twit!" the ghost shouted at her from where he stood by the window. "It's called emoting!"

I lowered my head to hide my smile. Finally, a ghost that didn't piss me off. Or make demands of me. Or ask for help. It—*he*—was a rarity.

It was only going to get worse the closer we got to Halloween. I had never seen this particular ghost before, and had no idea if he belonged to the school or Miss Chaisson, or someone else entirely.

I'd seen a few new ones today since my late arrival. One had been wandering the hall aimlessly with such a dejected look on his face that I actually risked stopping to ask him if he was okay. His name was Reggie White, and he was a former physics teacher who'd had a heart attack one day in class while freaking out on some noisy students. He didn't know why he was there as he normally spent his afterlife watching over his widow and her new husband. When I suggested that maybe one of his kids went to this school, he perked right up. That was exactly where he needed to be, and off he went. My good deed for the day.

It hadn't occurred to me that Halloween messed with ghosts as much as the living. I mean, it was annoying for me to see all of them, and hear them, and all that, but Reggie hadn't even known how he'd got to the school. His love for his kid had overridden his tether to his wife. That had to mess a spirit up.

But Reggie was my only good deed. I completely ignored the guy hanging in the stairwell. And I don't mean he was hanging out. He was *hanging*—by the neck. I ignored him and his attempts to get my attention because anyone who would hang themselves in a school stairway was an ass-hat. At least Dan had killed himself outside when there had been few people around.

Still, ghosts were shameless attention whores, and they usually haunted where there was the most chance of being seen. Kids—even teenagers—were more sensitive to ghosts than those over twenty; therefore, they increased their visibility profile.

As a theory, I thought it was a pretty damn good one. Still, it set me on edge, because I had to be that much more careful about who I looked at or spoke to, because there was always the chance I'd speak to a ghost and someone alive would hear me. I'd already been warned by the principal that I was on thin ice, and that it was only my grandmother's standing within the community that got me back into the school. The ghosts of Samuel Clemens High had gotten me into trouble before.

Which led me to develop a second theory. That attention-seeking mechanism was what led ghosts to places where they might be seen. And to people who might see them. People who could interact with them.

People like me. There wasn't a ghost in town that wouldn't rush me if they could. Halloween upped their chances of success. Maybe the school's increase in the life-challenged population was partly my fault.

So, there I was, trying to ignore the very entertaining ghost in my English class, when he suddenly turned his head and looked right at me with his gray eyes. He had gray hair, too, and grayish skin. He was wearing a gray sweater and gray pants. Had he never heard of blue? Maybe a little maroon to break things up?

"You," he said in that big, booming voice.

Roxi glanced at me from her seat across the aisle. Had she heard him? Could she see him? Now that she knew ghosts existed, she was much more open to their presence. I didn't look back at her—I didn't want the ghost to notice her.

I ignored Mr. One-Shade-of-Gray and tried to focus on Miss Chaisson.

"You are the one!" He came at me like a charging bull. "You can see me, can't you?"

He was standing right in Jeremy, who sat in front of me. That was rude. Any minute Jeremy was going to— Yup, there it was—he shivered.

My notebook was open to the page containing what little notes I'd been able to make during class. Carefully, in block print, my letters upside down, I wrote: MOVE.

One-Shade's eyes widened as he read what I'd written. Almost embarrassedly, he stepped out of poor, shivering Jeremy to stand in the aisle beside my seat. At the front of the room, Miss Chaisson had finished droning and was trying to get the class to partake in a discussion of the play—without much success. I couldn't help but feel like she was hoping we could explain it to her, because she didn't understand it, either.

"That woman is a menace," One-Shade sneered. "What were they thinking hiring her to teach English? She would be better suited for home economics."

Okay, so he was a rank misogynist and hadn't taught anything in the past couple of decades.

TRYING TO LEARN HERE, I wrote. Too bad upside-down printing wasn't a life skill that would do me any good. WHAT DO YOU WANT?

"You're not going to learn a darn thing from *her*," he informed me. Snotty much? He was much more entertaining when he stuck to dialogue that wasn't of his own making.

I shot him an impatient glare before locking my gaze on Miss Chaisson again. Looking at people who weren't there made the people around you uncomfortable, and it was a short jump from uncomfortable to thinking you were a nut. Been there, done that, yadda yadda.

I did have a Bell Hill T-shirt, actually. I should really throw it out.

Gray crouched beside my chair—nice of him because now

I didn't have to look up. "I've heard about you," he said. "You and your sister. The dead community is very tight in this town."

Wow. That was something I'd never, ever wondered about. Sadly, it was a good thing for me to know.

I nodded, giving him permission to continue. "There's something going on. Something big. Something bad. 'By the pricking of my thumbs, something wicked this way comes.'"

I rolled my eyes.

"Do you have something to contribute, Miss Noble?" Miss Chaisson asked.

My gaze locked with hers. How did she know my name and no one else's? Had Principal Grant told her about me? That I was trouble?

"Do you have something to say about Mark Antony's speech? What do you think the purpose of his repeated use of the phrase 'Brutus is an honorable man'?"

Oh, hell. I hadn't even heard most of it over Gray's repetition, and I'd heard even less since he started yammering at me. And now everyone was looking at me, some smirking, most bored, waiting to see if I screwed myself.

One-Shade set his gray hand upon my shoulder. It was like a hard slap to the head—but *inside* my skull.

"Antony makes a mockery of Brutus's own speech, and of Brutus himself by the repeated phrase. In his speech, Antony points out some of Caesar's virtues while using Brutus's own words against him to sway the crowd. In doing this, he downplays Caesar's ambition—which was Brutus's main argument against him—and calls attention to what could be seen as Brutus's own ambition to get rid of Caesar to further his own political career and popularity."

Beside me, Roxi covered her mouth to muffle her giggle. One-Shade squeezed my shoulder. "Well done," he said.

Miss Chaisson stared at me, her round cheeks flushing a bright pink. "Er, yes. Excellent point. Very good."

"Thank you," I said, but I wasn't talking to her. I shot my ghostly tutor a sideways glance. He smiled a little, but it faded quickly as Miss Chaisson went on to harass someone else.

"There's something going on at Haven Crest," Gray continued. "Sometime terrible—worse than Josiah Bent."

THE CONCERT? I wrote.

"It has to do with that, yes. A gathering like that, full of young people, is bound to produce elevated levels of psychic and spectral energy. Add that it's a tribute to a local ghost and on the grounds of the place where there has been the most death since the founding of this town, and you have the ingredients for something terrible indeed.

"The ghosts of New Devon are scared. If the evil of Haven Crest were to break through to this world, the entire town could be destroyed—not just the living, but the dead, too. We'll become its slaves, and no one will be safe, not your friends, not even your sister."

My head whipped around so fast, something in my neck snapped. I didn't care if anyone noticed.

"Yes." He answered my unspoken question. "Your sister is in danger. She's always in danger from the darkling dead of this town. Just as you are. She may be Dead Born, but it's you who are the shade, Lark. The Girl Who Is Her Own Shadow. The Girl Who Walks Between Life and Death. Only you can save Wren, and save the rest of us, as well."

WHAT DO I DO? My hand shook as I wrote. And what the hell was with all the freaking titles? Who was I, Harry Potter?

"What you have to."

DON'T GIVE ME THAT CRYPTIC CRAP NOW!

"Be prepared. Fight. And those of us who can will fight with you."

Ghosts? On my side? Garbage. No ghost was going to help me fight other ghosts. I looked at him for proof that he was lying—having fun with me.

He looked completely earnest. Honest. At that moment, I felt like I was the closest I'd ever gotten to knowing what I was, what Wren and I were.

And I realized I didn't want to know.

I found Ben, Roxi, Gage and Mace at lunch. Sarah was sitting with some of her cheerleader friends. I didn't miss her. She'd never gone out of her way to be friends with me, and I hadn't tried to make it easy for her. At that moment I was just relieved that she was one less person I had to worry about actual Halloween night. Not that I'd toss her in front of a ravenous spirit, but my sister and my friends took top priority.

Ben walked over to meet me before I made it to the table. He gave me a quick kiss—that sort of thing was frowned on at SC. "You okay?" he asked, dark brows coming together. "You look freaked."

"I am freaked," I replied. Wren wasn't there, and I really wished she had been. I could use her reassurance.

"Mace told me about him showing up at your house, if that has anything to do with it."

"Honestly? Not a bit." I hadn't even thought of trying to explain that in hours. "I'm sorry I didn't tell you about it first, but my mirror tried to kill me, or rather, something tried to use my mirror to kill me, and I forgot all about Mace."

Ben's frown deepened. His gaze lifted to the cut I'd tried so hard to conceal. "It hurt you."

"It tried. If Wren hadn't protected me, it would have been a lot worse. Can we go sit? If I'm going to tell this story, I only want to do it once."

He nodded, took my hand and led me to the rest of our friends.

"What happened in English?" Roxi asked. "We didn't have time to talk earlier."

I picked at my food—a turkey burger and fries. "Guys, it's in-freaking-sane. A ghost told me something bad is going to go down at the Dead Babies concert and that I'm the only person that can stop it."

They all stared at me—Gage actually had his mouth open.

"This just happened?" Mace asked. "Like, today?"

"Today has been crazy," I confessed. I told them about Emily and my bathroom mirror. "And I think it's going to keep getting crazier as the week goes on."

"What's going to happen at the concert?" Ben asked. "Have any of these ghosts given you useful information?"

"Not really. The only thing anyone has told me is that something terrible is coming for me—and for Wren, too, I assume. No, wait…not something terrible, *someone*. All I know is that it's male. Oh, and apparently the town's ghosts are willing to support me in fighting it. The ghost in class today said it had to do with Haven Crest and the spectral energy of the place."

Mace's eyebrows jacked. "You had a ghost in your class?"

I gave him a dry stare. Really? "They're all over this place. There's one hanging in the main stairwell."

He contemplated that. "So, when I felt like there was someone watching me in the bathroom between classes…?"

Gage punched him in the arm. "Dude, you were totally getting perved on by a ghost."

Mace scowled and punched him back. Gage almost fell off his chair, but he grinned. The only time I hadn't seen Gage in a good mood was when Josiah Bent had sent him to the hospital with some nasty spectral wounds.

"So, this ghost apocalypse," he said, rubbing his shoulder. "You're the only person who can stop it?"

I shrugged. "That's what he said." I nibbled on a fry. I was freaked, but I was still hungry, which meant I wasn't too flipped out. "It's a combination of Halloween, the concert and the number of ghosts at Haven Crest."

"Can we get the concert canceled?" Roxi asked. "I mean, a lot of people could get hurt."

I thought of Joe and the promise I'd made him. If the concert was canceled, how would I catch Olgilvie?

Mace spoke before I could. "If we go to the town and tell them ghosts are going to disrupt the concert and unleash hell on earth, they'll laugh in our faces. Or lock us up. And then they'll sell even more tickets because people will want to be there in case something *does* happen."

Roxi shook her head, as though she couldn't quite believe the human race. *Get in line, sister.* She'd been just as naive before she met me. Her dark gaze met mine. "Okay. So, what do you need us to do?"

"Yeah," Mace joined in. "Just name it."

I chewed another fry. I loved these people. "I don't suppose you all would stay home that night?"

Four brows lifted in unison. "No," they chorused.

I smiled. They were actually what friends should be. The idea of getting them hurt made me want to barf up all the deep-fried goodness in my gut. But the idea of not having them with me and Wren was worse.

"We'll have to sneak supplies onto the grounds," I said. "I doubt they'll let us in with salt and iron in our bags. Our rings will work against any ghost that gets close enough, but we're going to be so outnumbered." I felt guilty putting them in danger, even if they had volunteered for it.

"So, we know we're up against a male spirit, but not what his intent is?" Ben asked. "We're assuming he's old, yes? Older than Bent, even?"

"Yes." I squirted ketchup on my plate. "I think so."

Gage paled. "That's bad news."

I met his dark gaze. "I understand if you want to bail."

He actually frowned. "No effing way. I'm not letting another ghost make me his bitch."

Roxi put her arm around him and gave him a hug. "You're nobody's bitch, baby."

Ben continued, "And we know that ghosts around town are frightened enough that they've offered their help, so we've got backup?"

I nodded as he plucked one of my fries off my plate and ate it. "Yeah. The ghost I spoke to was nervous. Whatever— whoever this guy is, he believes it's going to be awful."

Gage tilted his head. "What does Wren think?"

"I haven't seen her to tell her," I confessed.

He looked confused. "But I thought she was always with you."

Hmm. That made my stomach clench. I set my fries aside. "She's got a boyfriend at Haven Crest."

My friends exchanged surprised glances. "The guy she brought to the party?" Roxi asked. "Maybe he's heard something."

That was a good point. A *very* good point. If ghosts around town had heard about something terrible coming to Haven Crest, why hadn't Noah mentioned it to Wren? Surely he'd know. And if there was all this doom and gloom lurking about the place, wouldn't Wren have felt it?

"I'll ask." Hell, yes, I was going to ask. Why the hell hadn't I asked before this? I wanted to slap myself in the head for being so lax.

Roxi pulled her phone out of her bag. "Speaking of that, I got a picture of Wren and her guy at the party, I think." She swiped her finger across the screen a couple of times. "There." She turned and held the screen toward me.

It was definitely Wren and Noah—their costumes were hard to miss. Wren didn't look as wild as she had in the photos of the dance, but she was still pretty frightening. It was Noah who bothered me. There was something ghoulish about his expression when he looked at Wren in one photo. There was a darkness around his eyes and mouth like smeared makeup, but it was black.

Ben peered over my shoulder. "He kinda looks like Kevin, only creepy."

Yeah, not going to go there—not when Kevin didn't know. "He's old," I said. I don't know if I was trying to assure him or myself. "Manifestations get scarier the older a ghost is." He probably couldn't help looking like he did.

God, I sounded lame even to my own ears. I had to get over this distrust of Noah. I had to give him the benefit of the doubt and stick with it for longer than a few hours. I just had to—for Wren.

"Wow," Gage enthused. "If that's true, I don't want to think about what Wren's going to look like in a few years."

I stared at him, a little surprised. My sister didn't look scary to me. She just looked like Wren. I mean, sometimes she got a little *wrong*, but she was still my twin.

Roxi nudged her boyfriend in the ribs. He frowned at her before taking the hint. He turned back to me. "I meant that as a compliment. I mean, she's awesome."

I smiled. "I'm not offended." I handed Roxi her phone. I resisted the urge to delete the photo. "But I hate going up against something I don't know how to fight."

Mace jabbed a fry in my direction. "We know there will be a lot of ghosts, so we'll make sure we're prepared for that. Back to supplies. How do we sneak them in?"

"I don't know. Wren, maybe. She's brought things out of the Shadow Lands, so maybe she can take items through there to Haven Crest."

"Will she tell her boyfriend?" Mace asked. "Do we know if we can trust this guy? He is at Haven Crest, after all."

I looked at him, and I knew he realized I'd been wondering the same thing. I trusted Wren with my soul, but Noah was another story. My vow to try trusting the guy hadn't even lasted five minutes. "We'll need to sneak it in by ourselves, then."

"I can do it," Roxi piped up. "Or, I think I can. My mom works at one of the renovated buildings. Her company just moved in last week."

Well, that was freaking convenient.

"Has she noticed any activity?" I asked.

She made a face. "My mom wouldn't notice if a ghost bit her on the ass. And if she did see one, she'd tell it to get the hell out of her space and keep going."

I laughed. "Okay, but we can't hide stuff in her building, because it will be locked up. Is there someplace outside where you can leave it?"

"I'll find one. If you can get the supplies to me tonight, I'll put the bag in the trunk of her car and pop by after school to hide it."

I felt like a weight had been lifted off my shoulders. "Rox, I could kiss you."

Gage grinned. "I'm totally okay with that."

Everyone laughed. It was something I really needed—a light moment. One-Shade-Of-Gray had scared me, and I didn't like being scared. What did he mean that I had to protect Wren? From the ghosts? Would they come for her like Bent had? There had been moments when I thought he might take her. How could I protect her against that many ghosts without somehow locking her in the Shadow Lands?

I didn't like not knowing what I was up against. And I really didn't like dragging my friends into a situation that might mean I couldn't keep them safe.

I would never forgive myself if I got one of them killed.

chapter fourteen

WREN

I'd never felt so powerful in my entire existence as I did scaring those kids. When they ran—and they ran screaming—I felt so vibrant, so complete.

So *alive*.

It was as though I found my reason for being, even though rationally, I knew my reason for being was something different. As a ghost, I was elated.

I wanted more.

"You were brilliant!" Noah enthused, sweeping me up and twirling me around. The building sparkled with spectral energy, appearing as it had a hundred years ago, gleaming and beautiful. The lot of us practically glowed with it. If someone were to look at this building, they would surely see rays of light pouring out of the battered and broken windows.

"I've never done that before," I confessed. "Not on that sort of scale. It was amazing!"

He laughed and twirled me again before finally setting me down. Both of us floated almost a full foot above the floor, we were so empowered.

My hair puffed out around me like a bloodred lion's mane. I could only imagine how terrifying I'd looked to the intruders, who had screamed themselves hoarse when I'd rushed toward them, my mouth a foot-long gaping black void, eyes burning like coals. I'd made people wet themselves before, but I'd never brought anyone so close to dying of sheer terror as I had that day.

"You should join us on All Hallows' Eve," Noah said.

"I'll be here for the concert," I told him. "What do you have planned?"

He grinned. "To walk among the humans, scaring them as we wish. It's always so much fun to make them wonder if we're people in costumes or actual spirits."

Miss April skipped by us. "It's our favorite night of the year! We get to walk among the living! And this year they're coming to us!"

I laughed at the joy on her face.

Noah pulled me close again, his eyes a bright blue as he stared down at me. "Say you'll come with us, Wren. Walk among the living with me."

I should spend that night with Lark. I should take the time to hug my friends and let them see me as I truly am. And I'd be lying if I said there wasn't a part of me that wanted to see Kevin, but more than any of those things, or all of them put together, I wanted to be with Noah. I wanted to feel like I did right at that very moment.

"Yes," I whispered. "Yes."

He grinned, and then he kissed me—right there in front of everyone. They hooted and hollered, clapping and stomping their feet until the very timbers of the building—each brick—vibrated.

Lark would understand. She'd be there with Ben, and she'd

never begrudge me the one night of the year where I could appreciate what it was like to be in her world—and not have to possess her to feel it.

"Do you sense that?" Noah asked when he lifted his head. I went still. A second later I felt what he meant. It was energy, flowing around us and through us. Before me, Noah took on an almost luminescent light that seemed to come from within him.

"What is it?" I asked, both mystified and excited.

"It's Haven Crest," he replied. Then, over his shoulder, he shouted, "Do you all feel it?"

Miss April twirled around in a perfect pirouette as Johnny, an older man who Noah said was "feeble-minded," clapped and laughed in delight. "It's our guardian spirit!" And she laughed.

"Guardian spirit?" I asked.

Noah took my face in his hands and kissed me again—as though he couldn't seem to help himself. It was obvious the inhabitants of this place were buoyed not just by the thrill of scaring, but also by this energy coursing through and around us.

"The spirit of Haven Crest," he explained. "The combined spectral energy of this place."

That was a lot of energy. "You mean, every ghost here can feel that?"

He nodded. "Every ghost in every building, lane or shrubbery." He laughed, and I had to smile at the thought of ghosts popping out of trees. "It's what unites us."

Like the Borg, I thought. That's what Lark called anything that seemed to have a unified mind or connection. I didn't know what the Borg were, exactly, except that they were keen on assimilation and had an "awesome kick-ass queen." Since

I felt pretty queenly after our little performance, it seemed appropriate.

Lark and I had theorized that Haven Crest had an energy of its own, but to feel it like this—so strong—was something else altogether. I didn't know whether to be awed or frightened—maybe both. I knew I ought to tell Lark about it, but she would want me to stay away in case something bad happened.

In case I was overwhelmed by the amount of energy present and went completely insane. I couldn't blame her for worrying. I worried about it, too, and that was why Lark could never know about my "collection"—because her idea of sanity and my idea of sanity were two completely different things.

And because I didn't want to be anything other than what I was.

She couldn't stop me from being there. And she couldn't expect me to stay away from Noah and my friends. I was accepted here, welcomed and wanted. I'd never felt that at Bell Hill. Never felt it anywhere except with Lark, and she was the blood to my spirit. It wasn't the same thing. She and I shared a bond neither of us had asked for. These ghosts welcomed me as one of their own, and they'd probably never know how much I appreciated that, since not even my own mother would accept I existed.

Yes, Lark would just have to learn to understand.

"If Haven Crest has its own spectral energy, how does it feel about the renovations?" I asked. It was a very Lark question to ask, which I wasn't certain was a good thing.

"She doesn't like it," Noah replied. "All those breathers stomping around, ruining our home."

"But the renovations will actually restore the buildings. Isn't that better than destroying the place? If nothing else, there will be plenty of the living around to scare." I smiled on that last part.

"Ghosts aren't big on change, Wren. You should know that."

His tone wasn't condescending, so I didn't get defensive. "Yes, but at least you'll still have homes. Anchors."

"Through which an endless stream of living will pass, polluting us with their stench."

Ghosts didn't really have a great sense of smell for the most part. I'd worked hard to develop what I had, but it still wasn't on par with a human's. "You can smell them?"

He waved a hand. "Figure of speech. The sentiment is the same. I would rather stay here alone forever, with the walls falling down around me, than spend my days surrounded by breathers."

"They're not all that bad," I said. "My sister is a breather."

"Lark is the exception, though I'm fairly certain she'd much rather salt my bones and burn them, just like Emily."

I froze, my gaze locked with his. "You knew Emily? Emily Murray? My ancestor?"

"Yes."

I was numb. After neglecting to mention his connection to Kevin, this was more than just a surprise. This felt purposeful. "And you're just telling me now?"

He seemed surprised by the hotness of my tone. "I didn't know her well. I saw her about town when I was alive, and then I saw her once or twice after I died. It's not like we were friends."

It hadn't occurred to me that he would have been alive when Emily was. It reminded me just how old he was. "I wish you had told me. Have you seen her lately?"

Noah shook his head. "Not for more years than I can count. I assumed she moved on."

"She hasn't," I confessed. "She's visited Lark and me a few times. We think she may be a prisoner."

Noah studied me intently. "What does she want?"

They really couldn't have been close if he didn't ask about her being held against her will. "To know what happened to her sister, Alys. Alys was…like me."

He smiled that charming smile of his. "There's never been anyone like you."

Flatterer. "Did you know Alys, too?"

He shook his head. "I never had the pleasure. As I said, I barely knew of Emily. I think I owe you an apology for not having told you sooner. Please, believe me that it never occurred to me to even bring it up—that's how little I knew her."

I put my hand on his arm. "Please, don't apologize. It's just that Lark and I know so little about what we are, that information on Emily and Alys would be very helpful."

"Then I will apologize for elevating your hopes only to dash them."

"You didn't dash them. I'm just disappointed."

"Wren, you are the dearest girl I've ever met." He set his hand over mine. "I would never want to upset you in any way."

I glanced away. "That's sweet, thank you."

A finger under my chin turned my head back so that our gazes locked. "I didn't say it to be sweet. Wren, you must know that I have the greatest admiration for you. I cannot remember the last time I was this drawn to anyone. We've known each other only a few days, but I feel, in my soul, that I've known you forever."

"Oh." It was like I was in a romance novel. I couldn't believe my ears.

Noah smiled. "'Oh'? Is that all you've got to say? You crush me."

"I like you, too," I said. "A lot."

The hand over mine tightened around my fingers and lifted them. "Come with me."

I let him pull me toward the stairs. On the next floor he turned the corner toward the men's wing. He took me into a room as abandoned and run-down as the others, but the moment we walked in, it began to change. Noah made it look the way it had been—or the way he wanted it to be. When it had finished, it was a beautiful space with cream walls and a huge four-poster bed.

"Is this your room?" I asked. "It's beautiful."

"Yes. Wealthy patients were allowed to bring their own furnishing. My father was already racked by guilt committing me to Haven Crest, so he spared no expense in making my environment as comfortable as possible."

I admired every detail, right down to the pattern of the huge rug that covered most of the floor. My gaze landed on a portrait hanging on the wall—it was of a beautiful dark-haired girl with bright blue eyes. The resemblance was obvious.

"Is that your sister?"

"Maureen. Yes, that's her."

"She was beautiful."

"She was."

I turned to face him. "You must miss her terribly."

His pain was reflected in the lines of his face. "I do."

"Where is she?" When he frowned, I immediately regretted asking. "I'm sorry. I don't mean to pry."

"No, it's fine. It's just been a while since I've spoken of her.

I assume she's wherever we go once we leave this place. She's not haunting anywhere, if that's what you wanted to know."

It was. "Why didn't you go with her after you died?"

He hesitated, and I wanted to stick iron in my eye for being so nosey. "Unfinished business," was his reply. There was a darkness to his gaze. "I'll see her again one day."

"That's a beautiful thought." I drifted closer to the picture. "Can I ask you how she died?"

"A fever." He moved to my side. "One of those diseases that, if she were alive today, would require nothing more than a few pills to recover."

I turned my head to look at him. "I'm sorry."

A sad smile tilted his lips. "Let's not talk about it anymore. She's not why I brought you up here. I brought you here so we could be alone."

A band of pressure surrounded my chest. "Why?"

He tugged me closer until the edges of our energy touched. "Have you ever melded with another ghost?"

I shook my head. "No." Melding was a very intimate experience. I'd only ever done it with Lark.

And Kevin. But they were alive, not another ghost. It was different when ghosts did it. With humans, you were aware of them, like they might be aware of a coat. It was possession but with the host aware. With ghosts, though, you really became one.

"Would you like to meld with me?" Noah asked softly. "It's all right if you don't."

Did I? It was such a trusting, vulnerable thing to do. For the duration of the meld we'd be the same creature. No me. No him. Just us.

"Yes," I murmured. There was a fluttery feeling inside

me, like there was a light inside me around which a thousand butterflies flapped their wings. "I want to meld with you."

He smiled. "Don't be nervous." He moved closer, and closer. I let down some of my guards, embraced being a being of pure energy and opened myself up to him. Slowly, our auras came together as I drew him in. He let me decide the pace, letting me know he'd stop if I asked him to.

I wasn't going to ask him to stop.

His lips pressed against mine, and we kissed until it wasn't his lips and my lips, but our lips, and then there weren't even any lips, because he was inside of me, and I was inside of him. There was nothing but just us.

It was beautiful.

LARK

Wren didn't meet me after school. Was I surprised? Not really. Was I disappointed? Yeah, a little. But, whatever. I assumed she was with Noah, and since I wasn't going to go to Haven Crest to hunt her down—because I'd hate it if she did that to me—I went home to change. I was going to do some kickboxing with Ben. He swore by it as his favorite way to work out, and I thought he looked hot all sweaty and stuff, so it was all good. Plus, ever since my run-in with Josiah Bent and his minions, I appreciated knowing how to throw a punch.

I could fight ghosts, but I still needed to know *how* to fight. It was a good skill for a girl to have.

Nan, being the living, breathing example of awesomeness that she was, had homemade organic granola bars on a plate in the kitchen when I walked in. I grabbed one and stuffed half of it in my mouth as I ran upstairs.

I changed into leggings, a sports bra and T-shirt and dug my sneakers out of the closet. I didn't wear them very much. I was more of a Fluevog girl. Most of my shoes came from secondhand stores or eBay because I had designer tastes and a nonexistent budget. My father had given me a credit card out of guilt, but I didn't use it very often. Although, I was tempted to run it to the max on shoes.

I stood in front of the full-length mirror in my room, twisting my hair up into a messy bun on the back of my head. My hair was getting too long—it grew like crazy. Sometimes I fantasized about chopping it all off and getting a really edgy cut, but I never followed through.

I had just finished wrapping a scrunchie around the bun when I caught a glimpse of movement in the mirror.

Sweet baby Jesus, what now? Hopefully she wouldn't explode this one.

I glanced up and met a gaze almost identical to mine in the mirror. Emily and I looked a lot alike. It wasn't just the eyes—which she had again—or the white hair; there was something to her expression that reminded me of my own face. She looked a bit older than me, which was funny because she had been an old woman when she died. A lot of ghosts were like starlets—they always wanted to look like they did in their prime.

"Thank goodness you're there," she said.

"You're not going to try to kill me again, are you?" I asked warily.

Her brows lowered in annoyance. "I didn't try to kill you, girl. I've done nothing but try to get your attention, but you don't listen all that well."

Now I knew where I got my prickly nature.

"What's going on with you?" I asked. "Where are you? Who are you afraid of?"

She ignored my questions, peering around the edge of the mirror as though looking for something—or someone. "Is Wren with you?"

"No." Thanks for the reminder that I'd been tossed over for a ghost.

She glanced over her shoulder. "Lark, listen to me. You're in a lot of danger. You can't trust him."

"Trust who?"

Another exasperated look. "You know who. Noah Mc-Crae."

Oh. This was fabulous. Why couldn't I have been wrong about him? Why couldn't he be an awesome guy who wanted nothing more from Wren than to hold her hand and do whatever it was that love-struck ghosts did? "Why not?"

"It's all about revenge." Emily's blue-eyed gaze was earnest as it met mine. "Against me."

"Revenge for what?"

She glanced away. "For what I did to his sister."

"The sister whose death sent him to the crazy house?" I'd read about it in his file.

"No, the other one."

It took me a second to realize she was being sarcastic. Another family trait, obviously.

"You toasted her, didn't you?" I'd like to think I was brilliant to have come to that conclusion, but I was just following along.

Emily nodded. Her hair glinted silver in the mirror. "She turned bad as a spirit. Really bad. Noah was a medium, so he was able to communicate with her, which was why his parents had him committed to Haven Crest. She drove him to the brink of real madness—she persuaded him to kill some-one. I couldn't let her continue. So, I snuck into the family crypt and sent her on to her rest. Or her torment. Or what-ever happens when we're allowed to move on."

"Someone's bitter," I muttered.

"Lark, Noah McCrae killed himself so he could take his revenge on me."

If she had reached through the mirror and slapped me, I wouldn't have been more shocked. "What was that?"

I swear on Wren's grave she rolled her eyes. "Listen to me— Noah McCrae blames me for what happened to his sister. It doesn't matter that perhaps I gave her the peace she sought. To him, I killed her more effectively than the fever she'd con-tracted. He killed himself shortly after. Do you know what happens to a medium when they die?"

I shook my head. "I'm kinda learning this stuff as I go."

Emily sighed. "That's because you've had no one to teach you. You and your sister are the first Melinoe in generations."

"Melinoe?"

She shook her head, as though that weird word wasn't important, even though she'd used it like it was. "When a medium becomes a ghost, they have some power over other ghosts—like a pied piper or snake charmer."

Well, that was just awesome. "How does he do that?"

"Ghosts are drawn to them when they're alive, and that charisma doesn't go away when they die. If left alone, it sim-ply makes for a ghost with a lot of charm and friends, but when nurtured and honed…"

I sighed. "You get Charles Manson and the Family."

Her expression turned grim. "Exactly."

I couldn't even enjoy the fact that she got the reference,

despite having died a good fifty years or more before *Helter Skelter* became more than just a Beatles song.

In the mirror, Emily glanced over her shoulder. I didn't blame her for being paranoid. "I wish I could explain everything to you and teach you what you need to know, but I can't so long as he's got me trapped here. With Alys and I separated, I'm weaker, and he's made me more so by polluting me with his own energy. I've only had this much time with you because he's with your sister. You have to keep her away from him, Lark. He's going to use her to further his own agenda."

"Which is?"

"I don't know."

Of course she didn't.

"He hasn't made me privy to his plans. I do know that what he plans to do isn't nearly as important to me as the fact that he plans to destroy the two of you to achieve it."

That got my attention. "Destroy us? Define *destroy*."

"If he kills you it will only make him stronger."

"I'm not going to let that happen." And then, "Wren thinks he's her boyfriend."

She grimaced. "I know. He will turn her against you if he can. He will turn you against each other and then destroy you both to give himself more power."

"How?"

"All Hallows' Eve is coming. The dead will walk among the living. Haven Crest will be at the apex of a huge energy surge. Noah will harness that energy and use it. He's going to rise, Lark. He will destroy everything in his path, and he will become the most powerful spirit the world has ever seen. Imagine the damage he could do."

This was what One-Shade-of-Gray had been talking

about—the terrible thing that was going to happen at Haven Crest.

It was Noah.

If somebody came into my room at that moment and offered me a full-on, needle-through-the-eye lobotomy with an electroshock-therapy chaser, I'd take it and I'd thank them for it. At least then I wouldn't know just how shitty the situation was, and I wouldn't care even if I did.

"We have to stop the concert," I said. Never mind that I'd said the opposite earlier. Never mind my promise to Joe. I hadn't known the full scope of Noah's douche-baggery when I made that promise. Joe would have to understand. Saving the town, and possibly the world—ego much?—had to be more important than a promise to one ghost.

At least, that's what I told myself.

"How?" she asked.

I couldn't think of a single way, other than arson or planting a body. Neither of those were an option, unless I could get Olgilvie to act early in the evening, but how? Going to the press would make me look nuts. And even if I could get in touch with the band, they'd think it was cool that ghosts were going to crash their party.

"Okay, then, if I can't stop the concert, what other option is there?"

"You know what you have to do."

Salt and burn his remains. Of course. But I didn't know where he was buried… Wait. Wasn't there a McCrae crypt in the graveyard? Kevin would know. He would definitely help me if it was for Wren.

In the mirror I met Emily's gaze. "I can do that," I told her, and I sounded so sure of myself even I believed it.

"Be careful," she warned. "He's stronger than he seems,

and the closer All Hallows' Eve comes, the more powerful he is, especially as connected as he is to Haven Crest."

"Won't Wren and I become more powerful, as well?"

Emily smiled softly at me. "My dear girl, the two of you have no idea how strong you are, and I hope if it comes down to it, you'll figure it out. I promise I'll rectify that as soon as I'm out of this prison. I'll rescue Alys, and then we'll make sure you girls are trained."

That sounded pretty awesome to me. "Why's Alys in the void?"

Emily's smile faded. "For something she did trying to save me. Lark, you and Wren are stronger together than you are apart, that's the way of the Melinoe, but you each have your own strengths. Don't let McCrae lure Wren to his side." She glanced over her shoulder, and I knew our chat was coming to an end.

"I have to go," she whispered. "But, Lark, there's something else I have to tell you before I go. It's very important, and you must trust me and not waver. Do you understand?"

I shrugged. "Sure."

She shook her head, her expression fierce. "No. You *must* heed me." She glanced over her shoulder again, then moved closer to the glass. If I touched the glass over her cheek, would it be warm? "This will be very, very difficult, but you must not give in. It is imperative that you do *not* fail."

"Seriously? Just tell me what it is!"

Blue eyes bore into mine with such intensity that I felt it right down to my toes.

"Noah has his hooks into Wren now. You must find a way to get her away from him, but you cannot, under any circumstances, let your guard down around her. Do you understand?"

I stared at her in shock. "You mean…"

Her expression was grim. "You cannot trust your sister."

And then she was gone, and I was left staring at my own shocked reflection.

chapter fifteen

WREN

Noah and I held hands as we walked through the graveyard at Haven Crest. My entire being still tingled from merging with him earlier. I'd done something similar with Kevin once, but it hadn't been nearly as amazing. Lark would probably be shocked if I told her I'd had the ghost equivalent of sex. It wasn't like I could get pregnant or contract some kind of terrible disease—that sort of thing was found only among the living.

To put it simply, Noah and I had become one being, our energy melding together, then re-forming. I felt closer to him than I had to anyone other than my sister, and even Lark and I had never blended so completely. I'd say it was impossible since she was alive, but my sister had died once, and she had been to the Shadow Lands, so I couldn't apply the same rules to her.

We walked among the ancient headstones—some of which were smashed beyond repair. Such disrespect for the dead. This was where they'd reburied the oldest of Haven Crest's dead. The rest lay beyond, with little plaques that contained nothing more than a number. It was so sad that they were left unnamed and unremembered.

At least my own grave was taken care of—by Lark, Nan, sometimes Kevin and even occasionally my parents. That stone was all they knew of me. My parents only ever saw Lark—their strange little girl with an unhealthy attachment to her dead sister, and an interest in the macabre.

"You know, our parents had Lark institutionalized after she tried to kill herself." He had told me about his past after I picked up parts of it during our merging.

Noah glanced at me. "Really?"

I nodded. "They didn't believe that she could really talk to me. They didn't believe in me at all."

"It seems your sister and I have something in common, after all."

"That and the fact that I like you both," I teased. I wasn't going to say I loved him, even though that had been the word that wanted to tumble out of my mouth.

He looked somewhere out in the distance. He had the love-liest profile. "Forgive me for saying so, but I do wonder if your sister feels the same loyalty to you as you have for her."

"What do you mean?"

Now he looked at the grass. Why wouldn't he look at me? "Only that she seems to treat you as though you were some sort of exotic animal—something she can admire and show off at her discretion, but always holds at a distance because she doesn't trust you not to attack."

I frowned. "No, that's not it at all."

"No?" He shrugged. "When she talks to you about me, is it with distrust? Does she talk to you about anything per-sonal, or is it always about information you've discovered? The one time she came here it wasn't to get to know me, or your

new friends, but because she wanted to hunt down Robert—
something she never even discussed with you beforehand."

He was right. But I hadn't exactly been there for my sister
over the past few days.

Still….a little needle of uncertainty dug at my mind. How
much gushing about Ben had I sat through? I mention Noah,
and Lark tells me to be careful. She didn't want to hear about
what I've done, or how happy I've been. It's all about Emily
and Alys, and the approach of Halloween.

"Lark's always been very protective of me," I informed
him, truthfully.

Now he looked at me. "Wren, *dearest*, she treats you like
a child. I mean neither of you disrespect, but if you want to
be treated as your sister's equal, you need to start demanding
her respect. You don't doubt her abilities as she doubts yours."

That was true, as well. "She worries that I'll be taken advantage of by other ghosts."

Noah made a scoffing noise. "And some breather could take
advantage of her, yet you do not seek to monitor her every
movement. I'm sorry, but I believe the reason she didn't ask
you about Robert was so she could just show up here and see
for herself what you'd gotten yourself up to."

I had wondered the same thing myself at the time—but
only for a moment. "My sister hasn't had many good experiences with ghosts."

"Knowing what it's like to be thought mad, I can tell you
that she hasn't had many good experiences with the living
either, but she's not out there setting fire to the ones who are
mean to her."

I laughed at the very idea. Although, there would be some
satisfaction in setting fire to that policeman Olgilvie. He
wasn't a nice man.

Noah smiled. "I love the way you laugh." He squeezed my hand as I glanced away, shy for some reason. "I don't mean to disparage your sister, I'm merely frustrated that a creature such as you has been basically kept in a box for her entire existence. You are a being of pure energy. You shine like a beacon in the dark, and yet you have been relegated to Lark's shadow. I think perhaps Lark's fear makes her keep a tight rein on you."

I couldn't argue with that. Part of me wanted to defend Lark and make him understand her, but...truthfully, he seemed to understand her very well already.

"I don't want you to dislike my sister."

Noah stopped walking and turned to face me. "Dislike her? No, sweet girl. I could never dislike someone who loves you so much. I might dislike some of her actions, but never her."

I smiled. "That makes me very happy."

He moved closer, lips curving in that way that made me feel both anxious and delighted. "Do *I* make you happy?"

I laughed. "I think you know the answer to that already."

"I want to hear you say it."

I rolled my eyes. "Yes, you make me happy. There. Are *you* happy now?"

His lips brushed mine. "I've never been as happy—living or dead—as I've been in the days since meeting you."

"Oh. How do you always know exactly the right thing to say?"

"I only speak how I feel." His gaze seemed to take in every aspect of my face. "My mother used to say that the truth was always the correct thing to say. That was before my father told her about his mistress."

I winced. "That must have been awkward."

He shrugged, and we began walking again. "It was a different time back then. Women were told to ignore their husbands' shortcomings."

"Did your mother ignore your father's?"

"For the most part. I think outliving him and inheriting his money gave her some satisfaction in the end. Oh, look. Here is where Miss April is buried."

I glanced down at the tiny little headstone. It was like the others with the numbers, but someone had set a little stone heart into the ground.

"There was a heart with her original grave," Noah explained. "Her fiancé had it placed there. I believe it was destroyed when they moved the graves. Then, one day, a descendant of Miss April's fellow was conducting research into the family. When the girl found our friend's grave and realized the heart was gone, she bought a new one. I've always thought that was a lovely gesture."

If I could cry I would have had tears trickling down my cheeks. As it was, I felt a burning sensation in my eyes. "That was very sweet of her." Sometimes the living amazed me.

"Yes, it was."

I looked about the stone garden. "Where are you buried?"

"Why?" he asked, his expression darkening. "So you can tell your sister, so she might salt and burn my bones?"

I drew back. "Of course not! How can you ask me that? And you call my sister distrusting."

His features softened. "You're right. Please, forgive me. I had no right to snap at you. It's just that I remember what she did to Josiah Bent."

"Lark might have salted and burned his bones, but I was the one who had to fight Bent to keep him from killing two teenagers. He would have killed them and several others. I

ripped him to shreds." Partially, anyway. "Are you so dis-
trustful of me?"

Regret shone in his eyes. "I trust you, but I'm afraid I'm
not so trusting of Lark."

I couldn't blame him. She wouldn't trust him either. "Come
with me," I said, taking his hand.

I took us to the town graveyard—just popped from one to
the other. Unlike the one at Haven Crest, the town graveyard was on consecrated ground and considered a sanctuary
by ghosts. No violence allowed.

Noah glanced around us. "Why are we here?"

I pointed at the ground in front of us and watched as he
read, as realization dawned.

"It's your grave," he whispered.

"Yes."

He frowned. "Who left the flowers? Your mother?"

"No."

"Your sister?"

"No." I should just make something up.

"Who?"

"Kevin."

"The McCrae boy?"

I nodded. "He and Lark are the only ones who ever come
here regularly."

His fingers squeezed mine. "Thank you for showing me
this."

"It felt like the right thing to do," I replied.

When he kissed me, standing on my grave, I felt a surge
of energy course through me. I didn't know what it was or
what it meant. I couldn't even tell if it was good or bad—it
was just incredibly intense. It was like how I imagined being
struck by lightning would feel.

It disappeared as quickly as it had come, and I chalked it up to a combination of our energies, mixed with the power of being so close to my mortal remains. It didn't matter. Noah was the only thing I cared about at the moment.

And I didn't even care that even though he knew where my grave was, he hadn't told me the location of his.

LARK

After kickboxing class, I went back to Ben's house. It was just the two of us, since his mom had taken his sister to dance class, his grandmother was at one of her social groups and his dad was still at work. His mother had left money for him to get food, so we ordered takeout from the local Thai place and ate in front of the television. His grandmother had left a bowl of peaches for us for dessert, and I'd learned something new about Korean culture—that peaches were thought to have supernatural powers, such as warding off ghosts.

I didn't want to think about how many peaches I'd have to eat to keep ghosts away. Still, I liked peaches, and I appreciated the gesture. She'd also left red bean cake for us—which was also supposed to ward off evil spirits.

"I think ghosts should be fought with food more often," Ben remarked.

"I can't believe all the ghost shows," I remarked as he scrolled through the menu. "I know it's Halloween week, but just how many reality shows about ghost hunters who never seem to find anything can TV support?"

"Seem? I always figured the ghosts didn't show up just to make them look stupid."

I nodded. "Some, but most times the crew just don't see

them. They have all their gadgets and gizmos, and they can't even see a ghost that's jumping up and down in front of them."

Ben gestured at the TV with his fork. "So, you can see ghosts when they're on TV?"

"Well, yeah." I'd never told anyone else that little talent. I'd always just assumed it went without saying. "They're just like real people to me."

He smiled slowly. "Cool. Apparently these guys have been trying to get into Haven Crest, but the town won't give them a permit." He glanced at me. "Do you think the ghosts there would put on a show for them?"

"I have no idea." And then, "Hey, isn't that Gretchen Jones?"

"It is." He turned up the volume so we could hear better.

Gretchen Jones was the lead singer of Dead Babies. Gretchen was also six foot four, had spiky purple hair and cited Alice Cooper as his biggest musical influence. He was hot, but completely nuts. Still, the band was awesome.

On-screen, one of the members of the *Supernatural Encounters* team looked earnestly at Gretchen and asked, "So, at your concert in New Devon Halloween night you intend to raise the spirit of Joe Hard."

Ben and I shared a glance. We knew the concert was in Joe's honor, and I'd assumed they'd make a spectacle out of it, but actually raise Joe? That was powerful and dangerous stuff. It wasn't the same as a summoning. A summoning called forth the lingering spirit. Raising someone meant you not only summoned them, but then you forced them to take some sort of form—usually a full-blown manifestation.

"Yeah," Gretchen rasped. He had a voice that sounded like sandpaper on stone. "Joe Hard was a major influence on my music. I can't think of any better way to honor his memory than to call him forth for one last encore, y'know?"

"Can he actually do that?" Ben asked.

"I have no freaking idea," I replied. "Maybe? It wouldn't surprise me. Shit."

"You think that's the 'big thing' that's supposed to happen at Haven Crest?"

"No. Joe's not evil." Of course I'd told him all about my conversation with Emily, and he was the only one I had any intention of telling, unless it was necessary. "But if the band tries to raise him, that's going to feed even more energy into the place."

Ben looked at the TV. "Shit."

I set my plate on the coffee table, half listening to Gretchen and the interviewer as I ran a list of possible scenarios in my head.

He cleared his throat. "I don't want you to go to Haven Crest. I don't want any of us anywhere near it." He didn't sound afraid, but he would have been stupid not to be, and my guy wasn't stupid.

"I don't want me to go either, but I've been thinking about that. The simple solution to all of this is to dust Noah now and ruin any plans he has."

Ben didn't blink. "Okay, but what are you going to tell Wren? She's not likely to forgive you for torching her boyfriend."

"I can live with that if he's as bad as Emily says."

"If Emily told Wren I was evil and Wren killed me without talking to you first, would you ever forgive her?"

"No." I didn't even need to think about it. God, I hated it when he used logic on me. "Fine, I'll talk to her."

"What about Joe Hard? Did he mention any of this when you talked to him?"

I shook my head. "I don't think he knows. I probably should tell him. I have to go to the concert. I promised Joe I'd make sure Olgilvie got caught." He was the only one I'd shared that information with, as well. It wasn't that I didn't trust my friends—I did. But knowing that a local cop was a murderer was dangerous, and being my friend was already dangerous enough.

Ben gathered me up with his arm around my shoulder. "We'll figure it out."

I leaned against him. It wasn't the danger that had me worried. Ghosts were scary, but there were things that scared me more than the dead. "Emily told me not to trust my sister."

He kissed my forehead. "I know. Have you noticed any personality changes in her?"

"Sure. It's Halloween, so there have been some changes. More than I remember her having before. It's not all the time, but sometimes I've caught her looking at me like she wants to gouge my eyes out."

"And you freaked out on her, too."

"At home, yeah. It was like I was the ghost. Freaky. I just want this all to be over. I'm scared. I don't know what's going on. I can't depend on Wren. I'm worried I'm going to get one of my friends hurt. People might die, and I don't know how to stop it." I was going to cry. I couldn't let that happen. If I started I wouldn't stop.

Ben took my plate from the coffee table and handed it to me. "Eat. And then go home. Find Wren and talk to her. Tell her what Emily said."

I wrapped noodles around my fork. "She's not going to like it. She probably won't believe me."

"But you will have told her. She'll find out about him eventually. If you've warned her, it won't be a total shock when he turns on her."

God. That made me want to puke. I ate anyway. "Emily said not to trust her. What if I tell her and she runs back and tells him?"

"Who do you trust more, Emily or Wren?"

I didn't need to answer that. I finished my food and then went home—after kissing Ben and promising to let him know how my conversation with Wren went. When I got home, I grabbed a quick shower and started in on my homework. I had just finished a history reading when I heard the text notification on my phone. I looked at the screen—there was no return number or name, but I didn't need one.

Staying with Noah. There's nothing wrong at Haven Crest. See you tomorrow.

I stared at it. I couldn't even text back to ask her to come home. I damn sure wasn't about to go to Haven Crest to get her. She'd never acted like this before, and I didn't know what to do about it. She deserved happiness, but didn't Noah raise any alarms for her? Didn't she suspect that he wasn't what he seemed?

Of course not. She thought he was everything she ever wanted—a reasonable replacement for the living boy she couldn't have. That might be harsh of me to think, but he and Kevin were blood relatives.

What was I supposed to do? Ask Dead Babies not to perform? That wasn't going to happen. Vandalism to sabotage the event would be tricky and wasn't worth juvenile jail time. The town wasn't going to shut it down—they had made a lot of money off this event, and were going to earn even more once the town filled up with concertgoers and Dead Babies fans. Who would listen to me? I was just some girl who'd spent time in a mental asylum.

God, if I caused trouble about the concert with the town, Nan would be the one who suffered for it. They'd all run bitching to her about me. I loved my grandmother—enough that I'd rather die than cause her any pain.

There wasn't enough salt or iron to protect everyone who would be at Haven Crest Halloween night, and using the stuff would prevent any help other ghosts wanted to give us. I couldn't count on Wren, who was either lying to me about Haven Crest or clueless about Noah's plans.

Maybe Emily was wrong. Maybe Noah wasn't evil. Maybe the concert would be just a concert and nothing bad would happen.

Yeah. *Right.*

I swiped my thumb across the screen and brought up my contacts list. I selected Kevin and lifted the phone to my ear. It rang a couple of times.

"Lark?"

"Hey, Kevin. Can I ask you a question?"

There was a second of hesitation. "Does it have anything to do with Mace or Sarah?"

"Not a bit."

"Then go ahead."

"Do you know if Noah McCrae is buried in your family crypt?"

More silence. "Wow. I didn't see that one coming. Um, I don't know."

I guess I ought to have expected that. I mean, did I think

he'd have a list or a chart lying around? "Well, do you know how old the earlier graves are?"

"There are a couple dating back to the 1700s. It's a big crypt. Not all the family is buried there. Most of the newer graves are outside, surrounding the building."

"Can you just walk in, or is it locked?"

"Seriously? Would you leave a crypt unlocked in this town?"

He had a point. Teenagers were pigs and horny enough to do the nasty on top of a centuries-old coffin with dusty bones rattling beneath them.

"Can you get a key?"

"Yes. What's this about, Lark?"

I sighed. I might as well tell him. Really, there was no good reason to keep it from him. He deserved to know just in case Noah had plans for him, too. "You know that guy Wren brought to the party?"

"Mr. Darcy? Yeah, I remember him." No, he didn't sound jealous at all.

"His name is Noah McCrae. He's your ancestor."

"Fuck off."

I laughed. How could I not? Kevin rarely swore.

"I'm not joking. I wish I was. Look, Kev, I've got reason to believe he's involved in something really bad. Worse than Josiah Bent bad, but the details are sketchy. Wren is in danger, and I *need* to get to Noah's grave."

A second ticked by. Was he even there? Had the call dropped? "You're going to smoke your sister's potentially evil boyfriend?"

"Yes."

"I'm in." *Oh, thank God.* "When?"

I checked the time. It wasn't even eight o'clock, and I had

my homework done. Nan would be okay with me going out. "Now?"

"I'll be right there."

"Thanks."

I hung up and changed into some dark jeans and a black sweater. I grabbed a pair of Fluevog boots out of my closet and put them on. Nan was in the kitchen making tea when I came down.

"I'm going out for a bit," I told her. "Ghost stuff."

She nodded, dipping a tea ball in and out of her cup. "Should I be worried?"

"No, and I won't be gone long."

She nodded, still dipping. "Is your homework done?"

"Yes, ma'am."

"Have you eaten?"

"Yup."

She nodded. "Okay. Be careful." She turned her gaze in my direction. "Call me if you're not going to be home by ten, or I'll start to worry."

I kissed her cheek. "It's nothing big, I promise."

She looked around. "Where's your sister?"

"With a friend." I did not want to get Nan's hopes up about that relationship.

"Hmm." She shook her head. "It seems so strange for her not to be with you. But I suppose you're getting older. It makes sense that she'd want a life of her own—no pun intended."

It did make sense. Perfect sense, but I didn't like it. Noah was using her; I knew it even without having talked to Emily. I'd known it from the night she met him, and not because he was a ghost, but because every instinct I had screamed that he wasn't to be trusted. I'd tried to like him, I really had. There'd even been a few moments when I thought I'd been wrong and that he really was a good guy. Not anymore.

Kevin pulled into the drive a little while later, and I dashed out to meet him with my "ghost-fightin'" backpack slung over my shoulder.

"Hey," I said as I climbed in.

"You're *sure* this guy is bad news?"

I buckled my seat belt as he backed out onto the street. "He's got one of my ancestors locked up, her sister in the void, and I'm told he wants to destroy me and Wren. Is that bad enough for you?"

His mouth tightened. "Yeah."

He drove quickly but not recklessly. The gates to the grave-yard were closed, but no one ever locked them. I had to jump out and open them so he could drive through. Then I closed the gate, so no one passing by would be curious, and jumped back into the car.

Of course we weren't the only car there. It didn't matter what day of the week it was; you were going to find people making out at the cemetery. I never got the appeal, and it seemed a little disrespectful to me. Normally ghosts avoided cemeteries, and they were considered "neutral" ground, but that wouldn't stop some pervy dead guy from peeking in your windows as you and your partner fogged them up.

Kevin parked the car and we got out. I slung my bag over my shoulder and followed after him down the gravel path. We had to walk by Wren's grave, and I blew it a kiss as we passed.

A few moments later we came up on a large stone crypt. The name *McCrae* was embossed into the heavy iron door. Kevin took a key from his coat and slipped it into the lock. The door creaked open.

He'd brought a flashlight, which produced just enough

light to make the crypt super creepy. I followed him inside. There were probably thirty graves in here that contained actual bodies, and another dozen that were mere urns upon a shelf.

The beam of Kevin's flashlight moved across the rows of dead McCraes.

"There!" I pointed at one on the far wall. "That's him."

Kevin shoved the flashlight under his arm and helped me pull off the front plate. Inside was an old, dusty coffin that we grabbed by the rails and slowly pulled from the cabinet. We didn't take it out all the way, but just enough to open the top portion of the lid.

Kevin pried open the casket as I got out my salt, lighter fluid and matches. I was really going to do this.

Forgive me, Wren.

"Um, Lark?"

"What?" I glanced up at him as I organized my supplies.

He pointed at the coffin. "Look."

Bracing myself for the sight of Noah's dried-up corpse, I moved closer and peered inside.

"Are you freaking serious?" I cried.

The coffin was empty.

chapter sixteen

LARK

"I don't believe it."

Kevin stood beside me, both of us staring into the empty casket. Well, it wasn't entirely empty—there were some scraps of fabric, dust and some other stuff I didn't care to try to identify.

But the majority of Noah's remains were gone. I could burn what was in front of me, but it wouldn't be enough to get rid of him.

"Now what do I do?" I demanded of the corpse-leavings. I wouldn't have to deal with Wren discovering I'd torched her boyfriend, which was good, but the realization that Noah had prepared for this weighed heavy on my shoulders. My sister was falling for a douche-bag ghost who knew I wanted to kill him. And who now had just sent me a big "F-You."

"How could this happen?" Kevin asked, his voice hoarse. "You have to have a key to get in here. Only my father and my uncle have a key."

"Someone could have picked the lock," I offered. I didn't

know why I made the suggestion until I saw the look on his face. He looked panicked.

"Kevin," I began cautiously. "Why do you look like you're going to puke?"

He turned his head to meet my gaze. He was so freaking pale that his eyes were unnaturally bright against the white of his skin. "I've been losing time lately."

I stared at him. This entire fiasco just kept getting better and better. Noah had me by the short-and-curlies at every freaking turn. "You mean, like, getting-possessed-by-my-asshole-dead-relative losing time?"

"I don't know." He ran a hand through his hair. "But there have been a couple of times I've been somewhere and not known how I got there."

"Did you happen to have a dusty old corpse in your hands one of those times?"

He hesitated, as though he were actually trying to remember. I didn't know whether to smack him or feel sorry for him. "No, but once I came out of it in the woods behind my grandmother's house, and another time I was in Paugussett."

"The state forest?"

"Yeah."

I stared at him. "Dude, that place is huge. It's like a thousand acres."

"More like eight hundred, and that's only on one side of the river. I came to in my car, so I don't even know what I was doing there."

I stared at the stained satin lining of Noah's casket. Douche-bag ooze, yummy.

Suddenly, the coffin lid slammed shut, and Kevin brought both of his fists down hard upon the aged wood. "Son of a bitch!"

I flinched as grave dust flew, but I let him get his aggression out. I knew how it felt, and I wasn't going to get in the way of that. I mean, if I'd found out some ghost had been using me as its personal meat suit, I'd be pissed, too. Wren had taken me over once without my knowledge—I'd been unconscious at the time—and that was enough of a pisser, even though she'd done it for good reason.

By the time Kevin had gotten his rage out, he was sweating and dirty, and the casket was still pretty much intact—they made those things sturdy.

"So," I began, keeping my voice as neutral as possible. "You know anyone who does hypnosis?"

He had his hands braced on the coffin. His knuckles were bloody, and when he turned his face toward me, he stared at me through a mess of curls. You know, he was kinda cute when he was mad. I could see why Wren had a crush.

And right now I'd so prefer her pining over Kevin than dating a seemingly brilliant, villainous dead guy powerful enough to possess his descendants to the point of complete takeover.

"No. Well, maybe Chuck."

Chuck was a weird guy who sold us iron rings and could see Wren but couldn't talk with her. He seemed a little too... stoned to be of much help. But we were in a tight spot. "Call him."

Kevin took out his cell and swiped his finger across the screen. A few seconds later he spoke. "Hey, Chuck. It's Kevin McCrae. Give me a call. I need to ask you a question."

"Of course you got voice mail," I moaned. "I'm losing more ground than I'm making. Come Halloween night I'm just going to be ripped apart by ghosts and not be able to do a single thing about it."

"Wren wouldn't let that happen."

I shook my head at the certainty in his voice. "She's not herself lately."

"She likes him."

"Yeah, well, she has rotten taste in guys—except for you, of course."

He actually smiled at me. "Flatterer." His smile faded. "I won't let him rip you apart."

Now I was the one who smiled. "Thanks. I guess we should get out of here before any of your other ancestors get curious and want to try you on."

"Good idea." We shoved the empty casket back into its notch and shut the door.

As we walked out into the darkening day, I said, "You know, it's funny. Wren and I have been back in town since the end of August. We grew up here, and this is the first time I've even heard of Noah."

"So?" Kevin pushed hair out of his eyes and slipped the lock into place. "I've been here my whole life and never heard of Josiah Bent."

"Yes, but you knew about Wren. And we've been to Haven Crest a few times now. I guess I just think it's weird that Noah chose the week of Halloween to suddenly appear and sweep my sister off her feet—and try walking in yours."

Behind his glasses, Kevin's bright blue eyes narrowed. "You think he planned it?"

I realized that it made me sound paranoid, but, hey, my paranoia had served me well in the past. "He's had his remains moved. That's a pretty good indication that he's up to no good. And, yeah, I think he did plan it. He didn't even let on he knew who you were when he asked Wren about you. I think knowing you're our friend gave him a little extra thrill when he possessed you and made you work against us."

"Bastard."

"Exactly. He needs Wren to take his revenge against Emily—our ancestor who was like me. She told me that Noah has her imprisoned somehow. He blames her for sending his sister's spirit on. She says he committed suicide so that he could become a vengeful spirit and get a little payback. He was like you—a medium. Apparently you guys can get really bitchy after you die."

Kevin shoved his hands in his pockets as we walked along the gravel path. "So, what you're saying is that our ancestors have bad blood between them."

"Yup. You and Wren are a regular Romeo and Juliet, except that she's already dead."

"I don't like to think of her as dead."

I couldn't help but notice the direction in which he glanced. He knew exactly where Wren's grave was located. "No, you don't. I appreciate that."

"Careful, Lark. Keep going like this and I'm going to think you like me or something."

I smiled, but I was only partly amused. "It's on us to stop this. We have to find his remains. And we have to keep him from possessing you again."

"I've been read—" Kevin suddenly stopped.

"What is it?" I asked.

He pointed, and I followed the line of his finger. Wren's grave. "I don't see anything," I whispered.

He lowered his hand and wrapped it around mine. It was like tuning a radio station. One moment there was nothing, and then I saw what he did.

It was Wren and Noah. They were faint—just a shadow of

how I normally saw them. Was this how ghosts looked to normal people? Maybe Kevin wasn't a great example of normal.

I watched them talk. Wren looked so happy, but she also looked...weird.

"Does she look different to you?" I asked. It wasn't like they could hear me—we were seeing something from the recent past, not really them. That was why I hadn't been able to see it without his help. Leftover spirit energy wasn't my thing—but mediums loved that stuff.

Kevin nodded. "She looks ghoulish. I don't like it."

It was true. Wren looked paper-white, with dark smudges around her eyes and mouth, like what I'd seen on Noah in Roxi's photo. Even her expression was wrong. She looked less like my sister and more like something you'd see in a Japanese horror movie.

"What's he done to her?" The back of my eyes burned with hot tears, and suddenly I was struck by a paralyzing fear.

What if he'd already ruined her? What if I was never going to get my sister back? What if I couldn't stop him?

Shitshitshitshit. I was going to hyperventilate.

I watched, lungs straining for breath, as Noah and Wren kissed. Kevin dropped my hand like it burned him. I hunched over, sucking in air in greedy gulps.

"Are you okay?" he asked.

I held up a finger—not the one I normally would have used, but a polite one to tell him to give me a minute. Slowly, I breathed in through my nose and out through my mouth. Once I was certain I wasn't going to drop, I straightened.

Head rush. I grabbed Kevin's arm to steady myself until the world stopped spinning.

"Sorry," he said. "I didn't know it would do that to you."

"That makes two of us."

"You really couldn't see them?"

I shook my head. "I see them on this plane. I think you must see them on a different channel or something. Weird."

"They were at her grave."

"Yeah." The ghost who had hidden his remains knew where my sister was buried. My sister, who was descended from a woman against whom he'd sworn revenge.

Fucknuts.

"Kevin," I asked, turning toward him with a new determination. Noah was not going to have my sister, the Mr. Darcy Casper-ass douche bag.

His gaze widened as it met mine. I guess he saw that I meant business. His jaw clenched. I guess he meant business, too. "What do you need?" he asked.

I looked back at the little square of land that held all of what was left on this earth of my twin. The spot where my parents had put her just a few days after we were born, the only evidence that'd she'd ever truly existed. If I were Noah, I'd have my human meat suit come back here as soon as I could swing it.

"A shovel."

WREN

I didn't know how long I'd been at Haven Crest, but when I glanced out the window and saw it was dark, I knew it had been too long. And not long enough.

Noah and I had spent most of the day and evening dancing, merging, dancing some more and talking. He told the most amazing stories of what life had been like when he lived, of the ghosts who had come and gone from this building and

Haven Crest in general. He knew so much about life—and death.

"I should probably go," I said. "You must be sick of me."

Noah ran his finger down my cheek. We were reclining on a chaise in his room. "I could never be sick of you. You are far too extraordinary."

I preened at his praise.

"Besides," he continued, "where are you going to go? Your sister is probably with her living friends, and those woeful souls in the Shadow Lands are far too dreary for someone like you. You may as well stay here. With me."

He had a point. A very good one. Part of me insisted that I should go to Lark, if for no other reason but to check in with her, but why disrupt her? This close to Halloween I didn't know if someone might see me. I didn't want to get Lark in any trouble.

And really, I didn't want to go anywhere. I was happy at Haven Crest.

"I have an appointment in the Shadow Lands on Wednesday."

"An appointment?" He seemed amused by the idea. "What manner of *appointment* could you possibly have in the Shadow Lands?"

"The book on Emily and Alys is in the Special Collections department. I had to make an appointment to look at it."

He frowned. "Why do you need a book? They were your ancestors, weren't they? Don't you already know all there is to know about them?"

"We know practically nothing about them. That's why I need to see the book. Emily's been trying to make contact with us—she completely ruined the bathroom mirror. We think that the book might be able to help us."

"You said she's been 'trying' to contact you. You've seen her?"

"Yes. We think she might be in trouble, and she's the only person who can tell Lark and me what we are."

"Then you had better keep that appointment." He smiled. "I want to tell you how honored I was that you took me to your place of rest. My own remains are in that very same graveyard. I should have shown you."

"Why don't we go now?" I suggested.

He pulled back, brows raised. "Really?"

"Why not? Do you have something else to do?"

"All right." He stood up and offered me his hand. "Let's go."

Instead of interdimensional travel as I'd used the night before, I pulled him along with me outside, so that we could drift over the grounds of Haven Crest. Even though it was dark, I saw the place as it was, regardless of time of day. The grass was still a rich green, and the trees were a riot of greens, golds and reds. Even some of the vines clinging to the brick buildings were shot with crimson. It was beautiful—despite the ugly stage the construction crew had almost completed. They'd put up some temporary fencing around the area as well, I supposed in an effort to keep people from sneaking in.

Was that Officer Olgilvie I saw, standing in the grass beyond the stage? What was he doing here?

"I will be so glad when that bloody concert is over and done with," Noah remarked. "It's such a nuisance."

I turned to him, the policeman forgotten. "There will be so many people here." I thought about them, all those living, breathing souls ignorantly trespassing on spirit territory. All those wide, gleaming eyes watching Dead Babies perform, catching glimpses of ghosts, glistening in my hand...

"Wren?"

I whipped my head around. "What?"

"You stopped moving." He was right, we were still. "Is everything all right?"

I laughed. "Daydreaming. Sorry."

"What about?" he asked.

Before I could stop myself, I blurted, "Eyes. I like eyeballs. I have a collection."

He didn't even blink as we started moving again. "I should like to see that—if you would show me."

Shouldn't I feel guilty for thinking about plucking the eyes right out of the sockets of the living? Probably, but I didn't. I didn't even care if it was because of Halloween or something else. It didn't matter. Being with Noah mattered. Feeling like I could be my real self with someone and not be judged for it mattered.

But...not even Lark knew about my collection. She'd never seen them. "Maybe I'll bring them with me someday."

He didn't push, and I was glad.

"I used to collect things," he said. "For the first thirty or forty years of being a ghost I would tuck away little keepsakes—hair from relatives because it was easy to collect. Once I was strong enough to interact with objects, I'd sometimes stash away handkerchiefs—not that I had any need for them." He laughed. "In the 1950s I became obsessed with collecting teeth."

I smiled. I loved how relaxed I felt with him. Not anxious like I had been with Kevin. I felt like we were two halves of the same whole—sort of like my connection to Lark, but different. More intense.

We drifted into the cemetery. It was serenely pretty under

the moonlight. There was no one here—no teenagers steaming up the windows of parked cars. It was nice.

"I envy you your freedom," Noah remarked. He was in the lead now, guiding me toward his place of rest. "You can go anywhere you want. You're not bound by a place or thing."

"I don't know why I'm that way," I replied. "I just am."

"I didn't mean any offense, dearest. I think it's wonderful that you can do all these things. And I'm happy to join you on any journey during which you wish to have my company."

"We can go anywhere you want within the town. I haven't tried to go any farther."

"I'll keep that in mind. It might be nice to visit the house where I grew up."

I'd take him there in an instant. "Whenever you want."

The McCrae crypt stood a little farther ahead. It was dark stone, bright and shadowed by the morning sun. We passed through the door—most ghosts chose to go through a door even though it was no different than a wall. Habit.

Inside the crypt was dark—the sun streaming through small stained glass windows, painting squares of red, yellow and blue on the dusty floor.

Noah moved to the back wall. "Someone's been here," he said.

I peered around him and saw that the compartment door had handprints in the dust.

Noah stuck his head through the wall. When he came out again he was frowning. "My remains are gone."

I went still. "What?"

He turned to me, anger and shock all over his face. "Some-one took my bones, Wren. Who would take my bones?"

I stuck my own head into the compartment, through the

coffin, and looked inside. It was indeed empty, but it was obvious that there had been a body in it at one time.

I slipped out to find Noah glaring at me. "Had to see for yourself?" he demanded. "You didn't believe me?"

"Of course I believe you. I just wanted to see if there was some sort of clue."

He pointed at the dirt-covered floor. "There's your clue."

I glanced down. There, near where my own foot hovered, was a clear shoe print. It was a woman's shoe with a round heel and a wide, rounded front. On its own it wouldn't be much of a clue, but the stylized *F* imprinted in the dirt was.

I went cold. I felt as though someone had reached inside me and ripped out something vital. I knew that *F*.

Lark.

chapter seventeen

LARK

How was I going to explain to Wren about her remains being missing? The question haunted me (pardon the pun) when I got home. I'd dug her up and brought the dirty tiny casket home to hide in Nan's garage, but I'd told Kevin I was going to bury her somewhere—and, no offense, but I wasn't going to tell him where, just in case Noah took him over again.

He'd dropped me off with the promise that he'd wear his iron rings all the time. And I'd drawn *pujok* symbols that Ben's granny had taught me on his inner arm in Sharpie to help. He promised me he'd look into better ways to protect himself, but I was worried about him. Noah used to be a medium as well, and now he was a powerful ghost. Kevin was going to have to be very strong to resist him.

"Eat peaches," I told him.

He looked at me like I was nuts. "Yeah, sure. Thanks." Then he backed his car out of the drive and onto the street.

I had an awful feeling as I went into the house that I might not see him again.

Lying in my bed, I almost texted Ben, but he'd had me

whining on his shoulder enough recently. And Ben would say all the right things, the things I needed to hear, whether I liked them or not.

I typed out a message and hit the Send key. A couple of minutes later my phone vibrated in my hand. On the screen was just one word: Yes.

Before I could talk myself out of it, I made the call.

"So, is this when I get to apologize for being such a tool for climbing in your bedroom window?" Mace asked when he answered. His voice was low. I wondered if his family was in bed.

"No," I replied with a slight smile. "This is when you tell me that ghosts are already dead, so it's not murder if I put one down."

"Why would I tell you what you already know?" And then, "Wait. Is this about the guy your sister's seeing? The ass-hat?"

"He knows I'm onto him. He's been possessing Kevin, and he moved his remains from the family crypt. I can't burn him if I can't find him."

"He possessed Kevin?"

"Yeah." I knew where he was going with this. "No, I don't think it was Noah who swapped spit with Sarah."

"You have such a kind and caring way with words, bitch." There was a trace of a smile in his voice, so I didn't take offense, and I didn't apologize.

I sighed. "Look, it's none of my business, but I don't think Kevin meant to hurt you. I heard him tell Sarah it was over. He felt terrible betraying you. He was just messed up, you know?"

"I don't want to talk about it."

"Neither do I. Stop stealing my thunder."

He actually laughed. "Look, you do whatever you need to do to this ghost, okay? I'm with you all the way. We all are."

Huh. Maybe Mace knew what I needed to hear, as well. "Hey, Joe Hard told me Olgilvie killed a girl. Her name was Laura."

"What?"

"You remember when you and I got arrested at Haven Crest?" As if he could have forgotten. Mace's father was the police chief, and I'm pretty sure he'd gotten in a lot of trouble that night. "When Joe showed up at the police station, he mentioned Laura."

"I believe you. I didn't know Laura, but my mom did."

Right. He told me that his mother knew Joe—that she used to have a crush on him. They probably grew up together. Joe also had a bit of a thing for my grandmother when he was younger, which I refused to think about.

"Were they friends?" I asked.

"Yeah. Olgilvie had a thing for her. She disappeared, though, years ago. Everyone thought she ran off to meet up with Joe on tour, but she never made it. No one heard from her again. You're saying Olgilvie killed her?"

"That's what Joe said. He showed me the spot where our creepy cop friend buried her. Joe thinks he's going to move her the night of the concert."

"Why would he do that? Even if someone found her, there probably isn't much in the way of evidence left."

"To prevent an investigation. I bet people had their suspicions about Olgilvie. In a small town like this, everybody knows everyone else. Even if nothing came of it, you can bet there were people who thought he did something to her. People who knew he wanted her for himself."

"Damn." Mace was silent for a second. "I know some of

the guys who are working the night of the concert. If we can find out when Olgilvie's going to do it, I can probably make sure he's found. It takes time to dig up a corpse."

"Yeah," I said drily. "I know." I'd dug up more graves than I would ever admit.

After making as much of a plan as we could—which basically hinged on Joe watching Olgilvie, his being able to contact me and Mace's credibility with his father's men—we hung up. I snuggled under the covers and waited for sleep to come.

I lay awake most of the night, worrying about Ben, my friends, the concert, Halloween, Noah and—most of all—Wren. I hadn't seen her since she'd gone off to ask Noah about being related to Kevin. I knew she was fine, because I could feel it.

The next morning I forced myself out of bed. My skin was itchy and tight—like it was stretched over my bones. I was exhausted, and had to use way more under-eye concealer than normal to make myself look half-presentable.

Ben had Roxi and Gage with him when he came by to pick me up for school. Roxi took one look at me and gave me a hug. I almost cried.

I was just about to get into the car when I felt my sister's arrival.

"Lark," she said, from behind me.

Gage's eyes went wide as he stared over my shoulder. I knew right then and there that this wasn't going to go well. Wren was manifesting.

I set my bag aside. "You guys should leave," I said.

Ben—who had gotten out of the car—shook his head. "I'm not leaving you."

I think I loved him at that moment, the idiot. I gave him a shaky smile before turning to face my sister.

God, she was scary. I'd seen her angry before, but it had always been directed toward someone else—not me. Her dark red hair stood out all around her head, caught in the static-charged breeze generated by her rage. Her eyes were entirely black, with dark smudges on the surrounding skin. There was darkness around her mouth as well, and her lips were dark gray, her face stark white. She was dressed in what looked to be layers of shadow—moving tendrils of darkness that swirled around her form like gossamer silk. There was nothing even vaguely human about her.

She was terrifying.

"Lark?" came Roxi's voice—high and soft. Scared.

"It's okay, Rox," I said, not taking my eyes off my sister. "Wren, what are you doing?"

She stood a couple of feet away from me—close enough that her energy nipped at me like tiny electric shocks. "Where are Noah's bones?"

Noah's bones? Not hers? What the hell?

Wren moved closer. My hair lifted in the breeze she created—like a blast of summer in the cold morning. "I saw your footprint in the dirt at the crypt. You shouldn't wear Fluevogs when you go looking to burn remains—it gives you away."

That *fucker*.

He'd known I'd go after him. He'd moved his own freaking bones and then made Wren believe it had been me.

"I don't have Noah's remains," I told her.

Wren reared up, stretching a foot above me. "Don't lie to me!"

My fists clenched. "You calm the hell down. I'm not lying."

"You were in the crypt."

"Yes, I was. But his bones were already gone."

Her energy came at me like a hot wind now—crackling like the approach of lightning. "Liar! You were going to burn him!"

"Yes, I was," I shouted. "And if his bones had been there I would have! But they *weren't* there!"

"Where are they?"

"I don't know. Ask your boyfriend. He's the one who possessed Kevin and used him to move his bones."

"What?" Gage asked. Behind me I heard him turn to either Ben or Roxi. "Did she say a ghost possessed Kev?"

Wren shot him a glare that spoke of torment and everlasting cold. "Shut up."

"Hey!" I stepped in front of her. "You don't talk to him like that. You're the one going full-on Amityville right now."

She turned that glare on me. It didn't have the same effect—I was surprisingly unmoved. I stared back—she actually flinched. "You don't want me to be happy. You went behind my back, Lark."

I scowled. "Oh, get off it. Of course I want you to be happy. What I don't want is for you to be involved with a psycho."

"You haven't even given him a chance. He makes me happy."

"He's using you."

"For what?"

I was not going to tell her that I didn't know. "Emily says he's the one that imprisoned her."

She shook her head. "Emily?"

"She came to me again. She told me that Noah imprisoned her as revenge for her dusting his sister's ghost. Wren, he killed himself so he could gain the power to use against her. And now he's going to take revenge not only on her, but on us."

"That's a lie!"

The lightbulb above the door exploded. Roxi and Gage cried out. Only Ben was silent. I had to fight the urge to look behind me to make sure he was okay.

Energy clawed up my spine like a thousand needles. My fingers tingled. "It's not a lie. He's using you."

"You think all ghosts are evil," she sneered at me. Even her teeth were black. "You can't stand that I've met someone nice—someone who actually likes me and I can be with."

"Now you're the one lying," I informed her. My voice didn't sound right in my ears—it was deeper, rougher. "Think about it, Wren. Isn't he a little too good to be true? A little too perfect for you? I bet he always says just the thing you want to hear. I bet he's even been nice about me, as he lists off all the ways I'm a terrible sister who doesn't understand you." I had no idea if he'd said such things or not, but if I were in his place, I would. It was classic divide and conquer.

"You *don't* understand me," she growled. It was a knife to the heart. "You never have. You don't know me half as well as Noah does. He understands me better than you ever will. You think you're better than me just because you're the one lucky enough to be born alive. You've always treated me like I was a bother."

I stared at her. My friends were silent, but I could feel their stares as I stood there, raw and exposed. I trembled with the strain of containing the emotions raging inside me. I choked on them.

"I died for you," I rasped. "I killed myself to prove that you were real. I went to Bell Hill because of you. My entire life you've been the most important person in it. I lost my mother because I refused to turn my back on you. Don't you *ever* tell me that I've treated you as something less! *I* would never let some guy I've only known a few days come between us!"

"Listen to her, Wren," came Ben's voice. "Any guy who truly cares about you would realize how much you and Lark mean to each other."

Oh, God. I knew he meant well, but I wished he hadn't said anything. That he hadn't caught her attention. Wren's head jerked so that she could look at him. I blinked and she lunged.

I whipped around as she tore past me. For a split second I could only watch as she attacked my boyfriend. She bent him over the hood of the car, perched on his chest, her fingers—like talons—going for his eyes. If she scratched him, it would cause a spectral infection like Bent had done.

Something inside me snapped. I think it was my humanity. I was not going to allow Wren to hurt someone, especially not Ben.

I went after her, running and leaping into the air like a cat. It wasn't right. It wasn't normal.

I didn't care.

My fingers fisted in her hair, close to her scalp, and yanked. She flew backward, off Ben, into the side of the house. The siding cracked.

"Fuuuuck," Gage muttered, awe dragging the word out.

"Lark?" That was Ben. I didn't look. He was only going to try to talk me down, and that was not going to happen. Not now.

"You don't touch him," I said to Wren as she stood. "You hear me? You *never* touch him."

"But you can kill Noah?" she demanded.

"Noah's a monster," I told her. I didn't have much proof—just Emily's word and my gut. And a sister who was acting like a ghost who needed putting down. That was proof enough. Noah had done this to her.

When she came at me, I caught a hint of something strange

just before she punched me in the face. Her aura wasn't right.
It swirled with darkness and a strange greenish tint, as though
she'd been poisoned.

The same color I'd noticed haloing Noah at Kevin's party.

My head jerked back from the force of the blow, but I
stood my ground. How, I don't know. I immediately went
into fighting stance and caught her with a kick to the chest.
She held her ground, too.

After that I don't remember much except the giving and
taking of pain. We traded punches and kicks with increas-
ing speed and ferocity, but we were a perfect match for one
another. We could do this forever, and neither one of us was
ever going to win—not while we fought against each other.

But neither of us was about to stop trying.

We'd never fought like this before. All we'd gone through
together, all we'd faced, and we were fighting over a freaking *boy*.

The door to the house flew open, and there was Nan,
dressed in her gym clothes. "What's going on out here?" she
cried.

Wren and I froze at the sound of her voice. We stood in
the driveway, practically toe to toe, both of us battered and
bloody.

Nan came down the steps toward us. She looked pissed.
"Look at the two of you! Fighting like a couple of cats. What's
wrong with you? You're sisters, not enemies!"

She could see both of us perfectly, I realized. And we could
certainly see her.

"You're both grounded," she announced. "I'm not going to
put up with this foolishness. You fight the bad things in this
world, not each other. You talk things out with your hearts
and your heads, not your fists. Am I understood? Now get

in that house and stay there until you can be civil to one another."

"I have school," I said.

Nan's brow arched. "Not today, you don't." Then to Ben and the others: "You three had better be on your way or you'll be late."

Ben—who luckily didn't have a scratch on him—nodded. "Yes, Mrs. Noble." Then he looked at me, and I knew he'd call later.

As the three of them got into the car, Nan turned back to us. Wren actually smirked at her. What the hell had Noah done to my sister? "You can't ground me," she said, her tone dripping mockery.

Oh, the look on our grandmother's face! She was a good and kind woman, and I loved her to death, but at that moment I'd rather go a hundred more rounds with Wren than be the recipient of *that look*.

"Wrenleigh Noble, as a child of my blood I bind you—" Nan put her finger to Wren's forehead and drew a crimson line on it. Blood? "—to this house until I give you release." She drew a line through the other to make a crude cross.

My sister gasped and disappeared. I jumped back. "What the hell?"

"Language," Nan warned, pointing a finger at me.

"Where'd she go?"

"Your room, I expect. I don't know. I'm new to this stuff. I'm surprised it even worked." She stuck the tip of her finger—the one that had drawn the cross—in her mouth.

"When did you learn to bind a ghost?"

"I found it in an old book of my father's. I suppose it had belonged to Emily—she mentioned it in her diary, and I thought it sounded familiar. I assumed a binding incantation might be a good thing to know, given our family history and the fact that I'm living with two teenage girls." She smiled. There was a little blood on her teeth.

I stared at her. "What else did you learn?"

The smile faded. "That Emily felt responsible for a young man's death because of what she'd done to the ghost of his sister, and that the young man vowed revenge upon her and her line."

Two guesses as to who the young man was.

"Now you go in there and settle things with your sister. I don't care what you have to do, but it's obvious she's not right. I'll be home after my yoga class, and if anything's broken, both of you are going to be sorry. Is that clear?"

I nodded. Dumbfounded. Maybe it was weak of me, but I spent so much of my time trying to figure out what to do that it was nice to have it decided for me.

My grandmother kissed me on the forehead. "Good girl. I'll see you in an hour."

As she went to get into her VW, I picked up my bag from the driveway and started for the house.

"Oh, Lark?" Nan called.

I turned. She stood with the driver's door open, smiling at me. "Clean up that glass and put a new bulb in, will you, dear?"

Right. The lightbulb. "You know, technically, that was Wren's fault."

She gave me *the look*.

"Sure, I'll do it now."

She smiled again, got into her car and pulled out of the drive. I got the broom and swept up the glass, and then dumped that in the garbage before getting another bulb. I had to use a ladder to remove what was left of the old one and install the new. My ribs—battered by my sister—protested almost every move I made, even descending the ladder.

Hopefully Wren had cooled down some in the time it took me to complete my task. I had, but Wren had more of a temper than I did.

I was cautious as I entered the house, every sense on alert, waiting for my sister's attack.

None came.

When I opened the door to my room, Wren stood in the middle of the carpet. She wasn't dressed in shadows anymore, but wore a boho dress that was more her style, and her hair hung smoothly around her shoulders. She turned to face me—there were still dark smudges around her eyes and mouth. She held out her bare arms—ivory pale except for gray-and-black veins just beneath the surface. Those veins climbed up her neck and framed her face, as well.

Her gaze was horrified as it met mine. "Lark, what's wrong with me?"

WREN

Lark grabbed my arms, holding them so she could look at the dark spiderwebs that hadn't been there an hour ago.

"Why do these things always happen to you?" she demanded. "Why can't these douche bags come after me for once?"

She wasn't mad at me anymore. Not like she had been. I wasn't mad at her, either. Well, maybe a little, but my fear won out over it for the moment.

"You really didn't take Noah's remains, did you?" I asked.

She shook her head. "He'd be dust if I had."

I believed her.

She lifted her head, and her gaze met mine. "I took yours, though."

I blinked. For a second, I forgot all about the blackness creeping over my form. "You dug up my grave?" My voice rose higher with every word.

"Yup. Hid your casket, too."

"Why?"

She arched a brow. "Uh, because if Noah can possess Kevin and make him hide his bones, he can make Kevin burn yours."

"Noah wouldn't do that."

My arms fell to my sides when she released them. "What did he say when you asked him why he never mentioned that he was related to Kevin? Did he tell you that he was afraid it might change things between you?"

"Yes. Sort of."

Her lips twitched. "Let me guess—he talks about not wanting to come between us, but tells you that I don't understand you, that I'm overprotective, stifling?"

I had that dropping feeling inside. "Maybe."

She didn't gloat like I expected her to. "I'm sorry, Wren."

I nodded. "I'm sorry I picked a fight with you." I frowned. "I was just so angry." In that moment I had hated her and wanted to destroy her. My God, I'd wanted to *kill* my sister. How could I have ever wanted that?

She took one of my hands and tugged me toward her vanity. "I need you to see something." She gestured to the mirror.

I bent down to look at myself.

"Oh, my God," I whispered. My hair was normal, but there was darkness around my eyes and mouth, and black veins like the ones on my arms. "My aura's not right." It had splotches of green in it. Like Noah's aura. "We merged," I whispered.

"I'd never done it before, and it was so incredible. But he left some of himself behind, inside me."

Lark made a face. "Didn't need to know all that, but, okay. Looks like Noah's infected you with a spectral STD. Which is, you know, gross."

I smiled—not that there was much to smile about. "You always do that."

"What?"

"Joke about a serious situation to make it seem less terrible. It's one of my favorite things about you."

She looked surprised. "Thanks."

"I don't like it when we fight."

"I don't either." She paused. A sheepish grin curved her lips. "But we were pretty freaking awesome, weren't we? I mean, I felt like we had at least a few more rounds before we tired each other out."

We laughed, and I felt like I might choke on it. "I don't want to believe Noah did this to me on purpose."

"Hold up. We don't know for sure that this is a bad thing. I mean, maybe it's some kind of protective spell. I mean, maybe Emily was wrong. Maybe Kevin's wrong, too. Hell, even I might be wrong. Maybe Noah's exactly as he presented himself to you."

She didn't believe any of what she'd just said. I knew that just by looking at her, but she wanted it to be true, for me. My sister would do anything for me, and I would do anything for her. Wouldn't I?

At the moment I was getting the oddest urge to attack her again. This anger was unfamiliar. Strange. It wasn't mine. It was Noah's. How could I have been so foolish?

"I don't think this is for my protection, and there's nothing good about it."

Lark put her arms around my shoulders and pulled me into a fierce hug. "No," she murmured. "But I'll fix it, Wrennie. Nobody's going to take you away from me."

I was so close to her I could rip her eye out of its socket before she could blink. I let that realization just hang there for a bit. I could bite her. Punch her. I could do all sorts of violence to her.

I hugged her tighter. "I'm scared," I whispered.

"It's going to be okay."

God, I wanted to rip her throat out. "I don't think it is."

She pulled away and looked at me. "You look like you want to kill me."

"I think I do," I replied. "I don't. But…I do."

Lark didn't look concerned. "Wreck this room, and I'll get Nan to bind you to a sewer drain."

"This isn't a joke, Lark!" Panic gripped me by the throat. "I want to hurt the only person who has ever loved me!"

"So do it."

I gaped at her. "What?"

"You're standing there flapping your lips about how much you want to hurt me, but you haven't even flicked me in the eye. Come on, then. Hurt me."

"I…I can't." Not now. Even though the urge was there, I couldn't bring myself to harm her.

"Then shut up about it. We've got bigger things to worry about. We've got to do something."

"We're grounded, remember?" It came out more snide than I intended. "I'm bound to this place until Nan lets me go."

Lark raised her gaze—to the bloody cross on my forehead, no doubt. "It's a neat trick. I think we need to take a look at some of the family books she's kept." Books. The living kept so much information in books. Lark and I had learned so much on our own when there had been books in this house that could have helped us if we'd only known.

"But first," she continued, "we need to find out what's wrong with you."

"Unless you've become an expert in spectral infections, I don't think you're going to have much luck."

"Not me," she replied. She gestured to the full-length mirror. "Emily."

"You really think we can summon her? That she'll even know what's wrong with me?"

"Hey, she knows we're Melinoe. That puts us ahead of us."

"Melinoe?" I echoed. "She said that?"

"Yeah. I've been meaning to look it up." She turned on the laptop on her desk. "How could I have forgotten? And why do you have that expression on your face?"

"Noah called me that the other day. When I asked what it meant, he told me it was ancient Greek for 'a pretty girl.'"

Lark glanced over her shoulder at me. "Sounds like he was fishing to see if we knew what it was." She turned back to the computer and started typing. "Let's find out."

I drew closer and peered over her shoulder at the screen. "How do we sort what's correct and what's not?"

"We look for anything that seems to describe us." She clicked on a link. "Nope." Then another. And another. And then..

"The daughter of Persephone and Hades—or Zeus, depending on what version you prefer." She scrolled down a bit. "Okay, here we go. 'Melinoe travels between the world of the living and the land of the dead, driving people mad with fear and defending the living from the vengeful dead. She rules over ghosts, hauntings, madness and restless spirits. She is often depicted as half white, half black, but early depictions show her as half white, half red. There are those who say she's not a single creature at all, but twins, one born to the living and one born to the dead, representing Persephone's agreement with Hades to spend part of the year in the Underworld and part of the year on earth.'"

Lark turned her head toward me.

"Well," I said, "that seems to describe us a bit."

My sister looked dumbfounded. "We're not goddesses. No freaking way."

"Of course not," I agreed. "But we're not human, Lark. Not entirely. We're something else." Two halves of the same whole. It was true.

"Greek, apparently." She made a sound that I thought was supposed to be laughter.

I crouched beside her, so that I wasn't bent over her shoulder. "Lark, we're not freaks. We're not some weird accident. We're meant to be. We have a *purpose*. Isn't that wonderful?"

The expression on her face made me wonder if maybe I was the one with domain over madness. "We're mythical!" Her voice was a hoarse squeak. "Like freaking Thor."

"He's very cute." She gave me an exasperated look, so I decided to leave the joke-making to her. "Lark, I know this is a lot to process, but I think you're missing the positive part of this."

"Enlighten me."

"We protect the world from vengeful spirits. According to Emily, Noah's a vengeful spirit. He never told me what *Melinoe* meant because he's afraid of us. If he's afraid of us, that means he sees us as a threat. We can stop him. Why else would he want to set us against each other?"

"We're stronger together than we are apart."

"Exactly. Now I'm going to go over by the window because I really want to eat your face." Oh, yes, I was definitely the crazy one. Strangely enough, I was fine with that realization. It made me suddenly make sense to myself.

"Touch my face, and I'll take you back to Noah myself."

I think she meant it.

chapter eighteen

LARK

The black veins were getting worse. And so was Wren's aggression. Her mood swings I could handle, but I didn't know what to do about the veins.

I went looking for books in the den, but the only one I found was the one that had given Nan the binding spell. It was an old book on *Protection From and For Restless Spirits* by Alexander Murray. A relative of Nan's, I guessed. It had lots of interesting information that I wanted to learn, but nothing that could help Wren at that moment.

She was on the bed, her pale skin completely crisscrossed with black. How did a ghost even have veins? Or was it just a manifestation of the infection? An easy way to make itself known? There was so much I didn't understand about my sister and what she was. So much I didn't understand about myself. I thought maybe the whole Melinoe thing would give us answers, and it did, but it brought more questions with it.

Nan would be home soon. I didn't know if lifting the binding spell would help Wren or not. I didn't know if my sister would try to hurt our grandmother, either. I really didn't know much of anything, except that if Noah McCrae weren't already dead I'd cheerfully kill him.

I sat down in front of my vanity mirror and tapped on the glass. "Hey, Emily? Are you there?"

Nothing.

The spirit board with the image of the red and white twins was in front of me. The last time I'd touched it Wren and I had ended up in the void, but what if I touched it by myself? Two days out from Halloween I probably shouldn't even look at it, but what the hell.

My instinct told me to place my hand on the white-haired twin, which made sense since I was the white-haired twin attempting to contact another white-haired twin. Why hadn't Emily told us what we were before this? How hard would it have been to tell us to research Melinoe?

We weren't really aspects of a goddess, were we? That was a bit much, even for me. But…well, I wasn't going to pretend it wouldn't be awesomely cool. All my life I'd felt like a freak—or at least since I was old enough to be called one— and the idea that there was something bigger to it, something with meaning, was incredible.

Still, I didn't know what would happen when I touched the board. Maybe nothing. I glanced at Wren. She looked to be asleep, but she didn't sleep. I didn't know what was wrong with her, and that was my biggest concern.

I put my hand on the board, directly on top of the white-haired twin. A jolt ran up my arm, like a little shock from a wall plug.

My reflection in the mirror swam, distorting my face, twisting it into something strange and gruesome, before putting it back together as someone else.

Emily.

My ancestor looked disoriented—probably the same way I appeared when she contacted me this way. Had I summoned her to a mirror, or was there one near her wherever she was?

She seemed startled to see me. "Lark. How did you do that?"

"There's something wrong with Wren," I told her. And then, "Are we really Melinoe?" tumbled from my mouth. So much for trying to be calm and focused. "I touched the spirit board, that's how."

Emily's gaze didn't quite meet mine but seemed to be fixed on a point above my left shoulder. I glanced up and saw Wren standing there, looking like a statue carved from black-and-white marble.

"He's with her," Wren said, tonelessly.

I heard a chuckle that sent a shiver down my spine. Noah. He stepped into the mirror, standing at Emily's side. She moved her arm, as though trying to avoid touching him. I didn't blame her.

God, I hated him and that smug smile of his.

"Miss Noble, so nice to see you again. Wren, darling, you look distressed. Come home, dearest, and all will be well." He looked right at me. "Your sister's condition will only worsen the longer she is away from me."

"What did you do to her?" I demanded.

"Why on earth would I confess to you?" His tone dripped sarcasm. "You'd only try to fix her, and that's not in my best interest at all. Give her back to me, and she'll be as good as new. You want to come home, don't you, darling?"

Wren's fingers bit into my shoulder. I tried not to let the pain show. "I don't want anything to do with you," she rasped. The words were true, but his hold over her was stronger than her own will. The moment Nan lifted the spell, Wren would run back to him.

Noah leaned closer, his gaze intent. "Did that clever sister of yours place a bind on you? I'm impressed, Miss Noble. I thought you more ignorant than you obviously are, but not as much as my dear Emily, who has clearly filled your head with nonsense about the Melinoe."

"You were the one who mentioned it first," I told him. "When you tried to find out how much Wren and I knew about it. And Wren's not coming back to you, so you can just get over it. As soon as I find your bones, you're history."

He laughed. It wasn't contagious. "You stupid cow. Haven't you figured out where I had my boy bring my bones?"

Bring. Not put, or hide, but bring. Oh, *hell*. Of course. If I were a powerful old ghost surrounded by dozens of other old, strong ghosts, where would I keep my bones? I'd keep them right freaking next to me, where any human would be stupid to go.

Haven Crest.

That's where his remains were. I don't know how he'd managed to do it, because he still would have had to use Kevin to bring them to the right spot on the property and risk getting caught, but he had managed it. I didn't doubt for a moment that he was telling the truth.

I put my hand over Wren's and pried her fingers open, then I wrapped mine tight around them. It was that or let her rip my arm out of its socket.

"So, what now?" I asked. "You fill me in on your dastardly plan, because you're obviously a genius and I don't stand a chance of defeating you, even if you spell it out?"

"I'm not foolish, young woman. I have no intention of telling you anything."

Wren pulled her hand from mine. "He's going to use the energy from the concert and the fact that it's All Hallows' Eve to fully cross over into this world, where he'll finally take revenge on Emily and Alys by destroying you and me, Nan, Mom, Dad and everyone in that line. And then he'll set the ghosts of Haven Crest free, and once he's harnessed the power of the buildings and the land, and all its dead, he'll make certain that any living person who sets foot on those grounds never leaves."

Noah glared at her. I watched as my sister smiled as smugly as he had just a moment before. She bent down so her face was right beside mine. "You infected me with your corruption to make certain I'd return to you, but you didn't realize just how strong that connection would be? Oh, my dear Noah—who's the ignorant one now?"

Noah's expression turned as hard and cold as stone. His gaze locked with mine. "Return her to me, breather. Or she'll only get worse, until she's nothing more than a mindless wraith."

"You have the power to stop him!" Emily cried. "The two of you together—"

They were gone, and I was left staring at myself and Wren in the mirror. My sister slumped to the floor, great sobs racking her body. I slid from my chair to the carpet beside her, pulling her close as I wrapped my arms around her. She might be a being of pure energy, but she was flesh and bone to me, and her tears soaked the shoulder of my shirt. I didn't need to ask her what was wrong. Any girl who had ever had her heart broken would recognize those sobs.

When she finally quieted, she lifted her head. The sight of all those black veins jarred me again—I'd forgotten about them somehow. Her eyes were red, but that was better than the black I'd seen lately.

"He's right," she said with a sniff. "I have to go back to him."

I shook my head. "No freaking way."

"Lark, if I stay here, I'll only get worse, and I can't help you. If I go back, I can help you stop him."

"No," I insisted. "He'll use you."

She actually smiled. It was sad. "At least now I'll know I'm being used. I can find his remains. I need to face him. I need him to know he didn't break me."

"I'm going to torch his ass," I vowed. My voice trembled with rage. "If it's the last thing I do, I'm going to turn him into a pile of smoldering ash."

Wren's bottom lip trembled, but she nodded. "He'll keep me from the appointment with Special Collections."

"That doesn't matter right—"

She stopped me—put her fingers against my mouth. "It matters more than ever. *You* have to go. You have to be the one to find out about Emily and Alys and how to help them. How to help us. Tell me you'll go." She removed her hand.

Was she nuts? "I don't know how to go to the Shadow Lands."

"Yes, you do. If I've always known how to come here, you know how to go there."

She made it sound so freaking easy. Instinctual. Maybe it was. But it was obvious that she couldn't tell me how to do it, and I would have to do that on my own—and it was going to mean more missed school.

There was a knock on the door. I looked up just as Nan stuck her head into the room. "Can I come— Oh, my dear girls. What's happened?" She might have been in her sixties, but our grandmother was in great shape, and as soon as she saw us, she was right there on her knees beside us, holding us both.

The only person I loved more than her at that moment was Wren.

"Nan, you've got to remove the binding spell," I said. "Wren has to leave, or she'll get worse. And I need you to show me every book, journal and possible ghost-related item that belonged to someone in our family."

Nan nodded. Her expression, which had been full of concern as she looked at Wren, turned to one of steely determination when she turned to me. "We're going to fix this, right? And make whoever is responsible for it sorry they ever crossed my girls?"

I smiled, blinking back tears I couldn't afford—not at that moment. "Yeah," I said, taking one of her hands in mine and one of Wren's. "We're going to make him very, very sorry."

WREN

The moment my grandmother wiped the blood from my forehead and said, "I release you," I felt myself pulled from the warmth of her house to the familiar ghosts of Haven Crest. A few hours ago I loved that building and its inhabitants. Now I despised it, and them.

My only comfort in the face of their sneers and smug smiles at having so thoroughly fooled me was that they didn't have Lark on their side. And they hadn't beaten me, no matter what they might think.

Immediately I began to feel better—stronger. It was being near Noah that did this. Whatever he'd infected me with, it wasn't so bad when I was with him. I wished I could say the same about the pain of his betrayal, but that was so much worse when I looked at him.

"You needn't look at me with such hostility, my love," he told me. "If it's any consolation, I was not as guarded with my own feelings as I ought to have been."

I stared at him. Silent.

He touched my cheek. I forced myself not to jerk away.

"I am rather fond of you," he murmured. "You are so deliciously frightening when you want to be, with a rather delightful mad bent to you."

I smiled bitterly. "I'm the crazy one," I replied.

He arched a brow. "Indeed?" He obviously didn't catch my reference to the Melinoe. Maybe he didn't know as much as he thought he did. That could come in handy.

"So, what's your plan, Noah? You'll use the concert to tap into the spectral energy of Haven Crest and bring yourself fully into this world, and then what? Will you be human? Ghost? Ghoul?"

He looked so proud of himself. "An immortal being of pure power."

"What happens when you've gotten your revenge? Surely it won't take you long to tie up whatever loose ends my sister and I represent. How will you amuse yourself once you've gotten your revenge?"

Surprise blinked in the depths of his bright eyes and then was hidden. "How I amuse myself will no longer be any concern of yours, my dear. Unless, of course, you'd care to spend eternity with me?"

"It's tempting," I replied. "But I doubt it would ever happen. You don't seem to have much of an attention span."

He stiffened but didn't lose that haughty look. "Well, to be fair, you didn't provide much of a challenge."

I laughed, even as the words cut me. I had been entirely too easy for him to take advantage of me. "Of course I didn't! I'm sixteen years old, Noah. And you should be glad of it. Had I any amount of experience with the opposite sex, I wouldn't have been attracted to you at all. It was only because you looked so much like Kevin that I was drawn to you in the first place."

Noah smirked. "Such remarks cannot touch me, little one."

"I'm not trying to insult you—we both know I haven't the necessary appreciation for depravity it would take to descend to your level." Let Mr. Fancy Vocabulary think on that one for a moment. "It's merely the truth. You've seen Kevin. You've *been* Kevin! I'm sure you've noticed the resemblance."

"Well, we *are* related."

"Oh, and it's so easy to tell. It's embarrassing, but there were times when I forgot that you weren't him." I let myself smile then—a little dreamy, faraway look. No man, no matter how young or how old, dead or alive, liked to be told that a woman had been thinking of someone else while she was with him. And Noah had hurt me deeply enough that I wanted to hurt him back.

His eyes turned cold, but that biting smile remained. "Yes, well, I suppose I should be grateful you don't have white hair, or I might have confused you with Emily."

"No," I corrected. "You wouldn't have made that mistake. It's obvious to me now that you're in love with her. Or rather, that you're obsessed with her. Have you always been? Because that must have been very painful for you when she dusted your sister. Oh, I'm sorry—when she sent your sister on to the next stage of her journey."

Suddenly, Noah was right there in front of me—his face just inches from my own. "Don't you *ever* talk about my sister. And the next time you insinuate that I feel anything but hate for Emily Murray, I'll make you sorry."

I grinned. "No, I don't think you will. You could try, but I'll still be right, and you'll still be in denial."

He hit me. Knocked me a few feet across the room. It didn't hurt like it had when Lark had tossed me into the side of the house, but it still smarted. And it gave me such satisfaction it wasn't even funny. I laughed all the same. I'd gotten to him, made him break that gentlemanly act of his.

"What are you laughing at?" he demanded.

"You," I chirped. "My sister hits harder than you."

"You want to be hit harder?" He clenched his fists. "I'll be glad to oblige."

I held my arms out to my sides. "Be my guest."

He scowled. "You actually want me to hit you?"

"You can hit me all you want. It's not like you can beat me to death, is it? You think you can hurt me that way because you used to be alive, but I don't have that reference. You can beat me all you want, if it makes you feel like a man. It won't make me afraid of you."

I'd struck a sore spot—I knew it from the blackness that overtook his eyes. I wasn't afraid of that, either. "Now you're getting interesting," I said.

For a moment I thought he was going to come at me again, but then Miss April stepped between us. "Don't you dare hit her, Noah McCrae. You were raised to never hit a girl."

"She's not a girl," he sneered. "She doesn't know what it is to have lived. She's just a dead thing."

Ouch. "I'm Dead Born," I informed him. "In the hierarchy of our world, that makes me better than you, and I know you understand class. Maybe I don't know what it is to live, but hanging around here, concocting some plan that will let you walk among the living again, tells me that you don't know what it is to be dead. Even if you succeed in your plans, you'll still be dead, Noah, and your sister will still be gone."

"That may be, but your sister will be dead, too."

I shrugged. "That only means we'll be together, so I'm fine with that."

"Death isn't pleasant."

"She's already died once."

He froze. "What?"

Hadn't I told him about this? I was sure I'd mentioned Lark's suicide—but maybe I hadn't mentioned that she'd actually died. That was important, apparently.

"That bothers you," I observed. "Does that change your plans?"

He didn't answer me. He just turned and walked away. He climbed the stairs, but I didn't follow. He wouldn't be foolish enough to keep his bones in his room. I would have seen them by now. He wasn't stupid, so he would hide them someplace safe.

I wondered where Lark had hidden mine.

In movies, ghosts are often portrayed as basement dwellers. People are always afraid of cellars and dark underground tunnels and structures. I have known of ghosts who linger in such places, but subterranean places remind most ghosts of their grave, and they avoid them. We exist in the dark because we're often not given a choice, but we're drawn to the light. That's why it's so unfair that many ghosts have to withdraw inside when the sun rises.

If I were going to hide my own remains, I'd choose one of those dark, underground places where neither ghost nor living liked to go, but not someplace obvious like a morgue, which often drew those curious ghost hunters. But I'd keep them close—where I could check on them, especially if I knew someone wanted to destroy me.

Noah's bones were in this building. Probably in the basement. I just had to find out where exactly, so Lark or someone could burn them down to ash.

"Where are you going?" April asked when I moved.

I turned to her. Was she expecting me to thank her for stepping in between Noah and me? If she was, she'd be waiting a long time.

"Not far," I told her. "Noah saw to that when he infected me with...whatever he infected me with."

"It was only a bit of himself, and a bit of this place."

The place? How had he managed that? "It was poison."

"That's a little melodramatic, don't you think?"

"No." I turned my back on her and left the main hall. She followed me. Noah had probably told all of his little sycophants not to let me out of their sight. It was annoying, but smart.

Instead of going to the basement, I walked all the way down the corridor to what used to be the dining room. I passed two residents who drew back into the wall as though they were afraid I might brush against them and taint them. If I could, I would.

The dining room was at the end of the corridor. It was a big room with large windows on the three outside walls. A lot of the panes were broken, and the rest were dirty. The tiled floor was covered in debris, including leaves and twigs that had blown in through those windows. There was an abandoned bird's nest on the chandelier. The last time I'd been in that room, Noah had made me see it as it used to be— beautiful, clean and whole. Now I saw it like I saw Noah— as it truly was.

It wasn't pretty.

"Noah says that soon this entire building will look like it used to all the time," Miss April informed me, "not just when we remember."

I turned to face her. The morning sun coming through the windows made her look tired and drawn. Not as fresh and pretty as she usually appeared. "How's he going to do that?" I asked.

She didn't respond.

"He hasn't told you, has he? He's filled your heads with all the things he plans to do, but he hasn't told you how. Are you all just going to go along with it?"

Miss April glared at me. "We trust him. He's always looked after us. He'd never hurt any of us."

I snorted. "Yeah, right." I sounded so much like Lark at that moment. "I'm sure Robert would disagree with you."

She grinned at me, showing all her teeth—yellow and a little crooked. "You're sure, are you? Good for you. It must be nice to be so sure." She giggled and pivoted on her heel, leaving me alone.

I didn't bother to wonder what she'd meant, because I really didn't care. I waited for a couple moments after she left, and then I left, as well.

I had a basement to search. I wondered if Noah knew how lucky he was that I couldn't interact with matches.

chapter nineteen

LARK

I tried not to worry about Wren after she left. After she was *taken*.

Nan and I went up to the attic to look for anything that might be useful. I found some old books on the occult and paranormal phenomena, and some old photos, but nothing that screamed at me as a beacon of ass-saving.

I'd been hoping that the answer would just be handed to me. I'd—*we'd*—been lucky with that in the past. I knew what we were now, but I still didn't know much about it, and the internet wasn't always the most trustworthy of sources.

I was going to have to keep that appointment tomorrow in the Shadow Lands, even though I had no idea how to get there. Wren said I'd figure it out. I hoped she was right, because ever since we'd gotten our first whiff of trouble I'd been running into wall after wall. We had a laundry list of things going on, but no idea how it all tied together.

And no idea how to stop any of it, short of burning Noah's bones, which we couldn't find. Maybe Wren would have some luck there.

Without my sister I was lost. Incomplete. I was missing an important piece of myself and only functioning at half power.

So it was time to stop dwelling on all the things I couldn't do and turn to what I could do instead.

I texted my friends and asked them all to come over after school. And I asked Nan if we could order pizza.

"Of course," she replied. "But only if I can help you."

Did Wren and I win the grandmother lottery or what?

I started getting replies a few minutes later. Within half an hour—during which I was at the kitchen table, drinking tea, eating waaay too many cookies as I went through the books and photos Nan and I had found.

One of the books was a family Bible. In itself it wasn't going to give me any information on how to fight Noah, but the family tree at the beginning of it did. It had belonged to my great-grandmother, and it went back several generations—even before Emily and Alys.

I started way back with the first of the family listed, and came forward. Twins popped up a fair bit, but in the line that led directly to me, there was a set of twins every other generation in which one was stillborn.

Including my grandmother's sister.

"Nan," I began. "You had a twin."

She was at the counter, making herself a cup of tea. She went very still for a moment. "Yes."

"But you're not... There's a set every other generation, and in the photos I found they had white hair." Not that there were that many photos of earlier generations, because photography had only started in the Victorian era. But there were descriptions, and tiny paintings that Nan called miniatures.

My grandmother brought her tea to the table and sat down across the butcher-block top from me. "When I was born, my mother said my hair was unnaturally red, and my sister's was white. She was stillborn, but I lived. And as I got older, my hair became lighter, until it was a more natural red."

I stared at her. "So you—"

"The wrong one lived." She took a sip of tea as I sat there, staring at her. "I didn't really figure it out until you girls came to live with me, and I accepted what you are. I believe I was supposed to be the one that died. I don't know why I didn't, and she did. I don't know where it went wrong." Her eyes looked wet. "I should have died, and she should have lived. We should have been here to help you and Wren, but it went wrong, and Emily and Alys weren't able to pass on their knowledge."

"They should have anyway," I retorted a little angrily. "It wasn't your fault. None of this is your fault."

"Oh, I know that, dear." She dabbed at her eyes with her fingers, wiping away all traces of tears. "Thank you for saying it. I know it was all out of my control, but I wish I had known her. I've always felt like I was missing an important part of myself."

"Why didn't you tell me about her before?"

Nan shrugged. "I didn't think it was important, and when I realized what it meant, and what I'd lost…well, I suppose it felt just a little too personal."

I sat there for a moment, feeling like an ass for bringing it up. "I'm sorry."

She smiled, but there was a sadness to it. "Well, it's hard to miss what you never had. Did you find anything of use?"

"No." I closed the Bible and reached for another cookie. "I'm hoping I'll have better luck tomorrow in the Shadow Lands."

Nan dunked her cookie in her tea and shook her head.

"There are times when I wish you weren't so honest with me as you are."

"Would you rather I just tell you I'm going to the library?"

"No. I want to know. Otherwise I can't figure out how to fix it."

Well, at least I knew where I got it. "I'll continue on with being my usual honest and open self."

She shot me a wry look that made me laugh.

After I finished my tea, I did some kickboxing to work off the cookies and all the angry energy knotting up my neck and shoulders. Plus, I had to practice if I was going to kick Noah's ass.

A few minutes after I got out of the shower, Kevin arrived.

"You're early," I said when I came downstairs. He was in the kitchen, eating cookies, talking to Nan.

"I only had two classes today," he explained. "I brought you a present. It's in my trunk."

"Is it a bag of douche-bag bones?"

"Lan-*guage*," Nan sing-songed from where she stood making yet more cookies. I was going to gain fifteen pounds by the time we put Noah down.

"It's his head." My grandmother made a small sound of distress as Kevin took another bite of cookie. "That's what was in the park. I haven't found the rest yet."

I grabbed a cookie off the plate beside him. I had no willpower. "If we only have one piece of him, the head's a good one to have."

"I can't believe how matter-of-fact the two of you are." Nan popped a tray of cookies into the oven. "I'd be scared out of my mind to be carrying around a skull. What if the police stopped you?" She looked at Kevin when she asked this.

He shrugged. "I'd tell them it's a prop for a Halloween party."

Nan gave him a soft smile. "Did you think of that before you came here, or just now?"

Kevin returned the smile. "Before I even took it out of the ground."

She patted his shoulder. "Good boy."

"This conversation is just so wrong." I grabbed a soda from the fridge and tossed it to Kevin before getting one for myself.

"Hey, my parents don't even believe in ghosts." He popped the tab on the can. "They'd think I was nuts if I told them I could communicate with the dead. I'd take a 'wrong' conversation over their 'right' any day."

"Nan is unbelievably cool," I allowed, grinning at my grandmother. "Life would be a lot more difficult if I didn't live here. It *was* a lot more difficult."

A wooden spoon was shaken in my direction. "Your mother never recovered from losing Wren. It's not her fault she's frail."

Kevin and I shared a glance. I rolled my eyes.

"Don't roll your eyes at me, young lady."

Kevin laughed. I stole another cookie. "C'mon, Sixth Sense, you can give me my present and help me set up."

"Set up for what?" he asked as we went outside.

I cast him a sideways glance. "A séance."

He stopped. "Have you forgotten what happened last time we had a séance?"

No, I hadn't. "It will go better this time."

"You can't possibly know that."

I gave him a shove out the door. "Well, you can't possibly know that it won't."

A sharp burst of laughter shot from his mouth. "I can't believe I let you talk me into these things."

I made a face at him. "I don't talk you into anything. You jump right in. You're a freaking ghost magnet just like I am, and you like it."

"Maybe I do, but that still doesn't mean I understand it."

We'd reached his car. He unlocked the trunk and took out a small tied garbage bag. He held it out to me. "Here you go. The head, I believe, of Noah McCrae."

I took it, my fingers wrapping around the knot in the plastic. I wasn't about to let my hands get any closer to it than they had to, just in case I got some sort of weird vibe or a shock or something. It wasn't like I handled a lot of bones. Normally I just doused everything with something flammable and tossed in a match. Easy.

How much would burning his head weaken Noah? It would have to, wouldn't it? It was worth a shot.

I went to the garage and got what I needed. The salt Nan put on snow and ice to melt it in the winter worked just as well as any other. Kevin followed me to the backyard where I built a small mound of paper, wood scraps and a couple pieces of wood in the stone-encircled fire pit. I put the plastic bag on top of the pile, dumped salt and a bit of lighter fluid on it, then struck a match and let it fall.

There was a whoosh of flame as the liquid ignited. The paper and kindling went up next. The bag melted so quickly I barely smelled it. The skull was another story. It was old, so there wasn't any flesh to "barbecue." When I first found out about burning bones, I did a lot of reading on cremation, and it's not the same thing. It can take about two and a half hours for a body to burn when cremated, but when you had bones, and old ones at that, it didn't take as long. Skulls are pretty brittle and can come apart during burning, especially if debris—like the top of an old coffin—falls on it.

In my experience, the bones didn't have to burn for long to send a ghost on its way. I had no idea what this would do to Noah, but I hoped it hurt.

I hoped it hurt a lot.

WREN

I'd just left the cellar when I heard the screams.

Everyone was in the dining room. I had to push my way past those clustered in the door.

It was terrible.

There in the middle of the dirty, dingy floor was the girl who had given me Emily's message. I couldn't even remember her name, and the fact that she was on fire didn't help to jog my memory.

Her screams. Oh, her screams.

"Help her!" I shouted to those gathered. They were all older than I was. Surely they knew what to do?

No one moved. They just stood there, staring in horror as her head was engulfed in flames.

Except for Noah. He didn't look horrified at all. In fact, he looked smug—actually pleased.

"This is because of you!" I hissed at him.

He raised a brow. "Me? It's your sister behind this, my dear. Oh, how I would love to see her face when she discovers that it wasn't my skull she lit up."

Lark would be horrified. Or, at least I hoped she would be. I, on the other hand, could listen to those screams no more.

I shouted in my head, focusing on the little electronic miracle my sister carried around with her at all times. I shouted for her to put out the fire as I threw myself at the burning girl and wrapped my energy around her. I didn't know what

I was doing, but when Lark took fire safety in school years ago they'd said to "Stop, drop and roll," and that's what I did.

Oh, it hurt! The flames—pure spectral energy—seared me. It was like being destroyed layer by tiny layer.

Greenish black smoke rose above me in angry tendrils, just like the smudge on my aura, and those awful veins.

Someone grabbed me, swearing. Their grip was tight and strong. They tried to pull me away from the girl, but the fire was dying, I could feel it.

Then, suddenly, it was gone. The hands pulling at me stopped, and I released the girl.

She looked awful—her hair mostly gone and her face blistered. Her nose had been totally destroyed. Burning her skull hadn't been enough to send her on, only to maim her in a terribly cruel way.

I looked down at my hands. They were pink and tender, but otherwise I was surprisingly unhurt. Underneath the burn I looked fine. Normal.

No black veins.

I turned my head to look at Noah. He'd done this to her on purpose. He had to know she was a friend of Emily's—they'd been here at the same time. And he'd only tried to pull me off her because he knew the fire—the very same spectral cleansing fire that forced us on to the next stage of our journeys—would burn the infection out of me.

I lunged at him, slamming him into the wall. Halloween was so close that he smashed into the plaster, leaving an imprint that his form then dissolved through.

He grabbed my hand and used me to pull himself out. As he did, the black veins reappeared on my arm, ugly and tarlike. The fire might have taken some of his infection from me, but whatever he'd done to me responded to his touch. I'd need more than just a little spectral fire to fix it.

Plaster dust clung to Noah's dark coat and hair. He brushed off his sleeves with a sneer. The ghosts gathered around us were silent—including the girl whose head had been on fire.

"You still haven't learned who is in charge here, have you, Wren?"

"I know the residents of this house deserve a better leader than you."

"Are you interested in the job?" he asked, stepping closer. "Because they'd rather have me."

There were a few murmurs of agreement behind me.

"You allowed that girl to be hurt."

"I allowed a traitor to be punished for her betrayal. So I buried someone else's bones in places for my boy Kevin to recover and hand over to your sister. It's not my fault she's so full of hate for our kind that she immediately sets our remains ablaze."

More murmurs. He had them all brainwashed. He'd had about a century to perfect it. I'd only known them a few days—not long enough to make a difference. The dead could be so stubborn.

"I wish I could see Lark's face right now," he went on, smiling. "She's probably so proud of herself, thinking that she might have caused me pain or slowed me down."

Maybe, but I doubted it. The fire had gone out pretty quickly after I "texted" Lark. She would have felt my pain and panic, as well. I didn't mention any of this, of course. I might have been terribly naive, but I wasn't stupid.

Instead, I said, "She'll only be that much more angry when she finds out the truth. Is that what you want?"

"The angrier she is when she comes here on All Hallows'

Eve, the better it will be. If I didn't need you, I would have destroyed you by now, just so she'd know what it's like to lose the most important person in the world."

"How is doing any of this getting revenge on Emily? She doesn't know me or Lark. Do you really think hurting us will hurt her?"

"It's not about Emily," he replied smoothly. "It's about you and your kind, and putting an end to it entirely. Do you have any idea how difficult it was to convince Alys to kill your grandmother's twin while the two of them were still in the womb? It was very difficult, but it worked out. I thought maybe that would be the end of you, but you're like syphilis— you just keep coming back."

There was a little laughter at this.

I held out my arms and tried to ignore that these people who I'd thought were my friends were the same ones laughing at me now. And I absolutely refused to let him see that I hadn't known Nan was a twin, or that the other was dead— and not Dead Born.

"What about this?" I asked, referring to the black veins. "How does this fit into your plan?"

"You and I are linked now, my dear." He leaned forward, plaster dust falling off him like snow. "I can't tell you how honored I am to have been your first merge." God, he made it sound…dirty.

I met his gaze. "But you weren't. Kevin was."

Hate flickered in his eyes. Good. If I could despise and mock him, then I couldn't love him, and I had been well on my way to feeling that very emotion. The bastard.

Noah straightened. "Regardless. I put some of my energy into you and took some of yours into me. We're connected now. Always. If you're away from me for too long, you'll start to feel sick and aggressive. It won't be long before you start to feel what I feel, want what I want. You see, turning you into my slave will be my final revenge on Emily Murray."

His slave? Now I was the one arching an eyebrow. "You know my sister will destroy me before she lets that happen."

An arrogant smile tilted the corners of his mouth. "She won't live long enough. An old friend of mine is going to be calling on your sister a little later. He'll take care of her."

I actually laughed. "If you think 'taking care' of my sister will be that easy, you're in for a nasty shock."

"If he doesn't get the job done, I know who will."

"Am I supposed to guess who you mean?"

"I would think it's obvious. By the time I've put my plans into motion on All Hallows' Eve, I will have the perfect assassin under my full control. *You.*"

chapter twenty

LARK

The fire pit was soaked and so was I.

I wound the garden hose back into its spool and ran back to where Kevin stood, watching me like he couldn't quite understand what I was doing.

"That wasn't Noah's skull," I told him.

His face fell. It was a terrible, horrified expression that made my throat tight. "He got me to hide other bones, too? So someone else would suffer if we found them?"

"Seems that way," I said, picking up a pair of long-handled tongs used for making s'mores. I tried to keep all emotion from my voice. "The text from Wren said it was the wrong skull and to stop. She also said that what I was looking for was in the basement of the house. Since she sucks at being cryptic, I'm assuming that means Noah's remains are in the cellar of the men's residence at Haven Crest."

He ran a hand through his already effed-up hair. "How the hell are we supposed to get them if he's practically sitting on them?" His brows came together in an anguished frown as he looked at the fire pit. "Why do that to another ghost?"

"To punish them. To mess with me. Now he knows that I'd burn him, and he wants me to know he's smarter than I am. I have to agree with him. I should never have assumed that skull was his just because he used you to dispose of it."

Kevin slumped into a nearby wooden chair as I bent over the charcoal soup that was the fire pit. "I don't remember going to Haven Crest."

"You only remembered the park because he left you there." I reached out with the tongs and snagged the skull by the jaw. "He's a smart bastard."

His gaze was on our charred and gruesome companion. "Did we just commit ghost murder?"

I shook my head. "More like aggravated assault, I think." I carried the skull—in the tongs—to an empty planter and put it inside.

We'd just started for the house when two cars pulled into the driveway—Ben's and Mace's. Ben had Gage and Roxi with him. Mace was alone. It was weird not to have Sarah as part of the group, but I can't say I was too upset that she was gone.

"What's up?" Gage asked as he approached. "Is that a skull in the planter?"

"Yep," I replied. "We thought it was Noah's. It wasn't."

Ben walked up beside me and put his arm around me. "How did you figure that out?"

"Wren just so happened to be with the ghost whose head burst into flames. She sent me a text, but I could feel her panic, too."

"That's a sneaky ghost," Gage remarked, doing what he always did—stating the obvious.

I nodded. "He is, but we're going to figure out how to blitz the douche bag and get my sister back."

"He took Wren?" Roxi looked horrified.

"Again?" asked Gage. "Didn't Bent take her, too?"

I sighed. My sister was primo hostage material for any hostile ghost. "Yeah, he did. Look, she's not stupid. She was lonely. All she wanted was a friend, and he took advantage of that." I didn't have to look at Kevin to know he felt guilty.

"What's his endgame?" Mace asked, hands in his pockets.

"Crossing over, general terror, destroying my family and probably eventual world domination."

"Crossing over?" Gage leaned against the hood of Ben's car. "You mean, like, coming back to life?"

"No. He'll be a ghost that exists on this plane. He'll be seen and heard—felt. And he'll do it with all the anger and insanity a ghost his age has built up."

Mace frowned. "I don't know about the rest of you, but I'm thinking about setting fire to the stage so the concert has to be canceled."

My gaze locked with his. He knew that would make keeping my promise to Joe practically impossible, not to mention the risk he'd be taking. "Not an option," I said. If anyone was going to risk getting arrested, hurt or even killed, it was me, and no one else.

Roxi pulled a mini candy bar from her purse, unwrapped it and shoved it into her mouth. She had a whole bag in there. I held out my hand for one. "We have to stop him, then." She chewed some more and slapped candy into my palm. "We just salt and burn him, right? Once we find him?"

I unwrapped the chocolate. "It's not that simple. Wren thinks his bones are in the basement of the residence Noah stayed in when he was a patient at Haven Crest."

"How did his bones get into the cellar?" This came from Ben as he draped his jacket over my shivering shoulders.

Ohmygoditwassowarm. I shoved the candy into my mouth. My hands were dirty. Grave dust. Gross. But I didn't spit out the bar.

"Me," confessed Kevin, stepping forward. "Noah's my ancestor and also a medium. Apparently that makes it easy for him to possess me. He used me to move his bones."

Mace gave him a hard look. "You're just fucking up all over the place, aren't you?"

I scowled at him. "Hey. It's not his fault. Kevin's in just as much danger as Wren and I are." If Noah decided he needed a body again, Kevin would be the one he came for. "I need Kevin to help deal with any ghosts that come our way, especially with Wren working the crowd at Haven Crest. The two of you can fight later. Now let's get inside."

They all followed after Ben and me, and I tried to ignore the twinge of guilt I felt for chastising Mace.

Inside the house, I ran upstairs to clean up and change while Nan played doting hostess. She seemed to really like my friends—especially the boys, because they ate everything she put in front of them. Seriously, there had been times when I thought Gage hadn't eaten for a week before coming over.

When I came back down in leggings and an oversized sweater, I found Ben at the bottom of the stairs.

"Hey," I said. "What's up?"

He took my head in both of his hands and stared at me for a couple of heartbeats before kissing me. He tasted like cookie. I smiled against his lips.

"Are you okay?" he asked when we finally drew apart. His dark eyes were bright with concern. "Is Wren?"

I nodded. "We've been better. This guy really played her. I want to torch him just for that."

"How can we prepare when we don't know what we're

preparing for? I don't like the idea of you going up against this guy."

He was worried about me. Most of my friends seemed to think I had all the answers. I appreciated their confidence, but knowing that someone cared about me and my well-being was awesome. If anything happened and Wren couldn't be with us, at least I knew Ben had my back.

"I guess we'll just have to prepare based on what we do know, and then multiply it by ten." I took his hand. "Come on, let's get to work. We're running low on time."

Before getting to the séance, the bunch of us gathered around the dining room table—upon which Nan had laid out a plethora of snacks. She seemed surprised when I asked her if she wanted to brainstorm with us.

"I would, yes." She sat down at the other end of the table, so that she and I were foot and head, respectively. A red twin and a white, as it should be.

I had a notebook in front of me—I worked better on paper. Gage liked to put everything on his laptop, but I found it hard to concentrate and type at the same time.

I filled everyone in on Noah's backstory—about his sister and Emily and how he'd sworn revenge. I told them about him setting up Alys so she'd get sent to the void for killing her own kind. Then I told them about how he'd infected Wren with part of his energy so she would suffer if she wasn't with him.

"Bastard," Kevin muttered. I gave him what I hoped was a sympathetic smile.

"Okay, so we know he's out for revenge," Ben began, "but if I had been a ghost for a century or so, waiting to get my revenge on someone, why wait until this Halloween? What's so special about this one? I mean, wouldn't you and Wren have been easier to get rid of when you were kids?"

That was a good question. I mean, aside from the months spent in Bell Hill, and the little time I'd spent in Massachusetts with my parents after that, I'd lived the entirety of my life in New Devon. I'd been on Haven Crest property before; so had Wren. So why had he waited until now?

"Maybe he wanted to make sure you were old enough to know what he was doing?" Mace suggested. "Make sure you suffered?"

"Maybe. It's not the anniversary of his sister's death," I said, consulting the notes I'd made earlier. "I don't see anything that makes this year special to him."

"Maybe it's not him," Nan suggested. "Maybe this year is special because it's the year you and your sister turned sixteen."

We all looked at her. "So?" I asked.

Nan smiled that smile that said she didn't know how I'd managed to survive this long in the world. "Sixteen has historically been the 'coming of age' year for many cultures. If you add one and six, you get seven, which has historically been a number of power in religious and mythical texts. In some versions of the Persephone-and-Hades story, it was seven pomegranate seeds that Persephone ate, sealing her fate to spend half the year as the underworld's queen."

I stared at her. Persephone and Hades—parents to the Melinoe. Nan had been doing her research, which made me feel stupid and totally out of my depth. I should have already known what she'd just said. I should have been better prepared for this, but Noah had made sure no one had been there to prepare Wren and me.

"Sounds good to me," Gage announced, giving Nan a grin.

"Yeah," I agreed. I hesitated. "There's something I have to

tell you guys. There's lore that suggests that Wren and I are descendants of Persephone and Hades."

One by one, each of their heads turned toward me. One by one, they looked at me in slack-jawed surprise.

"There's a story that they had a daughter that was split into twins—one had ties to the dead, the other to the living. It sounds crazy, I know, but..." What else could I say that wouldn't make me sound insane?

"From what we can tell, there have been twins like Lark and Wren in every other generation of my family line," Nan told them. "I was supposed to have been like Wren, but my twin died, breaking the cycle. I believe the four of you have spent enough time with my extraordinary granddaughters to see how special they are for yourselves."

Gage stared at me in wide-eyed wonder. "You're like Wonder Woman or something."

The rest of them laughed, which made me feel better. Ben still stared at me. I couldn't quite figure out the expression on his face. Was it amazement? Fear? No. I think it might have been respect. Maybe a little awe. Was he okay with this? Or was this the moment when he finally decided I was just too much of a freak?

"We know we can't stop the show, so how do we protect people?" It was Roxi who brought us all back to the problem at hand. "It's going to be a big crowd."

I turned to Mace. "Your dad has guys working the gate and security, right?"

"Yeah." He rested his forearms on the table and leaned forward. "Olgilvie's going to be there and a few other guys, along with outside security."

"I'm surprised Olgilvie would want to work it," Roxi remarked. "Wasn't he a patient?"

"Yes, but it wasn't anything major," I said. "Otherwise he probably wouldn't be allowed to be a cop." Still, he was a murderer, according to Joe. And a rapist.

I turned my attention back to Mace. "Do you know if they plan to use hand stamps?"

"Yeah, they do. Dad asked me to get some, after making me promise not to tell people so they could sneak in." He made a face. "Like I'd buy my own ticket but sneak someone else in."

"You haven't gotten the stamps yet, then?"

"No. I was going to get them tonight—less chance of someone figuring out which ones I got and getting their own." Mace popped a pretzel into his mouth. "Why?"

"You need to get stamps that have the Seal of Solomon on them."

His eyes crinkled at the corners. It was the same expression he made when he fought the urge to be sarcastic. "And where, pray tell, would I get stamps with the Seal of freaking Solomon on them?"

"I know!" Nan exclaimed. She got up from the table and rushed off into the living room. A few moments later she returned with her laptop, which she set on the table and began clicking away on the keys.

"Found some." She turned the laptop around so we could see it. There, at the bargain price of $4.99 with free shipping, was a wood-backed stamp depicting the Star of Solomon.

"We can have them by tomorrow if I buy them in the next five minutes."

I looked at Mace. He shrugged. "Sure. Can you get two, Mrs. Noble? Please?"

Nan smiled at him. "Mrs. Noble was my mother-in-law, and I couldn't stand her. Call me Charlotte. And, yes, I can get two."

"What does the seal do?" Gage asked.

"It's protection against evil ghosts or spirits," Kevin responded before I could. I didn't mind, since I would have said the same thing almost word for word.

"If the seal is stamped onto everyone who goes into the show, it will give some protection against whatever Noah has planned. At least in theory."

Gage smiled at me. He had really white teeth that looked even whiter next to his tanned skin. He and Roxi both looked like walking toothpaste commercials. "Your theories haven't steered us wrong yet."

I smiled back. It was either that or plant a big wet one on him for saying exactly what I needed to hear.

"The stamps are a good idea," Ben said. He squeezed my hand, and I knew he meant it. For a moment I believed it would all work out. But then I thought of Wren and those inky veins.

"Rox, can you still sneak some stuff onto the property with your mom?" I asked.

"Yup. Just give me what I need to take."

"Great. I have a bag with salt and iron already packed. I need all of you to make sure you're stamped Halloween night. Make sure you've got as much iron as possible, too. If Wren was right about Noah's bones, I may be able to sneak into the building during the concert and grab them, or torch them on-site."

Ben lifted his brows. "Not alone."

"Thank you, Ben," Nan said. "My granddaughter seems to think she's invincible."

I blushed and rolled my eyes. "Um, hello? I won't be alone, I'll have Wren."

"You said Noah made her sick," Ben reminded me. "It wouldn't hurt to have a backup."

Did he ever get tired of being right? I mean, I liked it, but it was infuriating at the same time. Still, I couldn't really be upset by it because he was right, and I'd be stupid to run in alone.

Roxi took a sip of her soda. "We should pick a place to meet so we can all go in together and get the gear."

"Someplace easy to find each other," Mace added. "Maybe meet outside the gate?"

We all agreed.

"Oh, there's one more thing," I said. When each head turned toward me, I took a deep breath. "If things go bad, I need to know you guys will protect yourselves and get out of there."

"We're not going to leave you," Ben insisted. I loved that he believed everyone else would share the sentiment.

"Yes, you are," I told him, and I meant it. "If it's that dangerous, I can't have you guys there. I can't worry about you and Wren and take on Noah. So before we go any further, I want you all to promise. Now."

They traded glances, but when they turned their attention back to me, they each made the promise. I just had to hope they kept it.

"Okay, then," I said. "Let's call up a ghost."

"Who is it?" Roxi asked.

I smiled. "Maureen McCrae. Noah's sister."

We took the snacks off the table and put them on the buffet against the wall. I ran up to my room and grabbed the spirit board to use as a focus. I didn't know for sure that it would work, or that it wouldn't whisk all of us into the void, but I had a feeling, and I'd come to trust them.

I also had a feeling that I could probably summon Maureen on my own, but I wasn't ready to test that theory. To be honest, it freaked me out a little. More importantly, I wanted my friends with me to hear what she had to say, because my first priority—after getting Wren back—was to protect the people I cared about. Once I knew they were safe, then I'd start taking risks.

"Ohhh," Roxi cooed when I set the board in the center of the table. "That's pretty."

"Is that supposed to be you and Wren?" Gage asked. "It looks way old."

"Spirit boards came about in the latter 1800s," Nan told him. "Spiritualism was popular back then. This board was made for my grandmother Emily and her twin, Alys."

Ben smiled at Nan. "My grandmother says Lark feels like powerful ancient energy. I guess she was right." He winked at me. I smiled.

"Okay, then." I sat down at the table once more. "Let's get started. I need you all to set your fingers on the edge of the board so that your thumbs touch, and your pinkies touch those of the person next to you." I didn't really know if this was absolutely necessary, but contact amplified energy, and ghosts were all about that.

I sat down in my chair and put my fingers on the board. The second my left pinky touched Ben's, closing the circuit, a tingle ran up my spine. Hello, spirit world.

I took a deep breath and slowly let it out through my mouth. Centering, it was called. I called it "okay, let's do this."

"Close your eyes," I instructed. "Clear your minds as much as possible. Let go of negative thoughts—and I mean it, because they will seriously mess this up." I heard a chuckle—I think it was Gage.

Two more breaths. "There's a light in the darkness. Just a tiny speck of light. Concentrate on that." Another two breaths. Behind the darkness of my eyelids there was a light, and I recognized it as Wren's. That poisonous green flickered within it, but she was still her—for now.

"Maureen McCrae," I said, opening myself up to all those tiny lights in the dark, "we summon you. We mean you no harm. Come to us." A second light appeared, growing closer, brighter. It hadn't worked like this when we'd summoned Bent, but then, he'd been hostile, and we hadn't had the spirit board.

A warm breeze lifted my hair. I didn't know where it came from, but it felt nice. "Please," I whispered.

Slowly, my head tilted back. Invisible fingers combed through my hair, pulling it free of the messy bun I'd twisted it into. I could hear music—guitar, heavy and melodic. A guy was singing in a rough and raspy voice, and all around me people screamed in unrestrained joy. The light was so bright now, it took up my entire lid. Someone jostled me.

I opened my eyes.

What the hell?

I wasn't in the dining room. I wasn't even in the house. I was in a theater, or an auditorium. I was standing in a crowd so tight I could barely breathe. There was a barricade in front of me; the people behind me pushed me into it as they fought to get closer to the stage. Hands reached out around me, above me—like leafless branches straining for the sun.

And there, on the stage above me, haloed by the glaring stage lights, was the most incredible thing I'd ever seen. He was tall and lean, wearing torn jeans and an old Led Zeppelin T-shirt. His dark hair hung over his shoulders, and he had a tattoo of angel wings on his biceps. His face shone with sweat, but he was smiling, and when he growled into the microphone—something about being young and naked in the backseat of her daddy's car—I felt the energy of the crowd ripple through me. It picked me up like a push from a giant hand, carrying me over the barricade, right up to the stage itself, until I stood directly in front of him.

Joe Hard looked at me, and his eyes went wide. "J.B.? What are you doing here?"

"I don't know," I replied. "I summoned someone else."

"Me," came a voice from behind me. I turned. Standing there was a young woman with pale skin, dark hair and familiar blue eyes. She was beautiful.

"Maureen."

She nodded and looked past me to Joe. "I'm sorry to have pulled you into this, but you were the closest spirit I could find to this girl that wouldn't alert my brother. I needed someone to hide behind, you see."

"Interference," I murmured.

"Exactly," she said, smile fading. "Noah knows my energy. He has some of it in him, and I have his. He'd know if I came here without the help of someone else."

"How can he have your energy if you moved on before he died?"

Now she just looked sad. "He summoned me. Merged with me." She looked away. "His love for me wasn't...normal."

I did not want to know. I held out my hand to her. Her fingers were cold. When she pointed at Joe, I held out my hand to him, as well.

He took it. And the world dropped out from beneath us so fast and hard my head swam. I opened my eyes and found myself standing near the table, holding hands with both Joe and Maureen. My friends stared at us.

"Oh, my God," Roxi whispered. She could see them, of course. Kevin and Maureen couldn't seem to take their eyes off each other. The resemblance was obvious.

Then Gage did something that made me blink. He reached out and poked Joe in the thigh.

"Touching's gonna cost extra, Emilio," Joe informed him with a grin.

"He's solid," Gage whispered, eyes like saucers. Then to Joe, "Dude, you're real. Who's Emilio?"

"Estevez," I answered. "He was popular in the '80s."

"He's not anymore?" Joe looked genuinely upset. "Damn, he was Billy the Kid, man. Why are you looking so freaked out, J.B.?"

My mouth opened. Words, that's what I wanted. Right, words. I looked at him, then Maureen. "How are you corporeal?"

He shrugged. "It is pretty close to All Hallows' Eve. Things get pretty funky around then—and around May Day."

"But I've never summoned anyone who was even remotely tangible before."

He smiled at me—a nice smile. "You didn't summon me, sweetness. You came into the Shadow Lands and brought me back with you. Her, too." He slapped his hand on his denim-clad thighs. "Feels weird to be in the world again."

I had gone into the Shadow Lands and brought him back. Okay, I could handle that. Wren had done it before with books and other small objects.

I'd done it with a freaking *person*. Two of them. I'd summoned Maureen from the Beyond into the Shadow Lands, and then brought her here.

Things were spiraling out of control faster than I could keep track. But, okay. It was nothing to panic over. It wasn't bad.

Holy shit. I took a deep breath. My knees buckled, but Joe and Maureen held me up. "If you let go, we'll disappear," Maureen informed me. "You are what anchors us to this place and this moment."

"Okay." I sucked in a breath. "Okay. I can do this."

"Does this have to do with the concert on Halloween?" Joe asked.

I nodded. "The band is going to try to raise you."

"They won't be the first to try."

"But they'll be the first on Halloween in a place already teeming with spiritual energy under the control of a nut job." I glanced at Maureen. "Do you know what your brother's planning?"

She shook her head. "I don't want to know. He was the reason I was vengeful in the first place. When Emily released me from this world, I left him behind me. I found peace for the first time in years."

I did not want to know what Noah had done to her.

I turned back to Joe. "If I help bring you into this world, will you help us fight Noah?"

He blinked. "Will you still help me get justice for Laura?"

I nodded. "I'm on it."

"Then, yes, I'll fight him."

Relief flooded my veins. "Oh, thank God." I turned to Maureen. "Will you?"

She looked horrified. "No! I won't face him. You can't make me."

"No," I agreed, "I can't. Don't you want to make him pay?"

"No." She shook her head. "I'm beyond that. I will tell you whatever you want to know about my brother. I will give you every weakness he has, but I won't confront him. He is evil incarnate, and I will not subject myself to that again, not after finally getting away."

Pressuring her or trying to force her wouldn't help. It would only make me feel bad, and make me like her brother in her eyes.

"Okay," I said. "Tell me how to fight him."

She stared at me. "You don't. You can't fight him. He's too strong."

"I don't believe that." I *couldn't*. "There has to be something."

"He's afraid of the dark," she said. "At least, he was in life."

Not terribly helpful.

"He's vain, and a bully."

Again, things I already knew. I had to try really hard not to be annoyed at her. She was as much Noah's victim as Wren was—even more so.

Maureen turned to Kevin. "He's possessed you. I can feel it."

Kevin nodded, a bitter expression on his face.

Maureen tugged on my hand, drawing me and Joe closer to Kevin. She reached out and wrapped her fingers around his. A warm rush of energy ran through me as the four of us connected.

"That was cool," Joe remarked. "Kind of like the first time I stepped out onstage."

Kevin looked stunned. "What did you just do?"

Maureen smiled. "I unlocked those things he would have you keep hidden. All the secrets he thought buried inside you are now yours to remember. I gave you some of my own memories, as well. Use them as you see fit." She turned to me, her face pale. "I can't stay here any longer. Please, release me."

I did. Hanging on to her would have felt cruel. She disappeared the moment we broke contact. Joe was still there.

Kevin rose to his feet. "I have to go. I think I know where there is something that might help us."

Joe spoke, as well. "You'd better let me go, too, J.B. Can't have you weakening yourself."

I felt fine. "I suppose it would be dangerous to let you walk around all corporeal. Women might start throwing their underwear at you," I joked. But then it occurred to me—wasn't this what Noah had planned? To make it so he was tangible, but with all the abilities of the dead? He would need a lot of power to do that.

I was going to have to make sure I was well protected that night, because I was starting to think that I was like a big ole battery for ghosts. If he had me, Wren and Emily to draw power from, there was no telling what he might be capable of.

No one would be able to stop him.

chapter twenty-one

WREN

I thought I was stronger than this.

I don't think returning to Haven Crest was the right thing to do. Noah said I would feel better, that the infection wouldn't be so bad if I returned to him. And now I can't leave.

I should have known he lied. He lies about everything.

I ache all over. I want to run wild. I want to feel eyeballs pop free under my thumbs. I want to feel that rush I felt when we scared away those college students.

I need that fear.

I don't know what he did to me.

But I want more.

LARK

The next day was Wednesday—the day before Halloween. I went to school for the morning—not because Nan made me, but because I wanted to talk to One-Shade-of-Gray again.

He found me in the bathroom closest to my locker between first and second class.

"Kinda pervy, don't you think?" I said when he drifted through the wall.

He looked around—all of the stall doors were open. "You're alone."

That was beside the point. I shrugged. "You were right, there is something big happening tomorrow night."

"I told you!" He looked strangely excited. "All the campus ghosts are ready to join you. Larry in the cafeteria also haunts the hospital. He says there are some there who want to join in as well, especially when they found out you were involved. You got rid of a bully for them last month?"

Bent. He'd managed to get to the hospital because of the infection he'd left in Gage, who we ended up taking to the emergency room. What he'd done to Gage and the others wasn't like what Noah had done to Wren. Theirs had looked like angry wounds. Other than the veins, my sister didn't have a mark on her.

That I knew of.

I hadn't heard from her since she sent me the text. I kept hoping she'd get in touch again. I reached out for her before going to bed last night, but all I'd gotten was a head rush, and I'd had to sit down for a minute until the world stopped spinning. Maybe I'd overdone it with the séance earlier.

Or maybe Wren was all kinds of messed up.

She wasn't gone, though. She was still here, still close and we were still connected. Until that changed, I could be concerned about her, but I couldn't afford to panic. I concentrated on Noah, and all my fear, anger and frustration went into that little box in my mind with his name on it. Whatever he had planned for us wouldn't happen until tomorrow, so I still had time.

"I don't know what is going to happen," I told One-Shade. "But we believe a ghost named Noah McCrae is going to try to use the combined energy of the concert and Haven Crest to cross over. Permanently."

He actually shuddered. "That would upset the balance. There'd be chaos." His gaze locked with mine. "You've seen what happens when the rules are broken—bad things happen."

I didn't admit my ignorance by saying, "Rules? What rules? There are rules?" I just nodded. "I appreciate your help. I really do."

He smiled. Then two girls walked in, chattering away to each other as though they were in their own private bubble, and One-Shade fled through the same wall he'd used to enter.

"Did you hear that Sarah and Mace broke up?" one of the girls—Beth was her name, I think—asked the other, whose name I didn't remember.

"Ohmigod, *yes.* Oh, the things I would do to him if I got the chance!"

My eyebrows crept up my forehead.

"What are you looking at, *freak*?" Beth demanded.

It took a second for me to realize she was talking to me, because I was looking at the older man who had followed them into the bathroom. He stood behind the other girl— Lucy, that was her name—with his hand on her shoulder. I watched as that hand crept lower over her chest, settling over her breast. She shuddered. I didn't blame her.

The man glanced up—right at me. He didn't move his hand. In fact, he brought his other one to the party as well, smirking at me the whole time.

"Hey." Beth snapped her fingers in my face. "I said what are you looking at?"

I pushed her aside. I was bigger than her, and I was stronger than most girls my age. She staggered into one of the stalls, books falling to the floor.

I didn't apologize; I was too intent on Lucy and the man molesting her. "Who is he?" I demanded.

She actually looked frightened of me, which was good, because if she'd called me a freak as well, I probably would have knocked her out just so I could deal with her abuser.

"The old man that likes to touch you in ways he shouldn't."

Her face went white. "I don't know what—"

Scowling, I looked her right in the eye. "Brown hair going gray. Blue eyes just like yours. Smarmy smile. Likes sweater vests. He's standing right behind you. He's the reason you feel cold, why sometimes you feel like you're being touched when there's no one there, and I'm willing to bet you dream about him and what he used to do to you. A lot. You thought it would stop when he died."

A tear rolled down her cheek. "My uncle Clark," she whispered. "Oh, my God, do you actually see him?"

"Blue shirt, gray sweater vest—argyle. Faded jeans and Top-Siders. Sound about right?"

She started crying harder. Uncle Clark removed his hands. He didn't look so confident right then. And seeing her upset made him shrink back.

Beth—who had come out of the stall—put her arms around her crying friend. She looked at me with an expression that was half pissed off, half respectful. "It's true what they say about you?"

"Most of it," I replied. I pulled an iron ring off one of my fingers. It was just an old nail a guy named Chuck had ham-

mered around a mandrel, but it was effective. I also pulled a
Sharpie from my bag. "Come here," I said.

Beth pulled Lucy toward me. Uncle Clark stayed back.

I gave Lucy the ring. "Put this on. Now give me your other
arm." She was still crying, but she did as I asked.

I pushed the sleeve of her sweater up, and then, with the
marker, I drew a Seal of Solomon—it was easier than the
Korean symbols Ben's grandmother had shown me, and required less need for precision—on the inside of her forearm.
"Redraw this if it fades or comes off in the shower. It will
protect you. What's his last name?"

"Williams," she replied, dabbing at her eyes. Her mascara
was everywhere.

I turned my attention to the ghost in the door. "Is he buried in the New Devon cemetery?"

She nodded. Beth gave her a wad of toilet paper to wipe
her face.

I smiled at the ghost. "Touch her again and I'll dig you up,
salt you and burn you. That's if I'm in a good mood. If I'm
not, I'm going to take it out on you until I'm happy again.
Sound fair?"

He nodded, but he didn't move.

"If he comes to you again, you tell me, okay? I'll end it
once and for all."

Beth stared at me as Lucy wiped at her face. Slowly, she
drew her friend toward one of the stalls.

I put the marker back in my bag before heading toward the
door. I needed to get some of this aggression out. I stopped
long enough to kick Clark Williams hard in the nuts, and
then drove my knee into his face while he was doubled over.

If only every day could be freaking Halloween.

I walked out into the empty corridor—class had already

started. I went to my locker and grabbed my coat. Then I called Nan on my cell and asked her to pick me up.

"Are you all right?" she asked.

"I'm fine," I told her, as I walked toward the stairwell. "I've just had enough of ghosts for the morning. I don't think this was a good idea."

"I'll be right there."

"Thanks." I slipped my phone into my purse and slipped into my coat.

I was on the bottom step when the ghost hanging in the stairwell moaned. "I'm so alone," he said in a quivering tone.

I glared at him. "Oh, fuck off." And just to be a bitch, I grabbed him by the legs, pulled him toward me as far as he would reach and then pushed him away, so that he swung back and forth across the stairs like a man-sized piñata.

He was just lucky I didn't have a stick.

Really, sometimes ghosts were *such* douche bags.

At home I tried to find out as much about Noah as I could online and in his Haven Crest file. I'd already been through most of it. I gave up at 12:45 p.m. I hadn't really found anything useful, and I'd already figured that his sister was his big weakness. So I pushed away from my desk and lay down on my bed.

Okay. Time to go to the Shadow Lands. Both times I'd done it lately had been accidents, and I had no idea how to replicate the procedure.

Just like Wren had no form here—except to me—I had no form in her world, so it was like astral projection. However, since I could interact with ghosts in this realm, I could in the Shadow Lands, as well—grabbing Joe had been proof of that.

Had all those people at his concert been ghosts? I didn't

even want to think about it, or how pissed off they must have been when I'd kidnapped the headliner.

I closed my eyes and thought about where I wanted to go. I thought about Wren, but I didn't reach for her. Instead, I tentatively peered outside of myself for something that *felt* like her. She had once told me that she didn't know how she'd first found me when we were babies, she just had. And now it was as natural to her as breathing was to me.

In my head it felt as though I were drifting through darkness, a pleasant breeze moving through my hair.

Only it wasn't in my head. I really was moving through darkness. Oh, crap. What did I do now? I teetered on the verge of panic—but it wasn't enough to send me flying back to my body.

And then it wasn't dark anymore, and I was standing inside a little house. It was pristine in its neatness, decorated with bright colors, throw cushions and lots of beads. I smiled. This place screamed of my boho, hippie-wannabe sister.

In dreams, it was said that a house represented the psyche of the dreamer. This place had been constructed by Wren, and it was an extension of her—a reflection.

The house was only a couple of rooms. It wasn't like she needed to cook, sleep or use the bathroom, so there was the main room and a smaller room off it decorated in a similar style. This room had photographs of our parents, a baby rattle and a doll I recognized from when I was very young. Had Wren brought these things here? Or were they replicas she'd created?

On top of an old dresser was a small lacquered box—the kind for keepsakes and mementos. It wasn't any of my business what Wren kept in it, but I was curious. I'd never gotten a peek into her life before, not like she had into mine. She knew every detail of my life practically, except for when I was alone with Ben. And that was good, because her hanging around when we were making out would be just plain weird.

I gave in to my interest and opened the lid. I looked inside...

I shut the box and left the room.

That would teach me to be nosy. Oh, my freaking balls! Eyeballs, to be exact. Like, a dozen of them, and none of them a pair that I could tell.

Since my sister had never maimed or killed a living being, I could only assume the eyes came from ghosts, who were technically already dead. Still, it freaked me out. Of the two of us, Wren was definitely the crazy side of the Melinoe equation. Which left me to be the scary one, a job I wasn't going to excel at if I got squeamish at the sight of eyeballs.

But I'd had that vision when we'd gone up against Bent, of Wren clutching a bouquet of eyeballs like they were wildflowers. Now I couldn't help but wonder if it had been a warning of some kind, especially since in the vision the eyes she'd held had belonged to our friends.

No. Wren would never hurt them. I had to believe that.

I left the little house as fast as my feet would take me and ended up on a quiet street that reminded me of a soundstage, or a movie backdrop. It looked perfect—too perfect. And when I rounded the corner I found myself on the same street I'd visited when I'd jumped between worlds outside of the Goodwill. God, that seemed so long ago now. That same woman was in the window. This time I waved at her.

She yanked the curtains shut.

So much for manners. Okay, then. I'd better get to the library. I didn't know where that was, but my feet seemed to have a direction in mind, so I followed them until they took me to a large columned building that practically screamed *Library!*

I climbed the long flight of shallow steps to the huge door and pushed. It swung open without even a hint of a creak, inviting me into a building that spread out so far from the center desk and so high, that it couldn't possibly fit into the dimensions of what I'd seen as I'd climbed the steps. This was trippy. *Dr. Who* trippy.

I walked up to the front desk. A woman with a 1950s hairdo and pencil skirt looked up at me through cat-eye glasses. She had the naughty librarian thing down to a science. Her very red lips fell open at the sight of me.

"Oh, my goodness," she said—in a tone so breathless I almost rolled my eyes. Was everything and everyone here a bizarre parody of the living world? "You're not supposed to be here."

"Yeah, sorry about that. My sister couldn't make her one o'clock appointment with Special Collections, so I came instead. My name's Lark Noble."

"I know *who* you are."

When she just kept staring at me, I leaned against the wooden countertop. "Are you going to tell me where Special Collections is, or do you want to talk fashion instead? Or, would you prefer that I just toddle off and find it on my own?"

"No!" She straightened her skirt. "I'll escort you."

"Awesome." I gave her my most sincerely fake smile. "Thanks."

As she came out from the behind the counter—and she definitely had the wiggle to go with that wiggle skirt—I said, "You must not get many breathers in here."

Her lips pursed. "That's such a vulgar term."

"But it's what you call us."

"I prefer 'non-dead' or 'death-challenged.'"

I laughed out loud. This time her whole face pinched up. She hadn't been joking.

"Sorry," I said, and I was sincere this time.

"The most common term we use is simply 'the living.' It seems to work fairly well."

I couldn't argue with that.

She led me up a flight of stairs that curved and wound upward in a wide, wooden spiral. The runner was a rich blood-red and didn't have a speck of dirt on it, or a fray. In fact, everything in this place was absolutely perfect. I bet they didn't even have dust.

No wonder most ghosts chose to either move on or remain in the human realm. This place would be utterly boring. A nice place to visit, but you wouldn't want to spend your death here.

Finally, we reached the top, and I didn't have to be distracted by the sway of her butt in front of me. There, on the opposite side of the hall, was a large double door with Special Collections above it on a large plaque.

"Here you are," the librarian said, unlocking the door and pulling it open.

"Thanks," I said, stepping up to the threshold. "Any rules I should know about?"

She looked at me as though I were stupid. "No talking. And don't blame me if the books don't cooperate."

Riiiight. I opened my mouth to make one of my usual witty retorts, but she was gone, and the door smacked me in the ass as it swung shut, knocking me into the room, which was as big as the entire library in New Devon. How was I supposed to find the book I needed?

I walked up to one of the long tables that had chairs in

front of them. It was the only table that had books on its surface. *The Melinoe*, one of them had in gold leaf on its front.

Creepy.

I pulled out a chair and sat down. The book was huge. I
opened it to the first page—it was blank.

"What the hell?"

Somewhere in the vast recesses of the room, someone
shushed me. I looked up. Really?

I turned back to the book. Black lettering began to appear
on the page changing from some language I didn't recognize
to English. Amazing.

HELLO, LARK NOBLE. PERMISSION GRANTED.

What? Did this book actually decide who was allowed to
read it?

This was the most awesome library ever.

I started reading. The book began with the story of how the
Melinoe came to be. Apparently, Persephone became pregnant
by Hades after she ate the pomegranate seeds that sentenced
her to spend half the year in the underworld. Coincidentally—
not really—the half of the year she spent in the underworld
began pretty much at All Hallows' Eve and ended a few days
into May.

According to the text, the child was born of both worlds
and spent equal time in both with her mother. She became
a goddess of the dead and the dying, a protector of the living and champion of ghosts who punished restless spirits and
helped the lost. She was terrifying and compassionate, rational and mad.

Hades, who hated losing both his wife and daughter for
half the year to his mother-in-law Demeter, split Melinoe into
two aspects—one living and one dead, so that he could have
her with him the whole year. Demeter, who had warred with

Hades for years over his abduction of her daughter, was placated by having the living version of her granddaughter with her year-round, and thus Melinoe continued on—two halves of one whole—until she grew weary of the separation. On the night that marked her mother's return to the underworld, Melinoe found a mortal woman who desperately wanted a child of her own. Melinoe told the woman she could give her twins, but that in return, she would have to lose one to the underworld, and that these children would be special and favored by Hades and Demeter, and that this favor would bring great responsibility with it. The woman agreed, and the first of the twins, called Melinoe for their creator, was born nine months later. One of them was stillborn.

As far as stories went, it wasn't bad. I'd read worse. The myth, or legend, only took up maybe ten to fifteen pages in the book. The rest was a history of the Melinoe twins, with biographies of each set. I skimmed through most of them on my way to the chapter about Emily and Alys. I didn't have time to read them. In fact, I didn't know how much time I had at all. An hour in the Shadow Lands could be an entire night in my world, or ten minutes. It was never consistent, so I had to be as quick as possible. It would really suck to leave here and discover that Halloween was over, and all my friends were dead because I'd been reading the history of my family tree.

Okay, so Emily and Alys Murray. I read quickly but carefully. Their grandmother had been one of the twins and taught them what they were supposed to know. That part made me sad, because it made me think of Nan and the twin she'd lost.

I flipped through a chronicle of all the ghosts and living people they'd dealt with until I found mention of the last name McCrae. I read how Noah's sister had died and become a tormented spirit. There was mention of his sister being mentally unstable, with the insinuation that this had been brought on by an "unnatural" relationship with her brother. As a medium, Noah had been able to keep in contact with his sister after her death, and it was wondered if he'd somehow helped to corrupt her in the afterlife. She became a violent ghost, and Emily had to destroy her. This sent Noah over the edge, and led to his being committed to Haven Crest. He then dedicated all of his time to finding out everything he could about ghosts, the afterlife and the Melinoe, which, thankfully, wasn't much. Shortly after that he committed suicide and began haunting Haven Crest. He did so peacefully, so as not to attract Emily's attention. It was only when he felt strong enough that he acted against her. And that wasn't until Emily herself had died.

This was the part that confused me. How had he managed to trap Emily? She'd been powerful in life, and I had to assume that when we Melinoe died we were still pretty strong. What had he done to capture her and lock her away as he had? Did it have something to do with Alys?

The book said that when Emily died, she and Alys were finally reunited in death, and they should have moved on, but they didn't because they didn't trust Noah. And they were right not to. My great-grandmother came to Haven Crest one day; it didn't say why, but it was during her pregnancy with Nan. Noah attacked her, and then he told Emily and Alys that the only way to save her was to kill one of her babies. Alys believed him, and she killed the red twin while it was still inside my great-grandmother. Only, it had been a deception, and she'd killed the white twin instead.

How? How had he managed to do that? Not even the book seemed to know. Although, there was talk that Alys was in league with Noah. She attacked Emily when her sister confronted her about the suspicions. Alys was sent to the void for killing her own blood, and for trying to destroy her own sister.

Emily didn't move on. She wouldn't while her sister was imprisoned. Because she lingered, Alys could occasionally appear to her family, but only briefly, or in dreams.

So it had been Alys I'd dreamed about.

And then last month, Emily disappeared.

I stared at the page. Disappeared? Emily hadn't disappeared. She'd been abducted. How could the book not know that Noah had taken her?

That's where the story of Emily and Alys ended. There was a brief paragraph about Nan and her dead twin, and then there was a chapter about me and Wren. It wasn't very long, and that was okay, because it was weird reading about myself, my suicide attempt and Bell Hill and seeing it presented in such a dry, emotionless way.

It ended with our fight against Bent. I supposed once Halloween was over, this latest "adventure" would appear on the pages, as well.

I was just about to close the book, when new writing appeared. I watched it spread out across the page:

LOOK OUT. BEHIND YOU.

I turned around just in time to have a fist slammed into my face. It knocked me into the table, but I shook it off and leaped to my feet. The chair went flying.

It was Woodstock.

Son of a bitch.

Of course he hadn't been dusted. God only knew whose bones I'd burned that night. Noah had tricked me, and I let him. I should have checked the patient number on the grave against Woodstock's file.

"What happened to your eye?" I asked with a smile when I saw the patch he wore. I was pretty sure it had been on the top of Wren's little collection.

His cocky grin faded.

"What payment did Noah give you for that eye, huh? Or did he tell you that losing an eye was better than being bar-becued?"

"You talk a lot," he said.

I nodded. "Yes, I do. You're here for a reason, Age of Aquarius. What is it?"

"I came for you. Noah said I could have you."

What was that all about? Noah wasn't going to just hand me over to this nut. I was too valuable. But Woodstock wasn't. Was Noah using me to tie up loose ends? "Bet he also told you that Wren wouldn't hurt you."

There was no trace of smugness now. "Time for you to shut up." He came at me. I shoved a chair in front of him, but he tossed it aside. I hopped onto the table and rolled off the other side, putting the furniture between us. He vaulted over it with ease. Not bad for a guy who smelled like patchouli and pot.

He hit me again. I was ready for it this time and got him with two good punches and a kick before he punched me hard in the face. I fell over onto the tabletop. Another punch and another. He jumped on top of me and pinned my arms with his knees.

Either he was happy to see me or he had more than fight-ing in mind. That was *not* going to happen. I'd had my fill of sexually abusive ghosts for the day—for the rest of my life.

I let the anger fill me until my skin crackled with it. My hair lifted into the air, floating like seaweed on water. Ah… manifestation. I smiled.

I pulled my arms free from his grip like he was as weak as

a child. I reached up and grabbed his hair, pulling his head down as I shoved mine up. Our skulls met like two coconuts. I threw him off me as stars danced in front of my eyes.

I started kicking him as he sat on the floor cradling his head. He swept out his leg, taking mine out from underneath me. I fell to the floor with a crash. There was that shushing sound again.

Woodstock's fingers fumbled with the button on my jeans. I got my left leg up so I could brace the sole of my boot against his throat. I pushed hard before easing up a bit. He relaxed a little, and I took the opportunity to then draw my foot back a bit and slam it into his throat, knocking him off me. He crashed into another table, knocking over two chairs in the process.

Now I was really pissed off. I grabbed his matted hair in my fist and slammed his face into the floor again and again and again...

This time the "shush" was followed by the door to the room opening. The librarian wiggled in like she and her hips owned the place.

"What is going on here?" she demanded. "This sort of noise and commotion is *not* allowed on these grounds. I'm afraid you're both going to have to leave."

"Sorry about this," I said, rising to my feet. I kicked Woodstock hard in the ribs as I stood. "I thought he was dead."

She blinked. "He is."

I almost rolled my eyes, but I'd walked right into that one. "I thought he was someplace where I didn't have to worry about him."

"Obviously not."

"Are you always so rude?"

"This isn't rude." Her eyes widened to a point that they

were too big for her face, giving her a creepy-doll look. "You don't want to see me get rude."

She had that right. "Okay, I'm going." I slowly walked around her. Woodstock had gotten up and was coming after me again. I doubted he'd let the librarian stand in his way.

I picked up one of the heavy wooden chairs and threw it at him. He only had one eye, and it wasn't on the side closest to me, so he didn't see it coming. It crashed into him, knocking him off his feet and sending him sprawling across another table.

The librarian let loose something that sounded like a cross between a squeal and the roar of a T. rex in *Jurassic Park*. I didn't stick around for the rest of her reaction or Woodstock's recovery. By the time she turned that anger toward me, I was already running out the door.

chapter twenty-two

WREN

It was pointless trying to fight him. This place and these ghosts did something to me. Pulled me in. Loved me. They whispered to me all the things I could do if I weren't bound by living morality, if I weren't afraid to be my true self.

And Noah talked to me of eyes, and how they reflected a person's soul. When we were alone, and it was just me and him, merged into one, he told me I could take as many eyes as I wanted—from both the living and the dead—on All Hallows' Eve. I could do whatever I pleased, and there'd be no one to stop me. No one strong enough, especially once my sister was dealt with.

I tried to hold on to Lark. I reached for her in the dark, but then the dark started swimming, seething with terrible creatures that wanted to tear me apart, and I shrank back in fear. Why had my sister left me to this place? Why hadn't she come for me? Why didn't she save me?

"She's more concerned about her breather friends," Noah whispered. "She's one of them. They're more important to her than you."

I wanted to tell him he was wrong, but I couldn't, because I wondered if maybe he was right. All she ever did was talk about protecting the living, and her friends, and her breather boyfriend whom she'd never even noticed when he was a fat, funny-looking kid. Shallow and disloyal, that was my sister.

I tried to run away from the things that nipped and bit, but there was nothing but darkness around me, and I didn't know where to go. I was scared, and I was angry. So angry.

Lark had done this.

Strong fingers wrapped around my wrist, and for a second I thought it was Noah, but it wasn't. It was a girl. Then I hoped it might be my sister, but of course it wasn't her. She wasn't coming.

Hair the color of blood broke through the darkness, followed by a face as pale as the grave, and eyes that glittered like ice. Lips, stained berry-red. I knew that face.

"You don't belong here," she told me, though her lips didn't move. "You need to leave. You have work to do." Her voice was soft but strong, and I believed what she said to me.

"I don't know the way out," I told her.

"Yes, you do," she said, and gave me a push.

Up and out I drifted, until the dense black gave way to moonlight and candles, something soft and scratchy on what Noah called "the phonograph." He was wrapped up in me, and I was wrapped up in him, so perfectly that we were one.

I'd fought him at first, but I soon learned I didn't have a choice.

"I thought I'd lost you for a moment," he said. "But I'll never lose you, will I, Wren? You're mine for as long as I want you."

"As long as I want you," I repeated, and he laughed, the sound reverberating through me like a wave moving through the ocean. I wanted to ask him what was so funny, but it didn't matter.

I laughed, too.

LARK

Halloween.

"You know, I used to love Halloween," I told Roxi as we got ready for the concert in my room.

"You loved it right up until Kevin's party," she reminded me. "Right before things got weird."

"My whole life is weird," I muttered, arranging my hair on top of my head. I'd gathered it up into a high ponytail and then wrapped it into a thick coil. I took two slender iron bars the size and shape of chopsticks and slid them through the bun, anchoring it to my head. To anyone else, they'd just look like hair decorations, but they were ghost-stickers. They were a little heavy, but wearing my hair high on my crown took the brunt of the weight, so I didn't feel like every strand was being pulled out at the root.

"Good thing you have friends who like weird."

I turned to her. "You know, normal people would have cut and run by now. I don't know why you guys stick around."

She shot me a dirty look. "Because we're stupid."

I nudged her with my boot. "That's not what I meant."

"I know what you meant." She didn't look at me. She was busy getting ready herself. "You're fishing—wondering if I really like you or if I think you're my best shot at surviving the concert. Well, news flash—it's both. I love you, despite the fact that you believe we hang around you because you saved our butts once and we might need you again. That's kinda rude, you know." She lifted her head and gave me a pointed look.

Well, if I didn't know my place before, I knew it now. "You're right. I'm sorry. Just because I don't think I'm great friend material doesn't mean you guys agree. Then again, you might actually *be* stupid."

She didn't just nudge me with her boot, she kicked me, and it hurt, the bitch. I laughed, though.

My costume was pretty lame if I had to say so myself. Black Doc Martens, black leggings, long black sweater. It was supposed to be a fairly warm night for the end of October, but this was still New England. It wasn't jeans-and-T-shirt weather. I'd clipped some fun-fur cat ears I'd made into my hair, and painted my face to look vaguely catlike. I felt like something out of one of those anime shows that always made me slightly uncomfortable.

It helped that Roxi, who was dressed as a werewolf, looked very similar. I knew someone would accuse us of trying to be sexy, but really we had gone for simple costumes that allowed for fighting, because that's what we needed.

We both had on our iron rings, and had all kinds of Sharpie tattoos underneath our clothes. I stuck to things that protected from evil spirits only, because I didn't want to hurt Wren, and after all this time with Noah, she might need me.

My sweater had a little zippered compartment in the left arm, and that's where I put some cash, my ticket and my ID. My phone was in a special pocket in my sports bra. Yeah, I'd heard all about the risks of breast cancer, but I figured one night wouldn't hurt. Anything else I might need was already on-site, tucked behind a shrub beside the building where Roxi's mother worked. Thankfully, it was inside the section of grounds roped off for the concert.

Although, once it got dark, I didn't know how security was going to make sure no one snuck in; but I'd heard that they had the place well barricaded, and of course there was a tall fence around most of it. The only way in that I knew of, other than the road, was the tree in the cemetery.

The concert didn't start until nine, but the grounds opened at eight so people could buy merchandise and snag a place near the front of the stage. It was almost eight now. Ben had to drop his sister off at a friend's house, and then he was going to pick up Gage and come get us. We'd meet everyone else at the grounds around eight-thirty. Then, I'd spend the entire opening act, intermission and most of the Dead Babies' set waiting for hell to break loose.

Because at midnight, the veil practically disappeared, and midnight was when Gretchen planned to summon Joe. And I assumed that was also when Noah planned to cross over.

Finally ready, Roxi and I went downstairs to wait for the guys.

Nan was handing out candy to trick-or-treaters. She'd just closed the door on two kids dressed like vampires when the guys arrived.

"Be careful," she said and gave me a hug.

"I will," I promised.

She squeezed me tighter. "Call me if you need me."

"I will." Only we both knew I wouldn't. I wasn't dragging her into this. I couldn't let myself think about how worried she had to be, or how much she wished that our family had been normal. If I thought about her worrying about me I wouldn't be able to do everything I needed to do that night.

We went outside. It was definitely sweater weather. I had a T-shirt on under mine for a little extra warmth, but at least it wasn't freezing. Some years we had snow on Halloween, but not tonight. The weather was the one thing we had in our favor. It would be really hard to fight ghosts in a freaking parka.

Gage jumped into the backseat when he saw us. It was kind of cute how he always gave me the front, like it was the gentlemanly thing to do. He was dressed like a lumberjack, which was hilarious because he was skinny and Latino and wouldn't know what to do with an ax if you gave him one. I knew this, because I'd once seen him attempt to cut firewood.

Ben was dressed entirely in black, had his hair all messed up and was wearing black eyeliner.

"What the hell are you?" I asked with a chuckle.

"I'm too tragic for this world," he informed me—entirely straight-faced.

"I'm a lumberjack!" Gage called from the backseat.

"I guessed that," I told him with a glance over my shoulder. "Nice beard, by the way." It was crooked.

He grinned.

I turned away with a smile. What would we do without him? Seriously, he found fun in everything. He rarely complained. He was just so cute and sweet—a genuinely good person.

I hoped I wouldn't get him killed.

Parking was a nightmare when we got to the Haven Crest grounds. We were directed into a lot across the street where the hospital used to store a lot of their grounds-keeping equipment. I was glad I hadn't worn heels by the time we finally got to the security check. None of us had bags so we were able to skip through. I didn't see any drug dogs, but they were checking people for weapons.

Then we had to get in line to have our tickets checked and get our bracelets—over-twenty-ones got a different color, so they could buy beer if they wanted. They also stamped our hands in case the bracelet came off—and so people couldn't hand bracelets over to people trying to sneak in without having bought a ticket. A perfect Seal of Solomon in black ink over the scar on my right wrist. By the time we got into the actual concert area, it was almost twenty to nine.

We met Mace and Kevin just inside. Neither Kevin nor Mace were sporting any bruises, so I assumed they'd made peace.

Roxi showed us where she'd hidden our supplies so we'd be able to get to them when we needed. We found a place to stand with a good view of the stage not far from there. The lights around the perimeter dimmed a bit as the stage lights came on, and the opening act—a local band—was announced. The crowd cheered, and more and more people herded in through the gate.

I turned my head, my gaze traveling from old building to old building, both reclaimed and derelict. There were people standing in front of them, people of all shapes and sizes, from all walks of life and spanning a couple of centuries. The ghosts of Haven Crest were lining up.

And then, drifting in from all directions, were more ghosts. Town ghosts. Some wore suits or dresses. Others wore jeans or uniforms. There were children and adults and senior citizens. Some were whole, and some were in pretty rough shape. I recognized a girl with no face as a ghost from the hospital. They gathered near the barricade and stopped. They were waiting, I realized. But for what, I didn't know.

And then the sound of an electric guitar ripped through the night, and I turned my attention to the stage. Might as well have some fun before Hell broke loose.

WREN

I heard music. Cheering.

The concert had started.

Something blossomed inside me—a feeling of awareness and warmth.

Lark. She was near. I smiled. Noah said he'd let me kill her. Silly boy. As though anyone else could.

I went to the window and looked outside. I could see the stage, all lit up. The band playing wasn't bad, but they weren't the main attraction. That's what we were waiting for. Energy hummed all around us, but it wasn't enough.

Noah stood beside me. "Soon," he said and lifted my hand to his mouth. I watched as he kissed my knuckles. The black veins running through me were everywhere, so stark against the pallor of my skin. They were almost pretty—like tree branches. Noah liked them.

I wondered if he noticed the red veins that crept out from beneath his collar and along his hairline, and I smiled. "Yes," I said. "Soon."

LARK

It was almost midnight.

Gretchen had just screamed the final note of "Bleak Wednesday," which was one of my favorites, though I was too wound up to enjoy it, and the crowd erupted into wild applause and screaming.

Gretchen held up his hands. "It's time," he shouted into the microphone.

More cheers. This time the ghosts joined in. I shivered. They pushed closer from all directions. All these humans were going to get caught in between. I could feel the ground it-self trembling beneath my feet. This whole place was about to implode with spectral energy.

And there was Joe, standing beside me. He looked anx-ious. "I've never been raised before," he said. "Does it hurt?"

"I don't think so," I said.

"Olgilvie is on the move." He looked around at the crowd. "How are you going to get through this to catch him?"

"I'm not." When he looked at me as though I'd just cut out his heart, I explained. "Mace is. His father's police chief. He knows the officers working here tonight. He's going to set them after Olgilvie." I took my phone out of my bra and typed a text to Mace. "See?"

Joe peered at the lit screen of my phone. "'Time to move.'" He glanced at me. "That's it?"

I nodded. "Mace will see that, wait a few minutes and then tell the other cops he saw Olgilvie in the field, and that he looks like he needs help. He'll lead them right to him." I didn't explain that earlier I'd shown Mace the spot where Laura was buried.

Joe looked away. "Thank you."

"Thank me when it's over."

A roadie came out and draped a black robe around Gretch-en's shoulders. A black robe? Really? Whatever. He also gave the singer a book. It looked old and leather-bound, but it could have been an early edition of *Little Women* for all I knew.

He began to read.

Ben turned to me. "Is that Latin?"

I shrugged. It could be *Little Women*, backward.

"It's Latin," Gage said. "He's invoking the spirit of Joe Hard to rise and join us."

I stared at him. "You awesome little freak. You constantly amaze me, you know that?"

He grinned. His moustache was crooked now, too.

The lights flickered. The crowd gasped. Beside us a guy yelled, "Fake!" He grinned at his friends, but he was afraid. I could see it. I could feel it. I was surrounded by fear and excitement. And hunger. Oh, such hunger. It wasn't human, it was dead.

And it made me angry.

"Repeat after me!" Gretchen yelled, and began reciting from the book again. The crowd chanted back. It was kind of creepy, all those voices in sync with each other. On the stage, a figure began to take shape, flickering in and out of sight like a bad connection. Joe. He wasn't beside me anymore.

The chanting grew louder and more frantic. I glanced behind us. Out of the darkness, a lone figure approached. It was Noah—I knew it without having to see his face. Of course he was going to want to be right in the middle of everything when the energy peaked.

And of course he was going to come for me.

"Guys," I said, making sure I had my friends' attention. "Go get our stuff." And they did. They didn't even notice I wasn't with them. But I didn't want Noah anywhere near them when things went down.

He stepped up beside me, straight and tall. When the light hit his face I noticed red veins creeping out along his cheekbones. That was new.

"Hey there, *Masterpiece Theatre*," I said.

The insult was lost on him. "Miss Noble. Don't you look plebian tonight."

Or maybe it hadn't been lost at all. "Enjoying the show? Sorry that Joe's going to steal some of your thunder."

KADY CROSS

Noah smiled. "There will still be plenty for me. Can you feel it?" He closed his eyes and tilted his head back, a blissful smile on his face. "Haven Crest is about to awaken."

I felt it—the second it became midnight. It was like a click inside my chest. On the stage, Joe Hard appeared, and Gretchen fell to his knees, mouth hanging open. I guess he hadn't expected it to work.

Beside me, Noah shuddered. His eyes, now wide, began to glow. Heat emanated from him as he began to absorb the energy around him. How was he doing that?

I didn't think, I just acted. I pulled one of the iron sticks from my hair and rammed it hard into his chest. The light in his eyes blinked and dimmed as he doubled over. Warmth spread over my fingers. It wasn't blood—it was energy.

I leaned close to his ear. "Being tangible sucks, doesn't it?" I gave the spike a final shove, pivoted on my heel and took off running toward the building he loved. The building where his bones were kept.

I didn't know if my friends had seen any of that. I didn't look. Right now they were safer away from me, and none of them would be foolish enough to go after Noah, but Noah would come for me. After all, he couldn't have his revenge without destroying both me and Wren.

Where was my sister?

And then I felt her, calling out to me. I looked around and saw a light in the distance. It was her. I knew it.

Security was too busy with the crazed crowd to pay much attention to a freaky white-haired cat-girl running in the opposite direction. In fact, no one paid me any attention at all until someone stepped right in my path. I barely managed to stop, the soles of my boots gripping at the grass.

Woodstock.

"Hey, Sweet Meat," he crooned. "Thought we might pick up where we left off."

"You are seriously beginning to piss me off."

I slid the other stick from my hair, the bun unraveling as he approached. I waited until he was almost on me, and I could smell the sweat and patchouli and grave rot that clung to him. I whipped my fist up hard. The iron stick plunged deep into his good eye. I felt it pop and give under the force of my strike. He screamed, his eye sizzling from the iron stuck in it.

For a moment, I just stood there, watching as ichor oozed between the fingers of the hand he'd slapped over his eye. He tried to pull the stick free with the other, but the damage was done.

He unraveled as he was sucked into the Shadow Lands. He wasn't destroyed, but he was out of my way for now, and that's what I needed.

I ran, continuing on toward the beacon of light ahead of me. Toward my sister. Toward Wren. I thought my lungs might explode, but I kept running. And then I saw her, standing in front of that building, dressed entirely in white, shining like a freaking angel.

If angels had veins of tar running through them.

She looked terrible and beautiful at the same time—those black smudges around her eyes and mouth looking goth-chic against the sheer white of her skin. She held out her hand and I reached for it.

Something struck me hard from behind, driving me to the earth. I barely got my hands out in time to keep my face from being ground into the old, crumbled pavement of the Haven Crest lane. I felt a snap inside, and pain shot through my torso so sharp I cried out.

I was flipped over so fast I lost my breath—not that I could breathe that well with at least one broken rib. Noah loomed over me like some kind of demon. His eyes had lost some of their glow, and I realized he'd put off sucking in energy to come after me.

How flattering.

"You bitch!" he cried, shaking me so hard my teeth rattled. "You meddling, sanctimonious worm! I'm going to rip you to shreds."

Was that blood I tasted? "Go for it." I reached up and wiggled the spike sticking out of his chest just for spite.

He backhanded me across the face. Now I definitely tasted blood. I punched him in the throat, hard. His head snapped back, but he hit me again and again and again. He was stronger than any ghost I'd ever faced before. I could literally feel my skull starting to come apart. I tried to manifest, but I couldn't do it. I wasn't angry enough, or scared enough.

Why the hell not?

Suddenly, he stopped. I looked up through tears and blood to see Wren standing there, her hand on his shoulder. "You said I could do it."

"No," I whispered. It wasn't just that her offer tore at my heart, it was the fact that she couldn't kill me. We both knew that—we were too perfectly matched. Too entwined. I didn't know if she was trying to trick him, or if she just wanted to hurt me for a while.

Noah grinned and rose to his feet. I could breathe a little without him on me. "Of course, my dear," he said, and stood back.

Wren crouched beside me, her long crimson hair brushing my face. Those awful black veins crisscrossing her cheeks.

"Do you know that when two ghosts merge, they can leave some of themselves behind?"

I nodded.

She smiled softly, her fingers stroking my cheek. "That's what Noah did to me. And I did to him. Do you know what happens when you and I merge?"

Blood trickled from my mouth. I stared up at her, through the haze of red that had pooled in my eyes. "We...become... one."

She leaned closer. "We become Melinoe. Let me *in*, Lark."

I did. I trusted her no matter what Noah had done to her, or how dark her eyes were. She was my sister. She was the other half of my soul. I knew that now. We were individual pieces of one powerful whole.

I heard Noah's shout as she sank into me, but I ignored it. My bones put themselves back together as Wren's energy filled me. I pushed the darkness of Noah's infection aside, cleansing and healing her as she healed me. My heart became her heart. My ribs became her ribs, whole and strong.

This wasn't possession. She wasn't wearing my body. This was her body. And it was mine. There was no me and no her.

There was only *us*.

chapter twenty-three

THE MELINOE

I was two. Then became one.

I rose, confused but steady and sure in this body. I looked down at my hands—they were long and pale, but strong. I wore a snug suit of leather, ancient armor from long ago. I knew what I was, and yet it was strange and new.

I was Lark. I was Wren. I was Melinoe. And I was not afraid.

Around me chaos reigned. I watched as earthbound spirits fought one another for reasons they didn't understand. I watched as others tried to possess humans marked by Solomon's protection. Some humans weren't quite so protected, and their frightened souls allowed them to be used as vessels.

This was not a fitting celebration for the night when the living and the dead walked together. This was not an honoring of those who had passed, nor a celebration of those who remained. This was chaos. And this place—so soaked in the tears of the living and the regrets of the dead—cried out in pain. So much pain.

I crouched and put my hand to the ground. "Easy," I whispered. "It will all be over soon."

I stood and turned my attention to the spirits gathered there—the ones who'd watched Noah beat on me. They stared at me, fear rendering them mute. They were no danger to me or to anyone else at the moment. They were sheep, just waiting to be led.

I would deal with them later.

"Where is he?" I asked.

They knew who I meant. An old man lifted his arm and pointed behind me. I turned and looked into the throng.

A scream rent the night, and I moved toward it, toward the stage where Gretchen stood speechless, staring at Joe as ghosts swept down upon the crowd. Joe's head turned. His gaze locked with mine across the churning sea of fans who didn't know what the hell was going on.

I nodded at Joe. His eyes widened. I must have looked very different to him in this form. *Look for Noah.* The thought drifted from my mind to his. He raised his hand—he had heard me.

Many of the living ran for the exit like frightened sheep, bunching up at the narrow exit, making themselves easy targets for predators. One such possessed ran by me, and I caught him by the collar, dragging him back until I could dangle him in front of me—a fish on a hook.

"Release this person," I commanded. The spirit slid free. He was shaggy and dirty and smelled of…patchouli.

"Woodstock," I murmured, setting the bewildered human aside. What was left of the spirit's one eye turned toward me. The iron-burnt flesh widened.

"What the hell are you?" he asked.

I smiled, placing my hands on either side of his head. "I'm where you end, little one."

He opened his mouth, but all that came out was a squeak. I

held him gently, as a mother might, shushing him as he struggled. His form shriveled in my hands, flaking like paper as I drained him of all his energy. I took his essence into myself like a long drink of cool water, until he was nothing but old dust caught up in a breeze and taken away.

I dusted his remains from my hands and rose. Humans and spirits ran in all directions around me, but my stride never altered. They moved for me.

A ghost with a badly burned face, her hair in patches, had her hands around the throat of a girl I recognized. Roxi. My friend. She had her up against the side of a building, slamming her against the rough brick. I recognized the ghost as the girl who had been on fire and I'd saved—the same girl whose skull I had lit on fire thinking it was Noah's.

I didn't even think, I simply acted, driving my fist through the bodice of the ghost's Victorian gown and out the other side of her. She crumbled away with a sigh, and I took in what was left. Where she went now was out of my control.

"Peaceful rest," I whispered. She deserved it.

I offered Roxi my hand. She had fallen when the girl released her. Warm fingers closed around mine.

"Lark?" Roxi said, as I helped her up. "Wren?"

"Yes," I said. I smiled. "It's complicated."

She looked wary. "Uh, yeah. Okay."

"Please, don't be afraid," I told her. "I won't hurt you. I couldn't. You're my friend."

Dark eyes met mine. "What color underwear am I wearing?"

A test? We were in the middle of a battle, and she tested me? "Purple. You don't own any other color."

She grinned. "Right. Okay, let's go."

"Stay with me, and you'll be safe." Then, I started forward

again. I found Gage and Mace, as well. Gage had lost his beard, and his sweet face was bruised, one eye swollen, but he was otherwise unharmed. Mace bled from a cut above his eye, and there was an angry red mark on his jaw.

"Olgilvie," he explained when he caught me looking. "He took a swing when I showed up with the cops."

"Did they find Laura?" I asked.

He nodded, his expression turning grim. "He'd already uncovered part of her when we arrived." And he had seen it. Poor thing.

I reached out and touched his face. He gasped but didn't pull away. The cut and welt disappeared. Then, I touched Gage and Roxi as well, healing their injuries.

"Follow me," I said. They fell into step behind me.

Every step filled me with more energy. This ground was steeped in it. I could feel its suffering in the soles of my feet and in my heart. The injustice of it angered me. I wanted to weep from the pain. So many spirits had suffered so much here.

A young woman ran in front of me, screaming as two laughing male ghosts chased after her. I cut them both down mid-stride. She didn't notice and ran off still screaming.

"The living can be such douche bags," I murmured. "Where are Ben and Kevin?"

"They went toward the stage," Mace replied. "Ben stayed with Kevin in case Noah showed up."

Ben. So brave and good. If Noah harmed him I would make him suffer a long time for it.

Finally, I stood before the stage. Security had come and ushered the singer and the rest of the band to safety, so the only other people on the stage were Joe, Noah and Kevin.

Ben was on the ground in front of the stage. On his back. Unmoving.

"Come any closer and I'll kill him!" Noah shouted. He had his arm locked around Kevin's neck, his hand curved into talons over his heart, ready to tear flesh and bone apart.

"Be quiet," I commanded. "I will deal with you in a moment." I went to Ben and crouched beside him. He wasn't one of mine. Not yet. And though he'd have a nasty headache when he woke up, there was no permanent damage done. I picked him up and carried him to where Roxi, Gage and Mace stood; the boys took him from me, staring at me in awe and wonder. And all because I'd lifted Ben as though he weighed no more than a child.

To me he didn't even weigh that.

I took one, two running steps and then leaped up to the stage, landing gracefully in front of Noah and Kevin.

"Stay back!" Noah commanded. His claws scratched through the fabric of Kevin's shirt and through his skin, drawing blood. Kevin hissed, but he didn't cry out. He just kept his gaze locked on me. What did he see when he looked at me? Did he see a terrifying creature with red-and-white hair? A goddess? Or did he see the dead girl he loved with all his heart? The answer was as obvious as it was heartbreakingly sweet.

But the other—the one who had lived long before Kevin—looked at me as though he thought he could bargain. As though he had any control over me. Stupid, stupid child. So desperate for power and worship. More broken and needy now than he had been in life, and he'd believed death would make him so much more.

Death only gave preference to a few of us, and this pathetic, dandyish boy was not one. Haven Crest had been given a choice the moment I merged; did it want to give its power to Noah, or to me?

It had been an easy decision. Noah would only rape this vulnerable place and exploit its pain. I offered peace.

"Let him go, Noah."

"No!"

I was tired of this. Tired of so much of *my* night being spent on this pathetic creature. He'd taken Emily, conspired against Alys, robbed Charlotte of her destiny and almost prevented me—Lark and Wren—from discovering what we were. What *I* was.

"You can't win, Noah. This is all of your own making."

The claws flexed deeper, and this time Kevin did cry out. It was a sound that echoed in my soul, because a part of me cared for him, deeply. And the other part of me hadn't been able to see just how much until then. Wren knew her heart so much better than Lark, which didn't surprise me, because Wren had no fear of having it broken.

"I'll kill him. I swear I will. Just like your predecessor killed my sister! Now back away, you filthy half-breed! Bow to me, or I'll rip his throat out."

"Bow to *you*?" Shadows drew close to me as my anger rose, wrapping around me like a loving embrace. "You have no dominion over Death, child. You have no dominion over *me*!" The words tore from my throat like a thunderstorm, knocking Noah back so sharply that Kevin fell from his grip. That's when I moved. In a blink I had Noah by the throat. He clawed at me, but I barely felt it.

"Your plan probably would have worked if you'd left us out of it," I said. "But you were so bent on revenge, so greedy for the power you thought Wren could give you. Did you not realize how much power you fed her at the same time?"

His eyes widened and I laughed. "You didn't even know, did you? You didn't notice those red veins creeping around your form? If not for you, we still wouldn't know what we truly are! Everything you did, every deceit and lie only worked against you. And it all started the day you killed your own sister."

Yes, that was Noah's terrible secret. Wren had gotten a glimpse when she began leaving some of her own essence behind in Noah. And Lark had already figured out part of the story.

"You killed her so, as a medium, you could have her all to yourself. But she became a vengeful spirit. You thought you could control her, but then along came Emily, who gave your sister release. Then you killed yourself because you thought you could be with your sister, but, no. She had moved on, and you couldn't because you were too deranged. You swore revenge on Emily, and you tricked Alys into destroying Charlotte's sister so the twin cycle would be interrupted. Emily couldn't move on with Alys in the void, and you imprisoned her. And then you came after me, because you thought you could destroy me."

Noah squirmed in my hand. His power was waning as Haven Crest slowly rejected him. *He* was the one causing it pain, who had demanded it feed him in return. He was the one who had helped Josiah Bent, and then sat back and watched just to see how strong I was, pitting my two selves against each other. He'd brought so much darkness to this place.

But his real mistake had been in thinking that he could turn me against myself.

"I don't regret any of it," he rasped.

"No. I don't think you do. Which is why I'm not going to send you on."

His eyes lit up. "If you don't send me on, you have to let me stay."

I smiled. "Oh, my dear Noah. You forgot the third option." I didn't need the spirit board or an infection-induced vision. For a few more hours I *was* Death—or at least the daughter of it—and imbued with all the power that brought with it.

The shadows that surrounded me rose up, swirling and twining around us, like dark vines. Below and over they climbed, until there was nothing but dark. Nothing but the void.

Noah realized where we were almost immediately. "No!" He clawed at my hand, but I held tight. Around us, the monsters in the dark circled. Waiting and hungry. But he wasn't for them.

I felt her approach. She was, after all, another part of me. Dear, mad Alys with her wild eyes and bloodstained mouth. She crept from the dark like a shadow herself.

"I've brought you a gift," I said.

Noah's wild gaze turned to me. "You can't do this!"

I shushed him and ran my hand down his cheek. "It was never the dark you were afraid of, was it, Noah? It was the things you knew dwelled in it."

Alys reached out her dark-stained hand, and I thrust Noah toward her. She grinned, pouncing on him like a cat on a mouse. His scream was the last thing I heard as I left.

The shadows receded, wrapping close to me once more. I was left on the stage with Joe. Ghosts continued to cause mayhem on the grounds, possessing humans and fighting one another, but the living were leaving at a steady pace, giving them fewer to choose from, and ruining all their fun.

I didn't have much work left. I turned to Joe. "Look at you," I said. "So young and alive."

"Well, I took that whole die-young-and-leave-a-gorgeous-corpse thing to heart."

I took his hand, feeling the energy that filled him. It was strong.

"Better than drugs," he joked.

"You absorbed a lot of power. Are you all right?"

"I'll be fine."

"I can take it," I told him. "I can give you rest, if you want. Peace. They found your Laura. Olgilvie's been arrested."

Dark-rimmed eyes narrowed. "If I stay here I can make sure he suffers."

Dear boy. He made me smile. I took his hand in mine, twining our fingers. "He will pay for what he did, Joe. I promise you. But now, I think there's someone who has been waiting a long time for you to give up your anger." I gazed beyond him, and nodded my head.

Joe turned. When he saw her, warmth blossomed within me. It hadn't taken much effort to call her. As one who had died a violent death, she would have felt the unearthing of her bones, and she would have hoped that Joe would finally come to her.

"Laura," he whispered. He ran to her.

On the ground, I heard Roxi give a little sob. It was rather romantic to see the two of them finally reunited after all these years. Sometimes the dead held on to old grudges for too long. So long, that they forgot what it meant to be alive. They forgot the things that had been important to them, and that was really what it meant to be haunted.

Joe and Laura, their arms around each other, broke apart

into little glimmering shards of light that drifted away on the breeze.

"They look like fireflies," Roxi said with a sniff.

I smiled. "Yes, they do."

When I descended from the stage, my friends were staring at me. Kevin was hurt, and Ben was awake. I walked up to Kevin and inspected the wounds. They weren't deep, but they looked painful.

"You'll be fine," I told him. I could have healed him, but he wanted the pain. He felt he deserved it, dear thing.

"What did you do with him?" he asked.

I patted his shoulder. "I sent him somewhere unpleasant."

"Will he ever come back?"

I shook my head. "No."

"What about Lark and Wren?" Ben asked. He touched the back of his head, and his fingers came away bloody. "Are they coming back?"

Dear boy. So brave. So accepting of Lark and what she was. "Yes, but first I have work to do." And the first of it was to heal him.

They all followed me across the lawn toward the building where Noah had done his damage. No one paid much attention to us now that a news crew had arrived. It seemed a good time for me to move out of frame.

"Stay out here," I told the living before I walked into the residence.

The spirits gathered as I walked inside. They watched me—a few even followed as I went down into the basement and collected the bones left there, wrapped in burlap. I brought them upstairs and set them on the floor of the entry hall.

"Is this all of you?" I asked.

They nodded, and I knew they were truthful.

I held out my arms. "Come here." And they did.

They came from other houses, too, from all over the grounds. Hundreds of them of all ages, shapes and sizes and social class. One by one, I sent them home.

Miss April was the last one. "I was mean to you," she said. I nodded.

Her chin quivered. "Are you going to send me to Hell?"

Hell was a concept of the living. I didn't know Hell, but I knew suffering, and that was the void. "No."

She stepped into my embrace. I felt her soul against mine—that joyful moment when she let go—and then she was gone. I was alone in the building with Noah's remains. There was no energy left here, good or bad. It was just an empty place.

Like a grave.

I picked up the sack of bones and walked outside. My friends sat on the walkway, eating candy from Roxi's un-ending supply, and talking. Someone had bandaged Kevin. Some distance away, the news people had their lights and cameras going. The campus was fairly empty now, except for emergency workers, police and those few living who re-mained behind.

"Isn't that your father?" Gage asked Mace, gesturing to where two police cars were parked, red-and-blue lights bright in the dark.

He nodded. "We should probably get out of here."

I took a step toward them and fell to my knees. I was ex-hausted. Depleted. Done.

"Lark!" Roxi cried, rushing toward me. I fell forward, my hands hitting the ground. This place still wept, but not like it had. I could feel peace where there had been only pain. I smiled as my vision doubled.

Hands clutched at me as I was split in half. I cried out at the loss.

And then I came apart.

LARK

I woke up in the hospital, Nan and Wren hovering over me.

"Is it over?" I asked. "It wasn't a dream, was it?" It felt like a dream, but all those ghosts...and Joe and Laura. I wanted that to be real.

"We were awesome!" Wren exclaimed.

Nan shot her a glance—obviously she could still see her. It would be nice if that continued. Wren would like that.

So, not a dream, then.

"Aside from being awesome, you apparently exhausted yourself mentally and physically. I thought the doctors were going to call Child Services on me—some of your levels were so low. One of them asked if you were anorexic."

"I'm sorry," I said.

She patted my hand. "I'm just glad you're all right. They did call your mother, though."

I made a face. "Was she overwhelmed by motherly love and concern?"

"Yes, of course."

Wren shook her head. Her hair wasn't as bright as it normally was, and neither were her eyes. Halloween must have taken its toll on her, too. "No. She wasn't. She told the doctors it was a cry for attention."

Nan frowned at her. "Wrenleigh, listening in on my telephone conversations is not allowed. Understood?"

Wren nodded. "Yes, Nan. But that's what she said."

I tried not to let on that it hurt. "That sounds like her. How long do I have to stay here?"

"The doctors gave you an IV loaded up with all kinds of nutrients and minerals and different solutions." Obviously medicine was not Nan's forte. "I confess I stopped listening after the doctor said you were going to live. They said if things continue to improve you can go home tomorrow. They're going to send home supplements for you, as well."

"Is this because of the merge?" I looked at Wren when I spoke.

"Yep," she replied. "It knocked me out, too. I was in the Shadow Lands until just a few hours ago. You've been out for almost twenty-four hours. Technically, they're saying you have a case of acute exhaustion. I told Nan there was nothing 'cute' about it." She giggled.

Nan arched a brow. "It's still not funny, dear."

I smiled. "Is everyone okay?"

"Kevin got hurt, but he's fine. They've all been by. Ben more than once."

Nan pulled her cell phone out of her purse. "That reminds me. I told the poor boy I'd let him know when you were awake." She stepped away from the bed as she dialed.

I turned to my sister. "Can you believe what happened? What we did?"

She shook her head. "No. It's like I was walking through someone else's dream. I know I was there, and I know the details, but it's like watching a movie." She smiled. "Kevin said that we were hot."

I laughed. "He would say that." I reached out and took her hand in mine. "I'm sorry you had to recover all alone while I was in here."

She gave me a sheepish look. "I wasn't alone."

"Kevin?"

"No. Well, yeah, a little." She leaned closer. "Emily."

"What?" I struggled to sit up a bit. "She's free?"

"Apparently when we left Noah in the void, his hold over her was broken."

"Where is she? Why isn't she here?"

Wren glanced over her shoulder. "She didn't want to scare Nan. She said she'll come see us once we've fully recovered. She said something about having a lot to teach us."

"That's kind of like putting on rubber boots when you're already in the mud puddle."

My sister frowned. "That makes no sense. Why would you do that?"

"Exactly." I played with her fingers. "Did she say anything else?"

"She said she wanted to get Alys out of the void."

"As long as we don't have to deal with Noah again, I don't care what she does. What did Kevin do with the bones?"

"No idea."

Nan came back to the side of the bed. "Ben and your friends want to know if they can come visit for a bit."

"They'd better," I said, loud enough for Ben to hear over the phone.

Twenty minutes later I was surrounded. Nan had left me with a kiss on the forehead and said she'd be back in the morning to take me home.

Ben stood up by my head and held my hand. He kept playing with my hair, too, and massaging my scalp. I felt like a cat, rubbing my head into his hand. It was awesome. I hadn't felt so relaxed in forever, though that might have been the drugs. They gave me something to make sure I got plenty of rest.

Kevin stood near Wren. Every once in a while, when he

thought no one would notice, I caught him looking at her. He could see her, I knew he could. He could see her as clearly as I could. Whatever Noah had done to him, it had made his abilities as a medium stronger.

I watched as he slowly reached out and laced his fingers with hers. My breath caught when she turned her head to look at him. I had no idea how it could ever possibly work between the two of them, but they'd figure it out.

Mace stayed down at the bottom of the bed, but every few minutes he'd tickle my feet to make sure I wasn't drifting off. He stopped once I kicked him. He smiled at me.

"Olgilvie's locked up," he told me. "They found some of Laura's things in his apartment."

"Creep," I muttered. "At least we don't have to worry about him anymore."

"Oh, hey," Roxi said, whipping out her phone. "I took a picture of you at the concert when you were all, like, Death Goddess. Where is it?" I watched as she swiped through the millions of photos on her phone. Wren made a noise when she paused at one of Wren and Noah at Kevin's party. Roxi didn't notice and thankfully kept swiping until she found the right one. "There. Look."

Wren leaned in closer. On the screen was a girl who could have been either one of us, but she looked super bad-ass confident. Half of her hair was white and the other half red— just like what I'd read online about the Melinoe myth. She was dressed in a leather suit that looked like something Catwoman would wear.

"That's me?" we chorused. And then we looked at each other. It was at that moment that I realized she really was my other half. Not in a weird way, because I knew who I was, and what I was. But it was nice knowing that no matter what, Wren would always be with me.

"We have to help Emily," I said. "And Alys."

Wren nodded.

"Emily? Alys?" Ben looked down at me. "You're not talking about more ghost stuff, are you? Lark, you're in the hospital."

I smiled and gave his hand a shake. "It's not anything big. Besides, the only ghost I want to see for a while is my sister."

"As if you had any choice," Wren chirped.

A nurse came by with a bouquet of flowers. I already had one from Ben and one from Nan. "Who sent those?" I asked. They were gorgeous—white and red roses. I really hoped they weren't from my parents.

Gage, who had taken the vase from the nurse, set them on the bedside table and opened the card.

"'J.B.—thanks for reminding me what it's like to be alive. You rock. Love, Joe.'"

We all exchanged glances.

"Joe?" Mace asked. "As in Joe Hard?"

"How is that even possible?" That was Roxi as she snatched the card from her boyfriend's hand. "Oh, my God. It really does say that."

Gage frowned at her. "Yeah—I didn't make it up."

She kissed him. "I know. I'm sorry." That's all it took to make Gage happy-smiley again.

I stared at the flowers. "How did he do that?" I wondered out loud. "He moved on. I saw him do it." How would he even place an order for flowers? Online? My head hurt just thinking about it.

Ben squeezed my hand. "How about you don't wonder *how* and just appreciate that he *did*?"

I smiled at him. "There you go being all wise and stuff." But he was right. It really didn't matter how Joe had done it. What mattered was that he had, and that Wren and I had helped him get back to Laura. That was all that mattered.

My friends stayed a little while longer but left when I started yawning. Ben gave me a kiss and told me to call him when I got home the next day. Since it was Saturday, he could come over and baby me if I wanted. Maybe watch a movie and get me caught up on homework.

"Sounds like a plan," I said, and pulled him in for another kiss.

When everyone was gone, it was just me and Wren. She wandered over to Joe's roses and gave them a sniff. "Do you think it's a coincidence that they're red and white?"

I laughed. "No. Not at all."

Smiling, she skipped back to the bed. "Are you tired?"

I nodded, yawning as if on cue. "I am, yeah."

"Do you want me to leave?"

I shook my head. "No." I patted the bed. "Crawl in. There's room."

She immediately slipped under the blanket, sliding in so that she faced me.

"I'm sorry," she whispered. "About Noah. About everything."

"I know."

"I'm going to make it up to you."

I looked her in the eye. "There's nothing to make up. You thought he liked you, and you turned the tables on him in the end. Just think, if you hadn't met him, we wouldn't know what we are, and Emily would still be his prisoner. Who knows what he would have gotten up to on Halloween if not for us? And we freed all those ghosts." I yawned as sleep came knocking. "We're rock stars."

I closed my eyes. I was just drifting off to sleep when she said, "Hey, Lark? What's red and white and black all over?"

I opened one eye. "You?"

"Yes!" She squealed, laughing like an idiot. "Or, I was." She grinned.

I made a noise that could have possibly been laughter, or a groan. "Are you going to talk all night?"

"No. I'm going to watch you sleep, and it won't be at all creepy."

I thought about the eyes I'd found in the Shadow Lands and all the other things we should probably talk about, and then I decided that it could wait. All of it could wait—and maybe we didn't need to talk about any of it. I really didn't care. I was going to be okay. Wren was okay. Our friends and Nan were okay, and our mother was still a selfish, clueless bitch. All was right with the world.

I wrapped my hand around one of hers. "I love you, Wren-nie."

She kissed my forehead. "I love you, too."

I fell asleep, and as far as I knew, she really did lie there all night watching me. And it wasn't at all creepy.

Well, maybe just a *little*. But that was just us.

★ ★ ★ ★ ★